WHAT WAS HER FATHER DOING
IN THE ATTIC?

Her father was standing at the foot of a long wooden box.

A coffin?

No way. That's ridiculous.

But shivers crawled up her back. He was staring down into the box. He was talking to someone or something in the box. Lane climbed higher. Dad didn't seem to notice. She looked over the edge of the box. And went numb.

It *was* a coffin, and it wasn't empty. This can't be happening, Lane thought. I must be sleeping, and . . .

He must be the one sleeping.

"I know," he said, but not to Lane. "But I'm afraid."

He nodded.

"I love you, too," he said. "But I love my wife and daughter. I can't give them up. Not even for you."

The fog in Lane's mind scattered at those words.

"Do you promise?" he asked.

He nodded. "All right. I'll do it." Leaning forward, he reached down toward the chest of the body, his fingers wrapped around the stake.

"DAD!"

BOOK YOUR PLACE ON OUR WEBSITE AND MAKE THE READING CONNECTION!

We've created a customized website just for our very special readers, where you can get the inside scoop on everything that's going on with Zebra, Pinnacle and Kensington books.

When you come online, you'll have the exciting opportunity to:

- View covers of upcoming books
- Read sample chapters
- Learn about our future publishing schedule (listed by publication month *and author*)
- Find out when your favorite authors will be visiting a city near you
- Search for and order backlist books from our online catalog
- Check out author bios and background information
- Send e-mail to your favorite authors
- Meet the Kensington staff online
- Join us in weekly chats with authors, readers and other guests
- Get writing guidelines
- AND MUCH MORE!

Visit our website at
http://www.pinnaclebooks.com

THE STAKE

Richard Laymon

PINNACLE BOOKS
Kensington Publishing Corp.
http://www.pinnaclebooks.com

This book is dedicated to
Frank, Kathy & Leah De Laratta
Great friends
Fellow explorers
&
Ghost town busters

Prologue

Charleston, Illinois
June 23, 1972

He had stalked the demon to her lair. Now he waited. Waited for dawn, when she would be most vulnerable.

The waiting was the worst part. Knowing what was to come. The legends, he'd learned, were not to be trusted. The legends were wrong in so many ways.

Vampires slept in beds, not coffins—a clever ruse to fool the unknowing. And although daylight sapped their powers, it did not render them helpless. Even after dawn they could wake from their sleep of the dead. They could fight him, hurt him.

He rubbed his cheek. His fingers trembled along crusty ridges of scab. She'd had sharp fingernails, the one in Urbana.

He shuddered with the memory.

He'd been lucky to save himself.

Maybe he'd used up his luck on that one. Maybe, this time, it wouldn't be fingernails ripping his cheek. Maybe, this time, teeth would find his throat.

Ducking down against the steering wheel, he reached under the driver's seat and pulled out a bottle of bourbon. He twisted off its cap. He drank. The liquor was lukewarm going down, but it spread soothing heat through his stomach. He wanted to drink more.

Later, he promised himself. No more until the task is done.

You must keep your wits about you, he thought. It was the liquor that almost got you killed last week. These monsters are clever.

Again he rubbed his scratched cheek.

He took one more drink, then forced himself to cap the bottle. He slid it under the seat. As he straightened up, a car turned the corner ahead. Its headlights were on, but the morning sky was light enough to show the rack on top. A patrol car.

He threw himself down across the passenger seat.

His mouth felt dry. His heart thundered.

It's not right, he thought. I shouldn't have to live like a fugitive. I'm as much a public servant as those police out there.

He held his breath as the patrol car cruised by. It passed so close that he could hear crackles, squawks, and a garbled voice from its radio. He regretted his decision to leave the windows down. They might find that suspicious. But his car would've been stifling if he'd kept it closed up.

He breathed again as the sounds faded.

He stayed low, counting slowly to one hundred. Then he sat up and peered out the rear window. The red taillights were mere specks.

Opening his door, he leaned out and studied the sky. It was still gray beyond the peaked roof of the vampire's dwelling. He placed a foot on the curb, straightened up and peered over the roof of his car. To the east the sky was pale blue.

From long experience, he knew that the sun would soon appear above the horizon.

It would be up by the time he was in position.

He sank back into the car. His silver crucifix hung against his chest. He fingered its chain and pulled the cross out from under his shirt. Then he lifted a leather briefcase off the floor in front of the passenger seat. Reaching into the case, he pulled out a necklace of garlic cloves. He looped it over his head.

Briefcase in hand, he stepped out of the car.

The overgrown lawn was surrounded by a picket fence. He swung the gate wide, kicking its bottom past tufts of weed that were high enough to hold it open. Coming out this way, he would be carrying the body. He didn't want the gate slowing him down.

The porch stairs creaked under his weight. The screen door groaned. Inside the porch he used a wicker chair to prop the door open.

Twisting the knob, he found that the front door wasn't locked. That made it easy. He wouldn't need his pry bar. He crept silently into the house, and didn't shut the door.

He knew where to find her room. Shortly after she'd entered, last night, lights had appeared in the front windows to the right of the porch. She'd stepped up to each of the windows and lowered the shades.

The house was silent. The faint light that found its way into the living room cast a gray shroud over the old sofa, the rocking chair, the lamps and piano. The wallpaper looked faded and stained. Above the piano hung an oil painting of a forest clearing with a peaceful, running brook. In the gloom, it looked dim and somber, as if dawn hadn't yet come to the forest scene.

At the far corner of the room was a wood-framed entrance to a hallway.

He crept to the hallway and followed it to the open door of the vampire's bedroom.

His mouth went dry and his heart pounded as he gazed in at her. She lay on a bed between the two windows, curled on her side, facing away from him. The first rays of the morning sun glowed against the blinds, filling the room with an amber hue. She was covered only by a sheet. Her dark hair was spread against the pillow.

Crouching, he set his briefcase on the floor. He spread its top, reached in and lifted out the hammer.

A sledge with a heavy steel head and a foot-long haft.

With his other hand he took out a pointed stake of ash wood.

He clamped the stake in his teeth.

He stood up. Staring at the vampire, he willed her to roll over. Face up or down, it didn't matter. He could pound the stake through her back as easily as her chest. But she had to be lying flat, not on her side.

Somehow, he'd known this would be a difficult kill.

Should he wait? Eventually she was bound to turn over.

The longer he waited, the more danger of being seen when he carried the body out. And he *had* to do that. Take it far away in the trunk of his car and hide it where it would never be found.

People vanished all the time, and for many reasons. But to be discovered here with a stake in her heart . . .

The police would stupidly mistake it as the work of a homicidal maniac. The news would spread. The populace would panic. Worst of all, a legion of vampires would suddenly be put on guard that a hunter was in their midst.

And this morning's efforts would be in vain, for the police or coroner were certain to pull the stake from her heart. She would live again to prowl the night.

No. She had to disappear.

A floorboard creaked as he stepped to the side of the bed. She moaned, squirmed a little beneath the sheet, but didn't turn over.

The stake still held in his teeth, he reached out with his left hand. He pinched the sheet where its edge curled over her shoulder. As he eased it down she continued to take long, slow breaths. But his own breathing quickened.

The sliding sheet revealed her naked back, the smooth curves of her buttocks, her sleek legs.

She was a vampire, a vile, murdering demon. But her

body was that of a slender young woman, and he felt a stir of heat in his groin as he studied her. He trembled with the familiar mingling of lust and terror—a sensation close to ecstasy, which always came upon him at such moments. He used to feel ashamed of his desire. Finally, however, he'd come to consider it a reward for his sacrifices. A payment, of sorts, bestowed upon him to balance out the risks.

Without it he would have lost the will, long ago, to continue his crusade. He knew this to be true. Confronting vampires of the male gender, he felt no such arousal. Only revulsion. As a result he had ceased to seek them out. He considered this to be his greatest failing, but often told himself that he was doing his share. He was one man against a horde. He couldn't dispatch them all. He had to be selective. So he selected the women. Horrid as they were, they excited him.

Her left arm lay against her side, bent at the elbow, the rest out of sight. Its skin was pebbled with tiny bumps from the cool, morning air. Leaning forward, he peered over her upper arm at the swell of her breast. It had gooseflesh, like her arm. Her nipple stood erect. From this position he couldn't see her other breast.

As he stared, saliva began to spill over his lip. He tried to shut his mouth, but the stake was in the way. He jerked his left hand up to catch the drool, but not in time.

A string of spit dribbled onto the vampire's arm.

Mumbling, she slid a hand out from under her pillow, brushed the wetness, rolled onto her back and frowned as if perplexed. Still, her eyes were shut. She took the hand away. It fell onto the mattress beside her hip. It rubbed the sheet, then rose and came to rest on her thigh, the end of her thumb sinking into the thick nest of hair at her groin.

As he watched, full of dread that she might awaken, yet trembling with a fever of desire, he took the stake from his teeth. He knew he should wait no longer.

But he hesitated. His eyes roamed her sleeping form.

Though she might be centuries old, her face and body were those of a teenage girl. She looked no older than seventeen or eighteen. She looked lovely, innocent, delicious.

If only she were human, and not a foul, loathsome creature of the night.

He ached to kiss those lips which had sucked so much innocent blood. He ached to caress those breasts, to savor their velvety smoothness, to feel the soft rub of those nipples against his palms. He ached to spread those legs and slide deep into her heat.

If only she weren't a vampire.

Such a shame. Such a waste.

Get it over with, he told himself.

He leaned farther forward, knees pressing against the side of the mattress, and raised his hammer high. His other hand twitched and fluttered as he lowered the tapered shaft toward her chest. The shaking point passed over her left breast, moved slightly higher, hovered half an inch above her skin.

There.

One strong blow and . . .

Her eyes leaped open. She gasped. She clutched his wrist, twisted it with all the might of her demonic powers. Crying out, he watched in horror as the stake dropped from his numb fingers and fell, blunt end first, toward her other breast.

A feeling of utter desolation swept through him like an icy flood.

Without the stake . . .

As it bounced off her breast he strained against her grip, praying to retrieve it. But her fierce hold was too powerful. The stake slid out of sight beyond her rib cage.

He knew, then, that all was lost.

Still, he swung the hammer down at her face. Crying

out, she yanked his trapped wrist. She flung up her other arm, blocking the blow as he fell toward her.

He sprawled across her chest. An arm clamped tight against his back and she bucked beneath him, squirming and turning, tumbling him over her body. He no sooner hit the mattress than she scurried onto him and smashed a knee into his groin.

His breath blasted out. Stunned with agony, he saw the wooden shaft in her hand. Watched her raise it above his face. He tried to ward off the blow, but his stricken muscles failed to obey.

He had just enough breath to choke out a scream as the stake's point punched through his eye.

EXPLORERS

One

"How about a little detour on the way home?" Pete asked. He started his van moving. Its tires crunched over the gravel of the parking lot.

A detour. Sounded good to Larry. But he said nothing. He knew that Pete's suggestion had been directed to those in the seats behind them. If the wives didn't go for it, the matter was closed.

"You aren't gonna get us lost again, are you?" Barbara asked.

"Who, me?"

"He gets us on those back roads, no telling where we'll end up."

"I always get us home, don't I?"

"Eventually."

Pete glanced at Larry. A corner of his mouth turned up, lifting that side of his mustache. "Why do I put up with this, I ask you?"

Before Larry could come up with an answer, Barbara leaned forward and hooked a tawny forearm across her husband's throat. "Because you love me, right?" she asked. She nipped the ridge of his ear.

"Hey, hey, calm down. You want to run me off the road?"

She wore a sleeveless blouse. A sprinkling of freckles showed on her deeply tanned shoulder. Though the air conditioner was blowing cool air into the van, the skin above her lip gleamed with moisture under a fine, curly down.

Larry didn't want to be caught staring, so he looked away. Just ahead, an old-timer dressed like a prospector was leading a burro along the road's dusty shoulder.

Larry wondered if the guy was for real. Silver Junction, the town they were leaving behind, was full of characters in old west getups. Some seemed like the real article, but he had no doubt that most were simply playing the role for the benefit of the tourists.

"So how about it?" Pete asked as Barbara released him. "Want to do some exploring?"

"I think it'd be fun," Jean said. "You in a hurry to get home, Larry?"

"Me? No."

"He always hates to lose a day," she explained. "I have an awful time trying to drag him out of the house."

"The day's already shot," he said.

"Same to you, fella," Barbara said.

"Whoops. Didn't mean it that way. It's been great." It *had* been a nice change from his usual seven-day work schedule. Fun being out with Pete and Barbara, wandering the old town, watching the gunfight on Main Street, having a burger and a couple of beers in the picturesque saloon. "I need to get out more, anyway, or I'd run dry."

"Everything we do ends up in his books," Jean explained, "but he still hates to be dragged away from his almighty word processor."

"That's what keeps a roof over our heads."

Pete tipped his head back as if to carom his voice off the top of the windshield, the better for Barbara to hear. "Let's take him to that ghost town."

A ghost town.

A warm, pleasant tightness came to Larry's chest and throat.

"You think you can find it?" Barbara asked.

"No sweat." He turned to Larry, grinning. "You'll love it. Just your kind of place."

"It's pretty spooky, all right," Barbara said.

"He'll be in hog heaven."

"I bet you get a book out of it," Pete told him. "Call it *The Horror of Sagebrush Flat*. Maybe have some weirdos lurking around, chopping up everyone."

Larry could feel himself blushing a little with the stir of pride that came whenever people started referring to his grisly novels. "If I did," he said, "you wouldn't read it."

"*I* will," Barbara assured him.

"I know you will. You're my best fan."

"I'll wait for the movie," Pete announced.

"You'll have a long wait."

"You're gonna make it," he said, nodding at Larry and narrowing one eye.

Barbara gave the back of his head a gentle whack. "He's *already* made it, dickhead."

"Hey, hey, watch it with the hands." He smoothed his mussed hair. The thick black hair was threaded with strands of gray. His mustache, with a lot more gray in it, looked as if it belonged on an older face.

"You'll be a wizened, silver-haired old coot," Larry said, "before they ever make a movie of one of my books."

"Ah, bull. You'll make it, mark my words." He tilted his head. *"The Beast of Sagebrush Flat.* I can see it now. I've gotta be one of the characters, right?"

"Of course. You're the guy driving."

"Who's gonna play me? Has to be someone suitably handsome and dashing."

"Pee-wee Herman," Barbara suggested.

"You about ready to die, honey?"

"De Niro," Larry said. "He'd be perfect."

Pete raised an eyebrow and stroked his mustache. "Think so? He's kind of old."

"You're no spring chicken," Barbara said.

"Hey. Thirty-nine. Hardly counts as one foot in the grave."

"Before you start losing your eyesight, you'd better watch for the turnoff."

"I know just where it is. Never fear. I've got a natural instinct for these things. De Niro, huh? Yeah, I like that."

"You'd better slow down," Barbara told him.

"Don't get your shorts in a knot, huh? I know exactly where we're going."

The van swept around a curve of the two-lane blacktop and shot past a road that led off to the left.

"That was it, smart guy."

He leaned against his door and watched the road recede in the side mirror. "Naw."

"Oh yes it was."

"They never listen to us," Jean said.

"That wasn't it," Pete muttered, stepping on the brake. The van slowed. He pulled onto the gravel shoulder, stopped, cranked his window down and stared back. "You really think that's it, honey?"

"If you don't believe me, keep going."

"Shit."

"Maybe we *won't* be visiting a ghost town today," Jean said, sounding amused.

Larry turned in his seat and looked at her. Smiling, she rolled her eyes upward. That expression was as good as words. *What've we gotten ourselves into?* Like Larry, she always got a kick out of the good-natured bickering that went on between Pete and Barbara. But they'd seen the arguments turn nasty, and had occasionally overheard quarrels that sounded truly vicious coming from the couple's next-door house.

"Why don't we give that road a try?" Larry suggested.

"It's not the one."

"Prince Henry the Navigator," Barbara muttered.

"Maybe we should flip a coin," Jean said.

"Do you have a map?" Larry asked.

"Pete doesn't believe in them," Barbara told him, her

voice pleasant. Amazing how she reserved the sarcasm for her husband. "It's up to you, Peter. I've offered my opinion. Feel free to ignore it."

"Oh, hell," he muttered. He started to turn the van around, and Larry saw the look of relief on Jean's face.

"If it's the wrong road," Larry told Barbara, "we hold you personally responsible."

She bared her teeth at him, then laughed softly.

"That's tellin' her, pal." Pete turned the van onto the side road and stepped on the gas. He drove up the middle, ignoring the faded white line. There wasn't enough left of the speed limit sign to read its numbers. The metal had been riddled with bullets. Some of the holes looked fresh, but many were fringed with rust. Pete pointed at the sign. "There's some local color for you. Ol' Barb's *really* gonna be in trouble if we not only take the wrong road, but get shot in the bargain."

"We'll duck if we see any bargain hunters," Larry said.

"Ha! Good one! I hate to tell you, they're in the backseat."

"Can't miss at this range," Jean said.

"We're dead meat."

"You've got nothing to worry about, Petey. You're no bargain."

"I know. I'm priceless. I'm also smart enough to know this isn't the road to Sagebrush Flat. But here we are anyway."

"It was a good decision," Larry assured him. "In my vast experience, I've found it always wiser to go along with female advice."

"That's because it's usually right," Jean said.

"Either way," he told Pete, "you can't lose. First, you make them happy by doing what they tell you. That's the main thing. Let them think they're in control. They love it. Then, if it turns out they were right, everything's cool. If it turns out they were wrong . . ."

"Which is usually the case," Pete added.

"Do they know what thin ice they're on?" Jean asked.

"If they're wrong," Larry went on, "then you have the pleasure of basking in the glow of superiority."

Pete grinned and nodded. "Hey, you oughta put that in one of your books."

"It *was* in one of his books," Barbara said. "If I'm not mistaken, a redneck cop spoke pretty much those very words in *Dead of Night.*"

"Yeah?"

"No kidding?" Larry asked, amazed that she had remembered such a thing.

"Don't you remember?"

He'd quoted one of his own characters without even realizing it? Odd, he thought. And a little disturbing. "I don't know," he admitted. "If you say so, I guess it's there."

"The philosophy at work," Pete said.

"No, I mean it. I write so much . . . That book was a long time ago."

"I have the advantage," Barbara said. "I just read it last month."

"Hey, maybe you're becoming that guy. Turning into your redneck cop. There's an idea for a story, huh? A writer starts turning into this character he made up."

"Has possibilities."

"Well, if you use it, remember where you got the idea."

"Ah-ha!" Barbara said. "Over on the left."

Looking across the road, Larry saw the ruins of an old structure. It no longer had a roof. The door and windowpanes, if it ever had them, were gone. The upper portions of the walls had crumbled away, and some of the rocks that might once have formed the square enclosure now lay in rubble around it—returning to the desert from which they'd been taken.

"Well," Pete said, "I guess this *is* the right road."

"Prince Henry."

"Doesn't look like much of a ghost town," Jean remarked.

"That isn't it," Barbara told her. "But we stopped and had a look around before we got to Sagebrush Flat."

"Nothing much there," Pete said. "Wanta take a quick look?"

"I'd rather get on to the main attraction."

In spite of Jean's earlier comments about her difficulties in getting him out of the house, they'd taken several day trips during the past year to explore the region. Sometimes with Pete and Barbara, a few times by themselves or with Lane—when they could drag their seventeen-year-old daughter away from home. On those outings, Larry had seen plenty of ruins similar to the one they were leaving behind. But not a real ghost town.

"Don't you always wonder who lived in places like that?" Jean asked.

"Prospectors, I should think," Pete said.

" 'Dead guys,' " Larry quoted.

"Leave it to you. The morbid touch."

"Actually, that was Lane's comment. 'Dead guys.' Remember, hon?"

"She went back to the car and waited for us that time. She wanted nothing to do with it."

"I know the feeling," Barbara said. "I think this stuff's interesting, but you gotta know that whoever lived there's been pushing up daisies for a while."

"Cactus," Pete said.

"Whatever. Anyway, dead. Makes it kind of spooky."

"All the better for Larry here."

"Doesn't bother me," Jean said. "I just think it's neat to see where they used to live, and, you know, imagine what it must've been like. It's history."

"Speaking of history," Larry said, "what do you know about this ghost town of yours?"

"Not much," Pete told him.

"He doesn't even know where it is."

"It must be in some of those guidebooks," Jean said.

"Nope. We checked."

"I guess it's nothing all that special," Pete said. "Maybe it's not an official ghost town, or whatever it takes to get noticed—just a wide spot in the road that got deserted." He suddenly grinned at Larry. "Hey, suppose it's just there for us? You know? Like a figment of our imaginations."

"A *ghost* ghost town."

"Yeah! How about that? Another idea for you. You're gonna have to start paying me a consultant's fee."

"You'd do better if you wrote the books yourself."

"Hey, maybe I oughta give it a try. How long does it take you to knock out one of those things?"

"Six months, maybe, to write one. About twenty-five years to learn how."

"You'd better just stick to repairing televisions," Barbara said.

"We coming up on the turnoff?" he asked.

"I'll let you know."

"We didn't get any chance to explore the place last time," Pete said. "Spent too much time screwing around back at that pile of rocks."

"Watch it, buster."

"Anyway, we had to get home for some party you were having, so we just drove right on through Sagebrush."

God, Larry thought, he'd meant it literally. Otherwise Barbara wouldn't have reacted that way. They'd actually screwed in that old ruin. Inside those tumbledown walls. No door. No roof. Right out in the open, almost.

For just a moment he was there. On top of Barbara. Her eyes were half shut, her lips peeled back, her naked body writhing under him as he thrust.

He banished the image, ashamed of his minor betrayal and the desire it stirred. No harm in daydreaming, he told himself. He had such fantasies often, and not just about

Barbara. But he'd never cheated on Jean. He planned to keep it that way.

"You're coming up on it," Barbara said.

Pete slowed nearly to a full stop by the time he made the right-hand turn. The road ahead looked as if it had gone ignored by a generation of repair crews. Only a few faint traces remained of its center line. The gray, sunbaked asphalt was cracked, crumbling, pocked with holes.

The van pitched and bounced, swerved to miss the worst of the potholes. Larry found himself hanging onto the armrest.

"You want to slow down?" Barbara suggested.

"You want to get there, don't you?"

"In one piece, if that's feasible."

A bump rammed the seat against Larry's rump. His teeth clashed.

"Goddamn it!" Barbara snapped.

"Okay, okay. Didn't see that one coming."

After he eased off the gas, the ride was still rough, but not punishing. Larry relaxed his grip on the armrest. Looking out his side window, he saw the rusted-out hulk of an overturned car. Its roof was mashed in and it had no wheels. It was well beyond the embankment bordering the road, surrounded by the desert's litter of broken rock, by cactus and scrub brush. He couldn't imagine how it had come to be belly-up. He considered mentioning the wreck, but decided to keep silent. The thing would probably inspire another story concept from Pete.

No doubt a perfectly mundane explanation for how it got there. Maybe it broke down and was abandoned by the roadside. People had come along later, pushed it out there for the hell of it, and flipped it over. Had nothing better to do. If someone wanted to salvage the tires, rolling the thing probably seemed more sensible than jacking it up one corner at a time.

Not just someone.

Larry felt a quick rush of joy.

A roving band of desert scavengers. A primitive, blood thirsty pack.

Maybe they don't just wait for breakdowns. Maybe they block the road or booby-trap it, then ambush the unlucky travelers. They slaughter the men. They take the women back to their lair—maybe an abandoned mine—for fun and games.

Not bad. Worth toying around with later to see if he could make it work. He needed a new idea. And soon.

"Just around the bend," Barbara said.

Larry peered out the windshield, but the view ahead was blocked by low, rocky slopes. The road curved through a gap between the desolate rises.

Maybe I can work the ghost town into the scavenger idea, he thought as they entered the narrow pass.

"Thar she blows!" Pete announced.

Two

Along the road leading into Sagebrush Flat were the remains of shacks that had been picked apart by the desert winds. Houses of stone, adobe, and brick had fared better, but even those looked battered, their doors hanging open or gone, their windows smashed. Here and there boards lay scattered on the ground near doorways and windows. Larry supposed that the lumber had once been used to seal the dwellings.

The weathered walls of the old houses were pocked with bullet holes, scribbled with sketches and messages in spray paint. Contributions from visitors to this dead town, making a playground of its carcass.

Many of the yards were bordered by broken-down fences. Along with cactus and brush, Larry saw pieces of old furniture in front of some houses: a sofa, a couple of cane chairs, an aluminum lawn chair with its frame twisted crooked. One house had a bathtub off to the side. Another had an overturned bathroom toilet that looked as if it had been the subject of target practice. The rusted hood of a car was leaning against a porch. Nearby lay a couple of tires, and Larry recalled the abandoned, tireless car he'd seen a few minutes ago.

"Isn't exactly Beverly Hills, huh?" Pete remarked.

"Love it," Larry said.

"Gee, and we forgot our spray cans," Jean said. "How can we properly deface the place without our paint?"

"We could shoot it up some." Pete reached beneath hi
seat and came up with a revolver. It was sheathed in
beltless holster. Larry recognized it as the .357 Smith &
Wesson that he'd fired a few times when they'd gon
shooting last month. A beauty.

"Put that away," Barbara said. "For godsake."

"Just kidding around. Don't get your balls in an uproar.'

As he concealed the handgun under his seat, Barbar
said, "Men and their toys."

Pete swung the van off the road and stopped beside
pair of gasoline pumps. He beeped the horn a couple o
times as if signaling for service.

"God," Barbara muttered.

"Hey, wouldn't it be something if a guy *showed up?*"

Larry gazed past the pumps. The porch stairs led up t
a country store with a screen door hanging by a singl
hinge. A faded wooden sign above the doorway identifie
the place as Holman's. A row of windows faced the road
Not a single pane was still intact. The window opening
looked like mouths with sharp glass teeth.

"Might as well start here," Pete said.

"Great," Larry said. He thought it might be interesting
to go through some of the houses they'd passed on th
way in, but those could wait for another day. He was mor
eager to explore the downtown area.

He climbed out of the van. The wind and heat hit him
Jean grimaced when she stepped down. The wind blew he
hair back, made her blouse and skirt cling to the front o
her slim body as if they were wet.

"Better lock up," Pete called.

"There's nobody around to steal anything," Barbara said

"Would you rather I take the magnum along?"

"Okay, okay, we'll lock the doors."

Larry took care of their side. They met Pete and Barbar
in front of the van.

"I would feel better if we took the gun with us," Pete said.

"Well, I wouldn't."

"You never know about a place like this."

"If you think it's dangerous, we shouldn't be here." Barbara tossed her head to clear her face of blowing blond hair. The wind parted her untucked blouse below the last button, and Larry glimpsed a triangle of tanned belly.

"Might be rattlers," Pete said.

"We'll watch our step," Jean told him. Like Larry, she was no doubt eager to end the gun debate before it could escalate into a quarrel.

"Yeah," Larry said. "And if we run into any bad guys, we'll send you back here for the artillery."

"Oh, thanks. While you guys hide."

"You wouldn't mind, would you, honey?"

He answered by clamping a hand on Barbara's rump. The way she flinched and jumped away, he must've done it hard. She whirled toward him. "Just watch it, huh?"

"Let's see what's in Holman's," Jean said, and hurried toward the stairs.

Larry went after her. "Careful," he said. The boards, bleached pale, were warped and threaded with splits. The one before the top was broken in the middle, half gone and half hanging down by rusty nails.

Jean held the railing, stepped over the demolished stair and made it safely across the porch. While she dragged the screen door open, Larry climbed the stairs. They creaked under his weight but held him.

"You better not try it," Pete warned Barbara, looking back at her as he trotted up the old planks. "You'll snap 'em like matchsticks."

"Give it a rest," she said.

Larry admired her restraint. It seemed so damn stupid of Pete to poke fun at his wife's size. She was big, probably a shade over six feet tall. Though not a beanpole, like

many tall women, she certainly wasn't overweight. Larry
had seen her in all kinds of attire, including swimsuits and
nightgowns, and considered her body terrific. He knew
that Pete was proud of her appearance. Pete was compact
and powerful, but lifting all the weights in the world
wouldn't give him the six inches of height he would need
to meet Barbara eye to eye.

Instead of calling him "short stuff" or "pip-squeak,"
she'd simply told him to give it a break. Admirable.

She climbed the stairs without bursting any of them.

Inside, Holman's smelled of dry, ancient wood. Larry
expected the place to be stifling, but the shade and the
breeze from the broken windows kept it bearable. A thin
layer of sand coated the hardwood floor. It had blown into
small drifts against the walls, the foot of the L-shaped
lunch counter, and the metal bases of the swivel stools
along the counter.

The eating area occupied about a third of the room.
There had probably once been tables between the counter
and the wall, but they were long gone.

"Bet they served great cheeseburgers," Jean said. She
was very fond of diners with character. To Jean, dumpy
old places that many people would disparage as "greasy
spoons" promised delights unattainable in clean and modern fast-food chains.

"Shakes," Barbara said. "I could go for one about now."

"I could go for a beer," Pete said.

"I think I saw a saloon up the road," Jean told him.

"But they only serve Ghost-Light," Larry said.

"Let's break a few out of the van before we move on."

"You've got a beer?" Larry could *taste* it.

"Surely you jest. The desert's one dry mother. You think
I'd brave her without my survival stash?"

"All *right!*"

Pete headed for the door.

"Aren't you going to look around?" Barbara asked.

"What's to see?" He hurried outside.

"I guess he's right," Jean said, scanning the room.

"The rest of it must've been a general store," Larry said. "I bet they carried everything."

Nothing remained, not even shelves. Except for the lunch counter and stools, the room was bare. Behind the counter was a serving window. Farther down, Larry saw a closed door that probably connected with the kitchen. Past the end of the counter was an alcove. "That's probably where the rest rooms were."

"I think I'll check out the ladies'," Barbara said.

"Lotsa luck," Jean told her.

"Can't hurt to have a look."

She walked into the alcove, opened a door, and whirled away clutching her mouth.

"Apparently," Larry said, "it did hurt to take a look."

Barbara scrunched up her face.

"You're a little green around the gills," Jean told her.

She lowered her hand and took a deep breath. "Guess I'll find a place around back."

They left Holman's. She followed the porch, jumped off, and disappeared around a corner of the building.

Larry and Jean went to the van. When Pete came out he had four bottles of beer clutched to his chest. "Where's Barb?"

"Went behind the building."

"Answering a call of nature," Jean said.

He scowled. "She shouldn't have gone off by herself."

"She may not want an audience," Jean explained.

"Damn it. Barb!" he yelled.

No answer. He called again, and Larry saw a trace of worry in his eyes.

"She probably can't hear you," Larry said. "The wind and everything."

"Take these, okay? I've gotta make sure she's okay."

Jean and Larry each took two bottles from his arms
"She's only been gone a couple of minutes."

"Yeah, well . . ." He hurried away, jogging toward th
far end of Holman's.

"Hope he doesn't tear her head off," Jean said.

"At least he's worried about her. That's something, any
way."

"I sure wish they'd quit bickering."

"They must enjoy it."

Jean wandered toward the road, and Larry stayed at he
side. The bottles of beer felt cold and wet in his hands
He took a drink from the one in his right.

"You'll be having to go yourself, if you don't watch it.'

"Don't let Pete come to my rescue," he said, and turne
his attention to the town.

The central road had broad, gravel shoulders for parking
The sidewalks were concrete, not the elevated planking
common to such old west towns as Silver Junction, wher
they'd spent the morning. The citizens had made som
modern improvements before leaving Sagebrush Flat to th
desert.

"I wonder why they left," Larry said.

"Wouldn't you?"

"I wouldn't live anywhere that doesn't have movie thea
ters."

"Well, I don't see any."

Neither did Larry. From his position in the middle of the
road, he could see the entire town. Not one of the building
had a movie marquee jutting over the sidewalk. He saw a
barber pole in front of one small shop; a place on the lef
with a faded sign that proclaimed it to be Sam's Saloon
about a dozen other enterprises altogether. He guessed tha
they'd once been hardware stores, cafés, possibly a bakery
clothing stores, maybe a pharmacy and a five-and-ten, a
dentist's and doctor's office—and how about an optimisti
realtor?—and certainly a sporting goods store. Not even the

smallest back-country town in California was without a place to buy guns and ammo. Way at the far end of town, on the left, stood an adobe building with a pair of bay doors and service islands in front. Babe's Garage.

The centerpiece of town appeared to be the three-story, wood-frame structure of the Sagebrush Flat Hotel, right next door to Sam's Saloon.

"That's the place I'd like to explore," Larry said.

"Sam's?"

"That, too. But the hotel. It looks like it's been around for a while."

"We'd better go there next, then. No telling how long this little expedition's going to last, those two start fighting."

"We'll have to come back by ourselves, sometime, and really check the place out."

"I don't know." She drank some beer. "I'm not sure I'd want to come here without some company."

"Hey, what am I, chopped liver?"

"You know what I mean."

He knew. Though he and Jean shared a desire for adventure, they were limited by a certain timidity. The presence of another couple seemed to erase that weakness. They needed backup.

Backup like Pete and Barbara. In spite of the bickering, each was endowed with self-confidence and force. Led by that pair, Larry and Jean were willing to venture where they wouldn't go on their own.

Even if we'd known about this place, Larry thought, we wouldn't have dared to explore it by ourselves. The chance of a return trip, at least in the near future, was slim.

Jean turned around and looked toward the corner of Holman's. "I wonder what's keeping them."

"Should we go find out?"

"I don't think so."

Larry took a swig of cold beer.

"Why don't we get out of the sun?" Jean suggested.

They wandered back past the van, climbed the rickety stairs to Holman's shaded porch and sat down. They rested the two extra beers on the wood between them. Jean crossed her legs. She rubbed her bare thighs with the base of her bottle. The wetness left slicks on her skin. She lifted the bottle to her face and slid it over her cheeks and forehead.

Larry imagined Jean opening her blouse, rolling the chilled, dripping bottle against her bare breasts. She wasn't the kind of woman who would ever do that, though. Hell, she wouldn't even step out of the house unless she had a bra on.

Too bad life can't be more like fiction, he told himself, and drank some more beer. A gal in one of his books would have that wet bottle sliding over her chest in about two shakes. Then, of course, the guy would get in on the action.

That'd be a scene worth writing.

You'll never get a chance to *live* it, not in this lifetime, but . . .

"Larry, I'm starting to get worried."

"They'll be along."

"Something must be wrong."

"Maybe she has a problem."

"Like the trots?"

"Who knows?"

"They'd be back by now if *something* hadn't happened," Jean said.

"Maybe Pete got lucky."

"They wouldn't do that."

"Obviously they did it back at that old ruin we passed."

"Sounded like it. But they were alone. They wouldn't do that here with us waiting."

"If you're so sure, why don't we go around back and look for them?"

"Go right on ahead." She gave him an annoyed glance.

"Nah." He put a hand on her back. Her blouse was damp. He untucked it and slipped his hand beneath it. She sat up straight, and sighed as he caressed her.

When he fingered the catches of her bra, she said, "Don't get carried away. They could show up any second."

"On the other hand, maybe they won't show up at all."

"Don't kid around like that, okay?"

"I'm not entirely kidding."

"Maybe they *are* screwing around."

"You said they wouldn't."

"Well, I don't know, damn it."

"Maybe we'd better go see."

Jean wrinkled her nose.

"If they did run into trouble," Larry said, "we aren't making matters any better by procrastinating. They might need help."

"Yeah, okay."

"Besides, their beers are getting warm."

He picked up the bottle for Pete, stood, and waited for Jean. Then they walked to the end of the porch. Larry peered around the corner. The area alongside the building was clear, so he leaped down. Jean covered the mouth of Barbara's bottle with her thumb and jumped.

"I don't know about this," she said.

"They can't expect us to wait forever."

Larry led the way, wanting to be a few strides ahead of Jean in case there really was trouble.

At times like this he wished his imagination would take a holiday. But it never left him alone. It was always busy churning up possibilities—most of them grim.

He pictured Pete and Barbara dead, of course. Slaughtered by the same pack of desert scavengers he'd dreamed up when he saw the overturned car.

Maybe Pete had been killed, Barbara abducted.

We'd have to go looking for her. Run back to the van first and get Pete's gun.

Maybe they both got killed by a criminal using the old town as a hideout.

Or by an old lunatic on the lookout for claim jumpers.

Maybe they'll just be gone. Vanished without a trace.

Pete has the keys to the van. We'd have to walk out of here.

He supposed the nearest town was Silver Junction.

God, it'd take hours to get there. And maybe someone would be after them, hunting them down.

"Better warn 'em we're coming," Jean said.

He stopped near the corner of the building, looked back at her and shook his head. "If they ran into someone . . ."

"Don't even think it, okay?"

From the look on Jean's face, he could see that she'd already considered the possibility.

"Just go ahead and call out," she said. "We don't want to barge in on something."

Speak for yourself, he thought. If Pete was having at her, he wouldn't mind a glimpse of it. Not at all. But he kept the thoughts to himself.

Without looking around the corner, he yelled, "Pete! Barbara! You all right?"

No answer came.

A second ago he'd pictured them rutting. Now he saw them sprawled dead, murderous savages hunched over their bodies, heads turning at the sound of his voice.

He gestured for Jean to wait, and stepped past the end of the building.

Three

"Where are they?" Jean whispered, pressing herself against his side.

Larry shook his head. He couldn't believe the couple was actually gone. "They probably just wandered off somewhere," he said. The idea that he would catch them fooling around had been the product of wishful thinking, and he knew that his worries about murder had been far-fetched. But so had his worries that they'd disappeared.

"We'd better find them," Jean said.

"Good plan."

But all he saw were the rear facades of the other buildings, and the desert stretching away toward a ridge of mountains to the south.

"Maybe they're playing some kind of trick on us," Jean suggested.

"I don't know. Pete was awfully eager for his beer."

"People don't go for a leak and vanish off the face of the earth."

"Only on occasion."

"It's not funny." Her voice was trembling.

"Look, they've got to be around."

"Maybe we'd better go and get the gun."

"It's locked in the van. I don't imagine Pete would be very happy about a broken window."

"Pete!" she suddenly shrieked. *"Barb!"*

A distant voice called, "Yo!"

Jean's eyebrows flew up. Her head snapped sideways and she squinted out at the desert.

Some fifty yards off, Pete's head and shoulders rose out of the wasteland. "Hey, y'gotta see this!" he shouted, and waved for them to approach.

Jean glanced at Larry, rolled her eyes and sagged as if her air had been let out.

He grinned.

"I think I may kill them myself," Jean said.

"I'll go get the gun."

"Break *all* the windows, while you're at it." Her voice sounded shaky.

"Come on, let's see what they found."

"It better be good."

They walked over the hard, baked earth, moving carefully as they stepped on broken rocks, avoided clumps of cactus and greasewood. Near the place where Pete waited was an old smoke tree. Larry guessed that Barbara had wandered farther and farther away from Holman's, looking for a suitably large bush or rock cluster, and had finally decided upon the tree. Its trunk was thick enough to afford privacy, and there was shade beneath its drooping branches.

Pete was standing some distance from the tree. At his back the ground dropped away.

"What'd you find?" Larry asked. "The Grand Canyon?"

"Hey, glad you brought the suds." He lifted the front of his knit shirt and wiped his face. "It's *nasty* out here."

Larry handed the full bottle to him.

The depression behind Pete was a dry streambed some fifteen or twenty feet lower than the surrounding flatlands. Barbara, sitting on a rock at the bottom, looked up and waved.

"Did you forget about us?" Jean asked Pete.

He finished taking a swig of beer, then shook his head. "I was just on my way to get you. Figured you might want to see this." He started down the steep embankment, and they followed.

"We were getting a little worried," Larry said, watching his feet as he descended the rocky slope. "Thought you might've fallen victim to a roving band of desert marauders."

"Yeah? That's a good one. Make a good story, huh?"

Barbara stood up and brushed off the seat of her white shorts. "God, it's hot as a huncher down here," she said, as they approached. Her blouse was unbuttoned, its front tied, leaving her midriff bare. The knot was loose enough to leave a gap. Her bra was black. Larry saw the pale sides of her breasts through its lace. "No breeze at all," she added.

"What's the big discovery?" Jean asked, handing a beer to her.

"It's no big deal, if you ask me." She tipped the bottle up. Larry saw a bead of sweat drop from her jaw, roll off her collarbone, and slide down her chest until it melted into the edge of her bra.

"Over here," Pete said. "Come on."

He led the way to a cut eroded into the wall of the embankment. There, lying in shadows and partly hidden by tangles of brush, was the demolished carcass of a jukebox. "Must've come from that café," he said, nudging its side with his shoe.

"How'd it get all the way out here?" Jean asked.

"Who knows?"

"The thing's no good, anyway," Barbara said.

"It's seen better days," Larry said, feeling a touch of nostalgia as he pictured it standing fresh and bright near the lunch counter in Holman's. He guessed that someone had dragged it out and used it for target practice. It would've made a tempting target, all decorated with bright chrome and plastic—if the shooter happened to be an asshole who took pleasure from destroying things of such beauty. After the box was blasted to smithereens, it had probably been shoved off the edge of the slope for the fun of watching it tumble and crash.

Larry crouched beside its shattered plastic top. The rows of record slots were empty. The tone arm dangled from its mount by a couple of wires.

"Probably worth a few of grand," Pete said.

"Forget it," Barbara told him. "He thinks we should take it with us."

"She's sure a beaut," Pete said. "A Wurlitzer."

"Think you could get it working?" Jean asked.

"Sure."

He probably could, Larry thought. The guy's house was a museum of resurrected junk: televisions, stereo components, a toaster oven, lamps, a dishwasher and vacuum cleaner, all once disgarded as useless, picked up by Pete and restored to working order.

"You might get it playing again," he said, "but it's too messed up to ever look like anything." Its chrome trim was dented and rusty, one side of the cabinet was smashed in, the speaker grills looked as if they'd been hit by shotgun blasts, and bullets had torn away at least half the square plastic buttons used for selecting tunes. "You probably can't even get replacement parts for a lot of this stuff," he added.

"Sure would be neat, though."

"Yeah." Turning his head sideways, Larry blew dust and sand from its chart of selections. Bullets and shotgun pellets had ripped away some of the labels. Those that remained were faint, washed out by rainfall and years of pounding sunlight. Still, he could make out the names of many titles and artists. Jean crouched and peered over his shoulder.

"There's 'Hound Dog,' " he said. " 'I Fall to Pieces,' 'Stand by Your Man.' "

"God, I used to love that one," Jean said.

"Sounds like it's mostly shit-kicker stuff," Pete said.

"Well, here's the Beatles. 'Hard Day's Night.' The Mamas and the Papas."

"Oh, they were good," Barbara said.

"This one's 'California Dreaming,' " Larry told her.

"Always makes me sad when I think about Mama Cass."

"All right!" Larry grinned. " 'The Battle of New Orleans.' Johnny Horton. Man, I must've been in junior high. I knew that sucker by heart."

"There's Haley Mills," Jean said, her breath stirring the hair above Larry's ear. " 'Let's Get Together.' And look, 'Soldier Boy.' "

"Here's the Beach Boys, 'Surfin' U.S.A.' "

"Now we're talking," Pete said.

"Dennis Wilson, too," Barbara said. "So many of those people are dead. Mama Cass, Elvis, Lennon. Jesus, this is getting depressing."

"Patsy Cline's dead, too," Jean told her.

"And Johnny Horton, I think," Larry said.

"What do you guys expect?" Pete said. "This stuff's all at least twenty, thirty years old."

Barbara took a few steps backward, stumbled when her sneaker came down on a rock, but managed to stay up. Sweaty face grimacing, she said, "Why don't we get out of this hellhole and look around town? That's what we came here for, isn't it?"

"Might as well." Jean pushed against Larry's shoulder and rose from her squat.

"Let's see if we can lift this thing," Pete muttered.

"Oh no you don't!" Barbara snapped. "No way! You're not carting that piece of trash home with us. Uh-uh."

"Well, shit."

"If you want an old jukebox so bad, go out and buy one, for godsake. Jesus, it's probably got scorpions in it."

"I think you'd better forget it," Larry said, rising to his feet. "The thing's beyond saving."

"Yeah, I guess. Shit." He gave his wife a sour look. "Thanks a heap, Barbara dear."

She ignored his remark and started climbing the slope. Below her rucked-up blouse her back looked tawny and slick. The rear of her shorts was smudged with yellow dust from the rock where she'd sat. The fabric hugged her buttocks, and Larry could see the outline of her panties—a narrow band inches lower than the belt of her shorts, a skimpy triangle curving down from it. Jean, climbing behind her, was hunched over slightly. Her blouse was still untucked. It clung to her back, and the loose tail draped her rump.

Pete was watching, too.

"Couple of good-looking chicks," he said.

"Not bad."

"You ever get the feeling they run our fucking lives for us?"

"Only about ninety-nine percent of the time."

Pete choked out a laugh, slapped Larry's arm, and took a long drink of beer. "Guess we'd better be good little boys and go with them." He glanced back at the jukebox. He sighed. He shrugged. "Adios. No more music for you, old pal."

"So much for that," Larry said when he saw the padlocked hasp across the double doors of the Sagebrush Flat Hotel.

Pete fingered the lock. "Doesn't look very old."

"Maybe someone's living here," Barbara said.

"Hey, Sherlock, it's locked from the outside. What does that tell you?"

"Tells me we'd be trespassing."

"Yeah," Jean said. "The doors are locked, the windows are boarded. Somebody's trying to keep people out."

"Kind of sparks my curiosity. What about you, Lar?"

"Sparks mine, too. But I don't know about breaking in."

"Who's gonna find out?" Pete turned away from the doors. He stepped off the sidewalk, bent over and swept his head slowly from side to side in a broad pantomime of scanning the town's only road. "I don't see anyone. Do you see anyone?"

"We get the point," Barbara told him.

"I'll just mosey on over to the van." He started across the pavement, walking at an angle toward Holman's.

"What's he got in mind?" Jean asked.

"God knows. Maybe he's planning to ram the doors open."

"That'd be rather drastic," Larry said.

"It's a matter of pride, at this point. A challenge. Pete wouldn't be Pete if he let a little thing like a lock keep him out."

Jean rolled her eyes upward. "I guess this means we're going to explore the hotel whether we want to or not."

"Just consider it an adventure," Larry suggested.

"Yeah, right. Jail would be an adventure, too."

Pete climbed into the rear of the van. A few seconds later he jumped down, swung the door shut, and waved a lug wrench overhead. It had a pry bar at one end. In his other hand was a flashlight.

He's really going to break in, Larry thought. Good Christ.

Barbara waited until he was closer, then called, "We've been having some second thoughts about this, Pete."

"Hey, what's life if you don't take a little chance now and then. Right, Lar?"

"Right," he answered, trying to sound game.

"You're a lot of help," Jean muttered.

Pete bounded onto the sidewalk, grinning and brandishing his tire iron. "Got my skeleton key right here," he announced. "Fits any lock."

"Anybody want to wait in the van?" Barbara asked.

"Ah, pussy."

"Well, I guess I'd like to have a look around," Larry said.

"Good man."

Pete gave the flashlight to Larry. Then he rammed the wedge end of the bar behind the metal strap of the hasp. He yanked with both hands, throwing his weight backward. Wood groaned and split. With a sound like a small explosion the staple burst out of the door, bolts and all. "Well, that was a cinch."

He shoved the bar under his belt, turned the knob on the right and pulled the door open.

"I suppose we could always say we found it like this," Barbara muttered.

"You won't have to *say* anything. Half an hour or so, we'll be long gone."

"If we don't get shot for trespassing."

Ignoring her remark, Pete leaned into the doorway and called, "Yoo-hoo. Anybody home?"

Larry winced.

"Here we come, ready or not!"

"Cut it out," Barbara whispered, slapping the back of his shoulder.

"Nobody home but us ghosts," he said in a low, scratchy voice, and turned around grinning.

"Real cute."

"So who's coming in?"

"I think we should all go in or none of us," Larry said, hoping Pete wouldn't figure him for a pussy. "I don't think we should split up. I'd be worried the whole time that something might happen to the gals while we're in there looking around."

"Good man," Barbara said, and patted his back.

"Guess you're right," Pete admitted. "If they got themselves raped and murdered while we were in there, boy would we feel like a couple of heels."

"Exactly."

"Real cute," Jean said, borrowing not only Barbara's phrase but also her disdainful tone.

"What do you say?" Barbara asked her.

"They'll hold it against us forever if they can't go in on our account."

"Admit it," Pete said. "You're dying to come with us."

"Let's get it over with," Barbara said.

Larry gave the flashlight back to Pete and followed him into the hotel. In spite of the closed doors and boarded windows, sand had found its way into the lobby. It made soft scraping sounds under their shoes.

"We probably shouldn't leave the door open," Jean said. There was a tremor in her hushed voice. "In case someone comes by." Without waiting for a reply, she closed the door, shutting out most of the daylight.

Light still came in around the doors, spilled through cracks and knotholes in the planks across the windows— pale, dusty streamers that slanted down to the floor. Pete turned his flashlight on, its beam pushing a tunnel of brightness into the gloom. He swept it from side to side.

"Boy, there's a lot to see in here," Barbara whispered. "What a find!"

The lobby was bare except for a registration counter. On the wall behind the counter were cubbyholes for mail or messages. Over to the left a wooden staircase rose steeply toward the upper floors.

"Should we check in before we have a look around?" Pete asked.

"Probably no vacancies," Larry whispered.

"A couple of real comedians," Jean muttered.

Pete led the way to the counter, pounded its top and

said in a loud voice, "How does a guy get some service around here?"

"Creep. You want to hold it down?"

"What's everybody whispering for?" He vaulted the counter, dropped into the space behind it and ducked out of sight. He reappeared, rising slowly, the flashlight at his chin to cast weird shadows up his face. Where the beam touched him, his skin gleamed with sweat.

Goofing off like a kid, Larry thought. But he sometimes pulled the same gag, especially around Halloween, more to amuse himself than to frighten Jean or Lane. They had come to expect such antics. The old flashlight-on-the-face routine hadn't scared Lane since she was about two.

It did make Pete look strange and menacing. Larry knew that if he let his mind go with it, he *would* get a shiver. "Mmm-yes?" Pete asked, pitching his voice high. "May I help zee veary travelers?"

"God, it's hot in here," Jean whispered.

"A damn oven," Barbara said.

"Anything back there?" Larry asked, carefully avoiding his friend's face.

"Only me and zee spirit of zee night clerk, who hung himself many years ago."

"If we're going to look around," Jean said, "why don't we, and get out of here?"

"I'd like to have a look upstairs," Larry said.

"Vait. Let me ring for zee bell captain."

"Oh, the hell with him," Barbara muttered. "Come on." She turned around and headed for the stairs. Jean went after her, and Larry followed. Barbara's legs and the bare part of her back were nearly invisible in the darkness. Her white shorts and blouse, pale blurs, seemed to float above the floor on their own. Jean, in darker clothes, was a faint smudge in front of him.

He heard Pete strike the floor and stride up behind him, sand crunching under his shoes. The flashlight beam flicked across the backs of the women, swung over to the staircase and swept upward, skimming past balusters, tossing their long shadows against the wall. Midway up was a small landing. The remaining stairs rose to the narrow opening of the second-floor corridor.

"You don't want to go first, do you?" Pete asked in his normal voice as Barbara started to climb.

"If I wait for you, we'll be here all day."

The light moved downward, gliding just above the stair treads, and something touched by the low edge of its aura winked like gold. A small, questioning breath of surprise came from Pete. The light skittered backward and down. Its bright center came to rest on a crucifix. "Christ," he whispered.

"That's right," Larry said.

The crucifix, directly below the landing, was attached to wood paneling that closed off the space beneath the staircase.

"What is it?" Barbara asked, leaning over the banister near the bottom of the stairs.

"Somebody left a crucifix on the wall," Larry told her.

"Is that all?" She leaned farther out, then shook her head. "Big deal," she said.

Jean stepped around the side of the staircase for a closer look.

"Anybody want a souvenir?" Pete asked. He strode toward the crucifix.

"No, don't," Larry warned.

"Hey, somebody just forgot it here. Finders keepers."

"Leave it alone," Barbara said from her perch on the stairs. "For godsake, you don't go around stealing crosses. That's sick."

The cross was made of wood. The suspended figure of Jesus looked as if it might be gold-plated. Pete reached for it.

"Please don't," Jean said.

He looked at her. "Oh," he said. "Oh, yeah." Apparently he had just remembered that Jean was Catholic. He lowered his hand. "Sorry. I was just kidding around."

"Reason prevails," Barbara muttered. She pushed herself away from the banister and resumed climbing.

She got as far as the landing.

The wood creaked under her weight, then burst with a hard flat crack like a gunshot.

Barbara sucked in her breath. She flung her arms up as if trying to find a handhold in the dark air as she dropped straight down.

Four

"My God!" Pete shouted.

Jean, racing up the stairs, called out, "Hang on!"

"I'm slipping! Hurry!"

Larry dashed toward the foot of the stairs. He didn't hear Pete coming. "Where *are* you, man?"

"Get up there and grab her!" Pete snapped.

"Oh shit," Barbara groaned.

Larry swung himself around the newel post. As he rushed up behind Jean he saw the hazy glow of Pete's flashlight ahead and to the right of the stairs. Hadn't the guy moved? Was he still down there in front of the crucifix?

Jean sank to her knees at the edge of the landing.

Barbara, her back to the lower stairs, looked like someone being swallowed by quicksand. She was hunched forward, pressing her chest against the remaining boards, bracing herself up with her elbows.

Jean crawled aside to make a space for Larry, then hooked an arm under Barbara's left armpit. "Gotcha," she gasped. "I gotcha. You're not gonna fall."

"Are you okay?" Pete called up.

"No, damn it!"

Larry dropped against the landing and stairs, looked down into a six-inch gap between the broken planks and the white of Barbara's blouse. Blackness.

A bottomless pit, he thought. An abyss.

Ridiculous, he told himself. Probably no more than a

six- or seven-foot drop, all told, from the landing to the lobby floor. She was already about halfway there.

What if the floor doesn't extend under the staircase? Or she breaks through that, too?

Even if she had only a four-foot fall, she would end up trapped under the staircase. And the broken boards might scrape her up pretty good on the way down.

He squirmed forward until his face met the hair on the back of Barbara's head. He wrapped his arms around her. They squeezed her breasts. Muttering "Sorry," he worked them lower and hugged her rib cage.

"Pete!" he yelled.

"You got her?" Pete's voice still came from below.

"Just barely. If you'd give us a goddamn hand!"

He heard a crack of splitting wood. For a moment he thought that more of the landing was giving out. Nothing happened, though.

"Yah!" Barbara yelped, jerking in Larry's embrace. "Something's *got me!*"

"It's just me, hon."

For an instant a pale tongue of light licked the darkness beside Larry's right shoulder. It had risen through the broken boards.

Pete's under us, he realized.

"How'd you get down there?" Jean asked. She sounded amazed, relieved.

"Tire tool magic," Pete said. "Okay, I've got you, hon. Let's lower her gently."

"No no no, don't! I'll fall."

"We gotta get you down outa there."

"Well, boost me up, okay?" Her voice was controlled, but tight with pain or fear. "If I try to go down, I'll get wracked up even more."

"All right. We'll give it a try. You guys ready up there? On the count of three."

"You gonna push her up by her legs?" Jean asked.

"That's the idea. One. Two."

"Take it easy," Barbara urged him, "or I'll end up with a bunch of wood in me."

"Okay. One. Two. Three."

Barbara came up slowly through the break as if she were standing on an elevator. Still hugging her chest, Larry struggled to his knees. She swayed back against him. He slid a hand down the slick, bare skin of her belly. She gasped and flinched. Then he grabbed her belt buckle, yanked upward, pulled her hard against him, and she came to rest sitting at the brink of the gap.

"Okay," she gasped. "I'm okay. Give me a second to catch my breath."

Larry and Jean held onto her arms.

"All right up there?" Pete asked. The beam of his flashlight swept back and forth through the break in front of Barbara's knees.

Barbara didn't answer.

"She's safe," Jean called down.

The beam slid away and only a faint glow drifted out of the opening.

"I want to go home," Barbara muttered. Larry and Jean held her steady while she leaned back and drew her legs up. She planted her shoes against the rim of splintered wood at the gap's far side.

"Jesus!" Startled, scared.

Barbara went rigid. "Pete! What's wrong!"

"Holy jumpin' . . . Oh, man." Not quite so scared now. Amazed. "Hey, you're not gonna believe this. Honest to motherin' God. Larry, get down here."

"What?"

Barbara leaned forward and peered between her spread legs. "What is it?"

"You don't want to know."

"This is no time for games, Peter."

"You're just damn lucky you didn't wind up down here."

For a moment no one said anything.

Then Pete's voice came up through the crevice. "You would've had company."

Shivers ran up Larry's back.

"There's an old stiff in here."

He's kidding, Larry thought. But his body knew that Pete was telling the truth. His cheeks suddenly felt numb. He had trouble getting enough breath. His bowels went shaky. His scrotum shriveled up tight, as if someone had just grabbed it with a handful of ice.

"Oh jeez," Barbara muttered. Jean and Larry got out of her way as she twisted around, grabbed the banister, and struggled to her feet. They followed her down the stairs. She held the railing and moved slowly, hunched over just a bit. Her blouse now hung all the way down her back.

"I knew I didn't like this place," Jean whispered.

Barbara went straight to the hotel door and threw it open. Daylight flooded in. She stopped in the doorway and turned sideways. She was squinting. Her teeth were bared. Though Larry was several feet away, he could see her trembling. Her hands shook as she pinched the edges of her blouse and spread its front wide. She gazed down at the raw band of skin across her belly.

Her breasts looked very white through the open patterns of her bra. Larry glimpsed the darker skin of her nipples. She was too hurt and dazed for modesty, and Larry felt like a cheap voyeur taking advantage of her carelessness. In spite of the guilt, he didn't want to look away. There was a dead body under the stairs. Somehow, the sight of Barbara's skin through the black lace bra eased his sick dread.

But he forced his eyes lower. The right leg of her shorts was rucked up higher than the left. Both thighs were scraped, her shins bleeding. The right was worse than the left, but both legs had been abraded in the fall.

Jean went to her. "You really *did* get wracked up."

"You're telling me."

"Where is everyone?" Pete called. His voice sounded muffled.

"Barbara's really banged up," Larry answered. "Come on out of there and let's go home."

"You've gotta see this! It'll just take a minute."

I don't want to see it.

"Man, your wife is hurt."

"What's one more minute or two? We've got a *dead body* here. You're a writer, for godsake. A *horror* writer. I'm telling you, this isn't something you want to miss. Come on."

"Go ahead if you want," Jean told him. "We'll start on over for the van."

Larry wrinkled his nose.

Barbara nodded, still grimacing and shaking. Her face and chest were shiny with sweat. Larry found himself looking again at her breasts. "Go on," she said. "It'll make him happy."

"You gals don't want to see it?"

"You've got to be kidding," Jean said.

"Just make it quick," Barbara told him.

He turned away from the door. He walked slowly across the lobby floor. Glancing back, he saw Jean and Barbara step outside.

He felt abandoned.

I don't have to be here, he thought. I could be out there with them.

He did not want to see a damn corpse.

But his weak legs kept moving him away from the sunlight.

Alongside the staircase a wide section of paneling had been ripped loose and gaped open a couple of feet. The glow of Pete's flashlight showed through the space. Larry turned sideways and stepped into the enclosure.

"Thought you were going to chicken out on me," Pete said.

"Can't miss a chance like this."

He found Pete standing on a couple of boards that had fallen from the landing. He looked frozen there, back rigid, his right arm straight out, aiming the flashlight almost as if it were a pistol. Aiming it at the coffin that was jammed headfirst against the underside of a low stair.

The body was covered, at least to the neck, by an old brown blanket. The blanket was rumpled as if it had been tossed into the coffin by someone who didn't care to straighten it.

The corpse had long yellow hair. The skin of its face looked tight and leathery. Larry saw sunken eyelids, hollow cheeks, lips that were stretched back in a mad grin that exposed teeth and gums.

"You believe this?" Pete whispered.

Larry shook his head. "Maybe it isn't real."

"My ass. I know a stiff when I see one."

"Looks almost mummified."

"Yeah. Guess we oughta check it out, huh?"

Shoulder to shoulder, they moved slowly forward. Pete kept his light on the corpse.

Hideous, Larry thought. He'd never seen such a thing. His experience with bodies was limited to three open-casket funerals. Those people had looked almost good enough to sit up and shake hands with you.

This one looked as if it might want to sit up and take a bite out of you.

Don't think that stuff, Larry told himself.

The underside of the stairway slanted down in front of them. They had to duck as they stepped to the foot of the coffin. Pete sank into a squat and waddled in farther. Larry started in, crouching. But after one step a sense of suffocation stopped him. The stairs seemed to be pressing down on him, wanting to shove him lower, to rub his face in the corpse. He dropped to his knees and reached out, ready to brace himself on the wooden edge of the coffin. Just before he touched it, he realized what he was about to do. He jerked his hands back and clutched his thighs.

The blanket piled on top of the corpse didn't cover its ankles and feet. They were bare, the color of stained wood, and bones showed through the tight skin. The nails were so long that they curled over the tops of the toes. Larry recalled that hair and nails supposedly continued to grow after death. But he'd heard that that was just a myth; they only *appeared* to grow because the skin sank in around them.

"Bet it's been here a long time," Pete whispered. He reached over the side of the coffin. With his index finger he brushed the corpse's forehead.

Larry moaned.

"What's wrong?"

"How can you *touch* it?"

"No big deal. Try it. Feels like shoe leather." He drew his finger across a blond eyebrow.

Larry imagined Pete's finger sliding down the ridge of the eye socket, touching the lid, denting it, sinking in to the second knuckle.

"Go on and touch it," Pete urged him. "How you going to write about this stuff if you don't experience it?"

"Thanks, anyway. I'll rely on my imagi—"

"We changed our minds."

He flinched at the sound of Barbara's voice. So did Pete. Pete's head slammed the underside of a stair. He cried, "Ah!" ducked down close to the face of the corpse and grabbed the back of his head. "Shit! Damn it, Barb!"

"Sorry."

Larry looked over his shoulder at the women and

smiled. Though his startled heart was drumming, he was *glad* they were here.

He felt as if some of the real world had come back.

"Guess you weren't kidding," Barbara whispered. "Jesus, look at that thing."

"Yuck," was all Jean said.

Barbara crouched over the end of the coffin. Jean stayed behind her and peered over her head.

"Didn't want us to have all the fun?" Larry asked.

"That's about the size of it," Jean said, her voice hushed.

"Curiosity got the best of us," Barbara added. Then she reached into the coffin and touched the foot of the corpse.

She's just like Pete, Larry thought. Whatever their differences, they're sure a set.

"I think I'm bleeding," Pete muttered.

"That makes two of us," Barbara said, still rubbing the dead foot. "It's like the skin on a salami."

"Salami's oily," Pete told her. "This is more like leather."

"Okay, we've seen it," Jean said. "Everyone ready to go?"

"Yeah, just about." Pete stopped rubbing his head, reached one arm down over the covered torso and snatched off the blanket. Larry lurched backward on his knees, wishing to God he'd known this was coming. He'd already seen too much.

Now the corpse was stretched in front of his face.

It was naked.

It was female.

It had a wooden stake in its chest.

"Holy shit," Barbara whispered.

"Let's get out of here!" Jean gasped in a high, tight voice. She didn't wait for a consensus. She bolted.

Pete threw the blanket down. It landed in a pile, covering the blunt top of the stake, the corpse's flat breasts and the slats of its ribs. Barbara leaned forward, grabbed a bit of the blanket and jerked it down to cover the groin.

Blond pubic hair.

Larry groaned.

Then he was scurrying after Barbara. The white seat of her shorts was still smudged with yellow from the rock where she'd rested in the creek bed.

Seemed like a century ago.

Why did we do this?

Larry followed her through the open section of paneling. Jean was still in the lobby. Her fists were clenched at her sides and she was prancing as if she had to pee. "Let's go, let's go!" she gasped.

Larry waited for Pete.

Together they pushed the slab of wood into place.

Shutting the door of the tomb.

Pete backed away as if afraid to take his eyes off it.

In the beam of his flashlight the crucified body of Jesus gleamed.

Five

Pete floored it out of Sagebrush Flat, and Barbara didn't say a word about the speed.

Nobody said a word about anything.

Larry slouched in the passenger seat, feeling dazed and exhausted. Though he stared out the windshield at the sunbright road and desert, he kept seeing the corpse. And the stake in its chest. And the crucifix.

It's behind us now, he told himself. We got away. We're all right.

His body felt leaden. There was a shaky tightness in his chest and throat that seemed like a peculiar mix of terror—subsiding terror—and elation. He remembered experiencing similar sensations a few years earlier. On a flight to New York the 747 had hit an air pocket and dropped straight down for a couple of seconds. Some of the passengers struck the ceiling. He and Jean and Lane, strapped in their seats, had been unharmed. But he'd felt this way afterward.

Probably shock, he thought. Shock, combined with great relief.

He sensed that if he didn't keep tight control of himself, he might start weeping or giggling.

This must be where they get the expression "scared silly."

"How's everybody doing?" Pete asked, breaking the long silence.

"I want a drink," Barbara said.

"There's more beer in the ice chest."

"Not beer, a *drink.*"

"Yeah, I could go for one myself. Or three or four. We should be home in less than an hour." He glanced at Larry. "You *believe* that back there? That was like right out of one of your books."

"He hasn't written any vampire books," Barbara said. "You'd know that, if you ever read them."

"Bet you will now, right?"

"I think I'd rather forget about it."

"Same here," Jean said. "God."

"That babe had a *stake* in her heart."

"We all saw it," Barbara reminded him.

"And how about that crucifix? I'll bet they put it there to keep her from getting out." He nodded, squinting at the road. "You know? In case the stake fell out, or something. To keep her from breaking through the wall."

"How would the damn stake fall out?" Barbara asked, sounding a little bit annoyed by his musings.

"Well, you know, a rat could get in there. A rat might pull it loose. Something like that."

"Give me a break."

"There's no such thing as vampires," Jean said. "Tell them, Larry."

"I don't know," he said.

"What do you mean, you don't know?"

"Well, there's plenty of legends about them. It goes way back. Back in the Middle Ages a lot of poor jerks wound up buried at crossroads with their heads cut off and garlic stuffed in their mouths."

"Guess ours got off lucky, huh?" Pete grinned at him. "All she got was the ol' stake-in-the-heart routine."

"She's not any vampire," Jean insisted.

"Somebody sure wasted her, though," Barbara said.

"That's right," Jean said. "Has it occurred to anyone that we found a dead body?"

Pete raised his hand like a school kid. "Me," he said. "I caught that right off the bat." He chuckled. "No pun intended."

"No, I mean shouldn't we tell the police?"

"She's got a point," Barbara admitted.

"So does our babe under the stairs," Pete said, laughing some more. "A point right in her chest."

"Give it a rest, would you? This is serious business. We can't just find a body and pretend it never happened."

"Right. We'll just tell the cops we broke into a locked hotel."

"You broke into a locked hotel."

"Hey, you want to be married to a jailbird?"

"We could make an anonymous call," Jean suggested. "Just explain where the body is, so they can go out and get it. Really. I mean, whoever she is, she deserves a decent burial."

"I wouldn't want it on my conscience," Pete said.

"What do you mean?"

"They won't bury her with that stake in her chest. Some poor slob'll pluck it right out. Next thing you know, he's a vampire cocktail."

"That's ridiculous," Jean muttered.

"Is it?" Making an evil laugh, he grinned over his shoulder at her.

"Watch where you're driving," Barbara said.

"I don't think we should call the cops," Larry said. "Even if we do it anonymously, there's still a chance we might get dragged into the situation."

"I don't see how," Jean told him.

"How do we know we weren't seen? Somebody might've driven through town and spotted the van while we were admiring the jukebox."

"Or the vampire," Pete added.

"And might've noticed the license plate number."

"Oh, there's a pleasant thought," Barbara muttered.

"You just never know. That's all I'm saying."

"Hey, somebody could've even been watching us from a window or something."

"Thanks, Peter. I really needed to hear that."

"Even if nobody did see us," Larry went on, "we undoubtedly left physical evidence behind. Fingerprints, footprints, tire-tread marks where the van drove over dirt. The police would probably treat the whole area as a crime scene. There's no telling what they might find. Next thing you know, they could be knocking on the door."

"We didn't kill her."

"Have you got an alibi," Pete asked, "for the night of September 3, 1901?"

"A pretty good one. I wasn't born yet. My *parents* weren't born yet."

"You think she's been dead that long?" Barbara asked.

"Sure looked old to me."

"I have no idea when she might've been killed," Larry said, "but I bet she hasn't been under the stairs there for much more than twenty years or so. I imagine she was put there *after* the hotel closed down."

"Why's that?" Pete asked.

"The guests would've smelled her."

"Gross," Jean muttered.

"Well, it's true. Assuming she was put in there right after she was killed, people would've noticed the stink. She doesn't smell now, but . . ."

"You're making me sick, Larry."

"Why do you say twenty years?" Barbara asked.

"The jukebox."

"Ah-ha. The oldies-but-goodies."

"I don't think any of the songs I noticed were much later than the mid-sixties. That's probably when Holman's went out of business. I figure the hotel might've closed its doors around the same time as Holman's."

"Makes sense," Barbara said. "So you think the body was put under the stairs sometime after, say, 'sixty-five?'"

"It's just a guess. Of course, she could've been dead fifty years before somebody put her under the stairs. I that's the way it went, there's no telling how long she' been there."

"Yeah," Pete said. "You eliminate the stink factor by having her someplace else while she's ripe, you could stick her under the stairs and nobody'd be the wiser."

"I don't see how it matters," Jean said. "The thing is she's dead. Who *cares* how long she's been under the stairs?"

Pete again raised his hand. "I myself find it to be o more than passing interest."

"So would the cops," Larry added. "I think it'd make a big difference in the way they look at the situation. I she's been dead half a century—and they have ways o figuring that stuff out—she's almost like an historical artifact. If she was only killed twenty years ago, they migh very well start an active homicide investigation."

"That's right," Barbara said. "Whoever put the stake in her could still be alive and kicking."

"Speaking of which," Pete said. He glanced at Larry arched an eyebrow and stroked his chin. "Wait'll you hear this one."

"We know," Barbara said, *"You* did it."

"Hey, I'm being serious here. Anybody happen to notice anything odd about the front doors of the hotel?"

"Aside from the fact that we were the first to break in?" Barbara asked.

"Very good, hon. That's one thing. The place was still sealed when we got there. Just about every other joint in town was wide open. People'd busted in and done some exploring. But not the hotel. What else?"

"Are we playing Twenty Questions? Is it bigger than a bread box?"

"Here's a clue. Bright and shiny and brand new."

"The padlock," Larry said. "The hasp."

"Right! The way those suckers looked, I'll bet they were sitting on the shelf of a hardware store a month ago."

"So?" Jean asked.

"Who put them on the doors? Who wanted to keep intruders out of the hotel?"

"Could've been anyone," Larry answered.

"Right. And it could've been someone who hid a body under the stairs. Someone who's still around and trying to make sure nobody stumbles onto his little secret."

"The same person who put the crucifix on the wall," Larry added.

"Right."

"Sort of a guardian, a keeper of the vampire."

"It's more likely," Barbara said, "that whoever put the lock on the doors doesn't know a thing about it."

"More interesting if he does," Pete told her.

"Maybe for you."

"Any chance we might stop talking about it?" Jean suggested. "I wish we'd never set foot in that damn hotel."

"You know," Pete said, "we *should've* pulled the stake. You know what I mean? Just to see what happens."

"Nothing would've happened," Jean said.

"Who knows?" He leered at Larry. "Hey, want to turn around and go back and do it?"

"No way."

"Aren't you curious?"

"Not that curious."

"Just try turning the van around," Barbara warned, "and *I'll* bite your neck."

"Pussy."

"Don't push it, buster. It was your big idea that got me messed up like this."

"You could've stayed outside. Nobody was holding a gun to your head."

"Just shut up, okay?"

He cast a glance at Larry. His expression was somewhat amused. "Guess I'd better shut up before I get her riled, huh?"

"I would if I were you."

"Whatever happened to freedom of speech?" Though the words were spoken quietly to Larry, they were aimed at Barbara.

"That freedom ends where my ears begin," she said.

Pete grinned at Larry, but said no more. He drove in silence.

Larry looked out at the desert. He still felt a little light-headed and nervous, but much better than before. He guessed that the discussion had helped. Putting words to it. Sharing their concerns. Especially the playful way Pete had turned the whole godawful experience into a vampire story. And the bickering between Pete and Barbara. Their nice, normal, everyday quarreling. It all helped a lot. Leeched the horror out of their encounter with the corpse. Like throwing sunlight onto a nightmare.

But his anxiety started to grow when they came to Mulehead Bend. Not even the familiar sights along Shoreline Drive were enough to dispel the dread that seemed to be swelling inside him.

Pete drove slowly through the traffic—a few automobiles surrounded by the usual mix of off-road vehicles, campers, vans, pickup trucks, and motorcycles. The road was bordered by motels, service stations, banks, shopping centers, restaurants, bars, and fast-food joints. Larry saw the bakery where he'd bought a dozen doughnuts early that morning. He saw the supermarket where Jean did her grocery shopping, the computer store where he regularly bought floppy disks, paper, and printer ribbons for his word processor, the movie theater where they had attended a horror double feature Wednesday afternoon.

Every now and then he caught glimpses of the Colorado River just east of the business district. A few people were still out, water skiing. He saw a houseboat. A shuttle boat was carrying passengers toward the casinos on the Nevada side of the river.

All so familiar, so normal. Larry thought he ought to feel some relief in returning to home turf, leaving behind the strangeness and desolation of the back roads.

But he didn't.

It's splitting up with Pete and Barbara, he realized. He didn't want to part with them. He was *afraid*. Like a kid who'd been telling spooky stories with his friends and now had to walk home alone in the dark.

I'm not a kid, he told himself. It's not dark. We just live next door. And I won't be going home alone, Jean will be with me and Lane's probably back by now.

"Why don't you guys stick around for a while?" Barbara suggested. "We'll have some cocktails, get the dust out of our throats."

"Great!" Larry told her, wondering if she, too, was reluctant for the group to break up.

"I'll make my famous margaritas," Pete said.

"Sounds good to me," Jean said.

Larry felt blessed.

Pete left the traffic of Shoreline Drive behind and steered up the curving road to Palm Court. When he turned onto Palm, their houses came into view.

It *was* good to be getting home.

Lane appeared from beside the porch. She wore cutoff blue jeans and her white bikini top, and carried a plastic bucket. Apparently she was preparing to wash the Mustang.

Pete beeped the horn as they approached. Lane turned to them and waved.

"Let's not say anything to her about the you-know-what," Jean said.

"Mum's the word," Pete said. He pulled into his driveway and stopped. Climbing from the van, he called to Lane, "Feel free to do this one when you get through over there."

"Hardy-har."

"Have fun shopping?" Jean asked her.

"Yeah, it was okay." She beamed at Larry as he stepped past the front of the van. "I spent *all kinds* of your money, Dad. You're gonna have to stay home and write like a dog."

"Thanks a lot, sweetheart."

"Consider me a motivating force. So, how was the excursion?"

"Had a good time," Jean told her. "We'll be over here for a while."

"Join us if you'd like," Barbara said, appearing behind the van with the ice chest in her hand.

"Jeez!" Lane blurted. "What happened to you?"

"Had a little accident."

"Are you okay?" she asked, frowning.

"Just some scrapes and bruises. I'll live."

"Wow."

"Come on over, if you'd like. We'll be having some drinks and snacks."

"Thanks anyway. I want to wash the car."

"Well, if you change your mind . . ."

"Sure. Thanks."

They entered the house. The air-conditioning felt cool and good after the brief walk through the heat. Larry sat in his usual chair at the kitchen table. Jean sat across from him. Pete began to gather bottles from the liquor cupboard.

It was all very familiar, very comforting.

"I'm going to get cleaned up a bit," Barbara said. "Back in a minute, then I'll dig up some goodies."

Pete sang a few lines of "Margaritaville" as he dumped tequila and Triple Sec into his blender. The blender was one of his finds. Someone had put it out for the trashmen. He'd spotted it while driving to work, picked it up and restored it to working order.

It reminded Larry of the jukebox down in the creek bed. He saw himself crouching over it, and then he was on his knees beside the coffin, staring in at the withered brown corpse.

He felt himself start to shrink inside.

It's history, he told himself. We're home. It's all over. That damn thing is fifty, sixty miles away.

"Sure is good to be here," he said.

"Better than a sharp stick in the eye. Or in the heart, as the case may be."

Jean grimaced.

Pete split open a couple of limes and squeezed them into the blender, then tossed in some ice cubes. He took long-stemmed margarita glasses down from the cupboard, rubbed their rims with lime, then dipped them into a plastic tub of salt. "Okay, baby, do your stuff," he told the blender as he capped it and pressed a button. After a few noisy seconds the machine went silent. Pete filled the glasses with his frothy concoction and carried them to the table.

As he sat down, Barbara returned.

"Are you okay?" Jean asked.

"Feeling a lot better."

She looked a lot better, too.

She was barefoot, wearing red gym shorts and a loose gray T-shirt that was chopped off just below her breasts. Larry guessed that she had taken a washcloth to her legs and belly. The filth and blood were gone, leaving her skin ruddy around the abrasions. The wood had scratched her like an angry cat, and there were broad scuffs that looked as if she'd been given swipes with some heavy-duty sand-paper.

Larry watched as she put together a tray of cheese and crackers.

The back of her looked fine. Tanned, smooth, unblemished.

She brought the snacks to the table and sat down. Pushing out her lower lip, she huffed a breath that stirred the hair on her forehead. "At last," she said.

Pete raised his glass. "May the vampire rest in peace and never come looking for our necks."

"I'm gonna brain you," Barbara said.

"I'll help," Jean said.

Pete grinned at Larry. "These gals, they've got no sense of humor."

Six

Larry woke up shivering. The covers were off him, twisted around Jean as she thrashed and whimpered. He shook her gently by the shoulder. She flinched. Gasped, "What's . . . what's . . . ?"

"You were having a nightmare," Larry whispered.

"Huh? Oh. Okay." She rolled onto her back. She was still panting for air. "Smothering," she muttered, and struggled to free herself from the blankets. She shoved and kicked them down to the foot of the bed.

"I'm going to need some of that," Larry said, sitting up.

"Huh? Oh. Sorry."

"No problem. I'll put some light on the subject," he warned, and gave Jean a moment to shield her eyes before he reached to the nightstand and turned on the lamp.

"Wait. I'll do it. You'll mess it up."

"Fine," he said, and smiled. Seconds ago Jean had been in the grips of a terrible nightmare. Now she was concerned that he might foul up the job of arranging the sheet and blankets. He leaned back, bracing himself up with locked arms, and watched her climb off the bed.

She looked as if she'd just taken a shower with her nightgown on. Her short hair was matted down, wet ringlets clinging around her ears and the nape of her neck. The sleek white fabric of her nightie was glued to her back and rump.

"You're drenched," Larry said. "Must've been a real corker."

"Probably. I don't remember." She bent over her side of the bed and pulled the top sheet out of the tangle. Her breasts swayed slightly inside the low-cut, lace bodice.

"You think it was about today?"

"Wouldn't be surprised." She swept the sheet high. As it fluttered down, Larry leaned forward and caught the edge. He drew it over his naked body and eased backward onto the mattress. The sheet was enough to block out the chill of the soft night breeze. But the lightweight blanket felt even better as Jean covered him with it. She smoothed it carefully over her side of the bed, then came around to his side. Bending over him, she straightened the blanket. He slipped his arm out and stroked her rump. The nightgown felt silken and damp. Her skin was smooth beneath it, and very warm. She glanced at him, eyebrows rising. He moved his hand down the back of her leg and slipped it under the hem of her nightgown.

Standing up straight, Jean reached out and turned off the lamp. Her gown, pale in the faint light from the windows, climbed her body and fell away. Larry swept aside the sheet and blanket that she had just finished arranging so neatly. But she didn't protest.

She crawled onto the bed, straddled his legs and eased down on top of him. As they kissed, he caressed her back and her small, firm buttocks. She lifted her legs onto his. She pressed his growing penis between her thighs and squirmed against him. Her breasts were warm, slick cushions rubbing his chest, and though the feel of her writhing body made him ache with need, her hipbones felt as if they were grinding into him.

He rolled, tumbling her onto the mattress, covering her with his body. He pushed himself up with elbows and knees to keep his weight off her. She squirmed as he kissed the side of her neck, moaned as he moved lower and kissed one nipple, then the other.

He pushed himself back. Kneeling between her open legs, he whispered, "Just a second."

Jean's fingers curled lightly around him, slid the length of his shaft. "I don't think you'll need one tonight."

"You sure?"

"Yeah."

"Great. I hate those damn rubbers."

"I know." She smiled.

Bright teeth in a faint blur of face. Patches of darkness where her eyes should be.

Larry was suddenly under the stairway again, kneeling over the corpse. He felt himself go cold and tight.

Don't think about it!

He realized that Jean was about the same size as the horrible, dried-up thing.

Stop it!

"What's wrong, honey?"

"Nothing," he said.

Her shadowed skin was dark, but not *that* dark. Her breasts were mounds, not slabs. But even in the dim light he could see the contours of her ribs. Below the rib cage she seemed shrunken in. Her hipbones jutted.

"Honey?"

Her hand felt leathery around his small, soft penis.

Its hand.

He pictured himself knocking it away.

But he knew that this was Jean. She hadn't turned into the corpse. He wasn't hallucinating, either. This was just Jean, and his damned imagination was simply messing with him.

Not going to let it win, he promised himself.

He scooted backward on the mattress. Her hand went away from him. He kissed her belly. Warm, soft, slick with sweat. Not dry and leathery.

Stop comparing!

But when his face rubbed Jean's moist curls, he remembered the thing's blond thicket of pubic hair. A shudder passed through him.

Jean thrust fingers into his hair.

He went lower. She writhed and moaned, thrusting herself against him, clenching his hair, and he lost all thought of the corpse.

Soon she was whimpering.

But not from any nightmare, Larry thought as she tugged his hair and he scurried up the mattress. He clamped his wet mouth to hers. He ran the hard length of his penis into her heat. She seemed to suck him in as if she were hungry to be filled.

"I should have . . . nightmares more often," she told him later.

"Yeah."

She was panting beneath him, lightly stroking his back. Then she turned her face away, worked her lips strangely, and raised a hand to her mouth. With her thumb and index finger, she pinched something and pulled it out.

"What's that?"

"A hair."

"Where'd that come from?"

"Your mouth," she said, shaking under him as she chuckled. She rubbed her hand on the sheet, then wrapped her arms around Larry and gave him a powerful squeeze. It was as if the hug used up the last of her strength. After a moment she released him and sprawled out limp. Then he eased away, sliding out of her.

He pulled the sheet and blanket up and scooted closer to her. He rested a hand on the warm curve of her thigh. Under his fingertips was a smear of stickiness. "Ooo, yuck," he said.

She laughed softly. "Don't complain, buster. *I've* got the wet spot."

"Want to trade places?"

"It's my wifely duty to sleep on the wet spot." Her hand covered his, caressed it, fooled with his fingers.

In the silence he began to worry that Jean might ask about his problem. He doubted that she would, though. Their sex life was something they rarely discussed. Besides, he'd made a rather spectacular recovery.

"Well," he said, "I'd better go to sleep or I won't be worth a damn tomorrow."

"You'll have to write like a dog to pay for Lane's new wardrobe."

"Bought out the store," he muttered, rolling away from Jean and curling up on his side.

She laughed, then surprised Larry by snuggling against him. Normally they slept at opposite sides of the bed.

But it felt good. Her breath warm on the nape of his neck. Her breasts and belly pressing his back. Her lap against his rump. The soft tickle of her pubic hair. Her thighs smooth against the backs of his legs. An arm came down over his side and fingers curled tenderly around his penis.

"You still horny?" he asked.

She kissed his back. "Wiseguy. I just want to be close to you."

"Well, I guess that's all right."

"Thanks."

"Are you okay?"

"I don't know," she whispered. "I guess so. How about you?"

"I wish we hadn't gone there today."

"Me, too. I've never seen anything so horrible." She pressed herself more tightly against him. "On the other hand, you're always looking for material."

"I could do without *that* sort of material."

"The real thing's too much for you, huh?" she teased.

"Darn right it is."

"Your fans would be appalled, you know, if they ever found out how squeamish you really are. Nasty Lawrence Dunbar, master of gore, pussy."

"Pussy, huh? You've been around Pete too much."

She laughed again. "Go to sleep, tough guy."

GOING FOR IT

Seven

"Happy trails to you," Dad said, and swatted her butt as she stepped out the door.

She smirked back at him.

"Say hi to Roy and Dale," he added.

"You should look so good," Lane said, then turned away and hurried toward the car. The red Mustang gleamed in the early morning sunlight. She stepped around to the driver's side, feeling fresh and eager in her new clothes: the mottled pink and blue T-shirt; the tie-dyed blue denim jumper with its white lace trim and pink flowerbud decorations on the bib, straps, and hem; and the white, fringed boots.

Dad was always poking fun at her clothes. She supposed this outfit *did* make her look like a cowgirl.

One hot, radical cowgirl, she thought, and grinned as she climbed into the car.

At least he hadn't made any remarks about the length of the skirt. Sitting down, she could feel the seat upholstery high on the backs of her legs. As she waited for the engine to warm up, she leaned close to the steering wheel and looked down. The skirt was short, all right. Any shorter might be embarrassing.

This was just right.

Sexy, but not outrageous.

She especially liked the lace around the hem of the skirt,

the way its long points lay like frilly spearheads against her thighs.

I'm going to drive Jim nuts when he sees me in this.

As if he needs any help along those lines.

Laughing softly, trembling just a little with the anticipation of being at school on such a fine day in such a grand outfit, Lane backed out of the driveway. She turned the car radio to "86.2 A.M., all the best in Country twenty-four hours a day!" Randy Travis was on. She turned the volume high and poked her elbow into the warm stream of air rushing past her window.

God, she felt great.

Seemed almost criminal to feel this great.

She leaned her shoulder against the door, tipped her head and felt the wind caress her face, tug at her hair.

To think that she'd put up such a fuss about leaving Los Angeles. She must've been crazy, wanting to stay in that lousy apartment in a city full of filthy air and creeps. But she'd grown up there. She was used to it. She'd known she would miss her friends and the beaches and Disneyland. This was so much better, though. She'd made new friends, she loved the river, and the clean, open spaces gave her a constant sense of freedom that made each day seem rich with promise.

Best of all, she supposed, was the release from fear. In L.A. you had to be so careful. The place was crawling with rapists and killers. Not a day went by when the TV news didn't broadcast stories of such horror and brutality that you dreaded stepping outside. Kids missing. Their bodies usually found days later, nude and mutilated and sexually abused. Not only kids, either. The same thing happened to teenagers, and even adults. If you weren't kidnapped and tortured, you might be gunned down at a restaurant or movie theater or shopping mall. And hiding at home was no guarantee of safety, either. There were plenty of nuts who simply drove around town, shooting into the windows of houses and apartment buildings.

Nowhere was safe.

Lane's joy slipped away as she suddenly remembered the chopping crashes of gunfire in the night. They had been home in their ground-level apartment in Los Angeles, sitting close together on the sofa, watching *Dallas* on TV. Lane had a tub of popcorn on her lap. Mom sat on one side, Dad on the other. All three were reaching in, hands sometimes colliding. The first blast made her jump so hard that the tub flew up, flinging popcorn everywhere. Then the night exploded as if someone on the street had opened up with a machine gun. Mom had screamed. Dad had shouted *"Get down!"* but didn't give Lane even an instant to respond before he grabbed the back of her neck and nearly broke her in half as he rammed her forward. The edge of the coffee table skinned the top of her head. She wept and held her head and shuddered as the roar pounded her ears. Then all she heard was a ringing. The gunfire had stopped. Dad still clutched her neck. "Jean?" he'd asked in a high, strange voice. Mom didn't answer. *"Jean!"* True panic. Then Mom had said, "Is it over?"

They stayed on the floor.

Then came sirens and the loud whap-whap-whap of a police helicopter low overhead. The front draperies were bright with flashes of red and blue. Dad had crawled to the window and looked out. "Holy Jesus," he said, "there must be twenty cop cars out there."

It turned out that the shots had been fired at a family in a duplex across the street. Both parents, and three children, had been killed by automatic fire from an Uzi. Only an infant had survived the shooting.

Lane hadn't known the family. That was another thing about L.A.—even most of your neighbors were strangers. But the fact that they'd been gunned down, right across the street, was shocking.

Just too damn close.

Dad had reminded them about a family gunned down by mistake a few years earlier. It was a drug hit. The killers had gone to the wrong house, the one next door to the residence of their intended victims.

"We're getting out of here," Dad had said, even while the street outside was still jammed with police cars.

Two weeks later they were on the way to Mulehead Bend.

They knew the town from having vacationed there just a month before the shooting. They'd spent a night in a motel, followed by a week in a houseboat on the river. They'd all enjoyed the area, it was fresh in their minds, and it seemed like a good place to find sanctuary from the mad, crowded hunting grounds of Los Angeles.

Sometimes the wind and heat were enough to drive you crazy. You had to watch out for scorpions and black widow spiders and several varieties of poisonous snakes. But the chances of catching a bullet in the head or getting abducted by a pervert were mighty slim.

Lane looked upon L.A. as a prison from which she and her family had escaped. The freedom was glorious.

She swung her car onto the dust and gravel in front of Betty's place and beeped the horn once. Betty lived in a mobile home, as did the majority of Mulehead Bend's population. It was firmly planted on a foundation. A porch and an extra room had been added on. It looked pretty much like a normal house from the outside, though the interior always seemed narrow and cramped when Lane visited.

Betty trudged down the porch stair as if laboring under the burden of her weight—which was considerable. She managed to raise her head and nod a greeting.

Leaning across the passenger seat, Lane opened the door for her. Betty swung her book bag into the backseat. The fabric of her tan shirt was already dark under the armpits.

The car rocked slightly as she climbed in. She shut the door so hard that Lane winced.

"Well, look at you," Betty said, her voice as slow and somber as always. "What'd you do, mug Dolly Parton?"

"Who'd *you* mug, Indiana Jones?"

"Yucka yucka," she muttered.

Lane steered onto the road. "We picking up Henry?"

"Only if you want to."

"Well, is he expecting us?"

"I suppose."

"You two aren't fighting again, are you?"

"Just the usual grief about my culinary preferences. I told him he's no prize himself, and if he thinks he can do better, he should go ahead and try, and good riddance."

"True love," Lane said.

She swung around a bend and accelerated up the road to Henry's house. He was out in front, sitting on a small, white-painted boulder next to the driveway, reading a paperback. When he saw them coming, he slipped the book into his leather briefcase. He stood up, ran a hand over the top of his crew cut, and stuck out his thumb as if hoping to hitch a ride with strangers.

"What a dork," Betty muttered.

"Oh, he's cute," Lane said.

"He's a nerd."

That was a fact, Lane supposed. In his running shoes, old blue jeans, plaid shirt, and sunglasses, he could almost pass for a regular guy. But the briefcase gave him away. So did the rather dopey, cheerful look on his lean face. And the way his head preceded the rest of his body made him look, to Lane, like an adventurous turtle.

He was a nerd, no doubt about it. But Lane liked him.

"Good morning, sports fans!"

"Yo!" Lane greeted him.

Betty climbed out, shoved the seat back forward, and ducked into the backseat. Henry got in after her. Hanging over the seat, he managed to pull the door shut. Then his head swiveled toward Lane. "Foxy outfit there, lady."

"Thanks."

" 'She had a body like a mountain road,' " he said. " 'Full of curves and places you'd like to stop for a picnic.' "

"Mike Hammer?" Lane asked.

"Mack Donovan, *Dead Low Tide.*" He dropped backward, or was yanked by Betty.

"You never talk to me that way," the girl grumbled.

He whispered something that Lane couldn't hear over Ronnie Milsap. She turned the radio down, and heard a giggly squeal from Betty. Making a U-turn, she headed down the hill.

"So, you have a big weekend?" Henry asked after a while.

"Okay," Lane said. "Nothing special. I went shopping yesterday."

"No dream date with Jim Dandy, King of the Studs?"

"He had to go out of town with his parents."

"*Too* bad. And I bet he didn't even have the courtesy to leave you his biceps."

"Nope, I had to go without."

"Rotten luck. Should've come to the drive-in with us. Saw a couple of dynamite films. *Trashed* and *Attack of the S.S. Zombie Queens.*"

"Sorry I missed them."

"Sorry *I* saw them," Betty said.

"Well, you didn't see much of them, that's for sure. Between your forays to the snack bar and the john—"

"Hush up."

"We think she got a bad hot dog," he explained.

"Henry!" she whined.

"On the other hand, could've been a bad burrito or cheeseburger."

"Lane doesn't want to hear all the gruesome details."

"What's going on with your dad?" Henry asked, leaning

forward and folding his arms over the seat back. "Have they started filming *The Beast?*"

"Not yet. They just renewed the option, though."

"Terrific. Man, I can't wait to see that one. I've got rubber bands holding that book together. Read it five, six times. It's a classic."

"I would've liked it better," Lane said, "if it hadn't been written by my father."

"Ah, he's cool."

"And apparently somewhat demented," Lane added.

Henry laughed.

At the bottom of the hill Lane turned onto Shoreline Drive. Most of the shops along the road weren't open yet, and the traffic was light. The station wagon ahead of her was filled with children on their way to the elementary school, which was across the road from Buford High at the south end of town. Quite a few older kids were on the sidewalks, hiking in that direction.

Henry, still resting on the seat back, swung his arm toward the passenger window. "Isn't that Jessica?"

Lane spotted the girl on the sidewalk ahead. Jessica, all right. Even from behind there was no mistaking her. The spiked hair, dyed bright orange, was enough to give her away.

Her left arm was in a cast.

"Wonder what happened," Lane muttered. "Anyone mind if I offer her a lift?"

"Yeah, do it," Henry said.

"Terrific," Betty muttered.

Lane swung the car to the curb, not far behind the swaggering girl, and leaned across the passenger seat. "How about a ride?" she called.

Jessica turned around.

Lane winced at the sight of her.

"God," Henry muttered.

Jessica was generally considered the foxiest gal in the junior class, maybe in the entire high school.

Not so foxy now, Lane thought.

From the looks of her now, she might've gone ten rounds over the weekend with the heavyweight champ.

The left side of her face was swollen and purple. Her cracked lips bulged like sausages. She had a flesh-colored bandage on her chin, another over her left eyebrow. Lane guessed that the pink-framed sunglasses concealed shiners. The girl usually wore huge, dangling rings in her pierced ears. Today the lobes of both ears were bandaged. The low neckline of her tank top revealed bruises on her chest. Others showed around her shoulder straps. Even her thighs were smudged with purple bruises below the frayed edges of her cutoff jeans.

"How about it?" Lane called to her.

She shrugged, and Lane heard a quiet intake of breath from Henry—likely at the way the gesture made Jessica's breast move under the tight, thin fabric of her top. Only one showed. The other was discretely hidden under the cloth sling that supported her broken arm. The visible one jiggled as she stepped toward the car.

Maybe she got herself gang-banged.

Nice, Lane. Real nice.

Would've been her own damn fault.

Cut it out.

Leaning across the passenger seat, she unlatched the door and swung it open.

"Thanks," Jessica said.

Henry dropped away from the seat back—no doubt with Betty's help—and lost his chance to watch the girl climb in. Too bad, Lane thought. He would've enjoyed seeing Jessica's leg come out through the slit side of her jeans. The bruises might've dampened his enthusiasm, but not by much.

She pulled the door shut. Lane checked the side mirror, waited for a Volkswagen to pass, then swung out.

"Are you sure you want to be going to school?" she asked.

"Shit. Would you, ib you looked like this?"

"I guess I'd probably call in sick."

"Yeah," Jessica replied through her split and swollen lips. "Well, better than habbing by old lady in by face all day. She's such a bain."

Lane rubbed her lips together, licked them. Listening to Jessica was almost enough to make them ache.

From the backseat came Betty's voice. "So, you going to let us in on it, or do we have to guess?"

Scowling, Jessica peered over her shoulder.

"It's none of our business," Lane said.

"Yeah. Well, I got trashed."

"Who did it to you?" Henry asked.

"Who the buck knows? A couple guys. Real asswibes. Beat the shit outa be and stole by burse."

"Where'd it happen?"

"Ober backa the Quick Stob."

"Behind the Quick Stop?" Betty asked. "What were you doing there?"

"They dragged be there. Saturday night. I went in bor cigarettes, and they got be when I cabe out."

"Bad news," Henry muttered.

"Yeah, I'll say." With one hand she opened a canvas satchel and took out a pack of Camels. She shook it, raised the pack to her mouth, and caught a cigarette between her fat, scabby lips. She lit it with a Bic, inhaled deeply, and sighed.

"Did they catch the guys who did it?" Lane asked.

Jessica shook her head.

"I didn't think stuff like that happened around here."

"It habbens, all right."

Lane pulled into the student parking lot, found an empty space, and shut off the car.

"Thanks a lot bor the ride," Jessica said.

"Glad to help. I'm awfully sorry you got messed up."

"Be too. So long." She climbed out and headed away.

"Wouldn't you just die to know what *really* happened?" Betty said.

"You think she lied?" Lane asked.

"Let's put it this way. Yes."

Henry shoved the seat back forward. "Why would she lie about a thing like that?"

"Why wouldn't she?"

Eight

Larry drank coffee and read a new Shaun Hutson paperback for an hour after Lane went off to school. Then he set the book aside, said, "I'd better get to it," and rose from his recliner.

"Have fun," Jean told him, glancing up from the newspaper as he strode past her.

He shut his office door and sat down in front of the word processor.

He had already decided not to work on *Night Stranger* today. The book was going well. Two more weeks should take care of it.

Then what?

Ah, he thought, there's the rub.

Normally, by the time he was this close to finishing a novel, the next was pretty well set in his mind. He would already have pages of notes in which he had explored the plot and characters, and have several of the major scenes worked out.

Not this time.

Gotta get cooking, he told himself.

When the day came to write "The End" on *Night Stranger,* he wanted to slip a fresh floppy disk into his computer and begin Chapter One. Of whatever.

Two weeks to go.

That should be plenty of time.

You'll come up with something.

You'd better.

Eighty, ninety pages to go. Then he would find himself facing an empty disk, a void, a taunting blank that would push him to the edge of despair.

It had happened a few times before. He dreaded going through a period like that again.

I won't, he told himself.

He formatted a new disk and brought up its directory; 321,536 bytes to play with.

Let's just use up a couple thousand today, he thought.

A page or two, that's all it'll take. Maybe.

He punched the Enter key and the screen went blank. A few seconds later he had eliminated the right margin justification, which would've left odd spaces between the words, spaces that drove him nuts when he tried to read the hard copy. He punched a few more keys. "Novel Notes—Monday, October 3," appeared in amber light at the upper left-hand corner of the screen.

Then he sat there.

He stared at the keyboard. Several of the keys were grimy. The filthy ones were those he used least often: the numbers, the space bar except for a clean area in the shape of his right thumb, some keys at the far sides that could apparently be used to give commands for a variety of mysterious functions. He didn't know what the hell half of them did. Sometimes he hit one by mistake. The consequences could be alarming.

He spent a while cleaning the keyboard, scratching paths through the gray smudges with a fingernail.

Stop screwing around, he told himself.

He scraped Saturday's ashes out of a pipe, filled it with fresh tobacco and lit it. The matchbook came from the Sir Francis Drake on Union Square. They'd had lunch there during a vacation along the California coast two summers ago. The vacation he thought of as the "wharf tour."

He set the matchbook down, puffed on his pipe, and stared at the screen.

"Novel Notes—Monday, October 3."

Okay.

His fingertips tapped at the keys.

"Come up with something hot. Original and big. Try for at least 500 pages, more if possible."

Right. That accomplished a lot.

He typed in, "How about a vampire book? Ha ha ha. Forget it. Vampires are done to death.

"Need something original. Some kind of a NEW threat."

Good luck, he thought.

How about a sequel? he wondered.

"Maybe a sequel. *The Beast II,* or something. Worth considering, if you can't turn up anything better."

Come on, something new.

Or a new variation on an old theme.

"Nobody but Brandner's done anything decent with werewolves. Come up with a fresh werewolf gimmick? Forget it. That TV show's got the whole thing covered. But that's not a book."

Larry scowled at the screen.

"Forget werewolves.

"What else is there?"

His pipe slurped. He twisted the stem off, blew a fine spray into the wastebasket beside his chair, put the pipe back together and lighted it again.

A few minutes later, he had a list:

> werewolves
> ghosts (boring)
> zombies
> aliens
> misc. beasts
> demonic possession (shit)

homicidal maniac (done to death)
curses
wishes granted ("Monkey's Paw")
possessed machinery (King's realm)
crazed animals (see above, and BIRDS)
haunted house (possibilities)

"How ABOUT a haunted house book?" he wrote.

He'd always wanted to do one, and always reached the same stumbling block. By and large, he didn't consider ghosts sufficiently scary. Something else had to be in the house. But what?

That question took him back to the list.

He stared at it for a long time.

"Something horrible inside the house," he wrote. "But what?"

How about a vampire under the staircase?

Right. Just thinking about it made his insides crawl.

He was on his knees beside the coffin again, staring at the withered corpse. Feeling fear and disgust.

He wanted to forget he ever saw the thing, not spend the next few months dwelling on it.

Would make a good story, though.

"A blond corpse under the hotel stairs," he wrote. "A stake in its chest. Found by some people exploring a ghost town. Could tell it just the way it happened. Fun and games."

He wrinkled his nose.

"But they don't run off, scared shitless, like we did. Maybe some of them do. But one is fascinated. Is this a vampire, or isn't it? A character like Pete, but a little crazier. He *has* to know. So he pulls the stake. Right in front of his eyes, the thing comes back to life. Changes from a hideous brown cadaver (use Barbara's line about looking like salami?) into a gorgeous young woman. A gorgeous, naked young woman. Pete character is enthralled. And turned on. He wants her. But she has a different idea, and bites his neck.

"They don't come out, and don't come out. The others get worried, go back into the hotel to see what's keeping the guy. Nobody under the stairs. The coffin is empty.

"Little problem, bud. Vampires don't screw around in the daytime. So how come our merry band is exploring a ghost town after dark?

"Easy. They're driving through town, on the way home from an outing in the desert, and the van breaks down. Flat tire, or something."

Ah, he thought, the old car-breaking-down-in-just-the-worst-possible-place gag.

It could work, though.

And it had a nice bonus: that wasn't the way things happened yesterday.

"Make it different enough from the truth," he typed, "and maybe you can handle it.

"How about taking One Big Step, and changing what's under the stairs? Not a dead gal with a stake in her chest, but a . . . a what? (A crate with a monster in it? Been done.) Could be anything. The body of a creature from outer space? A troll? Have open spaces between the stairs, and it reaches through and drags people in by the feet. Gobbles 'em up. He he he.

"Chicken.

"What's wrong with the way it really was?

"Yuck. Horror's supposed to be fun.

"But there's a real story there. Who is she? Who put the stake in her chest? Was the lock (brand new) put on the hotel doors by the same person who hid her under the stairs? Best of all, what happens if you pull the stake?

"Lies there. Dead meat.

"But what if life flows into her? Her dry, crusty skin becomes smooth and youthful. Her flat breasts swell into gorgeous mounds. Her sunken face fills out. She is beautiful beyond your wildest imagination. She is breathtaking. (And bloodtaking.)

"She doesn't bite your neck, after all.

"That's because she's grateful to you for freeing her to live again. Feels so indebted that she'll do anything for you. You're her master, and she will do your bidding. In effect, you have this gorgeous thing as your slave.

"Real possibilities."

Nine

Lane shoved her books onto the locker shelf, took out her lunch bag and shut the metal door. As she gave the combination lock a twirl, an arm slipped around her stomach, a mouth pressed the side of her neck. She cringed as chills scurried up her skin.

"Stop it," she said, whirling around.

"Couldn't help myself," Jim said.

Lane looked past him. The hallway was crowded. Kids were wandering by, talking and laughing. Those who weren't with friends all seemed to be in a great hurry. Lockers slammed. Teachers stood near their classroom doorways, on the lookout for trouble. Nobody seemed to be paying any attention to Lane and Jim.

"Did you miss me?" Jim asked.

"I survived."

"Uh-oh. Am I in trouble?"

"I don't much care to be grabbed in public. How many times do I have to tell you that?"

"Oooh, touchy. Are we on the rag?"

Lane felt heat rush to her face. "Real nice," she muttered. "Who died and made you king of the jerks?"

He smiled, but there was no humor in his eyes. "I was just kidding. Can't you take a joke?"

"Obviously not."

He dropped the smile. "I don't need this."

"Good. Adios."

Scowling, he muttered something Lane couldn't hear, turned away and joined the flow of the hallway crowd. He walked about twenty feet, then glanced over his shoulder as if he expected Lane to come rushing after him.

She gave him a glare.

He smirked as if to say, "Your loss, bitch," then continued down the hall.

Creep, she thought.

On the rag. What a shitty thing to say.

She leaned back against her locker and took a deep breath, trying to calm herself. She felt hot with embarrassment and anger. Her heart thudded. She was trembling.

Who needs him, anyhow? she told herself.

I *was* pretty rough on him, she thought as she started down the hallway. It wasn't as if he did anything all that awful. Just kissed my neck, really. No big crime. But he shouldn't have done it right in front of everyone. He knows how I feel about that kind of thing.

Even if I did give him a hard time, it was no reason to make a crude remark like that.

She *had* missed him. All weekend she'd looked forward to seeing him again.

She suddenly felt cheated and sad. Her new outfit made it worse. Like getting all dressed up for a party and being left at home.

Why did he have to act like that?

He can be such a jerk sometimes.

Whenever he didn't get his way, Lane got to see his snotty side. Afterward, though, he was usually quick to apologize, and he could be so sweet that she found it difficult to hold onto her anger.

She supposed the same thing would happen this time.

One of these days, she told herself, he'll go too far and that'll be the end of it.

Maybe he just did.

But the thought of breaking up with Jim made her feel

empty and alone. He was the only real boyfriend she'd had since starting at Buford High—ever, for that matter. They'd shared so much. He might act like a creep sometimes, but nobody's perfect.

You're just too chicken to dump him, she thought.

In no time at all everyone in school would know they had split up. When that happened, she would be fair game. She'd either have to become a hermit or risk going out with virtual strangers—and some of them were bound to be creeps.

At least you know you can handle Jim.

True love, she thought. *I must be out of my gourd. You don't keep going with a guy forever just because he's okay and you're afraid you might do worse.*

When he tries to make up this time, I should just tell him to drop dead.

On the rag. A, I'm not. B, screw him anyway.

In the cafeteria she spotted Jim at one of the long lunch tables, surrounded by his jock friends. Betty and Henry were at a corner table, sitting across from each other at its far end, several empty chairs between them and the rowdy clique of girls occupying the other end.

After buying a Pepsi at the "drinks only" window, she went to join them. "Mind if I sit here?" she asked.

"Okay with me," Henry said. "Just don't embarrass us by sticking a straw up your nostril."

"The hell with that. How'll I drink my pop?"

"Take a load off," Betty said.

She pulled out the metal folding chair and sat down beside Henry.

"So how come you're not eating with Jim Dandy?" he asked. "Did your taste buds finally rebel at the prospect?"

"Something like that. We had a little problem."

Betty, about to take a bite, frowned and set her sandwich down. "Are you all right?"

Lane realized she suddenly had a lump in her throat. She didn't trust herself to speak, so she nodded.

"The dirt bag," Betty said.

"Want me to kick his butt?" Henry asked.

"You'd need the Seventh Cavalry," Betty told him. "And they already bought it at the Little Big Horn."

"Very funny."

"I don't know why you put up with him," she said. Her cheeks wobbled as she shook her head. "Good Lord, girl, you know darn well you could have any guy in the school. Except for Henry, of course. I'd be forced to kill him if he made a play for you."

"You ladies could *share* me," he suggested.

"But I mean it, though. Seriously. Jim's always giving you grief about one thing or another. Why do you stand for it?"

"I don't know."

"Because he's so cute," Henry said.

"Stick it in your ear. This is serious."

"Maybe I will dump him," Lane said. "It's just getting worse all the time."

Grinning, Henry leaned sideways and slipped an arm around her back. "Saturday night. You and me. We'll make beautiful music together."

Lane saw a quick look of alarm on Betty's face. Then the girl narrowed her eyes and said, "Prepare to meet your maker, Henrietta."

"Sorry," Lane told him. "I'd hold myself responsible for your demise. I can't have that on my conscience."

"I'd die happy."

Betty's face went red. She pressed her lips together.

"That's enough, Henry," Lane said.

He tried to hang on to his silly grin but it fell off. He pulled his arm in. "Just kidding," he said.

Just kidding. That's what Jim had said. What was it, the standard excuse when a guy makes an ass of himself?

Lane opened her bag and took out the sandwich. It was wrapped in cellophane. She saw egg salad bulging out between the bread.

"Just trying to make you jealous, sweet stuff," he said to Betty.

"You'd stand as much chance with Lane as an ice cube in a hot skillet."

Tears suddenly burned Lane's eyes. She slapped her sandwich down hard on the table. "I'm sorry!" she blurted. "Goddamn it! Don't do this! You're my friends!"

They both gaped at her.

"I'm sorry. Okay?"

"Gee," Henry said.

"It's all right," Betty murmured. "You okay?"

Lane shook her head.

"I know just the thing to make you feel better."

"What?" Lane asked.

"Let me eat that sandwich for you."

She gasped out a laugh. "Not a chance."

"Grab it off her, Hen, and I'll forgive you."

He reached for it. Lane caught his wrist and pinned it to the table. "Try it again," she warned, "and you'll be picking your nose left-handed."

"He's such a klutz, he'd put out his eye."

Lane let go. When she finished unwrapping her sandwich, she tore it down the middle and offered half to Betty. The girl leered at it but shook her head. "Go on," Lane told her. "I don't have much of an appetite, anyway."

"If you're sure . . ." She took it.

They ate their lunches and chatted, and everything seemed normal again. But Lane knew that damage had been done. Obviously, Betty had seen through Henry's joking around—realized he would dump her in an eyeblink if he thought he stood a chance with Lane.

Break up with Jim, and sooner or later Henry probably

will ask you out. Then you'll be minus your two best friends.

Jessica's assigned seat in Mr. Kramer's sixth-period English class was at the front of the room, just to the left of Lane's desk. Today Riley Benson swaggered down the aisle and sat there. He slumped against the backrest, stretched out his legs and crossed his motorcycle boots. He looked at Lane. His face, with half-shut, sullen eyes, never failed to remind her of television news photos that showed men who put bullets into people for the fun of it.

Twisting around, she saw Jessica in Riley's usual seat at the rear corner.

"We traded," he said. "You got a problem?"

"None of my business."

She turned to the front. The final bell hadn't clamored yet, and Mr. Kramer rarely entered the classroom before the bell. She hoped he would show up soon. Riley had a reputation for starting trouble, and she was pretty sure that she'd already been chosen as today's target.

Thanks a heap, Jessica.

The trade had to be Jessica's idea. Lane could understand that. Battered the way she was, the girl probably wanted to be as inconspicuous as possible.

It crossed her mind that Riley might be the guy who'd beaten up Jessica. She knew they'd been going together, and he sure seemed capable of such things. Maybe Jessica gave him some lip. She could've made up the mugging story.

Lane looked over at him. His fingers were rapping out a rhythm on the edge of the desk. He had dirty knuckles, but they weren't bruised or scraped. He might've been wearing gloves, though. Or done the damage with a blunt instrument of some kind.

"You got a problem?" he asked.

"No. Uh-uh." She turned her eyes to the front.

"Bitch."

This is really my day.

She stared at Mr. Kramer's empty desk. Her back felt rigid. Her heart was thumping hard and her face was hot.

Come on, teacher. Where are you?

"Fuckin' twat."

Her head snapped toward him. "Blow it out your ass, Benson."

The bell blared and she flinched.

Riley's lip curled up. "See ya after class. Count on it."

"Oh, I'm so scared. I'm trembling."

"Ya oughta be."

In fact, she was. Now I've done it, she thought. Why didn't I keep my mouth shut?

It was little consolation when Mr. Kramer entered the room.

If only he'd shown up a couple of minutes ago.

Roll book in hand, he settled down against the front edge of his desk and fixed his eyes on Riley. "I believe you're in the wrong seat, Mr. Benson."

"You got a problem with that?"

"As a matter of fact, yes, I do."

Lane felt a grin spreading across her face.

Give it to him, Kramer.

"Please return to your assigned seat. Now."

From the back of the room came Jessica's voice. "I asked Riley to trade with be," she said.

"Neverthe—" For an instant, he looked surprised. Then concern furrowed his brow. "My God, what happened to you?"

"I got wracked ub. Okay? Can I just stay here?"

"Did somebody do that to you?"

"No, I fell down the stairs."

Maybe she had a different story for everyone.

"I'm very sorry to hear that, Jessica. But I'm afraid I'll have to insist that you both resume your proper seats."

Riley mumbled something, gathered his books, and headed for the back of the classroom.

Good show! Lane thought.

No wonder Kramer was one of the most popular teachers at Buford High. Not only young, handsome, and clever, but he had the guts to keep discipline. Plenty of other teachers would've backed off and let Riley stay.

Lane suddenly remembered Riley's threat. She felt herself go hot and shaky again.

Jessica slid into her seat. She sat up straight, facing Kramer. "Thanks a lot, teach," she muttered.

"You're not outside, now. Take off those sunglasses."

That's going a little too far, Lane thought.

Jessica dropped her sunglasses onto the desktop. Lane could only see her right eye. It was swollen nearly shut. Her upper lid, shiny and purple, bulged as if someone had jammed half a golf ball underneath it.

Kramer pursed his lips. He shook his head. "You may put the glasses back on," he said.

"Thanks a heab."

"Okay, we've wasted enough time. Take out your texts and turn to page fifty-eight."

Lane watched the clock. This was the last class of the day. It had forty-five minutes to go.

He won't try anything, she told herself. He wouldn't dare.

I'll be okay if I can just get to my car.

Thirty minutes to go.

Ten.

In spite of the air-conditioning, Lane was bathed with sweat. Her T-shirt felt sodden against her armpits. Cool dribbles trickled down between her breasts. Her panties were glued to her rump.

With one minute to go she piled her books on top of her binder, ready to bolt for the door.

The bell rang.

She pressed the books to her chest, slid out of the seat and stood up.

Kramer met her eyes. "Miss Dunbar, I'd like to speak with you for a minute."

No!

"Yes sir," she said.

She sank back onto her seat and put the books down.

Why was he doing this to her? Was he annoyed because she'd seemed in such a rush to get out?

I'm doomed, she thought.

Mr. Kramer stepped behind his desk and stuffed books into his briefcase. The kids hurried out. The room had doors at the front and rear. Riley didn't leave by the front. He'd probably used the other door, but Lane forced herself not to look.

Maybe he forgot about me.

Fat chance.

Mr. Kramer came around his desk and sat on its edge, facing her. He held some typed sheets in his hand.

He wants to discuss one of my themes?

But Lane could see that it wasn't hers. It looked like erasable paper. The stuff always felt sticky, and the ink had a tendency to smear if you rubbed it, but she'd used it anyway until her father had told her to "throw away that junk and use some decent bond." He'd gone on to say that only amateurs fooled with erasable paper, and editors hated it with a passion.

"That isn't mine," she said.

Mr. Kramer smiled. "I'm aware of that. What I have here is a book report that I found very interesting. It was written by Henry Peidmont. Is he a friend of yours?"

"Yes."

Henry, she knew, had Kramer for second period.

"He's quite a good student, but he does have a peculiar taste in literature. He seems to relish the macabre."

"Yeah, I've noticed."

Kramer fluttered the pages a bit. "This particular report deals with a book called *Night Watcher,* by Lawrence Dunbar." He tipped his head sideways and smiled at Lane.

So that's it, she thought.

I'm not in trouble, after all.

Just in trouble with Riley.

"He's my dad," she admitted, feeling a mix of pride and embarrassment.

"Henry mentions that in his report."

Thanks, Hen.

"We don't have many real authors living here in Mulehead Bend. In fact, your father is the only one I'm aware of. Do you suppose he might be willing to come in sometime and talk to the class?"

"He might. He's kind of busy, but—"

"I'm sure he is. We wouldn't want to impose on him, but I think that the class might enjoy hearing what he has to say. I've never read any of his books myself. They're not exactly my cup of tea."

"A lot of people feel that way," Lane said.

"I've seen his books on the stands, though. And I've seen any number of students with them."

"They need more parental supervision."

Kramer laughed softly.

He may be a teacher, Lane thought, but he's sure a neat guy.

"I understand that the novels are pretty nasty."

"You were misinformed. They're *extremely* nasty. I'm under strict orders not to read any until I'm thirty-five."

"I'll bet you've disobeyed, though, haven't you?"

Lane grinned. "I've read 'em all."

"Under the bedcovers, I presume."

"Some of the time."

"Well, I'd really appreciate it if you would talk to him. If he could find the time to come in, I think the kids would get quite a charge out of it. He might want to tell them about how he became a writer, why he chose to specialize in 'extremely nasty' novels, that kind of thing."

"I'll check with him about it."

"Fine. I won't keep you any longer now. But let me know, okay?"

"Sure." She picked up her books. As she scooted off the seat, she saw him glance at her legs and look away quickly.

At least somebody appreciates the dress, she thought.

Too bad he has to be a teacher.

Heading toward the door, she was hit again by the knowledge that Riley might be waiting for her.

What if I ask Mr. Kramer to walk me out to the parking lot?

No way, she told herself. He might get the wrong idea. Unless I explain about Riley. And that might get Riley in hot water, and then I'd *really* be in trouble.

"See you tomorrow," she called over her shoulder.

"Have a nice evening, Lane."

She stepped into the hallway. Leaning against the lockers on the other side was Jim. He lifted a hand in greeting.

"I wouldn't blame you if you told me to get lost," he said, coming toward her. "I don't know what got into me this morning. I'm really sorry."

"You should be."

"You can wash my mouth out with soap, if that'd help any."

"That's an idea." She took hold of his hand. "Next time, I just might."

"Am I forgiven, then?"

"I guess so. This time."

Together they walked down the hall.

So much for dumping him, she thought. Guess I wasn't ready for it, after all.

Though she was a little disappointed in herself, she mostly felt relieved.

"I was afraid I'd really blown it," Jim said. "All day I kept thinking about it, and how much I'd miss you. I really love you, Lane. I don't know what I would've done if . . . well, anyway. We're okay again, right?"

"Yeah. We're okay."

He squeezed her hand.

In the parking lot Lane spotted Riley Benson sitting on the hood of her Mustang. They were still some distance away, and Jim hadn't noticed him yet.

But Riley saw them, scurried down and swaggered off.

Ten

She was waterskiing on the river at night. She didn't want to be there. She was frightened.

She wanted to stop but didn't dare. The thing in the water would get her before the boat had time to swing around and pick her up.

She didn't know what it was in the water. But something. Something awful.

The boat sped faster and faster, as if it wanted to help her escape. She skimmed over the smooth black surface, clinging to the handle of the tow line, whimpering with terror.

Somehow, she knew that the boat wasn't quick enough. The thing in the water was gaining on her.

If they were closer to shore! If the boat took her near enough to a dock, she might let go of the line and her speed might take her gliding to safety.

But she couldn't see the shore.

On both sides there was only darkness.

That's impossible, she thought. The river's no more than a quarter mile wide.

Where are we?

Sick with dread, she thought, We're not on the Colorado anymore.

Clutching the wooden handle with her right hand, she raised her left and waved for the boat to head ashore.

Wherever that might be.

It kept its straight course.

Look at me! her mind shrieked. Damn it, pay attention!

She suddenly realized that she didn't know who was steering the boat.

Then she saw that it was drawing away from her.

As if the tow line were stretching.

Slowly, the running lights faded with distance, until they vanished entirely. Even the sound of the outboards died away.

There was silence except for the hiss of her skis.

The tow rope led into darkness.

She was alone.

Except for the thing under the river.

Oh God, what am I going to . . .

Cold hands grabbed her ankles, tugged her straight down. She was still on her skis, still speeding at the end of the tow line, but under the surface. The water pushed at her. It filled her open mouth, muffling her scream as the hands scurried up her legs.

She felt the thing's icy flesh against her back. It was standing on the skies behind her, riding them, reaching around her front, grabbing her hands, trying to rip them from the wooden bar. She held on with all her might.

If I let go, he'll have me!

He snapped her left arm. Broke it off at the elbow. Her hand still clutched the bar for a moment, trailing its severed forearm. Then the rushing current took them away.

A hand clamped over her mouth. It pinched her nostrils shut.

She fought to suck in air.

Somehow, she'd been able to breathe in spite of the water gushing down her throat, but the hand was different. It was solid. Her lungs burned.

She grabbed the hand and woke up and the hand was still there, mashing her bruised mouth, pinching her nostrils shut.

"Don't make a sound, Jessica."

Frantic for a breath, she nodded. The hand lifted. She sucked air into her starved lungs.

"Had a little nightmare?" he whispered.

He was on the bed, sitting on her, leaning forward and holding her by the shoulders. Jessica was no longer covered by her sheet. In the glow of moonlight from the windows, she saw that Kramer was shirtless. From the hot feel of his skin where he sat on her, she knew that he'd removed all his clothes before climbing onto her. He had slipped her nightshirt up, too. Her left forearm rested against her chest, its cast heavy and cool.

"You bastard."

"Shhh. If you wake up your parents, I'll have to kill them. And you. I'll have to kill everyone. You wouldn't want that to happen, would you?"

"No," she whispered.

"I didn't imagine you would."

"What do you want?" she asked. The stupid question of the year. What he wanted was obvious. But she'd thought it was over.

Saturday night she'd told him it was over, told him that he could find another girl, threatened to get him fired if he didn't stop. That had been the stupid threat of the year. But after finishing his little "lesson," he'd said, "I'm sick of you anyway, you disgusting slut."

"I've been thinking," he whispered. "I've been worrying."

"I'b not going to tell."

"How do I know that?"

"Don't hurt be. Blease."

"I didn't come here to hurt you, Jessica. I'm here for only one reason. Well, maybe two." He laughed softly. She squirmed as a hand slid down from her shoulder and squeezed her breast. "I'm here to teach you a lesson. A lesson about safety. For you, there is no safety. Do you understand?"

She nodded.

"If you should ever happen to tell someone about me, I'll come into your home just as I did tonight. There will be one difference. I'll have a straight razor in my hand. I'll begin by slashing the throats of your parents while they sleep. And then I'll come to you." A fingernail circled her nipple. "I'll cut you very badly. Everywhere. It may take all night. And just before dawn I'll open your throat from ear to ear. Do you understand?"

"Yes."

"Very good." The pale blur of his face drifted down. He kissed her sore lips. "Very good," he whispered again.

Eleven

Except for the struggle on Monday morning to come up with a new story, Larry had spent the entire week on *Night Stranger*. That book was coming along fine. But what about the next?

He didn't feel like wracking his mind for a new idea. So much easier to stick with the familiar territory of *Night Stranger*. He knew where that book was going, and enjoyed the excitement of guiding it there.

This was Friday.

He couldn't keep avoiding the problem forever.

Think how much better you'll feel, he told himself, once you've come up with a great plan for the next book.

A great plan that does not include a stiff under the stairs with a stake in its heart.

He found the disk from Monday, put it into his word processor and tapped out commands until "Novel Notes— Monday, October 3" appeared at the corner of the screen. As he cleaned a pipe and loaded it with fresh tobacco, he skimmed the amber lines. About three pages worth of material. And nothing.

A lot of crap about their vampire.

"In effect," he read, "you have this gorgeous thing as your slave.

"Real possibilities."

Sure.

Better luck today.

Larry lit his pipe. Below "Real possibilities" he typed, "Notes—Friday, October 7.

"How about a tribe of desert scavengers?" he wrote, recalling the idea he'd toyed around with shortly before the van reached Sagebrush Flat. "They arrange 'accidents' on the back roads, then fall upon the unlucky travelers.

"Too much like *The Hills Have Eyes*. Besides, I already did something along those lines in *Savage Timber.*"

Larry scowled at the screen. He wished he hadn't reminded himself of *Savage Timber.* That damn novel, his second, had nearly destroyed his career. A major release, and all it did was sit in the stores, thanks to that damn green foil artsy-fart cover.

Don't think about it, he told himself.

Come on, a new idea.

"How about a guy who finds the remains of an old jukebox? He restores it to working order, and . . ."

And what?

"It doesn't have any records in it. He puts in his own. But it doesn't play the new ones. All it will play are the oldies-but-goodies that used to be in it. Back before it was shot to pieces by . . . Hey, maybe it wants revenge on the vandals who used it for target practice.

"Great. A pissed-off jukebox. What does it do, scoot around and electrocute people?

"Could be like a time machine. The guy gets it working, and it shoves him into the past. So he finds himself stranded in Holman's—or a dive of some kind—back in the mid-sixties.

"Has possibilities.

"Maybe the box wants him there to have a showdown with the jerks who plugged it. A motorcycle gang, or something. A real nasty bunch.

"The poor guy doesn't know what's in store for him. But he's plenty upset. It's Twilight Zone time. One minute he's with his wife and kids, has a nice house and a good job. Suddenly, bam, he finds himself in a diner in a dying town twenty-five years in the past. Freaks him out. All he wants to do is get home.

"Until he finds himself falling for a beautiful young waitress. At that point he begins to appreciate his situation.

"Things start to get ugly when a gang of biker thugs thunders into town.

"Suppose the real reason the jukebox took him there was to save the waitress? Neat. The jukebox *likes* her. Sometimes, alone at night after the diner closes, she has it play her favorite tunes, and she dances alone in the dark.

"The way things went down, first time around, the bikers raped and murdered her. The jukebox has brought our hero back to the diner to alter the course of history—to save her.

"Which, of course, he does.

"Mission accomplished, the box lets him go home again. But he misses the beautiful waitress. (Okay, he didn't have a wonderful wife and kids. He was divorced, or something.) He goes looking for the gal. Finds her.

"She's his mother. He's his own father. He got her pregnant during their brief time together back in '65, and he was the baby she had.

"He'd have to be about thirty years old in the present. She could be about twenty-five when he met her in the diner.

"She had to give up the baby (our hero) for some reason. He was adopted, and always curious about the identity of his parents.

"If she is his mother, we could give him back his wife and kids.

"Neater if he finds the waitress in the present and they resume as lovers. But how would that work with their ages? Say he's thirty in the present. How could the gal be anywhere near his age when he finds her again? If she's thirty now, she would've been five when he saved her from the bikers.

"What if the waitress he fell in love with was her mother? That would make the daughter just his age in the present. And she is the spitting image of her mother, the gal he loved.

"Not bad. Might work."

Larry's pipe had gone out. He could tell by the easy draw that nothing remained in the bowl but ash. He set the pipe into its holder and returned his fingers to the keyboard.

"Our main guy resurrects the jukebox. It seems evil at first, but turns out to be a force for good. And a matchmaker. He falls for the waitress, who happens to have a really cute little girl at the time. Plenty of thrills and spills and nasty crap with the bikers (make them total degenerates, monsters). By facing them down (he's scared, but comes through, proving to himself that he's a man), he ends up saving the kid who will later become his true love.

"Why not?"

Larry grinned at the screen.

All right! You've got it. Spend the next couple of days working out the details, and . . .

The next couple of days.

He muttered a curse.

The weekend was shot. As soon as Lane got home from school today, they would be hitting the road for Los Angeles to visit with Jean's folks.

Just what he wanted to do.

Especially now, with the new idea sizzling in his mind.

Can't get out of it, though. You'll just have to put the idea on hold till Monday.

It would give him something to think about while he drove. He might be able to work out a few of the main scenes, maybe even come up with some nifty new angles. But he knew very well that daydreaming about the story while he steered down the freeway would accomplish very little compared to working at the word processor. The act of typing out his thoughts seemed to give them a focus that wasn't there when he simply let his mind wander. Daydreams seemed to meander and drift. But sentences were solid, and one led to another.

Not this weekend, they won't.

This weekend's down the toilet.

Well, he tried to console himself, Jean's folks are okay. And it is their anniversary. I'll probably end up having a good time, even though I'd rather be . . .

He heard the doorbell ring.

Jean would take care of it.

He wondered whether he should get back to *Night Stranger* or spend the rest of the day fleshing out his jukebox story.

Call it *The Box,* he suddenly thought.

And grinned.

"THE BOX," he typed. "Great title. Has a mysterious ring to it. And Box not only refers to the jukebox that sends him back in time, but also the 'box' or trap he finds himself stuck in. He's boxed in by circumstances. No apparent way out. Also, the sex thing. Have one of the bikers refer to the main gal as a box. 'Foxy box.' And maybe the main guy is a former boxer—killed an opponent in the ring, and swore off fighting? No, that'd be pushing it. Trite, too. But maybe there are some other 'box' angles. Fool around with it."

He heard Jean's footsteps approaching. She might come in and look over his shoulder, so he scrolled down until "foxy box" climbed out of sight at the top of the screen.

She rapped on the office door and pushed it open. In her hand was an Overnight Mail bag that looked large enough to hold a manuscript. "This just came for you," she said. "It's from Chandler House."

His publisher.

Jean watched while he tore open the bag. Inside, he

found a fat manuscript held together by rubber bands. And a typewritten note from his editor, Susan Anderson:

Larry

Here is the copyedited manuscript of MAD-HOUSE. The corrections are light, so I'm sure you'll be pleased.

We would like you to make whatever changes you consider appropriate, and return it to us if possible by October 13.

Best,

Susan

Larry grimaced.

"What?" Jean asked.

"It's *Madhouse.* The copyedited version. I'm supposed to send it back by the thirteenth." He glanced at his calendar. "Christ, that's next Thursday."

"They didn't give you much time."

"That's for sure," he muttered. "They've had it for about a year and a half, and now I get . . . six days."

"Have fun," Jean said. She left the room, closing the door again to keep his pipe smoke from contaminating the rest of the house.

Larry pushed his chair back, crossed a leg, rested the thick manuscript on his thigh and rolled the rubber bands off. He tossed Susan's note and the title page onto the cluttered TV tray beside his chair.

Then he groaned.

For "light" corrections, page one seemed to have an awful lot of changes.

Halfway down the page his paragraph used to read, "She

tugged at the door. Locked. God, no! She whirled around and choked out a whimper. He was already off the autopsy table, staggering toward her, his head bobbing and swaying on its broken neck. In his hand was the scalpel."

Larry struggled to decipher the changes. Words had been crossed out, others added. The paragraph was a map of lines and arrows. At last he figured it out.

"Tugging at the door, she found it to be locked. No! Snapping her head around, she whimpered in despair, for she saw that the corpse was staggering toward her with a scalpel in his hand. His head was swinging from side to side atop its snapped neck."

"Jesus H. Christ on a crutch," Larry muttered.

He found Jean in their bedroom, gathering clothes from an open drawer of her bureau and taking them to her suitcase. Both suitcases lay open on the bed.

He sat down at the end of the mattress. "We've got a problem."

"The manuscript?"

"I just looked through the whole thing. It's been wrecked."

"Not again."

"Yeah." *Madhouse* was his twelfth novel, and the third to be demolished by a copyeditor.

"What're you going to do?" Jean asked.

"I have to fix it. I don't have any choice." He scowled at the carpet. "Maybe I could get them to take my name off and publish it under the name of the copyeditor."

"It's that bad?"

"And then some."

"Why do they let it happen?"

"God, I don't know. It's the luck of the draw, I guess. This time, they happened to send my book to some idiot who thinks she's a writer."

"Or he," Jean said, standing up for her gender.

"Or it."

"Couldn't you just write a letter to Susan, or something, and explain the situation? Maybe they could send a fresh copy to someone else."

He shook his head. "I don't think she'd appreciate that. It'd be like calling them jerks for sending it to some illiterate butcher. Besides, they already paid to have it done. And they're on a tight time schedule by now, or they wouldn't want the damn thing back in six days."

"Maybe you should phone Susan."

"The last thing I need is to get a reputation as a troublemaker."

"So you're just going to take it lying down?"

"I'm going to take it sitting on my butt with a red pen in one hand and a copy of my British edition in the other. If the people in London didn't fix it, it didn't need fixing." He hung his head and sighed.

Jean stepped in front of him. She rubbed his shoulders. "I'm sorry, honey."

"Fortunes of war. The thing is . . . it'll have to be mailed Wednesday for next-day delivery. If I go to your folks' place, that only gives me about three days to go through the whole damn thing and try to . . . save it."

"You could take it along."

"I wouldn't be fit to live with, anyway. Maybe you and Lane should just go ahead without me." As he spoke the words, he realized that he didn't want to be left behind. Not for this. But he couldn't go. "If I spend the whole weekend working on it, maybe I'll be feeling human again by the time you get back."

"I suppose we could call it off," she said, stroking his hair. "Go up next weekend instead."

"No, don't do that. It's their anniversary. Besides, you've been looking forward to it. No need for all of us to suffer because of this crap."

"If you're sure," she muttered.

"I don't see any choice."

Larry went back to his office. His throat felt tight.

You didn't want to go in the first place, he reminded himself.

But that was before he found out he would have to be laboring over *Madhouse*.

He stared at his computer screen.

"Maybe there are some other 'box' angles. Fool around with it."

Right. Sure thing. Maybe sometime next week.

No more working out the details for *The Box*. No more plunging toward the conclusion of *Night Stranger*.

The next few days belonged to *Madhouse,* a book that he'd finished eighteen months ago. A book that had already been published in England—and about all they had changed over there was "windshield" to "windscreen" and added u's to words like color.

"So who said life is fair?" he muttered, and shut his computer off.

Twelve

"I have a special announcement to make," Mr. Kramer said with two minutes remaining before the bell. "As I've mentioned before, the drama department at the city college is putting on *Hamlet* next week. I'm sure the production will be well worth seeing for all of you, and I urge every one of you to attend if you can. Now, here's the thing. I've obtained four free tickets to the Saturday night performance. Only four of you will be able to participate, but for those lucky students, I'll provide tickets and transportation." He smiled. "That way, you won't have to bug your parents to borrow a car." A few of the kids laughed. "If any of you would like to take advantage of the opportunity, just stay in your seats after the bell rings."

Lane gnawed her lower lip. Should she stay? Jim might ask her out for that night.

We can always go out Friday night instead, she told herself.

It *would* be neat to see the play, especially with Mr. Kramer. Couldn't hurt, either, in the Brownie points department.

The bell rang. Lane remained in her seat.

As Jessica stepped by, she glanced at Lane and shook her head.

Probably thinks I'm an idiot, wanting to give up a Saturday night to see Shakespeare.

Maybe I am. If it turns out that Jim's busy Friday night, I'm going to kick myself. He was gone last weekend, I'll be gone this weekend. That'll make three weeks in a row if I go to the play and he can't make it on Friday.

This Saturday night was when she'd wanted to go out with him. All week he'd been especially nice. Trying to make up, Lane supposed, for being such a creep Monday morning.

She turned on her seat. Five other kids had remained in the room.

There're six of us, and he can only take four. If I'm not picked, that'll solve the problem right there.

"I see I've got more Shakespeare fans than tickets," Mr. Kramer said. "That's certainly gratifying, but it does present a little difficulty. We want to be fair about this." He dug a hand into a pocket of his slacks and pulled out a quarter. "I'll flip a coin. The first two of you to lose will have to bow out. Does that sound okay to everyone?"

Nobody objected.

"Okay, Lane, you first. Call it in the air." He rested the coin on his thumbnail and flicked it high.

"Heads," Lane said.

It landed in the palm of his right hand. He slapped it onto the back of his left, kept it covered and smiled at her. "Want to change your mind?"

"Nope. I'll stick with heads."

He looked. "Heads it is," he said, tipping his hand and letting the coin drop into the other.

He didn't let anyone see it, Lane realized.

What the heck, they're his tickets.

"Okay, George, your turn."

George won. So did Aaron and Sandra.

Jerry and Heidi, the losers, called the coin again to determine who would be first choice as an alternate in case one of the chosen was unable to attend. Heidi won.

"Okay," Mr. Kramer said, "I'll fill you in on the details later. In the meantime, have a good weekend. Don't do anything I wouldn't."

That comment brought a few chuckles.

Lane gathered her books and stood up. "I'm glad you're one of the lucky four," he said. "Maybe I'll get a chance to meet your father when I pick you up for the play."

"I'm sure he'll be glad to meet you."

"I'll have to pick up one of his books and get an autograph."

"That'll make his day."

"And maybe we can firm up the date he'll be coming in."

"Yeah. He said any time after the first."

"Well, maybe we can make it more definite."

Lane nodded. "Have a nice weekend, Mr. Kramer."

"You, too. Try to stay out of trouble." He winked.

"What would be the fun of that?" she said, blushing.

As he laughed, Lane waved good-bye and left the room.

The hallway was crowded with kids, noisy with slamming lockers, shouts, and laughter. She leaned against a wall and waited for Jim. A few minutes later he came along.

"I have to drop some stuff off at my locker," Lane said. They started up the hall together.

"When are you leaving for Los Angeles?" he asked.

"As soon as I get home."

"What a drag."

"There's always next weekend. Next Friday, anyway. I have to go to a play Saturday night with Mr. Kramer."

"Yeah?" He glanced at her, lifting an eyebrow. "Isn't he a little old for you?"

"Get real. It's a school function. He's taking four of us from his sixth-period class."

"Great."

"Oh now, don't start pouting. I've got nothing on Friday night."

"Nothing on, huh? I'd like to see that."

"I just bet you would." She felt a hand slide over the seat of her skirt. "Quit it."

"Sorry. Just trying to refresh my memory. It's been two whole weeks, you know, and now it'll be another."

"I'm not overjoyed about it myself. Nothing I can do, though." She arrived at her locker and started spinning the combination dial.

"Maybe you could pretend to be sick," he suggested. "What if you did that, and they let you stay home by yourself? I could come over to your house tomorrow night and—"

"Dream on, MacDuff."

She opened the locker and switched books, taking out those she would need for homework. Then she shut the metal door. "Even if I did stay home, boys aren't allowed in the house when my parents are gone."

"Who would ever know?"

"I would. Anyway, you might as well forget it. Ain't gonna happen." They started down the hallway. "If you promise to behave," Lane said, "I'll give you a ride home."

"What about your goofball friends, Fat and Ugly."

Lane frowned at him. "I don't know who you mean."

"You know, all right. Betty and Henry."

"Why don't you refer to them that way, okay? They are my friends."

"God knows why."

"Are you trying to start something?"

"No, no. Just kidding. They're wonderful people, the salt of the earth."

"You could stand to be a little more like Henry."

"Uh, duh." He put a dopey smile on his face and started bobbing his head.

"Very funny," she said, but couldn't hold back a smile. "Stop it. That's not nice."

"Duh, okay."

"Anyway, Betty's mom was picking them up after school and taking them to violin lessons."

"So it'll just be you and me, huh?"

"If you can fit your big head into the car."

"I can try."

At the end of the hallway Jim held the door open for her. She stepped out and looked toward the student parking lot. She spotted her red Mustang.

No sign of Riley Benson.

After Monday, she'd expected each afternoon to find him perched on the hood. So far he hadn't tried it again. Though they crossed paths several times a day, he'd done no more than give her tough-guy looks.

He must've given up on his big plan for revenge, she decided.

Maybe Jessica had talked him out of it.

Pays to be nice to people, she thought. Especially if they're buddy-buddy with someone who wants to wipe up the floor with you.

When Lane opened the car door, hot air poured out. They cranked down all the windows. She took a beach towel from the trunk and spread it over the driver's seat so she wouldn't burn her legs on the upholstery.

"You don't have one for me?" Jim asked.

"You're not wearing a skirt."

"You sure are," he said, and bent forward as if trying for a glimpse of her panties when she climbed in. "Pink," he announced.

"Wrong."

She started the engine. She twisted around to look out the rear window as she backed out of the space. She could feel her blouse pull tight against her breasts. Jim, of course, was staring at them.

"If they match your bra, they're white," he said.

"Don't you ever think about anything but sex?" she asked, grinning at him.

"Sure. Instead sometimes I think about sex."

She shook her head, faced forward again and steered for the parking lot exit.

"Must be hot, wearing a bra all the time."

"What makes you think I wear one *all* the time?"

"Every time I've seen you."

"Are you sure?"

"Are you kidding? I can tell a mile away if a babe's got one on."

"That's impressive. . . . How long is your car going to be out of commission?" Lane asked, hoping to change the subject.

"I'll have it off the blocks tomorrow. I wanted it ready so we could go out tomorrow night."

"Sorry about that."

"Maybe I'll give Candi a call."

"I know, just kidding."

Jim said nothing. Lane got a tight, sickish feeling deep inside. She kept her eyes on the road.

"You wouldn't mind, would you?"

"Be my guest."

She knew that Jim was teasing. He had no intention of taking out Candi. He'd dumped Candi in order to start going out with her. The threat of taking up with Candi again was nothing more than a form of punishment.

"You know what they say about a bird in the hand," Jim said.

"A good way to get a dirty hand."

"Also, she's a lot more cooperative than some people I might mention."

"And probably has the diseases to prove it."

"Oooh. Mean."

"But feel free to take her out. It's your life."

He reached over and put a hand on Lane's leg. "You know I wouldn't do that."

"I only know what you tell me."

"I miss you, that's all."

"I miss you, too. But there's nothing I can do about this weekend."

"Yeah, I know." He squeezed her knee, and his hand moved slowly up her bare leg to the hem of her skirt. He caressed her thigh. It felt good.

"Just don't go throwing Candi at me every time you get upset."

"Jealous?"

"Suppose I was always threatening to dump you for Cliff Ryker?"

"That shithead?"

"You think you'd enjoy it?"

"You wouldn't. Not if you went ahead with it."

"He's cute."

"Not as cute as me." Jim's hand crept under her skirt. She pushed it away. "He's no gentleman, either."

"And you are?"

"I'm not like Cliff. He isn't the kind of guy who takes no for an answer. First time out with him, and he'd bang you till you couldn't see straight. If that's what you want, I'll be glad to take care of it for you."

"You go out with Candi, and you'll never get the chance."

"Hmmmm. I like the sound of that. You mean, if I don't, I do?"

"Where there's life, there's hope."

She pulled the Mustang over to the curb in front of Jim's house. Checking the windows and rearview mirror, she saw nobody nearby. She turned to Jim. She slipped a hand around the back of his neck. "No funny stuff," she said. "Just a quick kiss."

"How about coming in for a Pepsi, or something?"

She shook her head. "I have to get home. My folks are waiting."

"Ten minutes? That won't throw off your trip by much. Tell them you had to stay after class."

I *did* have to stay after class, she thought. It wouldn't be a lie.

"Is your mother home?"

Jim answered by swinging a thumb over his shoulder, pointing out the Mazda in the driveway.

"Okay," Lane said. "Ten minutes. No longer, though."

She took her hand away from his neck and climbed out. Jim stayed in the lead as she walked up the flagstones to the front stoop. He unlocked the door and held it open for her.

The air was cool.

The house was silent except for the hum of the air-conditioning system.

Jim didn't call out to announce that he was home.

"Are you sure she's here?" Lane asked.

"Might be sleeping. Or taking a bath. Who knows?"

They entered the kitchen. Lane leaned against a counter while Jim took a couple of cans from the refrigerator. The air smelled fresh. It was almost too cold on her skin. It chilled the damp back of her blouse.

Jim found glasses, dropped ice cubes into them, and filled them with soda.

A glass in each hand, he stepped in front of Lane. She reached for her drink. Instead of giving it to her, he stretched both arms past her sides and set the glasses on the counter. His arms closed around her, pulled her gently forward until their bodies met.

"What if your mother walks in?" Lane whispered close to his mouth.

"I don't think she will." He tugged the tail of her blouse out of her skirt and slid his hands underneath.

Lane let herself sink against him. She kissed him.

Shouldn't be doing this, she thought.

But she'd intended to kiss him good-bye, anyway. And

his hands felt good roaming the bare skin of her back. And she liked the feel of his chest tight against her breasts. She could feel his breathing and his heartbeat.

He started to fumble with the catches of her bra.

She pulled her mouth away. "Oh no you don't."

"It's all right."

"No, it isn't."

He unfastened the bra anyway. She felt it go loose.

She grabbed Jim's arms and pushed them down to his sides. "I said no, and I meant it."

"Come on, what's the harm?"

"For one thing, your mother."

"She might be in town at the beauty parlor," he said, smiling as if he expected Lane to appreciate the news.

"The car . . ."

"She usually goes with Mary from next door. Right about three on Fridays."

"You *knew* she wasn't here?"

Still smiling, Jim shrugged.

"You lied to me."

"Just a little fib."

"Terrific," she muttered, reaching up under the back of her blouse to fasten the bra.

"Come on, don't do that." He lifted his hands to her breasts.

"Cut it out."

"Come on, you like it."

"I told you . . ." She got one of the hooks fastened. He was squeezing, rubbing. She *did* like it. "Damn it, Jim." Not bothering with the other hook, she swung her hands around and pushed him away. "I have to leave."

"No you don't. Hey, come on."

"This is what I get for trusting you, huh?"

"Look, I'm sorry I lied about Mom being here. Okay?" He looked into her eyes and gently held her shoulders. "I just figured you wouldn't come in, and . . . we haven't been together for weeks. I get crazy wanting to be with you. Sometimes, all I can think about is kissing you and how it feels to hold you. Especially after last time."

"That was nice," Lane said, remembering.

She had been under orders to be home by eleven, so they'd skipped the second feature at the movies and parked in the desert outside town. She'd refused Jim's suggestion to get into the backseat. Staying in the front, they twisted themselves awkwardly to embrace and kiss. But it was wonderful. She felt daring and romantic and sexy in the moonlit car. Her blouse came off early. She managed to keep her bra on, though. In spite of Jim's begging and his attempts to remove it. In spite of her own desire to rid herself of the garment and feel his touch without a stiff layer of cloth in the way. Finally she'd told him, "It's almost time to leave." He didn't protest, simply nodded and murmured, "I guess so." Reaching behind her back, Lane unhooked her bra. She took it off. His mouth fell open and he stared for a long time before touching. When he did touch her breasts, his hands were trembling.

Softened by the memories of that night, she stepped forward and put her arms around Jim. She kissed him gently on the mouth. "Apology accepted," she whispered. "But I really do have to leave now."

His hands slid down her back and caressed her rump. "What about your Pepsi?"

"Time's all up. You can walk me to the car, though."

He squeezed her against him and kissed her hard, then stepped away. "Guess I'll just have to wait for next Friday, huh?"

"It'll get here."

"Not soon enough."

"I'll miss you," she said.

"I'll miss you more."

"No you won't."

"Yes I will."

"Wanta fight about it?"

"Yeah," he said. "Let's wrestle."

"Oh, you'd like that."

"So would you."

"Maybe."

Holding hands, they walked to the door.

Thirteen

Larry stood at the end of the driveway, waving good-bye to Jean and Lane as the car headed off down the road. It seemed strange, being left behind.

He knew he would miss them. Hell, he *already* missed them.

On the other hand, he rather liked the prospect of being on his own for the weekend. He could do whatever he pleased, and not have to answer to anyone.

Freedom.

He felt like a kid being left home without parents or baby-sitter.

The car vanished around the corner. Larry turned toward the house, then raised a hand in greeting as Barbara trotted down the steps next door. A handbag swung at her hip. Larry supposed she was leaving on an errand.

"So, they took off without you."

"Sure did."

"Jean told me about that manuscript." She stopped beside her car in the driveway. "Sounds like the pits to me."

"Gives me a good excuse to stay behind," he said, smiling.

"If you're not too busy, why don't you come over for dinner? We'll throw some steaks on the barbecue."

"Sounds great."

"Good. Drop in around five, then, all right?"

"I'll be there."

She climbed into her car, and Larry headed for the house.

Things are perking up already, he thought.

In his office he glanced at the savaged manuscript and realized he was in no mood to struggle with it. He'd already fought his way through more than a hundred pages today, scratching out the copyeditor's misguided corrections and replacing them with scribbles to match the printed lines as they'd originally been written. That was plenty for one day's work.

He settled down in the living room with a beer and the Shaun Hutson novel he'd started reading that morning. Though his eyes traveled over the words, his mind kept slipping out of the story. He found himself imagining what Jean's folks might say when they realized he'd stayed home, wondering what he should wear over to Pete and Barbara's, thinking about how much he would like to spend all day tomorrow working on ideas for *The Box*.

Then he was speculating about the jukebox in the ditch. He wondered how much it weighed. Could two men lift it? In his book they would have to carry it to the van. Would that be possible?

Have the women lend a hand with it. My main guy isn't married. Might have a girlfriend with him, though.

Still occupied with his thoughts, Larry set the book aside. He drained the last of his beer, wandered into the bedroom and took off his clothes.

Have one of the gals fall while they're lugging the jukebox up the slope. Good. Foreshadowing that the box is going to cause trouble.

In the bathroom he turned on the shower and stepped under its beating spray.

She tumbles down the embankment, he thought as he began to soap himself. Gets banged up pretty much like Barbara did in the hotel.

He remembered the way Barbara had looked, standing

in the doorway afterward. How her legs and belly were scraped. How her blouse hung open.

The images stirred a pleasant heat in his groin.

Which turned cold when he suddenly saw himself kneeling under the staircase, gazing at the shriveled corpse.

God, he wished he'd never seen that thing!

It always seemed to be with him. Waiting. Like some kind of spook lurking in a dark closet of his mind, every now and then throwing open the door to give him another look.

So damn grisly and repulsive.

But fascinating, too.

As Larry washed his hair, his mind ran through the familiar questions. Who was she? Who drove the stake into her chest? Was her presence under the stairway known to the person who put the brand-new lock on the hotel doors? Could she really be a vampire? What might happen if someone pulled out the stake?

He had no answers.

He told himself, as always, that he didn't *want* to know the answers. He only wanted to forget about the thing.

Which wasn't about to happen.

Maybe we should've reported it, he thought. He'd been against that at the time. Now, however, he saw how it might've been for the best. A call to the cops would've relieved them of responsibility. Like passing the baton.

We did our part, now it's your turn.

Part of the problem, he realized, was carrying the burden of knowledge.

We're the only ones who know it's there.

But we didn't do anything about it.

So the damn corpse is more than just a grisly memory, it's unfinished business.

According to the shrinks, that's what messes up your head more than anything—unfinished business.

Maybe we need to deal with it, Larry told himself. Take some kind of action to get the thing out of our systems.

"Let's drive out and get it," Pete said.

Larry felt as if his breath had been knocked out. "You're kidding," he said.

"You're out of your gourd," Barbara said.

"Hey, if he's going to write a book about that jukebox, he ought to *have* it. Or better yet, *I* ought to have it. Larry can keep track of my progress repairing the thing so he gets the details right. You know? There's nothing like first-hand experience to give a book . . ."

"Verisimilitude," Larry put in.

"Yeah, that's it."

"I don't know," Larry said.

He took a sip of his vodka tonic and shook his head. He wished he hadn't mentioned *The Box*. Normally, he didn't discuss story ideas with anyone. But Pete and Barbara were part of this one. They'd discovered the jukebox. Pete's desire to take it home had really been the inspiration. So the story had rolled out.

Should've kept my mouth shut.

The last thing I want to do is go driving out to Sage-brush Flat.

Pete got up from his lawn chair and checked the barbecue. The flames had died away, but Larry could tell from where he sat that the briquettes were burning. The air over the grill shimmered with heat waves. "Be another ten, fifteen minutes," Pete said. He turned to Barbara, arched a dark eyebrow. "Don't you need to go inside and do something?"

"Trying to get rid of me?"

"Just trying to be helpful. We're going to have those sauteed mushrooms, we'll want them *with* our steaks."

"They only take a few minutes," she said. "I'll do them up when you put the meat on."

Good, Larry thought. He wasn't eager for her to leave. Not only was she the best defense against Pete's crazy urge to fetch the jukebox, but it felt good to look at her.

She sat on a lounge in front of him, bare legs stretched out on its cushion. Her long, slim legs looked wonderful in spite of the scabbed areas. She wore red shorts and a plain white T-shirt. The shorts were very short. The T-shirt lay softly against her flat belly and the rises of her breasts. Its fabric was thin enough to show a faint pink hue of the skin underneath, the dark crust of the scabs above Barbara's waist, the white of her bra.

He watched the way her muscles moved as she sat up straight to take a drink of her cocktail and settled back again and rested the glass on the moist disk it had left just below the hip of her shorts.

"You don't want to go back there, do you?" she asked Larry.

"Not a whole lot."

"I didn't think so."

"It's probably too heavy for the two of us to carry, anyway," he told Pete.

"Barbara will come along and lend a hand. Won't you, hon?"

"Not on your life."

"She's just scared of the vampire."

"You know it. Besides, we don't need that piece of junk cluttering up the garage."

"It'd be great for Larry's book. He can come over and check it out whenever he needs some inspiration." Looking at Larry, he added, "And we can take pictures of it. You know? A photo of the actual jukebox, all shot up the way it is, that'll be terrific on your cover."

"That would be pretty neat," he admitted.

"Jeez, don't encourage him."

Larry smiled at her. "I have no intention of going back to that place."

"You're scared of the vampire, too, huh?" Pete said. "Hey, it can't hurt you. Not as long as it's got that stake in its heart."

"I'm not worried about any 'vampire,' " Larry told him. "I don't think it *is* a vampire. But stiffs give me the creeps."

"That's a good one, coming from you."

"I'm scared of my own shadow, man. That's what makes me good at writing those books. And I tell you, Sagebrush Flat is a lot scarier to me than my shadow. My shadow pales by comparison."

Barbara chuckled at his pun.

"Even if there *were* no corpse under the stairway, I'd still want to stay away from that town. Just the fact that it's deserted is enough to spook me. There's something basically frightening about a place where people are supposed to be but aren't. An abandoned town, an office building at night . . ."

"That's really true, you know," Barbara said. "Like a hotel really late at night when everyone's asleep."

"Or a school," Larry added. "Or a church."

"Yeah." Her eyes widened. "Church's are *really* spooky when nobody's there. I used to go for choir practice when I was in high school. We'd meet on Wednesday nights at eight." She leaned forward and gazed at Larry. "One night . . . God, I'm getting goose bumps just thinking about it." Hunching up her shoulders, she squeezed her arms tight against her sides. "One night, practice had been called off and I didn't know about it. I think we'd been out of town. Anyway, the choir director was sick, and everybody knew it but me. So my dad dropped me off in the parking lot and I went in."

"You taking notes, Lar? Maybe you can use this."

"Sounds promising so far." He could feel himself shivering slightly as if Barbara's fear were contagious.

"There was a light on in the narthex. But the stairway

to the choir loft was dark. I went up there, anyway. I figured I was just the first to arrive. The choir loft was dark,
too."

"Why didn't you turn on some lights?" Pete asked.

"I don't know. I guess I thought I shouldn't mess with
anything like light switches. But also, I was afraid somebody might . . . turning on lights, you know, that'd be like
giving away that I was there." Her mouth stretched, baring
her teeth.

"That's the thing," Larry said. "When a place seems
deserted, you're afraid you aren't *really* alone."

"That's it. Exactly. Because you can't see what's out there.
God, I started thinking someone was roaming around, sneaking up on me. I even thought I heard someone creeping up
the stairs." Her right hand still held the glass on her lap.
Her other hand crossed over to that arm and rubbed it as if
she wanted to smooth away the goose bumps. Larry saw
that her thighs were pebbled. Though she wore a bra, it was
apparently of a light, stretchy fabric. Her nipples made small
points against her T-shirt.

I'll have to remember that, Larry thought. A woman has
gooseflesh, the nipples get erect.

Fear makes them hard.

Or is she turned on?

Turned on by the fear?

Barbara kept frowning, rubbing her arm. She seemed
lost in her memory of that night.

"So what happened?" Pete asked.

She shook her head. "Nothing."

"Oh, that's a great story."

"I waited around for about fifteen minutes. I was almost
too scared to move. I kept staring down at the nave and
pulpit and everything, and thought someone was down
there in the dark. You know, *aware* of me. Watching me."

"Coming for you," Pete added.

"Damn right."

" 'They're *coming* for you,' " he said, mimicking the voice of the jerky brother in the graveyard scene of *The Night of the Living Dead.* "They're *coming* for—"

"Knock it off, would you?"

"Nobody ever showed up?" Larry asked.

She shook her head. "I finally beat it. I was never so glad to get out of a place in my life."

"Not even the hole in the landing of the Sagebrush Flat Hotel?" Pete asked.

"That was different. I was in pain. That's not the same as being scared half to death."

"So you finally just bolted out of the church?" Larry asked.

"Sure did. I didn't even stop to use the phone and call home. I waited in the parking lot, and Dad finally came along at the usual time to pick me up."

"That's it, huh?" Pete asked.

"It was enough. I quit the choir after that. Nothing was ever going to get me back into the church after dark."

"Pretty drastic, considering that nothing happened."

"It wasn't exactly as if nothing happened," Larry pointed out.

"That's right. All these years have passed, and it still gives me the creeps if I think about it."

"Still isn't much of a story," Pete said.

"A good setup for one," Larry told him.

"Think you might use it?" Pete asked.

"I can just see it," Barbara said, smiling. "You'd probably have a homicidal maniac chasing me through the pews."

"Something like that. Maybe Jesus gets down off the cross and stalks the gal through the church."

"Oh, sick."

Pete laughed. "Hey, goes after her with a nail in each hand."

"You guys."

"That's good," Larry said. "Next morning, the preacher shows up and *she's* the one on the cross."

"God's gonna get you for that," Barbara warned.

"More than likely."

"I'd better put the steaks on," Pete said. "Feed him quick before a lightning bolt comes down and knocks him out of his shoes."

After dinner, Pete presented his surprise—a plastic bag containing three videotapes. "Thought we'd have a movie marathon, unless you're in a big hurry to get home."

With three vodka tonics under his belt, and the two beers he'd had with dinner, Larry knew he was in no condition to write, make corrections on his copyedited manuscript, or even read the Hutson novel.

Nor was he eager to be alone in his empty house.

"Sounds good to me," he said. "Let's see what you've got." He inspected the tapes through their clear plastic boxes: *Cameron's Closet, Blood Frenzy,* and *Floater.*

"Barb phoned me at the shop," Pete explained. "So I picked these up on the way home." He looked quite pleased with himself.

"Oh, this'll be neat," Larry said.

"These should put you in a great mood," Barbara said, "for when it's time to go home."

"They freak you out, you can spend the night here."

"I imagine I'll be all right."

They started with *Blood Frenzy.* Pete watched from a recliner beside the sofa. Larry sat at one end of the sofa, Barbara at the other. After a while she tossed a cushion onto the coffee table and propped her feet up.

When the movie ended, Pete made popcorn. Barbara disappeared for a few minutes. She came back wearing a knee-length blue robe. She filled glasses with Pepsi for everyone. Pete separated the popcorn into three bowls.

Before returning to her place on the sofa, Barbara turned off all the lights.

They munched popcorn, drank their sodas, and watched *Cameron's Closet* in a room that was dark except for the glow from the television screen.

Every now and then Larry glanced at Barbara. She was slumped against the back of the sofa, popcorn bowl on her lap, her legs stretched out, feet resting on the cushion she had earlier placed on the coffee table. When she twisted sideways to set her empty bowl on the lamp table, the robe slipped off her left leg. She wore a pink, diaphanous nightgown. It was shorter than the robe. It didn't reach down much farther than her hip. With a quiet moan of annoyance, she flung the fallen section of the robe back on top of her thigh.

This is sure better than being home, Larry thought.

A few minutes later she took the cushion out from under her feet. She tilted it against the armrest, swiveled herself around and swung her legs onto the sofa. She lay down on her side, head propped on the cushion. "Let me know if I kick you," she said.

"Maybe I should get out of your way."

"No, that's fine."

Pete looked over. "Oh, here we go. For godsake, Barb, sit up. You won't last five minutes."

"I'm wide awake."

"You won't be. I'm warning you, I'm not gonna rewind. You drift off, it's your hard luck."

"I'm not going to drift off."

"Famous last words," Pete said. "Lar, you catch her dropping off, pinch her."

"Don't you dare." She tucked the robe in between the backs of her legs as if to prevent Larry from reaching up inside it for the pinch.

It was the sort of thing that Jean might do.

The casual warning and precaution hinted at an intimacy that was both comforting and exciting.

Larry used the remote to rewind the few seconds of the movie that he'd missed while complaining to Barbara.

She lasted more than five minutes. But not more than ten. Larry realized she was asleep when her legs straightened and one of her bare feet pushed against the side of his thigh. Her touch made warmth flow through him.

He waited for a while, enjoying the sensation. But it made him feel guilty. "Pete," he finally said. "She's zonked."

"Barrr-bra."

She flinched, lifted her face off the cushion. "No, I'm fine."

"You dosed off."

"No, I didn't. I'm fine." Her head settled down again. Her eyes drifted shut.

"Forget it," Pete said. "She can watch it in the morning if she wants to."

"I'm watching," she mumbled.

Larry tried to watch the movie. Her right foot made it difficult. So did the way the top of her robe hung open, revealing most of her right breast through the flimsy pink nightgown. The show on the TV screen was good, but the stolen glimpses were better. Sometimes the foot rubbed him.

Near the end of the movie she stretched out her left leg. Its foot pushed across the top of his thigh and rested on his lap. The pressure there made him squirm. He wrapped his hand around Barbara's ankle and guided her foot down beside the other.

"Huh?" she moaned. "Sorry. Kicking you?"

"It's all right," he said.

Pete looked around, frowning. "Christ, Barb, you're screwing up the movie. Why don't you just go to bed."

"Yeah, maybe I better."

Shit, Larry thought.

She pushed herself up and staggered to her feet. "Night, guys. Sorry I pooped out on you, Larry."

"No problem. Thanks for the dinner and everything."

"Glad you could make it. See ya." She made her way around the coffee table. Larry could see through her robe when she stepped in front of him. Her breasts swayed a little as she bent over and kissed Pete good night.

Then she was gone.

The room seemed empty without her.

During the final moments of *Cameron's Closet* Larry heard a toilet flush.

Pete removed the tape from the VCR. He grinned over his shoulder. "Free at last, free at last," he said. "Thank God Almighty, free at last."

"If you want to turn in . . ."

"Are you kidding?" He pushed the tape of *Floater* into the machine and started it playing. "Back in a second." He hurried away.

He came back while the screen still showed its warning against unauthorized use of the videotape. He had a bottle of Irish whiskey in one hand and two glasses in the other. He sat next to Larry on the sofa. He filled the two glasses. "Party time," he said.

"I'm gonna be wasted tomorrow."

"The cats are away. Gotta live it up."

They watched the movie until their glasses were empty. Pete refilled them both, then pressed the Stop button on his remote. The horror film was replaced by a black and white John Wayne movie. Larry recognized it immediately as *The Sands of Iwo Jima*.

"Why'd you turn it off?" he asked.

A grin stretched the corners of Pete's mouth.

Fourteen

"How about a little excursion?" Pete said.

"What do you mean?"

"Sagebrush Flat."

"You're kidding," Larry said.

"Who's gonna stop us?"

"I don't want to go out there."

Pete clapped a hand down on Larry's knee. His eyes gleamed with mischief, but he wasn't smiling. He looked like a kid, a kid with a mustache and some gray in his hair and with big plans to pull off a caper. "We take the van. We drive out there, pick up the jukebox, and we'll be back in two, three hours. Barb's zonked. She'll never know."

"She'll know when she finds the thing in your garage."

"Okay, so we'll leave it over at your place. What do you say, Lar?"

"I think it's crazy."

"Hey, man, an adventure. It'll be great. You can use it in your book. You know, tell all about how the two guys sneak off in the middle of the night to bring the thing back. You can write it the way it happens, you know? Won't have to tax the ol' imagination."

"It's crazy."

"Don't you want the box?"

"Not that badly."

"What about a photo for the cover of your book?"

"Well, that'd be neat, but—"

"So we'll take my camera. Maybe we won't bring the thing back, you know? Maybe we can't even lift it. But at least we'll have some pictures."

"We could do that during the day."

"You know the kind of heat I'd get from Barbara. She'd give me all kinds of shit. How about it?"

"You really want to go *now?*" The digital clock on the VCR showed 12:05.

"No time like the present. A midnight mission."

The idea frightened Larry. It also excited him. He felt a vibration that seemed to hum through his nerves.

When was the last time, he wondered, that you did something really daring?

If you chicken out, you'll regret it. And Pete'll think you're a pussy.

A real adventure.

"Just like Tom and Huck," he said.

"Huh?"

"Tom Sawyer climbed out his window in the middle of the night and went with Huck to a graveyard to cure their warts. I always wished I could do something like that."

"You got warts, man?"

"Let's go for it."

Grinning, Pete refilled the glasses. "Fun and games," he toasted. They clinked their glasses and drank.

Pete took his glass with him. He turned on a lamp at the end of the sofa. Then he removed the tape from the VCR, flicked off the television and left the room. Larry sipped whiskey while he waited. It warmed him but didn't ease the thrumming vibrations.

When Pete returned he wore a gunbelt. His .357 hung in the holster against his right leg. Dangling by a strap around his neck was a camera with a flash attachment. "I checked the bedroom," he said in a low voice. "Barb's out like a light."

Pete set his empty glass down. He capped the whiskey bottle and handed it to Larry. "You be the keeper of the hooch."

"We shouldn't take it with us."

"Fuck that. Who's gonna know?"

"If we get stopped—"

"We won't. Calm down, you'll live longer."

They went to the door. Pete turned off the lamp.

They stepped outside. Standing under the porch light, Pete locked the front door with his key.

Larry, shivering, hugged his chest as he hurried toward the van at the curb. A chilly wind pushed at him. He thought about stopping by his house for a jacket. But Pete wasn't bundled up. Pete still wore his short-sleeved knit shirt and blue jeans.

If he can take it, I can, Larry told himself.

Besides, it'll be all right once we're in the van.

The van felt warm. It must've been like an oven before the sun went down, and it still retained a lot of heat. Larry settled into the passenger seat and sighed.

"Pass it over."

He handed the bottle to Pete, who took a swig and gave it back. Larry took a drink. "Are you all right to drive?" he asked.

"You kidding? I don't hardly even have a good buzz on."

I do, Larry thought. I'm buzzing, all right. But it isn't the booze. Just good old-fashioned excitement. And maybe fear.

Pete started the van. He kept the headlights off for a while. After turning the first corner, he put them on. They drilled into the night. "Hey, this is something, you know that?"

"You think you can find the town?"

"No sweat."

"We stay away from the hotel, though, right?"

"If you say so." Pete drove in silence for several minutes. They were on Riverfront Drive before he looked at Larry and said, "You know what I don't understand? How come you want to write about the jukebox instead of the vampire?"

"Vampire books are a dime a dozen."

"Not true ones. Don't get me wrong, I think your jukebox story sounds pretty neat. But I'd think the true story of how you found a vampire in a ghost town would be . . . different, you know?"

"Different, all right."

"Remember that movie, *The Amityville Horror?* That was supposed to be a true story."

"It was supposed to be," Larry said. "But I've heard the whole thing was made up."

"Maybe it was, maybe it wasn't. The thing is, they *claimed* it was true. And that's what made it. Would've been just another haunted house movie except for that. You're supposed to think it actually happened, right?"

"Right."

"It was based on a book, wasn't it?"

"Yeah. And the book was pushed as nonfiction."

"Did the book sell okay?"

"Are you kidding? It sold a ton."

"So what's to keep you from writing up this vampire thing as nonfiction? Have a big best-seller, they make a movie out of it, presto! You're rich and famous."

"Shit."

"What do you mean, shit? You got something against money?"

"I'm doing okay."

"Sure, you're doing okay. But how many best-sellers have you had?"

"You can do just fine without ever having a book on the best-seller lists. Those guys on the lists, they're making millions."

Pete whistled softly. "That much?"

"Sure. Some of those guys get a million up front. Or more. That's before paperback rights, foreign rights, movie sales."

"Christ, and you're not interested?"

"I didn't say I'm not interested. I just don't want to mess with any vampire."

"Hey, let's not kid ourselves here. The thing's not a vampire. It's just some broad with a stake in her chest. But we don't *know* that. Not for sure. Neither will your readers. That's what keeps the story going. Wait till the very end, then you pull the stake. That's like the final chapter, you know? You pull the stake and see what happens."

"I don't know."

They left the lights of Mulehead Bend behind. Pete turned off the main road and headed west into the desert. There were no more streetlamps. The headlights pushed paths of brightness up the lane in front of them. The moon cast a pale glow over the bleak landscape of boulders, scrub bushes, cacti, and the jagged mountains in the distance. It looked cold and forlorn out there. Larry suddenly wanted to turn back.

It was bad enough, driving through this bleak terrain on the way to a jukebox.

But that obviously wasn't what Pete had in mind.

"What are we *really* doing?" Larry asked.

"Just what we planned. Bring the jukebox back. Or just take some pictures, if we can't carry it."

"Then what's this vampire business?"

"Just a thought. Hey, you don't like the idea, fine. I'm not trying to push you into something. But Jesus, why on earth would you want to pass up a chance to make a million bucks?"

"The thing scares me."

"That's the point." He reached over, took the bottle from

Larry, drank from it and handed it back. "The point is, you're in the business of scaring people. Right?"

"Scaring them with fiction. Not the real thing. They want real scares, they can watch the TV news."

"This wouldn't be all that different from your novels. Hey, we are talking about vampires, not homicides or nuclear war. The only difference is, this would be a true story. And it'd fit right in with your image, you know? This is the sort of thing that'd make publicity people drool. Get this, 'Renowned horror writer discovers vampire on weekend outing.' It's a natural. They'd put you on the tube, man. And here's the best part, you could *take her with you.*"

"Oh, wonderful."

"Just let 'em *try* to say you made the whole thing up."

"Great. You've got me carting a corpse around on the talk-show circuit."

"We're talking about a million bucks, Lar. I'd sure do it."

"Be my guest."

"I can't write for shit. And you've got—" His head snapped around. "I've *got* it! I'll be the main guy. You can be the guy who takes it all down."

"Your Watson, your Boswell."

"Yeah, whatever. God, I wish we had a recorder. We oughta have all this on tape for the book."

"You're really serious."

"Damn straight. Can you remember all this? Hell, we should've laid off the booze."

"Right." Larry took another swallow of it.

"I see this as a major book and movie. It's a natural."

"It does have potential," Larry admitted.

"Potential? It'll be a blockbuster."

"It'd need a story, though."

"Hey, man, we're living the story right now. You start it off with last Sunday when we found the thing. You write it just the way it happened. That's a few chapters worth, right there. Then you've got tonight. And how we go off to get the jukebox, but I talk you into getting the vampire instead."

"That's maybe fifty pages," Larry said. "Then what?"

"You just tell it like it happens. Describe us going into the hotel, taking out the corpse, putting it in the van and taking it home."

"To whose house?"

"Have you got any good hiding places?"

"Nowhere that Jean wouldn't find it. Besides, I don't like keeping secrets from her."

"How do you think she'd react?"

"To having a corpse in the house?"

"In the garage, say."

"I don't think she'd be delighted by the idea."

"Barb would just shit."

"So much for the blockbuster," Larry said.

Pete went silent.

Thank God, Larry thought. Good thing we're both married. That ought to nip the idea right in the bud.

He felt enormous relief. He took a drink of whiskey and sighed.

"I've got it!" Pete blurted. "That's part of the story! We need stuff to happen after we get the thing, right? You can put all the stuff in there about Jean and Barbara giving us grief about the thing. But we talk them into letting us keep it."

"Now you're talking fiction."

"We just explain to them, you know? It's not like we'll be keeping the thing forever. Just a couple of months, maybe, while you're working on the book. With a big jackpot at the end. I think the gals might go for it."

"Where's the big jackpot for Barbara?"

"I'm getting a cut, right?"

"Yeah, I may cut your throat. Then I can do a book on that while I'm in prison."

"What do you say, twenty percent? My idea, after all. You wouldn't do it at all if it weren't for me."

"True enough. Not that I'm planning to do it at all, regardless. The whole thing's crazy."

"That's what makes it so great. It's crazy. It's wild! You think Stephen King would pass up a chance like this? Hell, he'd probably do it for the fun of it."

"Why don't you give *him* a try? I've got his address."

" 'Cause you're my pal. I don't want to take this away from you. This is your big chance."

"Thanks."

"So, what do you say? Are you in?"

If you tell him no, Larry thought, he'll never forgive you. He's probably already calculated twenty percent of a million bucks. It'd be like robbing him. No more outings with him and Barbara, no more drinks and dinner with them. The end of all that.

He thought about the fun they'd had during the past year.

He thought about Barbara stretched out on the sofa, and the way she had tucked the back of her robe between her legs.

Wouldn't necessarily end the friendship, he told himself. But it would sure put a strain on it.

And Pete was right about the book. It could be big. It could be another *Amityville Horror.*

Doing it would mean spending a lot more time with Pete, too. With Pete and Barbara.

It would also mean bringing the corpse into your life.

Probably not so bad, once you got used to it.

"I think we'll have real trouble with the wives," he said.

"Nothing we can't handle. What do you say, man?"

"I guess we could rent a room for it, or something, if they won't let us keep it around."

"Sure. We'll figure something out. Are you in?"

"Maybe."

"Ah-ha!"

"Let's just play it by ear, okay? We'll have a look at the thing. But I still want to do the jukebox book, so let's take care of that first, and see how it goes."

"Oh, man. Hey, this is the start of something big."

"We ought to have our heads examined."

Fifteen

When the reaching headlights found Babe's Garage at the east end of Sagebrush Flat, Pete killed the beams and eased off the gas pedal.

They entered the town, moving slowly.

Larry studied the moonlit street ahead of them. He felt trapped by their crazy plan, but he held on to a hope that something might intercede to stop it. They needed privacy. If a car were here . . . if light came from a doorway or window . . .

But the street looked abandoned. The buildings were dark.

The van rolled to a halt in front of the Sagebrush Flat Hotel. Leaning forward, Pete peered past Larry.

They both stared toward the doors. But the hotel blocked the moonlight, throwing a black shroud of shadow all the way to the sidewalk. The blackness looked solid.

Unable to see the doors, Larry imagined them standing wide open, imagined he was gazing deep into the lobby, pictured the cadaver on her withered feet beside the staircase, staring out at them.

His skin crawled. His scrotum shriveled, tingling as if spiders were scurrying on it.

"Drive on ahead," he whispered.

"Right. The box."

The van moved forward.

He lifted a hand to his chest and fingered a nipple through the fabric of his shirt. It felt like a pebble.

True of guys, too, he thought. You get goose bumps, your nipples get hard.

He remembered the way Barbara had looked as she told her story about the dark church. Focusing his mind on that, he lost the image of the corpse. But he felt guilty about using Barbara that way, so he thought about Jean. Jean on Sunday night after her nightmare. Slipping out of her gown, climbing onto him. But then he was kneeling above her and her slim body looked cadaverous in the shadows, and he was suddenly in the hotel on his knees beside the coffin, staring at the corpse. Dried brown skin, ghastly grin, flat breasts, pubic hair shining like gold in the flashlight's beam.

He shook his head to dislodge the images, and let out a shaky breath. "I don't know if I can hack this," he muttered.

"Never fear, Peter's here."

Pete drove past Holman's, made a U-turn and parked in front of the gasoline pumps. He shut off the engine.

They each took a drink of whiskey.

"Let's take it with us," Pete said.

"Let's not. I want my hands free." Larry capped the bottle and set it on the floor.

They climbed out. Leaning against the chilly wind, Larry trudged to the rear of the van. Pete met him there. He had his flashlight but left it dark. Side by side they walked past the corner of Holman's. The desert ahead of them looked gray, as if its rock-littered surface, boulders, and bushes were painted with dirty cream.

They were almost to the rear corner of Holman's when a vague shape darted in front of them. Larry flinched. Pete, gasping, crouched and snatched out his gun. The wind-tossed tumbleweed bounded on by.

"Shit," Pete muttered, holstering his weapon.

"Good going, Quickdraw."

I'm not the only one nervous around here, he thought. It pleased him to know that Pete was also feeling jumpy.

"Maybe you should turn on the flashlight," he suggested.

"It'd give us away."

"To whom?"

"You never know, man. You never know."

They left Holman's behind and headed out into the desert, angling toward the far-off smoke tree that marked the edge of the stream bed. Another tumbleweed crossed their path, but Pete saw this one coming and didn't draw down on it.

Larry studied the landscape ahead. He wished it didn't have so many clumps of rock and brush. Hiding places. Each time he approached one, he tightened with fear. Each time he passed one, he quickly looked behind it, half expecting to find someone crouched and ready to pounce.

Nobody's here except us, he kept telling himself.

But he couldn't convince himself.

At last they reached the rim of the embankment. Larry turned around. He scanned the area they had just finished crossing.

Pete did the same.

Then they faced forward. The area below them lay in shadow. Pete turned on his flashlight. He played its beam over the slope and started down. Larry stayed close to his side. They stopped a few times while Pete waved his light across the bottom of the gully as if to assure himself that no surprises were waiting down there. The streambed didn't look familiar to Larry. He was sure it hadn't changed since Sunday, but it seemed very different in the darkness. He couldn't even tell for certain which was the rock that Barbara had been sitting on.

We might not be here now, he thought, if she hadn't wandered away from Holman's looking for a place to relieve herself. We wouldn't have found the jukebox. Maybe the corpse, but I never would've started out tonight except for the jukebox.

He realized that he had to urinate, himself.

When they reached the bottom of the embankment, he said, "Hang on a minute. I've gotta take a leak."

"Don't get any on you," Pete said. "Want the light?"

"Yeah, thanks." He took the flashlight. Pete waited while he wandered to the left, stepping around blocks of stone. He clamped the light under his arm to free his hands. With his back to Pete, he opened his pants. The wind felt good against his penis. He aimed his stream straight out. The wind flapped it sideways, but not back at him.

When he was done, he zipped up his pants and started to turn around. The pale beam of the flashlight passed across a circle of black surrounded by rocks. "Hey, Pete. Come here."

"I don't want to get my feet wet."

"Come here." He took the flashlight out from under his arm while Pete came up beside him. He pointed it at the circle. "Look at that."

"A campfire."

"Was that here before?"

"I don't know. Might've been, but I didn't see it."

They walked toward it. The center of the fire circle was black with ashes and the charred remains of wood.

And bones. Larry saw half a dozen bones, intact among the dead cinders—gray and knobbed at each end.

"Holy shit," Pete muttered.

"Rabbit, you think?"

Pete squatted. He picked up a bone that was nearly a foot in length. "This sucker didn't come from any rabbit," he said. "A coyote, maybe."

"Who the hell would eat a coyote?"

"The fuckin' Madman of the Desert, that's who." Pete tossed the bone down. "This'll go good in our book."

"Great," Larry muttered.

Pete pressed a hand against one of the sooty rocks. "Still warm."

"Don't give me that."

"It is."

Crouching, Larry touched one of the rocks for himself. It was cold. "Asshole."

Pete laughed. "Had you going there, huh?"

"Prick."

"Get out of the way. I'm gonna take some pictures."

He backed off but kept the light on the fire circle while Pete removed the lens cap, switched on the camera and its flash attachment.

"What if the guy who did this is still around here?"

"No sweat. He's already eaten."

"A guy who eats coyotes isn't someone I want to meet."

"He's probably long gone." Pete raised the camera to his eye, bent over the remains of the fire for a close-up, and took a shot. The flash strobed, hitting the area with a quick blast of white.

He stepped backward. One stride. Two. Then another flash split the darkness.

In that blink of white Larry saw something beyond the fire circle. He found it with the beam of his flashlight. "Oh, my God," he muttered.

Three rocks were stacked up. At the top rested the head of a coyote, its gray fur matted with blood, a bone held crosswise between its teeth. It had bloody holes where its eyes should've been.

Pete lowered his camera and stared. "Wow," he muttered.

"Maybe we ought to get out of here."

Pete flapped a hand at him and stepped closer to the thing. He raised the camera. He took a shot. In the stark flick of light Larry saw *into* the empty sockets. He started gagging as Pete stepped right up in front of it, crouched, and snapped another picture.

He turned aside and vomited. When he finished, he backed away from the mess. He took out his handkerchief, blew his nose and wiped his lips. He blinked tears from his eyes. He rubbed them with the back of a hand.

"You all right?" Pete asked, coming up behind him.

"Christ," he muttered.

"Feeling a little queasy myself. Bad scene. Guy that did that must be a fuckin' lunatic. You see the way he poked out its eyes? Wonder if he did that *before* he ate."

Larry shook his head. "Let's do the jukebox and get out of here."

"Give me the light. I want to check around, see what else we can find."

"Are you nuts?" He kept the flashlight and started walking through the gully toward the place where they'd found the jukebox.

"Ah," Pete said. "What the hell. Don't want to lose *my* supper. Wouldn't taste half as good on the way out." His head swung around.

A shiver rushed up Larry's back. "What is it?"

"Nothing, I guess."

"Did you hear something?"

"Probably just the wind. Unless it's our crazy fuckin' coyote muncher sneaking up on us."

"Cut it out."

"Wonder if he talked to the thing while he ate. You know? Like put the head up there for a dinner companion. Had a little chat with it. Talked to the head while he ate the body."

It was an image, Larry realized, that had passed through his own mind while he was vomiting.

"Wonder if he ate the eyes."

Larry *hadn't* thought of that. "He probably just didn't like the thing staring at him."

"Maybe. Guess we'll never know. Unless we get a chance to ask him." Pete chuckled.

"Give me a break."

Larry stepped around a large rock. He pointed the light at it. "Is that where Barbara was sitting?"

"I think so."

He swept the beam forward until it found a thick clump of bushes on the right. He glimpsed chrome and dirty red plastic through the foliage. "There."

They hurried the final distance.

Larry stared down at the machine resting smashed and bullet-riddled in the bushes. He imagined a photograph of it on the cover of his book. *The Box* by Lawrence Dunbar.

That's the book I'm going to write, he told himself. Not some damn thing about a vampire.

"See if we can lift it?" Pete asked, squatting down.

He saw them struggling to carry it up the steep embankment. He saw himself stumble, fall, roll down the slope. The box tumbled and crashed down on top of him. Pete lifted it off. *We'd better not try to move you, Lar. I'll go get help.* Pete left the revolver with him and hurried away. He lay there, alone and half paralyzed. Soon he heard someone creeping toward him. A ragged hermit dripping coyote blood, a knife in his hand. What makes me think there's only one of them? he wondered.

"What do you think?" Pete asked.

"Let's not try it."

"Yeah, maybe you're right. God knows what's under the thing. Or inside it, for that matter. Don't want to go upsetting a rattler. Or a nest of scorpions, or something."

"That's what I like about you," Larry said. "Adventurous, but not foolish."

"My mama didn't raise no morons." Pete got to his feet. He backed away from the box and lifted the camera.

Larry stepped aside. He faced the length of the gully and probed its darkness with the flashlight. The campfire and the grisly remains of the coyote were well beyond the range of the pale beam. He swept the light from side to side. None of the rocks or bushes in sight seemed large enough to conceal a person.

"You spot Ragu the Desert Rat," Pete said, "give us a yell."

"I won't yell, I'll scream."

Pete laughed.

Larry kept watch, his back to Pete. In his peripheral vision, he noticed four blinks of light.

"Why don't you get into the picture?" Pete suggested. "We'll get a couple of you with the famous jukebox."

Though reluctant to abandon his guard duty, he stepped backward until he came to the box. He crouched beside it. A red light on the flash attachment beamed a ray at his face.

"Say 'cheese.'"

"Come on, get it over with."

"Say 'head cheese.'"

"Screw you."

White light hit his eyes. Pete took another photo, then stepped closer and fired two more. "That oughta do it."

"Sure did my night vision." He stood up, shutting his eyes and rubbing them. Bright sparks and balls fluttered under his lids.

"We done down here?" Pete asked.

"I sure hope so."

"Want to go back and pick up a souvenir? Take it home with us, put it in the freezer?"

"Yeah. Why don't you do that."

"Hah! You think I'm out of my tree?"

"You want to take the corpse back," Larry said, stepping past the bushes and starting to climb the slope. "What's the big difference?"

"The corpse isn't all bloody and gross."

"It looked pretty gross to me."

"Well, the coyote head ain't worth a million bucks. For

a million smackaroonies, I'd pick the thing up in my bare hands and *walk* home with it."

"Would you eat it?" Larry asked, starting to feel almost cheerful as he approached the top of the embankment.

"Who'd give me a million bucks to eat it?"

"It's hypothetical."

"Would I get to cook it up first?"

"Nope, gotta chow it down raw."

"You're sick, man."

"Me?"

They reached the top and the wind pushed against Larry. It seemed to be blowing much harder up here than in the gully. But he was glad to be out. He felt as if he had been an intruder in the lair of the coyote eater. Ragu the Desert Rat. He hurried forward, wanting to put as much distance as possible between himself and the madman's domain.

Now and then he glanced back. So did Pete, but not as often.

At last they reached the van. Larry flung himself onto the passenger seat, slammed the door shut and locked it. The warmth felt wonderful. And it was good to be out of the wind. The skin of his face and arms felt tingly from the buffeting. He opened the whiskey bottle and took a couple of sips while Pete climbed in behind the steering wheel.

He offered the bottle to Pete.

Pete shook his head. He flicked a switch and light filled the van. With a nervous glance at Larry, he slipped between the seats.

Larry watched him move in a crouch toward the rear of the van—head darting from side to side, fingers wrapped around the handle of his holstered magnum.

Christ, he's afraid someone might've gotten in.

Pete searched the length of the van and turned around. "It's cool," he said, coming back.

In his seat again, he shut off the interior lights. He

started the engine. He reached out, and Larry put the bottle in his hand. He drank, then gave it back. "Now, are we ready for the real fun?"

"I think I've had enough fun for one night."

"You aren't going yellow on me, are you?"

"What'll we do with the corpse if we *do* take it home?"

"You write a book about it."

"About what? Having a pseudovampire as a house guest?"

"Exactly."

"It'll just lie there. That's if the women don't make us get rid of it."

"You're right. We'll have to do something with it. Maybe we can find out who she is."

"How would we do that?"

"First things first, Lar. Let's take her home, then figure out what's next."

"Why don't we *not* take her home till we figure that out."

"Hey, we're already here. When'll we get another chance like this? Come on, man, we agreed. Don't bail out on me now."

"I'm not bailing out. I just don't see what we'll accomplish. Our book has to be a lot more than a couple of goofs taking a stiff home and freaking out their wives. Even a true story needs action along the way, drama, a climax. Especially a climax. We've got nothing."

"Well, eventually we pull the stake."

"And the damn thing *still* just lies there."

"Maybe, maybe not."

"Oh, come on. You said yourself she's not a vampire."

"We don't know that for sure. Obviously, *someone* thinks she is."

"Okay. Suppose we pull the stake and she *is* a vampire?"

"That'd be something, huh? Then we've got a best-seller for sure."

"If she doesn't bite our necks."

"We'll take precautions when the time comes. You know, have plenty of crucifixes and garlic handy. Maybe buy some handcuffs or tie her up."

"So what happens if we pull the stake and nothing happens? Which is the way it's bound to go down. Then what?"

Pete started the van moving forward.

"A big dud, that's what," Larry told him.

Pete eased the van onto the road. It rolled slowly toward the Sagebrush Flat Hotel.

"Let's just go home and forget about it."

"You said we should play it by ear."

"My ear tells me to forget it."

"I've got a better idea." Pete's head turned toward Larry. In the hazy moonlight his teeth seemed to glow as he smiled. "You say we've got a dud if we pull the stake and she just lies there. Well, let's find out tonight if she's a vampire." He eased the van to the other side of the street and stopped in front of the hotel. "Let's go in there and pull the stake."

ENCOUNTERS

Sixteen

Larry stood in front of the van, shivering, and aimed his flashlight at the doors of the hotel. They were shut. The padlock hung from the hasp, but nobody had repaired Pete's damage. The staple was still ripped from the right-hand door.

Pete came up beside him. He held the tire iron.

"You won't need that to break in," Larry whispered.

Nodding, Pete slipped the rod under his belt. He glanced up and down the street. Then he raised the camera and snapped a shot of the doors.

As he stepped onto the sidewalk, Larry clutched his shoulder. "Wait a minute."

"I'm going in there. If you're scared—"

"Aren't you?"

"Hey, sure. But I'm not gonna let that stop me. You can wait out here if you want."

Larry let his hand drop. He followed Pete across the sidewalk. The muscles of his legs felt soft and shaky. His bowels ached. His heart thudded and he panted, trying to get enough air into his tight lungs.

Who's going to write Pete's book, he thought, if I have a heart attack and keel over dead?

Pete opened the door. Larry shined his light into the lobby. Its beam trembled on the stairs to the left, jerked past the banister and downward, sweeping over the empty space to the right.

They stepped inside. Pete shut the door.

I'm in, Larry thought. Good Christ.

The wind was gone. He heard it, but it no longer blew against him. The hotel was warm. Not as warm as the van, though. He couldn't stop shivering. His skin felt tight. He knew he was goose bumps from head to toe. An icy hand seemed to be squeezing his genitals.

He swung the flashlight back and forth. Over the sandy, hardwood floor. Across the registration counter. Along the walls. Turning slowly, he lit the boarded windows at the front. The closed doors.

The click and blink of the camera made him flinch. Its automatic film advance buzzed.

"Wanta get the general layout," Pete whispered. He took several more photos, turning in a full circle to capture every foot of the lobby's empty interior.

While he reloaded, Larry squatted down to ease a cramped feeling in his bowels.

"You okay?" Pete whispered.

"Hardly."

"Crap your pants, you'll have to walk home."

"Ha ha."

"I'm going up and get a couple of the landing."

Larry stood but didn't go with him. He aimed the light at the stairs. Pete climbed them, holding the camera in both hands. And stopped abruptly.

"Very interesting. Have a look."

Grimacing, Larry forced his wobbly legs to carry him to the stairway. He made his way upward until he reached Pete's side.

Four dirty, weathered planks lay across the landing. They covered the hole left by Barbara when the boards gave out beneath her.

"You know what this means," Pete said.

"Let's get out of here."

"God, I hope he didn't take our vampire."

God, I hope he did, Larry thought.

Hope he doesn't *show up*.

What if he's the coyote eater?

Larry shined his light up the stairs. It reached into the second-floor corridor, threw a faint glow high on the wall. He stared, half expecting a wildman to shamble into the beam.

Pete's got a gun, he reminded himself.

But the scare will probably kill me.

He wished he could make himself look away from the upstairs corridor. But he didn't dare take his eyes off it.

Pete drew the revolver. "Hang onto this for a minute."

Larry switched the flashlight to his left hand and took the gun in his right. He aimed both toward the top of the stairs.

The solid, heavy feel of the .357 was comforting.

Very comforting.

Almost like putting on a coat, the way it soothed his chills and calmed him. But better.

No wonder Pete's been so cool about most of this. He's had the pig-iron on his hip.

Pete snapped a photo of the landing. Then, letting the camera dangle by its strap, he crouched and lifted one of the boards. He propped it upright against the wall. When all four planks had been removed, he took two shots of the gaping hole.

No longer worried much about an intruder, Larry lowered his gaze to the break in the landing. He saw the splintered edges of wood that had gouged and scraped Barbara. He remembered the feel of her body when he'd wrapped his arms around her. The soft warmth of her breasts against his forearm. The way she'd looked later, standing in the sunlit doorway with her blouse open.

His mind came back to the present as Pete began setting the boards back into place. He realized he was no longer shivering at all. He wondered if it was having the gun or thinking about Barbara that had taken away the shakes. Probably both, he thought.

"Okay," Pete said, getting to his feet. He held out his hand for the weapon.

"Let me keep it," Larry said.

Pete was silent for a moment. Then he shrugged and said, "Sure, why not?"

They turned around and started down the stairs.

"We're gonna have a lot of good shots of this place. Did that *Amityville* book have photos?"

"Nope."

"Great. We'll be going it one better."

They reached the bottom of the stairway and stepped around the newel post, shoes crunching on the sandy floor.

The panel alongside the staircase was shut, just as they had left it. The body of Christ on the crucifix gleamed golden.

Pete took a few strides backward and snapped a photograph to show the staircase enclosure.

Stepping up to it, he ran his hands along a seam in the paneling. He tried to dig his fingers in, then gave up and took out the tire iron. He pushed its wedge into the crack. Slowly, as if trying not to make a sound, he pressed the bar.

"Open, sesame," he whispered.

With a soft groan and squeak of nails, the slab of wood moved outward half an inch.

Pete slipped the fingers of his left hand into the gap. He shoved the bar under his belt. Using both hands, he eased the panel toward him. Nails squawked. The gap widened.

At last the panel came off completely. It was about four feet across. Pete stretched out his arms and grabbed both edges. He looked like a life-size imitation of the body on the cross as he lifted the panel and carried it aside—the crucifix almost touching his cheek. He propped the slab against the staircase, rubbed his hands on the front of his pants, then moved backward and took a shot of the opening.

Larry waited until Pete was beside him. Together they stepped under the staircase.

Let the thing be gone, he thought as he swung the flashlight to the left.

It lit the foot of the coffin. Raising the beam slightly, he saw the old brown blanket covering the body. The blanket was propped up like a small tent over the stake. Beyond the upthrust area of blanket was the corpse's dark face.

Pete nudged him with an elbow.

"What?" Larry whispered.

"Nobody absconded with it."

"Too bad."

"I'll get a shot from here," Pete said.

A small patch of red light from the camera's flash attachment appeared on the blanket. It floated upward to the underside of a stair just above the corpse's head, then found the face. Over the pounding of his heartbeat Larry heard the camera make brief, whiny buzzing sounds as its autofocus made adjustments. The red light trembled on the tawny forehead, touched a sunken eyelid, roamed down a hollow cheek and settled on the upper row of teeth.

Larry shut his eyes in time to miss the sudden shock of brightness. He saw it through his lids. Then another.

"Come on," Pete whispered.

He opened his eyes. He followed Pete. Though he kept the coffin lighted, he avoided looking at it.

Crouching, Pete reached the end of the coffin and grabbed its edge. He gave it a yank. The coffin moved toward him, scraping on the floor. Larry stepped out of the way, and Pete dragged it past him.

Dragged it out from under the staircase and into the lobby. Larry followed it out.

"What are you *doing?*" he blurted in a loud whisper.

"Don't like it under there," Pete said.

"Christ."

Larry, himself, was glad to be free of the enclosure. But this was going too far. Way, way too far. The thing didn't belong out here. It belonged under the stairs, for godsake, not in the lobby.

"We've gotta put it back."

Instead of responding, Pete took a photo.

The white of the flash hit the sandy floor, the coffin, the feet and face of the corpse, its blond hair, the blanket.

The blanket.

Larry's chest tightened. "Pete."

"Stop whining, would you?"

"The blanket."

"What about it?"

"We didn't leave it that way."

"Hey, you're right."

Sunday, Pete had flung the blanket carelessly onto the corpse, leaving it heaped on the chest and belly. Barbara had pulled a corner down to cover the groin. Now the blanket was spread out smoothly, shrouding the body from shoulders to ankles.

"Must've been the same guy who did the landing," Pete said. He sounded pretty calm about it. Even without the gun.

"That means he knows we found the body."

"He doesn't know *we* found the body. Just that someone did."

"I don't like this."

"He's not here, is he?"

"He might be." Larry pointed his light toward the top of the stairway. He saw no one.

"He shows up, we can ask him about this."

"Right. Sure. What if he doesn't like the idea of a couple guys messing with his vampire?"

"You got any idea what a .357 does to a person? Just wing him, he'll think he got hit by a Mack truck. So don't shoot unless you have to."

"God," Larry muttered.

"Keep me covered while I get some skin shots." Pete bent down and tossed the blanket off the corpse.

Larry's eyes and flashlight went straight to the stake protruding from the center of its chest.

Pete wandered around the coffin, snapping half a dozen pictures. Then he faced Larry and lowered the camera against his belly. "Okay, pal. Time to see if she's for real."

Cold streaked up his spine.

"Don't."

Pete grinned, raised his eyebrows. "You said we don't want her if she's a dud."

"For Christsake, it's *night.*"

Pete stepped toward him. He lifted the camera strap over his head. "Maybe you should record this for posterity." He slipped the strap over Larry's head. The weight of the camera pulled against the back of his neck.

Pete stepped to the far side of the coffin and sank to his knees. He wrapped a hand around the end of the stake.

"Don't. I mean it."

"Don't be a pussy, man."

Larry aimed the revolver at him.

Pete's smile fell away. "Jesus Christ."

"Take your hand off it."

The hand jumped off the stake as if burnt. "It's off, it's off. Jesus!"

Larry lowered the gun.

He shook his head. He couldn't believe he'd actually threatened his friend with the magnum. He felt sick. "I'm sorry. God, I'm sorry, Pete."

"Jesus, man."

"I'm sorry. Look, we'll take it with us. We'll take it home. We'll do the book. Okay? And you can take the stake out, but not till the right time. We'll do it in daylight. We'll cuff her first, or something, like you said. We'll do it right, so nobody gets hurt. Okay?"

Pete nodded and got to his feet. He stepped around the coffin.

Larry met him beside it. "Here, you'd better take this thing."

Pete took the revolver from him. "I oughta stick it in your face and see how you like it," he said. "God*damn,* man, you know?"

"Go ahead. I deserve it."

"Nah." He holstered the weapon. He clasped Larry's upper arm and looked him in the eyes. "We're partners, man. We're gonna be *rich* partners."

"I shouldn't have pulled down on you, Pete. I don't know what . . . I'm sorry. I'm really sorry."

"No sweat."

They shook hands. Larry felt his throat go tight. He knew he was close to tears.

"Okay, *compadre,*" Pete said. "Let's haul this bitch out of here and head for home."

Seventeen

"Don't do it! I'm warning you!"

"Ah, don't be a pussy." Pete started to pull the stake from the chest of the corpse. It slid slowly upward.

Larry fired. The slug punched Pete's forehead. A spray of blood and brains flew up behind him. As he tumbled backward, Larry saw that he still clutched the stake. It came all the way out.

"No!" Larry shrieked.

Hurling the revolver aside, he ran toward the coffin, toward Pete sprawled on the lobby floor, toward the pointed shaft clenched in his dead hand.

You bastard! he thought. You bastard, how could you do this to me!

Gotta get the stake! Gotta shove it back in! Fast! Before it's too late.

But he couldn't run fast enough. The sand sucked at his feet. Moments ago, it had just been a thin layer. Now the sand was thick, heaped like dunes on a beach. Had somebody left the door open? He looked back. The door was open, all right.

A man stood there, ankle deep in the sand, the wind at his back flapping his dark, hooded robe. A robe like a monk. The hood concealed his face. In his upraised right hand he held a crucifix. "You're screwed now," the stranger called. "Up shit creek without a paddle."

Terrified, Larry turned his eyes away from the stranger and tried to run faster over the soft, shifting sand.

I'll never make it in time, he thought.

He was still far from the corpse. It still looked like a dried-up mummy. But he could hear it *breathing.*

Maybe that guy will lend me his crucifix.

He glanced back. The hood fell away. The stranger had the eyeless, bloody head of a coyote. The crucifix, now clamped in its maw, crunched as the thing chewed.

When he looked forward again, he gasped.

The coffin was empty.

But then he saw that Pete was sitting up. He suddenly felt so overwhelmed with relief that he nearly wept. *I didn't kill him, after all! Thank God! Thank*— He felt himself shrivel inside.

Pete wasn't sitting up because he was alive. He was being held by the brown hag on the floor behind him. Its withered legs were crossed around his waist. Its arms hugged his chest. Its mouth sucked and chewed on the exit wound at the back of his head.

Larry yelled and woke up.

He was alone in bed. The room was dark. Rolling onto his side, he checked the alarm clock: 4:50. He groaned as he realized this was Saturday morning and he'd been in bed less than an hour.

He remembered what they had done.

God, if only the whole thing had been a nightmare. What if I only *dreamed* that we went out there.

He knew it was too much to hope for.

They'd done it, all right.

At least I didn't shoot Pete, he thought. Thank God *that* was just in the nightmare.

He climbed out of bed. Naked, sweaty, and shaking, he stepped to the window. The moon hung low over the roof of the garage.

He didn't want to think about what was inside the garage.

We've gotta call this off, he told himself. We've gotta take it back, put it back under the staircase.

He wondered if he could do it by himself.

No. Alone, he wouldn't be able to face the thing, much less drive it out to Sagebrush Flat and drag it into that damn hotel.

He returned to the bed, sat down on the edge of the mattress, slumped forward and rubbed his face. He felt wasted. He needed sleep. A lot of sleep. But he knew the kind of dream that waited for him.

Never should've done it, he thought. Never should've.

He wandered into the bathroom, turned on the shower and stepped under the hot spray. The water felt wonderful splashing against his chilled body. It soothed his shivers, eased the tightness of his muscles. But it didn't help the fog in his head. His mind seemed numb.

Won't be able to write today, he thought. Not unless I get some sleep.

Work on correcting the manuscript?

That's why you didn't go with Jean and Lane.

God, he wished he had gone with them. None of this would've happened.

He saw himself in the hotel again, aiming the revolver at Pete.

Hell, I wouldn't have shot him.

But even to aim at him . . .

That was the worst part. That was even worse than the damn corpse in his garage.

Just have to live with it, he told himself. It happened, you can't make it go away.

The thing is to do the book for him. Even if it doesn't hit the big-time like he hopes, it ought to sell. Give him a chunk, he'll be happy. He'll figure it was worth having a gun pointed at him. Then maybe I can stop feeling guilty.

So write the book.

Larry shut off the shower, stepped out of the tub and dried himself. He made his way sluggishly into the bedroom. He took a sweatsuit and socks from his dresser, dropped onto the bed and struggled into the soft shirt and pants.

Write the book, he thought. But not today. Too wasted.

In the kitchen he made a pot of coffee. He carried his mug into the living room, settled down in his recliner and started to read. His eyes moved over the lines of the paperback. But the words seemed disconnected, meaningless.

One hour of sleep, he thought. What do you expect?

He closed the book. He gazed into space while he sipped his coffee.

Can't just sit here like a zombie.

Work on *Madhouse,* he thought. Should be capable of that, just going through and changing it back to the way it was in the first place.

He pushed himself off the chair, picked up his empty mug and headed for the kitchen.

Damn copyeditor. Hadn't been for her, I'd be in L.A. right now. Wouldn't have gone out to that damn town. None of this shit would've happened.

He filled his mug with coffee, carried it into his work room and gazed at the manuscript. He sighed. The chore seemed too great.

Maybe make some notes for *The Box* first. Work something in about the guys going out to bring it home, stumbling across the campfire . . . the coyote eater . . . what if he's a guy who's connected to the past somehow? Could be a character in the sixties section. One of the bikers? He's stuck around for some reason, mad as a hatter, living off the land.

Maybe a dumb idea, he thought. Who's in any shape to judge? Might as well put it down, though. Decide later whether it's worth pursuing.

He turned on the word processor and brought up the notes he'd made yesterday. He scrolled down to the last entry. "But maybe there are some other 'box' angles. Fool around with it."

A coffin is a box. There's an angle for you.

He typed, "Notes—Saturday, October 8."

Spaced down, tapped out, "Guys go to fetch jukebox. In ditch nearby, they find campfire and disgusting remains of a coyote someone had eaten for dinner. Who? A crazy hermit who was the main badass biker in the sixties section. He's still around after all those years."

Who *really* ate the coyote? he wondered. What if it's the same guy who fixed the hotel landing and straightened the blanket on the stiff?

What if he was watching us?

What if he followed us?

Larry downspaced a couple of times.

"Somebody," he wrote, "hammered a pointed shaft of wood through the heart of a woman. He left her inside a lidless coffin, and hid her corpse beneath the stairway of an abandoned hotel in the town of Sagebrush Flat.

"We found it there.

"My name is Lawrence Dunbar. I am a writer of horror fiction. This book is not fiction. You may judge for yourself whether it is horror.

"This is what happened.

"On Sunday, October 2, we left our home in Mulehead Bend for a day trip to visit an old west town in the desert to the west. The morning was clear and warm as we started off. Pete drove his van. I rode shotgun. Our wives poured coffee from a thermos bottle, passed the plastic cups to us, and gave us first dibs at the assortment of doughnuts I'd bought earlier that morning."

Not bad for a space cadet, he thought.

And kept writing.

It flowed. He finished his coffee. He fired up his pipe.

The words came so easily. As if a voice were speaking in his head and he merely had to copy the dictation.

He introduced Jean and Pete and Barbara. He described the beauty and desolation of the desert they drove through on the way to Silver Junction. He told about the old west town: the quaint shops they'd visited, the characters in cowboy garb, the gunfight staged on Main Street, their sandwiches and beer in the saloon. Finally they were ready to leave the picturesque town. They climbed into the van. Pete said, "How about a little detour on the way home?"

Larry returned to the start. He numbered the pages, then shook his head in astonishment. He'd written *fifteen*. He couldn't believe it. He looked at the wall clock. Eight-thirty. He'd been working for nearly three hours. That's about five pages per hour, he realized. Usually, he averaged two.

I should always write when I'm zoned, he thought.

Maybe it's garbage.

He read the chapter. Sure didn't *seem* like garbage. It seemed as good as anything he'd ever done. Maybe better. He felt as if he had transformed the somewhat mundane visit to Silver Junction into a sharp, colorful portrait, rich with incident, fast-paced.

The characters lived. Perhaps too well, in the case of Barbara. Her presence dominated the chapter.

That's as it should be, he told himself. Barbara is certainly a major figure in this tale.

But he worried that his infatuation with her might be too apparent. After all, Jean would eventually read the book. So would Barbara. Even Pete, the nonreader, was certain to plow through this one.

Can't let them get the wrong idea.

Better be careful, he warned himself. Watch out when you revise. Take out anything too suggestive.

Though eager to continue, Larry felt hot. He pulled off his sweatshirt and stretched, sighing with pleasure as his muscles drew taut and a warm breeze caressed his skin. He stood up, stretched some more, then went into the bathroom. He rolled deodorant onto his armpits. He urinated. Then he entered the bedroom and tossed his sweat clothes onto a chair. He put on shorts and a T-shirt. The loose, lightweight garments let the air in. Feeling a lot better, he headed for the kitchen.

He found a hardboiled egg in the refrigerator. He peeled off its shell and started to eat it over the wastebasket. It was dry in his mouth. He knew it would taste much better sprinkled with salt. But he couldn't be bothered. He stood at the wastebasket until the egg was gone. Then he refilled his coffee mug and returned to the office.

The second chapter went nearly as well as the first. But he was more cautious with it. He censored the voice in his head, refusing to tap out several descriptions it provided of Barbara's appearance. When he came to the part about the ruin of the old stone house they'd passed shortly before arriving at Sagebrush Flat, he stopped himself. He lit a fresh pipe and stared at the screen. Should he omit Pete and Barbara's dialogue about screwing in that place?

This is supposed to be a true story. They *did* say those things.

It's already strayed from the truth, he realized. I've certainly tampered with my own side of it.

Hell, the conversation happened. Tell it like it was. Besides, it'll say a lot about their relationship, help to flesh them out, make them seem more real.

" 'We spent too much time screwing around in there.' "

" 'Watch it, mister.' "

"From the tone of Barbara's voice, I realized that Pete hadn't been speaking figuratively. I imagined what it must have been like, picturing myself with Jean inside the tumble down walls of the ruin. Hard on the knees, probably. But exciting. I found myself wishing we were there now,

rather than riding with Pete and Barbara toward the remains of a dead town."

Larry grinned at the screen.

Nicely done.

He kept on writing. It went smoothly until the time
came for Barbara to answer nature's call. Should he put
that in? Without it, how would he get her over to the
streambed behind Holman's?

Tell it like it was, he decided.

And he did: Barbara wandering away, Pete going in
search of her, the waiting, the worry, he and Jean finally
going to look for them. All four were down in the gully
studying the jukebox when the doorbell rang.

Larry looked at the clock. Ten to eleven. He groaned as
he got to his feet. He made his way through the house on
legs that felt nearly too weak to support him. He blinked
sweat out of his eyes and opened the front door.

Pete, in a knit shirt and jeans, looked well rested, alert,
cool, chipper. "You taken up exercise?" he asked as he
stepped inside.

"I've been writing."

"Didn't know writing was such hard work. You oughta
turn the air on, man, it's hotter than hell in here."

"Yeah," Larry muttered. He peeled the seat of his shorts
away from his rear. "Want some coffee or something?"

Pete shook his head. "Already had my morning dose."

"You look so bright-eyed and bushy-tailed, it makes me
want to barf."

He laughed. "You look like death warmed over. How
about cleaning up and coming with us? Barb and I are
going across the river and checking out the casino action.
You're welcome to come along."

Larry felt the fuzz coming back into his head. "You've
gotta be kidding. I'd probably collapse." He rubbed his
face, yawned.

"Stay out too late last night?"

"Ha ha. I got about an hour of sleep."

"Should've slept in like I did. I feel like a million bucks."

"Speaking of which . . . I started on the book."

"The book?"

"Yeah."

"Fantastic! Man, you didn't waste any time."

"Maybe I just want to get it over with."

"You're actually *writing* it?"

He nodded. His head felt heavy. "Almost done with the third chapter. It's . . . I'm on a roll, I guess. It's really moving."

"Well, God, don't let me stop you. Forget I mentioned the casinos. I'll tell Barb I couldn't drag you away."

"You didn't tell her about . . . the thing?"

Pete looked as if he thought Larry had lost his mind.

"She's gonna find out sooner or later."

"The later the better. How much can you write before Jean and Lane get back?"

"I don't know."

"You've got the rest of today and tomorrow. And the coffin's pretty well hidden. Might be a week or so before anyone catches on. Hell, by then, who knows? You might be so far along in the book that it won't even matter."

"I don't know," Larry said again.

"How many pages you got?"

He shrugged. "Around thirty, I think."

Pete's face lit up. "All *right!* Thirty! That's incredible. You did all that this morning? No wonder you look like shit."

"Thanks."

"Hey, I'm getting out of here. Go back and pound out some more pages. This is terrific." He stepped out the door and faced Larry again. "If you feel up for drinks and dinner, stop by around five."

"Okay. Thanks. I don't know, though."

When Pete was gone, Larry staggered into the bedroom. He peeled off his wet clothes and flopped on the mattress.

Just a quick nap, he thought.

He woke up, gasping for air and drenched with sweat. The clock on the nightstand showed 2:15.

Eighteen

Larry toweled himself dry and stepped into his shorts. They were still damp, but they felt cool. In the kitchen he poured himself a glass of iced tea. He put salami and cheese on a few crackers and took them along with his drink to the workroom.

Just stick with it for a couple of hours, he thought. Then have a nice, cool shower, get dressed, and head on over to Pete and Barbara's.

It would be wonderful. Sit out in back with them like yesterday, have a few cocktails . . .

He read the last few sentences on the screen, and added a new one. Then another. Then it was flowing again, the words in his mind rushing ahead of his typing fingers.

He was in the story. He was living it.

The iced tea and crackers disappeared. He smoked his pipe. He had another glass of tea. After that was gone, he couldn't force himself away from the story to get another. He wrote and wrote. He rubbed the sweat off his face with slick forearms. Drops dribbled down his chest and sides, tickling until they stopped at the waist band of his shorts. Later, a breeze cooled his wet skin. Dried him. His mouth was parched. He told himself he would quit soon and go over to Pete and Barbara's and drink up a storm. After this page. Or after the next.

Suddenly he noticed that his room was dark except for the amber glow of the words on the computer screen. Dark and cold. A chill night breeze blew through the open window. He realized that he was sitting rigid, shivering, teeth clenched as the breeze scurried over his bare skin.

Feeling disoriented, he squinted up at the dim face of the clock.

Ten after seven.

Impossible. What had happened to the time? He knew he'd been deeply involved in the story, but he could hardly believe he'd been so immersed that he'd allowed himself to miss the cocktails and dinner.

He hadn't even been aware for the past hour that he'd been writing in the dark, nearly naked and freezing.

He read the final sentence.

"It was with a strange mixture of sadness and expectation that I watched the car vanish around the corner, carrying my wife and daughter away from me for the weekend."

He muttered, "Good God."

He scrolled upward to the start of the chapter. It was labeled Chapter Six. No page number. How many pages *had* he written today? Seventy? Eighty?

His normal output was seven to ten pages.

The most he'd *ever* done before in a single day was thirty. That was on a piece-of-garbage romance novel a few years ago when money was short and his agent had lined up a lousy deal for two romances at a thousand bucks a whack.

This was more than twice his record.

And I'm not done yet, he thought.

Holy smoke.

He folded his arms across his chest for warmth and shook his head.

Well, he thought, this is a true story. I'm just more or less reporting what happened.

It was astonishing, anyway.

If he'd gone over to Pete and Barbara's . . . He realized

he ought to give them a call and apologize. He left his workroom and wandered through the house, turning on a few lights. In the bedroom he got rid of the shorts and put on his sweatsuit and socks. As if his skin resented the loss of cold, it tingled and itched. Larry rubbed himself through the soft fabric while he walked to the kitchen.

Tacked to a bulletin board beside the wall phone was a card on which Jean had written emergency numbers along with those of repair people and friends. Larry found the number for Pete and Barbara.

Do I really want to call them? he wondered. It had been an open invitation, not the kind of thing that required much of an apology. No big deal that I didn't show up.

They're sure to ask me over.

I'll probably go. And that'll be the end of today's writing.

For godsake, I've written enough for one day. Enough for a week.

But if I stick with it, I can bring the story all the way up to the present. And be done with it. Nothing more to tell, once I get to where we hid the coffin in the garage. Tomorrow I'll be able to finish the corrections on *Madhouse,* get it into the mail on Monday, and spend next week finishing *Night Stranger.* Then start on *The Box.*

Only if I don't go over to Pete and Barbara's tonight.

He wondered if Barbara was in her nightgown. And he realized that he didn't much care.

He stepped away from the telephone and opened the refrigerator's freezer compartment. His eyes roamed its contents. A lot to choose from. The lasagna would be easy. Just throw it in the microwave for a few minutes.

Too much trouble.

He shut the freezer door and checked the refrigerator. There he found a pack of hot dogs. He opened it, slid out a wet frank, and poked it into his mouth. Holding it there like a pink cigar, he put away the package. He took out a bottle of Michelob beer, twisted off its cap and returned to his workroom.

He wrote. The hot dog and beer distracted him for a few minutes, but when they were gone he sank deeply into the story. He was there, over at Pete and Barbara's, first on their patio and then in their house, telling it all just as it had happened. Almost. Censoring, as if by reflex, every mention of Barbara's appearance and his own reactions to her. Then he was in the van with Pete. Then in the gully behind Holman's.

As he tapped out, " 'I've got to take a leak,' " he realized that he did need to do exactly that. He went to the bathroom. As he urinated he thought about what would come next in the story.

Finding the campfire of the coyote eater.

Shivers crawled up his back.

He flushed the toilet, walked back to his workroom and stared through the doorway at his waiting chair.

I'm not sure I want to write about that tonight, he thought. Not about the coyote eater, not about what happened in the hotel.

He turned away from the workroom. He wandered into the kitchen and looked at the clock. A quarter past ten.

That's no time of night to be writing scary shit, he told himself.

I'm so close to the finish, though.

Hang in there for a couple more hours, you'll be done with it.

Right, hang in there.

With a little help.

He dropped a few ice cubes into a glass, filled the glass with vodka, and added a touch of Rose's Lime Juice. He took a sip. Sighed with pleasure. Drank some more. Then carried the glass to his room, slumped against the back of the chair and gazed at the screen.

Once this stuff hits the system, you won't be able to write.

Hell, this isn't writing. This is typing.

The beer had been enough to turn his typing a trifle sloppy. This should really mess it up.

Who cares? he asked himself. Just fix it when you revise. Or don't. Give the copyeditor something constructive to do for a change. If she has to correct real errors, maybe she won't mess with the good stuff.

He took a few more swallows, then set the glass down and faced the dead campfire, the bones, the severed eyeless head of the coyote.

He was glad to have the vodka in him. Though the words flowed, he felt slightly disconnected, more an observer than a participant. He described the Larry character's fear and revulsion, but hardly felt them at all.

Then they were out of the ditch. Then in the van. Then about to enter the dark lobby of the hotel.

His glass was empty. He took it into the kitchen. This time he didn't bother adding lime juice to the vodka. He felt very fine as he sauntered back to his computer. He took a drink. He filled a pipe and lit it. He looked at the last sentence on the screen.

"Side bu side, we stoppped across teh threshold and entered the black mouth og the hotel."

Grinning, he shook his head.

"Take care of that later," he muttered.

He puffed his pipe, checked the keyboard to make sure his fingers were positioned correctly, and continued.

He wrote, and sipped vodka and smoked his pipe.

Somehow, a while later, the stem flipped over between his teeth and the briar bowl turned upside down, dumping ashes down the front of his sweatshirt and onto his lap. Luckily, no embers fell out. Larry brushed the gray dust off his clothes, put the pipe aside, and took another drink.

When he looked at the screen, he saw double.

"Oh, am I fucked up," he muttered.

With a little effort, however, he was able to line up his eyes and read the amber print.

" 'Take you're hand off of that steak!' "

"Pete let go teh thing real fast. 'If's off! Christ! Don-t shoot1' "

Larry muttered, "Oh, shit."

Concentrating hard, knowing he could lose a lot if he messed up, he fingered the save key and followed his usual procedure for exiting the computer. He put the disks away, then turned off the machine.

"Better hit the ol' sacko," he mumbled.

Larry woke up, but couldn't bring himself to open his eyes. He felt as if the back of his head had been split open with an axe. His dry tongue was glued to the roof of his mouth. He was shuddering with cold, and his bed felt like concrete. As he struggled to free his tongue, he reached down. He found the blanket near his waist and pulled it up. That helped a little, but not much. The real coldness was under him.

I am on concrete!

Larry forced his eyes open.

Though the light was faint, he knew that day had come and he knew where he was.

In his garage.

His heart suddenly pounded hot spikes of pain up the back of his neck and into his head.

He was curled on his side, the coffin near enough to touch.

Oh, Jesus H. Christ!

Turning his face away from the coffin, he bolted up. The pain in his head brought tears to his eyes. As he staggered backward, his bare foot landed in a mat of vomit.

It flew out from under him. His bare rump smacked the garage floor.

Sitting there, he clutched his head with both hands and blinked his eyes clear.

He saw that he was naked.

He saw that the blanket heaped on the floor near the coffin, the one he had used to cover himself, was the same old brown blanket that had shrouded the corpse.

It was on me! Touching me!

A whiny noise started coming from him. He slapped a hand across his mouth and gazed down at himself. Nothing on his skin.

What'd you expect? he thought. Cooties?

"Oh Jesus," he said, his voice coming out high and girlish.

He moved his left foot out of the glop and stood up.

The withered cadaver was still inside the coffin, the stake still in its chest. Thank God.

At least he hadn't pulled the stake.

What *had* he done? What was he doing here?

He didn't know. But he knew that he had to get out. He had to shower, and fast, to rid himself of the horrible crawly feeling left by the blanket.

His left foot was caked with vomit. Not wanting to spread the mess, he hopped through the cluttered garage until he reached the side door. It was open. The sunlight made his eyes ache. Squinting, he held onto the door frame. From the coolness of the air he guessed it was still early morning. Maybe seven o'clock.

What day? He struggled to concentrate. Saturday night was when he got himself bombed. So this was Sunday.

It sure better be, he thought.

Jean and Lane shouldn't be home till tonight.

What if they came home early?

What if this is Monday?

Shit, he thought. You've got enough problems without

inventing more. If they were home, they would've found me.

Naked in the garage with a goddamn corpse.

That would've been . . . don't think about it. Didn't happen.

The yard was fenced, so at least he had some privacy.

He hopped across the walkway. When he reached the lawn, he wiped his foot on the dewy grass. There was still vomit between his toes. He went over to the garden hose, turned it on and sprayed his foot clean.

Then he hurried down the driveway and entered his kitchen through the sliding glass door. The house was silent except for the soft hum of the refrigerator.

His damp feet left bits of grass on the floor as he made his way to the bathroom. He would have to clean that up later.

He would have to clean up a lot.

Later.

The blanket. It was on me.

But it has two sides, he told himself. Fifty-fifty chance the side that touched the corpse was up . . .

Fifty-fifty it wasn't.

If I took the blanket off her . . .

Did I touch her?

Horrified by the thought, he gazed at his trembling hands.

I wouldn't have.

How do you know?

Oh God! I could've done *anything!*

He lurched into the bathroom, threw the door shut and staggered to the tub. Falling to his knees, he reached out and turned the faucet handles. Water gushed from the spout. He held his hands under it.

All the perfumes of Arabia . . .

"I didn't touch her," he said.

It's bad enough I used the blanket.

He turned the knob to activate the shower, then climbed into the tub and slid the glass door shut. The hot water pounded against the top of his head. It ran down his body, soothing the chill, easing some of the tightness out of his muscles. When he stopped trembling, he lathered himself with soap. He rinsed the suds off, then soaped his body and rinsed again before shampooing his hair.

By the time he stepped out, he felt a lot better.

If only he could remember what happened!

Maybe just as well that you don't, he thought.

After drying, he took Alka-Seltzer. Then he washed down two aspirin for good measure.

He left the steamy bathroom. In his bedroom he found his sweat clothes heaped on the floor. His side of the bed had been turned down, the pillow dented, the bottom sheet mussed.

So you *did* go to bed last night, he told himself. But you got up again, and went out to the garage. Must've decided to take a look at the corpse, God knows why.

Must've had a reason.

Maybe she *willed* you to do it.

"Terrific," he muttered.

He sat on the edge of the bed and rubbed his face.

Never should've had that vodka.

Keeping his back to the coffin, Larry used paper towels to clean his vomit off the garage floor. He put them in a plastic garbage bag, then dropped the bag into the bottom of his trash barrel and covered it with a heap of debris from the grass catcher of his lawn mower. Satisfied that Jean would never find the evidence, he returned to the garage. He filled a bucket and scoured the area with a wet sponge. Afterward, he cleaned the bucket and sponge carefully.

All that remained, now, was a patch of wetness on the concrete. The heat of the day would soon take care of that.

He slid the bay door open to let in fresh air and sunlight.

From here the garage looked perfectly normal. The damp area, the blanket and coffin, were safely out of sight behind standing shelves and stacks of boxes.

He shook his head. Whatever his condition last night, he'd been aware enough to negotiate a virtual obstacle course in order to reach the corner where the coffin was hidden. In the dark, apparently.

What do you write about this? he wondered.

You don't.

I've got to. It's part of the story.

And you need to fill up more pages if you're going to make a book out of this thing.

Just leave out the business about being naked, he thought. Write it like it happened, but keep your clothes on. Otherwise, people might start thinking you . . .

I didn't, he told himself. No way.

What were you doing in there?

Suddenly he realized that he needed to take a close look at the corpse.

Besides, I've got to cover it up again.

He entered the garage. His heart started thudding, stirring the remnants of his headache.

He made his way among the shelves and trunks and boxes, and soon he reached the dim corner where the coffin rested. The wet spot on the concrete was nearly gone. He stepped over the blanket and stared down into the coffin.

The body looked ghastly, as usual: shrunken and bony, its skin dried out and brown, its breasts flat, its mouth open and lips twisted in an awful, toothy grin.

The body didn't look as if it had been disturbed. It lay flat on the bottom of the coffin, the stake jutting upright in the same position as usual, one withered hand on its hip.

Larry frowned.

The left arm, on the far side of the corpse, was bent at the elbow. The hand rested, palm down, against the hip bone. Its fingertips lay among dull blond curls of pubic hair.

Before (Larry was almost certain), both hands had been out of sight in the dark, narrow gap between the body and the sides of the coffin.

He was sure that he would've noticed if a hand had been in plain view.

Especially since this one wore a ring.

He bent down for a closer look.

A school ring? Surrounding the garnet stone was a tarnished silver border that appeared to be engraved.

"Holy Toledo," he muttered.

This could give a clue to the corpse's identity!

But how did the hand find its way onto the hip? Obviously, she hadn't placed it there.

I must've done it last night, he thought.

I did touch the damn thing.

Larry heard himself groan.

Disgust mixing with his excitement, he hurried to the section of the garage where he kept the yard tools. Maybe he had touched the corpse last night, but he sure didn't intend to do it again. He found some old gardening gloves and put them on as he hurried back to the coffin.

On his knees, he reached over the body. With his left hand he gently held the bony wrist. With the thumb and forefinger of his right hand he slipped the ring off.

Pete, he realized, was bound to visit the corpse sooner or later, and was sure to notice the new position of the hand. It had to be put back down where it belonged.

Wrinkling his nose, Larry tightened his grip on the wrist and gave it a slight push. It resisted him. He pushed a little harder, forcing it. This time the hand moved. Larry cringed at the quiet crackling sounds that came from the arm. Sounds like dry leaves being crumbled. His eyes darted to the cadaver's face. It looked as if it were grimacing, teeth bared in pain.

"Christ," he whispered.

Has to be done, he told himself.

Letting go, he switched the ring to his left hand and clutched the corpse's wrist with his right. He shoved down hard, jamming the arm toward the floor of the coffin. The shoulder lifted. The head began to rise. He yelled. Then came gristly snapping sounds, a pop. The arm went limp in his grip and the body sank back into position. He tucked the arm against its side, then lurched away.

He dashed through the garage, dodging his way through the maze of clutter, and didn't stop running until he reached the safety of the house.

He shoved the sliding door shut. He locked it.

He pressed his face to the glass and stared at the open garage.

Acting like an idiot, he thought.

But *God!*

After catching his breath, he opened his trembling hand. He lifted the ring close to his face.

Engraved in the silver that surrounded the garnet were the words "Buford High School," and the date "1968."

He looked into the middle of the loop.

Inside the band was a name.

"Bonnie Saxon."

Nineteen

"I gazed at the ring, dumbfounded. The hideous corpse in my garage now had a name. Bonnie. A pleasant, rather cheerful name.

"Perhaps she is a vampire. Somebody thought so, killed her with a stake and used a crucifix to seal her makeshift tomb. But a vampire by the name of Bonnie?

"She seems, to me, less frightening than before.

"The gruesome, mummified thing in the coffin may indeed be a demonic beast that would drink my blood if unleashed from death. But it was a girl once. A 'Bonnie' lass.

"She attended the same high school as my daughter, Lane. She walked the same halls, perhaps sat in the same classrooms, may even have had some of the very same teachers as Lane. She was a girl who ate lunch in the school cafeteria, who probably struggled against dozing off during her afternoon classes, who worried about pop quizzes and homework and zits.

"A teenager. Who studied schoolwork. Who watched television. Who listened to the latest music with the volume blaring. Who went to movies, to the school's football games and sock hops and the prom. Who had boyfriends.

"The vile thing in my garage was once a teenaged girl named Bonnie . . ."

The door bell chimed. Larry flinched. He scrolled up to remove his words from the computer screen, then hid the class ring under the matchbooks and scraps of notepaper scattered on his desktop. He hurried into the living room.

He half expected the person at the front door to be Pete. He was right.

"Hey, bud!" After a glance toward his house, Pete gave Larry a sly look. "Barb's off grocery shopping. Thought I'd drop by and see how our best-seller's coming along."

"Not too bad."

He entered, and Larry shut the door.

"I guess you really whaled on the thing yesterday," he said.

"Yeah, it went pretty well. Sorry I didn't make it over for supper. Time just got away from me and—"

"No sweat. So how many pages you finish?"

"I don't know. Quite a bunch."

"Terrific. Gonna let me read 'em?" he asked, flopping onto a chair.

Larry hoped his alarm didn't show.

"They aren't printed up yet," he said.

"Well, go do it. Don't let me stop you."

"It'd take hours," Larry said. He sat on the sofa, rested his elbows on his knees and shook his head at Pete. "Besides, I'll have to make a lot of corrections. It's pretty much of a mess right now."

"So when'll I get to read it?"

"How about when it's all done?" Larry suggested, trying to smile.

"Hey, come *on.*"

"No, really. I think it'd be best if you don't read any of the thing while I'm still working on it. It'd make me too self-conscious."

"Oh, bull."

"I mean it."

"What about my input? Maybe you forgot some stuff."

"I'll give you a copy when it's finished. If there's anything you want added or changed, I can revise it then. Okay?"

"That's kind of late in the ball game," he said, frowning slightly.

"You want me to write the thing, don't you?"

"Yeah, sure. But—"

"I can't do it if I have to pass every chapter along to you for inspection as I go along. I'll quit right now—"

"Jeez, don't get in a huff. Do it your way. I'm just curious, is all."

"Well, that's all right," Larry said, relieved that he had backed off. "I didn't mean to get testy about it."

"What's a testi between friends," Pete said, and smiled. "Anyway, it's going pretty good?"

"I think so."

"What's next on the agenda?"

"Well, I need to do those revisions."

"I guess we've gotta start thinking about how we break the news to the women," Pete said. "Jean'll be home tonight, won't she?"

"Yeah. Tonight."

"Should we just walk her and Barb out to the garage and show them? Or work up to it more gradually?"

" 'Guess what we brought home Saturday night?' "

"Something like that."

"Suppose we just keep the whole thing secret?"

"Are you kidding?"

Larry shook his head. "They won't let us keep a body around. No way. I don't care what we tell them, they'll make us get rid of it."

"They've *got* to find out sooner or later."

"Let's wait. We can tell them about it when everything's set to pull the stake. By then the book'll be almost done."

"Yeah. 'Course, they might give us shit about pulling the stake."

"Good point."

"No pun intended," Pete said.

Larry frowned for a moment, thinking. "Okay. Let's pull the stake and *then* tell them what we've done. After the fact. By that time it'll be too late for the gals to screw things up for us."

Pete grinned. "Man, will they be pissed!"

"That's for sure. The book's bound to find a publisher, though. Best-seller or not, I'm sure we'll be seeing a pretty good chunk of money from it. That should get us out of the doghouse."

"Maybe they don't have to find out about it," Pete said, "until you make the sale."

"If we work it right. What we have to do is hide the thing better. Right now, anybody wandering into the garage might stumble onto it."

"We *use* our garage."

"I know, I know," Larry said. He was well aware that Pete and Barbara often parked their cars in it, while he and Jean only used their garage for storage.

"There's a crawl space under our house," Pete said. "I suppose we could shove the casket under there. If we do it quick before Barb gets back from the store. We'd have to lift it over the fence. Wouldn't wanta be seen lugging it around the front."

"Not necessary," Larry said. "I know just the place to stash the thing."

Should've put it there in the first place, he thought. Maybe I wouldn't have ended up spending the night with it.

"Where?" Pete asked.

"Come on. We'll take care of it right now."

They went out the kitchen door and walked up the driveway to the garage. Its bay door was still open. As they entered the shade, Larry hoped that the wet spot on the floor had dried.

Must've, he told himself.

A few yards beyond the door was a square wooden platform half a foot high. Larry stepped onto it, reached up and caught hold of a dangling rope. He pulled the rope's knotted end. A plywood ceiling panel swung down on hinges.

"All *right*," Pete said. "A trapdoor."

Fixed to its top was a ladder folded into three sections. Larry lowered the ladder until the shoes of its side rails rested firmly against the platform.

"Gonna be a bitch getting our stiff up there," Pete said.

He was right. Though the ladder stood at an angle like a flight of stairs, it was much steeper than a stairway.

"It's the perfect place," Larry told him. "Nobody's going to find her."

He stepped aside. Pete climbed to the top and looked around. "Yeah," he said. "Great if we can manage it." He started down. "How come you don't use it for storage?"

"Never got around to it."

"Pretty neat up there. Floorboards and everything. Hotter than shit, though." He grinned. "Guess our friendly local vampire won't mind, huh?"

"Probably not."

They stepped off the platform. Larry led the way toward the far corner of the garage.

"Almost need a map to find the thing," Pete said.

I can find it in the dark.

"We're almost there."

Larry slipped through the passage between stacks of boxes and entered the small open area near the corner.

The concrete had dried.

The blanket lay heaped on the floor beside the coffin.

No!

He'd raced from the garage, near panic after dealing with the arm, and had totally forgotten to cover the body.

Now it was too late.

Pete appeared at his side, stepped forward and picked up the blanket.

Larry felt as if his skin were on fire.

"Been checking her out, huh?"

Deny it?

Pretend you don't know how the blanket got on the floor?

Pete's no idiot. He'd spot that lie in an instant.

"Yeah," Larry said, trying to sound lecherous. "Just had to. She's such a doll I just couldn't help myself."

"Can't blame you. What a mug. What a bod."

"Gives a new definition to feminine pulchritude."

"Gives a new definition to ugly," Pete said.

"Seriously, though, I *did* have to take a look at her yesterday. Research. Came time to describe her for the book, and I wanted to get it right."

"Right, sure." It was apparent from his tone that Pete believed the story. He shook open the blanket and spread it over the corpse, covering Bonnie from her shoulders to her ankles. Then he bent down again and pulled it up to hide her face. "That's better," he muttered.

"Why don't I take the front?" he suggested.

They lifted the coffin and carried it back through the garage.

"I'll go first," Pete said. "Should work better that way, since you're taller. Try to keep your end high."

He started up the ladder backward, moving slowly. As the box tipped upward, Bonnie slid toward Larry until the casket stopped her feet. The blanket dropped away from her face.

Larry raised his end of the box. Bracing it against his chest, he stepped closer to the ladder. The front kept rising. The blanket slipped down. The stake caught it, and the blanket hung from the wooden shaft like a cape tossed over a wall hook.

When Larry reached the base of the ladder, he realized he wouldn't be able to climb with the coffin pressing against his chest. "Wait," he called.

Pete stopped.

Larry lowered it to his waist.

"Okay."

Pete resumed climbing.

Larry mounted the ladder's first rung. Bonnie stood almost vertical inside the coffin.

"Oh, boy," Larry muttered.

"You okay?"

"So far."

"I'm just about there."

Larry shoved the casket upward with his knee, planted the toe of his shoe on the next rung and tried to rise. His foot slipped. As it dropped to the rung below, he lost his grip. The bottom edge of the casket pounded the ladder.

"Shit!" Pete yelled.

Larry grabbed the box's sides.

Something moved above him. He looked up.

He shouted, *"No!"*

Bonnie, standing rigid, teetered forward and plunged straight down at him.

It seemed to happen very slowly. The blanket fell from the stake and drifted toward her feet. Her dull blond hair flowed behind her head. Her right arm stayed tight against her side, but her left arm swayed down from the elbow as if reaching for him. Her mouth seemed to be stretched into a delighted grin.

He heard himself squeal.

He heard Pete shout, "Watch out!"

Hurling himself off the ladder, he staggered away and flung up his hands. He caught Bonnie by the sides, just under her armpits, and tried to shove her away. But her weight drove him backward. He stumbled off the edge of the platform.

He seemed to fall for a long time.

His back slammed the concrete floor.

His hands lost their grip, and the body crashed onto

him, the blunt end of the stake ramming his chest. He twisted his head aside. Dry teeth struck his cheek. Hair floated down, tickling his face like spiderwebs.

Larry bucked, throwing her off, rolled away and scurried to his feet. He stared at her. He gasped for breath. He felt as if a horde of ants were crawling on his skin, but he looked down at himself. Except for a snag and a smudge of dirt on the chest of his T-shirt, he saw no evidence of the encounter.

"Are you all right?" Pete asked.

Larry moaned. "I've been better."

"Right with you," Pete said, and dragged the empty casket up through the opening. Larry heard it scoot along the attic floorboards. Then Pete rushed down the ladder. "Guess maybe we should've tied her in."

"Yeah." Larry wanted to rub his crawly skin, but not with hands that had touched the body. "I've gotta shower," he said.

"Don't blame you. Gross-out. Let's take her up, though, huh?" Pete crouched over Bonnie's head and slipped his hands beneath her shoulders. "Take the legs, buddy."

Larry shook his head. "I . . . uh . . ."

"Come on, don't be a pussy."

He looked at his hands. "Don't wanta touch—"

"For God's sake, Lar! She was all *over* you. Come on, grab hold. We can't just leave her here."

Pete lifted. The rigid body didn't bend. Bonnie slanted down, straight as a plank, from her head at Pete's waist to her heels against the garage floor. "Guess I can just drag her," he said. "Save you from messing your hands. You can bring the blanket, can't you?"

"Yeah." Relieved, Larry crouched and picked up the blanket.

He watched Pete turn the corpse around and walk backward. Bonnie's heels sounded like newspapers sliding along the concrete.

Pete backed onto the platform. When he stepped onto the first rung of the ladder, Bonnie's feet rose off the floor. Her Achilles' tendons scraped the edge of the platform.

And left flakes of brown skin behind.

Larry winced.

He didn't want to touch her. But it pained him to see her getting hurt.

She's *not* getting hurt, he told himself.

The backs of her feet pounded the ladder rungs as Pete climbed higher.

Larry rushed forward. He tucked the blanket under his right arm, grabbed Bonnie's ankles and raised them. Holding both feet against his left side, he started up the ladder.

"Good man," Pete said.

Larry climbed carefully. He kept his eyes away from the corpse. At the top the heat was stifling.

They lowered Bonnie into the coffin. He spread the blanket over her, then hurried down. Pete came after him. They folded the ladder. A yank on the rope sent the trap-door swinging upward on its springed hinges. It slammed shut.

As they headed for the house, Larry realized that he felt guilty about leaving Bonnie in such a dark, hot place.

Don't be ridiculous, he thought. She's dead. She doesn't feel a thing.

"When do you think we oughta pull the stake?" Pete asked when they reached the living room.

"The sooner the better, I guess. I'll want to do some research on Sagebrush Flat, though."

"Right, good idea. Maybe they had some vampire troubles. Maybe that's how come the place was abandoned."

"We'll see. Anyway, I need to fill up more pages somehow."

"Right. And I need to pick up a video camera before the big event. I want to tape the whole thing, you know? It'll be great."

"Yeah." Larry opened the front door for him.

"See you later, bud. Going good, huh?"

"Well, at least we don't have to worry about the women catching on."

Grinning, Pete slapped his arm. "See you later. Don't let your meat loaf."

When Pete was gone, Larry hurried to the bathroom. He threw his clothes into the hamper and rushed to the tub.

As he stood under the hot spray of the shower, he wondered why he hadn't mentioned finding the ring. He *should've* told Pete about it, told him that the body was a girl named Bonnie Saxon who was graduated from Buford High in 1968.

How come I didn't? he asked himself.

Pete'll find out sooner or later. He'll realize I kept it from him.

So what?

Twenty

"Good morning, ma'am."

Lane swung her locker shut and turned around. "Well, hi, stranger."

Jim's hands were pushed into the front pockets of his jeans. Smiling, he drew them out for her to see, and slipped them in again. "Keeping 'em to myself," he said.

"Good for you. You're learning."

"Did you have a nice trip?"

"It was okay. I missed you. How was Candi?"

"Oh, she was grateful. She'd like you to go away more often."

Lane tried to hold onto her smile, but she felt it being tugged down. Her arms tightened around the binder and school books clutched to her chest.

"I was *kidding*."

"I know."

"*You* brought her up."

"I know. Dumb, huh?"

"I wouldn't go out with Candi. Or anyone else. Not as long as I've got you."

Lane's smile came back. She lifted an eyebrow. "Think you've *got* me, do you?"

"Hell, you know what I mean."

"Yeah. Give me one of those hands." She moved to his side, dropped one arm away from her load of books and squeezed his hand when he offered it. "Want to walk me to the library?" she asked.

"The library?"

"I've got an errand."

"It's only ten minutes before the first bell."

"Shouldn't take very long."

Holding hands, they made their way through the crowded hall.

"Is it still on for Friday night?" she asked.

"Sure. I hope so. Rather go out Saturday, but . . ."

"Hamlet."

"I know. What a drag."

Outside, they cut across the quad. Jim opened the library door for her. "Guess I'll make myself scarce," he said. "Ol' lady Swanson and me don't exactly hit it off. See you at lunch?"

"Fine. See you." Lane gave his hand another squeeze, then let go and entered the library. She headed straight for the circulation desk. There, Miss Swanson was busy checking out books to several students.

"Ol' lady Swanson" was probably no older than forty, an attractive woman with very short red hair and a freckled face. But Lane knew what Jim meant. Though the woman was hardly ancient, her rigid posture and high, thin eyebrows suggested a severity that made her seem older than her years.

She'd always been nice to Lane, but she seemed to enjoy visiting grief upon students who acted up. Kids usually referred to her as "the bitch." She was also known as "the dyke" and "the shithead." Henry, perhaps the most literate of her detractors, preferred to call her "the Scarlet Pimple."

After the last student wandered off, Lane stepped up to the desk.

"Good morning, Miss Swanson."

"Lane? How are you?"

"Fine. I was wondering if you could help me. Are old yearbooks kept around somewhere?"

"Indeed they are. We're missing certain years, of course. Books *fly* out of here if I'm not constantly on the alert. The students are a pack of thieves. And several of the teachers are just as bad, if I do say so myself." Her left eyebrow climbed her forehead. "What year would you be interested in?"

"Nineteen sixty-eight."

"That's long before I took over. Matters were an absolute shambles back then. I'll take a look, but don't be at all surprised if 'sixty-eight is among the missing."

Lane smiled politely and said, "Thank you."

Miss Swanson entered the office behind the circulation desk and stepped out of sight.

Lane leaned forward. She propped her elbows on the desk and crossed her feet. She waited.

"And how are you this fine morning?"

Before she could turn around, Mr. Kramer appeared beside her. "Oh, hi!" she blurted, and felt the warmth of a blush.

"All rested up and rarin' to hit the books?"

"Sure. I managed to reread *Hamlet* over the weekend," she said, hoping he would be pleased by the news.

"Wonderful."

He smelled wonderful. After-shave lotion? His cheeks looked smooth. They had a faint bluish hue where his beard would be if he grew one. She wondered if he ever had trouble shaving the deep cleft in his chin.

She met his eyes for a moment. They were *so* blue. She looked away and said, "It's really amazing. I get more out of the play each time I read it."

"Well, old Billy Shakespeare was no slouch."

She laughed, then faced forward as Miss Swanson returned to the desk. The librarian held the tall, thin volume of a yearbook. Seeing Mr. Kramer, she smiled and color came to her face. She suddenly looked softer, more feminine, younger.

"Good morning, Shirley."

"Mr. Kramer. May I help you with something?"

He shook his head. "Just visiting with one of my ace students, here."

Miss Swanson nodded, and turned her smile to Lane. "You're in luck, young lady."

"Terrific. How long can I check it out for?"

"I'm afraid you won't be *able* to check it out. Rules of the house. You may peruse it to your heart's content, but it remains in the library."

Lane wrinkled her nose. "Not even overnight?"

"I'm afraid not." She glanced at Mr. Kramer as if seeking approval. "If we allow the yearbooks to leave the library, we soon won't have any at all. You understand."

"Yeah." Lane shrugged. "Well . . ."

"Now please, those are the rules."

"This is my fault," Mr. Kramer said. "I asked Lane to pick the book up for me."

"Oh?"

He reached out and slipped it from Miss Swanson's hands. He nodded. "Yes, this is it. 'Sixty-eight. Is there a problem with *me* checking it out?"

"Why, no. Of course not. Let me write up a card." She slid open a drawer, took out a blank card, and jotted down, *"Buford Memories,* 1968."

"I really appreciate it," Mr. Kramer said as he signed the card.

Miss Swanson blushed even more. "Quite all right. Will you be able to return it tomorrow?"

He glanced at Lane. She nodded. "I should be done with it by then." Lifting the book, he said, "Thanks again, Shirley." He tucked the book under his arm, gestured for Lane to follow him, and walked out to the quad. "Here

you go." Handing it to her, he gave his face a silly, terrified expression. "For heaven's sake, don't lose it."

Lane laughed. "I'll be careful."

They walked together. "How come you're interested in
a yearbook that old?" he asked.

"Oh, it's for Dad. He's planning a novel that has stuff
happening in 'sixty-eight. He wants to check out the hair
styles, clothes, that kind of thing. Thanks an awful lot for
handling Miss Swanson."

"That's what friends are for."

Lane felt a pleasant glow spread through her. "I wish
there was something I could do for *you*."

"Well, if you mean that, I can always use an able hand
to help me correct papers."

"Great. When?"

"Can you spare half an hour after school? I still have
those spelling tests from Friday that need to be marked."

"Sure." The bell rang.

"Uh-oh. We'd better get to first period. See you later."

Nodding, Lane watched him hurry away. She took a
trembling breath, then forced her weak legs to carry her
forward.

She set her lunch bag and drink down on the table beside Jim, then peered across the cafeteria. Henry and Betty
weren't at their usual table. Someone else must've beaten
them to it. But she spotted her friends at the other side of
the crowded room. "Back in a minute," she told Jim.

"Forget something?"

"I have to see Henry and Betty."

Jim rolled his eyes upward, suffering.

Lane patted his shoulder, then hurried away.

She found them sitting across from each other, Betty
ripping open a bag of taco chips with her teeth while
Henry lifted a brown paper sack out of his briefcase.

"Hiya, guys," she said.

Henry twisted around and grinned up at her. "Salutations, my darling."

"Eat road apples," Betty told him.

"I have to stay after school today," Lane said. "I guess you'll need to get home under your own power."

"No prob-*lem,*" Henry said.

"Detention?" Betty asked.

"Ha! Me? Don't you wish."

"So what gives?"

"I'm staying late to help Kramer grade papers."

Betty pounded a chubby hand against her chest. "Be still, my heart. How'd you wangle that?"

"Just lucky, I guess."

"He's not Tom Cruise, you know," Henry pointed out.

"You wouldn't know a hunk if one fell on you," Betty said.

"They fall on me every time I go to P.E. It's among their favorite sports."

"Anyway, I'd better get back to Jim. I just wanted to let you know."

Betty leered, advised, "Keep your shorts on," and jammed a taco chip into her mouth.

"Degenerate," Lane said.

The girl nodded eagerly as she chewed.

Lane made her way back to Jim's table and sat down beside him. "See? Back already."

"Have a nice chat with Tweedle Dee and Dumb-dumb?"

"If you aren't going to be nice, I'll scram."

"Okay, okay. Just kidding. So what gives?"

"Aren't you the curious one?"

Shrugging, Jim turned away and took a bite out of his apple. For lunch each day he ate two apples and a chocolate bar, and washed them down with Pepsi. He was on his second apple. Only a core remained of the first. It was turning brown. Glad that she had *real* food, Lane unwrapped her salami-and-cheese sandwich. She bit into it and sighed.

Jim glanced at her. "You're eating poison, you know. All them preservatives."

"I'm counting on them preserving me."

"Ha ha."

"Cheer up."

"So what's the big deal with Hen-house and Betty Boob?"

"I'm staying after, that's all. I had to let them know."

"How come you're staying after?"

"I'm helping Kramer mark tests."

Jim wrinkled his face, baring his upper teeth. They were caulked with white mush from his apples. "Judas priest. Grades slipping, or something? Isn't enough, you giving up Saturday night for that bozo? Now you're doing slave labor? Shit! All of a sudden you're sure into some major league brown-nosing."

"If you don't know what you're talking about," Lane said calmly, "you ought to keep your mouth shut. Besides, it's disgusting me."

He opened his mouth wide and shook his head at her.

"Real cute. God, you can be so juvenile sometimes. To think I've actually kissed you."

"And will again, no doubt." He closed his mouth and commenced chewing with a blissful smile on his face.

Why do I even bother with him? Lane wondered. She took another bite of her sandwich, looked at the cafeteria clock and wished sixth period would hurry up and come.

In her fifth-period physiology class, Lane had to scribble notes furiously to keep up with the lecture. The time sped by. When the bell rang, it took her by surprise.

She hurried into the hall and ducked into the smoky rest room. There, she leaned close to a mirror and checked her teeth for remnants of her lunch. They looked fine. She brushed her hair, then opened her denim skirt and tucked in her blouse so that it slanted down, smooth and taut, from her breasts to her waist. The straps and lacy pattern of her bra cups showed faintly through the blouse's white fabric. She fastened her skirt, turned around once to make sure of every angle, then left the rest room and headed for class.

You'd think you were going out with him, she thought, feeling a little foolish. He's just a teacher. He's not interested in a *kid*.

So? It doesn't hurt to look nice.

Lane entered the classroom by its front door. Mr. Kramer wasn't there yet. She sat at her front-row desk, put away the books she wouldn't be needing, and waited.

Just before the bell rang, Riley Benson and Jessica came in. Jessica's left arm was still in a cast, but her right arm was around Benson. She glanced at Lane as she sauntered by. Her face looked better: though she still wore bandages on her chin and left eyebrow, the swelling had gone down; her lips no longer bulged; her bruises had faded to a sickly greenish yellow; some of her scabs had come off, leaving patches of shiny pink flesh.

She stepped to the other side of her desk. Benson rubbed her rear end, then ambled down the aisle. Jessica sat down.

"How are you doing?" Lane asked.

The girl sneered at her. "What do you think?"

"Just asking. Sorry."

"Blow it out your ass," she said, and turned away.

Whoops, Lane thought. Obviously, Benson had told her about the quarrel. Why'd she wait a whole week to sound off about it?

Bitch, she thought. Never should've bothered trying to be nice to her.

"Keep outa my way and keep your fuckin' nose outa

my business," Jessica suddenly added, "or I'll let Riley go ahead and ream you out."

"Okay. Jeez!"

Lane slumped in her seat and stared straight ahead.

She imagined herself telling Jessica to take a flying leap, but realized she'd better keep quiet. It wouldn't take much, she thought, to set the girl off. Jessica, alone, could probably take her apart. Not to mention what her scumbag boyfriend might do.

Mr. Kramer entered the room.

Lane sat up fast, pulling in her legs and swinging her knees together. She straightened her back. She folded her hands on the desktop.

Kramer took off his sport coat. He draped it over the back of his chair and began rolling up his shirtsleeves as he stepped to his usual position at the front of the table. His forearms were tanned under thick, black hair. He sat on the edge of the table.

Lane smiled when he met her eyes.

He acted as if he didn't see it, picked up his roll book and gave the classroom a quick scan. "Mr. Billings is apparently having himself another holiday," he said, and marked the student absent.

"Okay. This week's spelling words. Who'll volunteer to write them on the board?"

Lane raised her hand. He chose Heidi.

No big deal, Lane told herself. But she couldn't help feeling a small letdown. First, he hadn't returned her smile. Now he'd called on someone else to go to the board. Was he ignoring her?

Don't be ridiculous, she thought. I'm not the only kid in the room.

But as the class went on, Kramer continued to ignore her. He rarely gave her a glance. He called on other students to read from the poetry book, to answer questions about rhythm and meter, to offer interpretations.

Lane's uneasiness grew.

Is he mad at me, or something? What did I do? Maybe he thinks I took advantage of him at the library. But hell, I didn't *ask* him to check out the book. That was his idea.

She began wondering whether he still wanted her to stay after class.

Go on, get out of here.

He wouldn't say that.

Lane imagined herself sitting alone in the room, humiliated. "But you asked me to stay and help you."

"I don't care. Leave me alone."

Maybe I should go ahead and leave when the bell rings, she thought. But I *said* I'd stay. I can't just walk out. He'd think I'm nuts.

"Lane?"

Startled, she looked up at Kramer.

"Would you like to read the next stanza?"

"Uh . . ." She felt herself shriveling inside. "I'm afraid I've lost the place."

A few sniggers came from the back of the room.

Kramer shook his head slightly. He looked amused. "You *should* try to follow along in the book."

"Yes sir." She lowered her eyes to the page.

"Aaron, will you read the next stanza?"

Aaron began to read. Lane hunched over her book, shielded her eyes with one hand and studied the page.

Where the hell are we?

Shit!

She couldn't find the stanza.

Dipstick, you *wanted* him to call on you. And he did. He sure did.

Why don't I just die now, and make it easy on myself?

Aaron finished.

A hand appeared beneath Lane's face. Kramer's hand. It turned the page for her, pointed to a middle stanza, and went away.

"Thanks," she muttered.

Everyone else in the classroom seemed to find this quite amusing.

Lane kept her head down.

"Would you care to favor us with a rendition?" Kramer asked.

She nodded against her sheltering hand and began to read aloud.

She was halfway through the stanza when the bell rang.

"That'll be fine," Kramer said. Raising his voice, he announced, "Don't forget your spelling sentences for tomorrow. In *ink*, please. Class dismissed."

Lane shut her book and stared at it. Kids walked past her. Someone rubbed the top of her head. She looked up. Benson grinned down at her. "You gotta pay *attention*, babe."

She sneered at him.

He sauntered out with Jessica, a hand on her rump.

Soon the room was empty except for Lane and Kramer.

Lane forced her head up. Kramer stood behind his table, busy stuffing books and folders into his briefcase. He seemed unaware of her presence.

I should've left with the rest of them, she thought. God, how did I get into this?

Dad and his yearbook. Thanks a bunch, Dad.

She wondered if she should say something.

"Do you have a red pen?" Kramer asked, and finally looked at her.

The tension spilled out of her. "Uh . . . no. I don't think so."

"No problem. Let me get you one." He stepped over to his desk and opened the top drawer. He found a pen, shut the drawer, and searched through a stack of folders on the corner of his desk. "Here we go. I'll give you first period. How does that sound?"

"Fine."

He came toward her. "If you get done with these and want some more, I've got plenty. Don't want to keep you all afternoon, though."

Lane nodded.

I don't believe this, she thought. He's acting as if nothing happened.

What do you want, a lecture?

She cleared her desk. Kramer set the folder and pen in front of her. "It's five points a word," he said. "But I guess you know that."

"Yeah."

"Any questions, just ask."

"All right."

He turned away.

"Mr. Kramer?"

He turned to her again, a pleasant smile spreading across his face.

"I'm sorry about losing my place."

"Daydreaming?"

"I guess so."

"Well, no harm in that. I hope you weren't too embarrassed."

"I was pretty embarrassed."

"You're the best student in the class, Lane. Don't let one little lapse of attention throw you. Happens to everyone."

"Okay. Thanks."

"Of course, I had to give you an F for the day."

"Oh."

Laughing softly, he squeezed Lane's shoulder. "That was supposed to be a joke."

"Oh."

His hand stayed there. Lane felt as if its warmth were spreading down through her. He rubbed her shoulder gently, then let go.

"I really appreciate your staying after to help like this. It takes some of the pressure off."

"Glad to help." She could still feel where his hand had been.

"Teaching ain't all it's cracked up to be. Sometimes, I feel like I'm being consumed by paperwork. All I seem to have time for is grading papers, preparing lessons." He shook his head. "A real drag."

"If you'd like me to, I'll stay more often and help you out."

Her heart thudded. She couldn't believe she'd said that. *He'll think I've got the hots for him.*

Kramer's head tilted slightly to one side. He pressed his lips together and raised his eyebrows. "Well, I sure appreciate the offer. You must have better things to do with your time, though."

"I wouldn't mind. Really."

"It's up to you. I'd certainly be glad to have the help." Smiling, he knuckled the folder on her desk. "Now, get cracking. Talk's cheap, and time's a-wasting."

Lane laughed. "You're a real slave driver."

"Start correcting those papers, or I'll give you a taste of the lash."

"Yes sir."

He turned and headed for his desk. Lane's eyes stayed on him.

His sport shirt tapered down from his broad shoulders to his slim waist. The tail, just a bit untucked, puffed out over his belt. His wallet made a bulge over his left buttock. There seemed to be nothing in his right rear pocket. That side of his slacks was smooth against his rump, and Lane watched the way it moved as he walked.

Twenty-one

Jean, peeling potatoes at the sink, looked around at Larry as he entered the kitchen. "Quitting a little early, aren't you?" she asked.

He glanced at the clock. Almost four. He usually worked until four-thirty.

"I finished the damn corrections," he said. He took a beer from the refrigerator. "Too late to get started on anything else." He twisted the cap off the bottle. "Where's Lane?"

"Not home yet."

"I know *that*. Did she have some kind of plans for after school?"

"Not that she mentioned. Maybe she stopped over at Betty's, or something."

"Yeah." He poured the beer into a stein, sucked off the head of white froth, and emptied the bottle. "What're you going to do with the potatoes?"

"French fries."

"All *right!*" He dropped the bottle into the trash. It landed with a thunk.

He carried his beer into the living room, sank into his easy chair and started thumbing through the new issue of *Mystery Scene* that had arrived in the day's mail. Jean had probably already looked it over. She would've told him if she'd found any mention of him. So he went straight to Brian Garfield's "Letter from Hollywood."

He tried to read it.

But the day was mild. The air conditioner was off, the windows open. Each time Larry heard a car on the street, his eyes shifted to the window.

Where is she?

Patience, he told himself.

They might not even *have* the '68 yearbook.

They've got to.

He wished he'd asked Lane to phone him from school. Then he wouldn't have spent the whole day worrying. But he didn't want her to think it was any big deal.

"Try for the 'sixty-eight," he'd told her. "That's the year I'll be working on. If they don't have it, though, 'sixty-seven or 'sixty-six will be okay. Even 'sixty-five. In fact, if you could get the annuals for each of those years . . ."

"You've got to be joking," Lane had said. "I'll be lucky if Swanson lets me check out *any* of them, much less four."

"Just go for 'sixty-eight, then, okay?"

He heard another approaching car. He knew the Mustang's sound—a low grumble—and this wasn't it. He looked out the window anyway. A station wagon swept by.

He drank some beer, finished the Garfield piece, and looked for Warren Murphy's "Curmudgeon's Corner." This issue didn't seem to have one.

He muttered, "Shit."

Probably a story behind its absence. Have to ask Ed next time we talk.

At least de Lint's horror reviews weren't missing. Larry scanned the columns. Half the books were by writers he couldn't stand. But he spotted reviews of new books by Daniel Ransom, Joe Lansdale, and Chet Williamson. He'd already read the three books under discussion. Good. That way, the reviews couldn't spoil anything for him.

He took a drink of beer.

Started to read.

Heard the Mustang.

About time!

The shiny red car appeared on the street, slowed down, swung into the driveway and vanished from sight. The engine went silent. A door thumped shut. When he heard Lane's boots scraping on the walkway, he tossed the magazine aside and hurried to the door.

"Hi ho," he said, opening the door. Lane had her keys in one hand. Her other hand was empty. "How was your day?"

"Terrific."

Must've been, Larry thought. She looked even more chipper than usual.

He stepped out of her way and shut the door. Lane slung her book bag off her shoulders. Trying to keep his voice calm, Larry said, "So, did you have any luck with the yearbook?"

"Swanson didn't want to check it out to me. You really lucked out, though. Mr. Kramer was there, and she let him have it."

"But you've got it?"

"But of course." She dropped her denim bag on the sofa, unstrapped its top and slipped out a tall, thin volume. "It has to be returned tomorrow morning."

"No problem." Larry reached for it.

Lane clutched it to her chest and shook her head. "You owe me."

"What do you want?"

"Well, that's open to negotiation. I've had to make considerable sacrifices on your behalf. In particular, I'm obliged to help Mr. Kramer grade papers after school every day this week to pay him back for the favor."

"You're kidding."

"I wouldn't kid you."

"He shouldn't make you do that."

"Well, I kind of made the offer, and he didn't refuse."

"Ah. Well, that's different."

"It's still because of this," she said and, grinning, rapped her knuckles against the back of the yearbook.

"Okay. What do you want?"

Her eyes rolled upward. "Let me think. My services don't come cheap, you understand."

"They never have."

"Daaad!"

"Laaane."

"You make me sound absolutely mercenary."

"But you're not."

"Of course not. However, I just happened to notice an absolutely radical pair of denim boots a while back."

"And you didn't buy them?"

"I didn't think I should. I'd already made a few purchases that day."

"If you're talking about the day your mother and I went on our last outing with Pete and Barbara, I remember it well."

"I *really* wanted those boots. But I held back. For your sake."

"I'm touched. Truly."

"So, can I have them?"

"Sure, why not?"

"Oh, Dad, you're great!" She thrust the book at him. As Larry took it, she threw herself against him and gave him a quick kiss. Then she hurried toward the kitchen.

Larry retrieved his beer.

He heard Lane call out, "Yo! Mom! What've we got to eat around here? I'm dying."

Larry shut the door to his office. He placed his beer on the coaster beside his word processor. He leaned back in his chair and rested the bottom of the book against his stomach. The blue cover was embossed with gold lettering that read, BUFORD MEMORIES '68.

This is it, he thought. My God, this is it.

His heart was racing. His stomach felt tight and shaky.

He opened the book. A quick riffle revealed glossy pages of black and white photographs. At the back was an index. The final page of the index listed students with S names. Larry slid his eyes down the column:

> Sakai, Joan
> Samilson, Pamela
> Sanders, Timothy
> Satmary, Maureen
> Schaefer, Ronald

No Saxon, Bonnie.

Come on! Larry thought. She *has* to be in here.

Despairing, he flipped pages toward the front of the index. And spotted a subheading: FRESHMEN.

"Thank God," he muttered.

In 1968, Bonnie was a senior, not a freshman.

He thumbed the pages over, passing the lists of sophomores and juniors. Just above the heading JUNIORS was the name Zimmerman, Rhonda. Tail end of the senior class. He lifted his eyes to the left-hand corner. A senior named Simpson, Kenneth.

Simpson. An S!

Larry clamped his lower lip between his teeth. He turned the page and worked his way up from the bottom:

> Simmons, Dan
> Seigel, Susan
> Sefridge, John
> Sclar, Toni
> Schultz, Fred

Just another name in the index. Saxon, Bonnie. Not printed in red. Not in bold lettering or italics. But it seemed to explode off the page and slam through Larry's head.

To the right of her name were page numbers. Six of them.

Six pages with photos of Bonnie Saxon.

God almighty!

Larry scanned the column. Plenty of the names were followed by a single page number, several by two or three. Few had more than three.

Bonnie had six.

She must've been busy, Larry thought. And popular.

Popular girls are almost always pretty.

The first page number after her name was 34. Larry slipped a matchbook into the index to mark his place, turned to the front of the annual and thumbed through its pages until he found page 34. Blocks of small, individual photos showing members of the senior class. Boys in sport coats and neckties. Girls in dark pullover sweaters, each wearing a necklace.

The first name in the upper left-hand corner was Bonnie Saxon.

Larry shifted his eyes to the photo.

He moaned.

She was lovely. Radiant, adorable. Her gleaming blond hair swept softly across her brow, flowed down to her shoulders. Her eyes seemed to be directed at something wonderful just beyond the camera. They looked eager, cheerful. She had a small, cute nose. Her high cheeks curved smoothly above the corners of her mouth, as if lifted and shaped by her smile.

This was Bonnie.

She looked quite a bit like Lane.

She looked very little like the corpse in the attic of his garage, but her hair and teeth and the general shape of her face convinced him that he had made no mistake: the body was Bonnie Saxon. No doubt about it.

The hideous cadaver had once been the girl in this photo—beautiful, glowing with youth.

Larry gazed at the picture.

Bonnie.

He felt very strange: excited by his find, enthralled by her beauty, depressed. When the photo was taken, she must've thought a whole, wonderful life waited in her future. But she had only months, and then someone ended it all by pounding a stake through her chest.

This was no vampire.

This was a sweet, innocent kid.

Probably a real heartbreaker. Every guy in school must've longed for her.

Had one of them killed her? A jealous boyfriend? She'd broken his heart, so he drove a stake through hers? Possible, Larry thought. But the stake in her chest and the crucifix on the staircase wall sure made it seem that somebody believed she was a vampire.

Larry gazed a little longer at the photo, then checked the index and turned to page 124. There, he found group pictures of the Public Relations Committee, the Program Committee, and the Art Club. He didn't bother studying the lists of names. He wanted to search for Bonnie, to pick her out, to enjoy the surprise of recognition.

The Public Relations Committee photo was overexposed. Most of the faces were little more than pale blurs, their features washed out and faint. Bonnie didn't seem to be in this group, but Larry glanced at the names to make sure.

Then he went on to the Program Committee photo. He half expected to find her here. Though he wasn't sure about the functions of the Program Committee, Bonnie looked like the sort of girl you might find in charge of decorating the gym for a dance. He studied the face of each girl in the picture. No Bonnie.

He found her with the Art Club.

In the front row, second from the left, between a couple of gals who looked fat and dumpy.

Bonnie looked grand. She stood straight, arms at her
sides, head up, smiling at the camera. This wasn't a close-
up like the senior photo, but it made up for that by showing her from head to foot. She wore a short-sleeved white
blouse, a straight skirt that hung to the tops of her knees,
white socks and white sneakers.

Larry lifted the book, watching her grow as the page
neared his eyes. He studied her face. In spite of the distance from which the photo had been taken, it had very
good definition. All her features were clear. The collar of
her blouse was open. He looked at her neck and saw the
hollow of her throat, the faint curves of her collar bones.
Lower, the rise of her breasts was no more than a hint.
Larry followed her arms down to her hands. Her hands
were open, fingers curled slightly inward against the fabric
of her skirt. His gaze lingered on the slender curves of
her bare legs.

One of her white socks was slightly lower than the other.
If she'd known that, she probably would've fixed it. Larry
could almost see her bending over and pulling up the sock.
The image gave him a little ache, as if he'd missed something important by not being there.

He lowered the book and read a short description of the
Art Club's activities. Bonnie, he learned, had been the sec-
retary.

Must've been smart. You don't appoint someone secre-
tary unless she's intelligent and responsible.

Probably a straight-A student, he thought. One of those
kids who has everything going for her—looks, a terrific
personality, brains.

He checked the index again, and discovered that the next
photo was on page 126. He turned back to the Art Club,
flipped the next page, and immediately recognized Bonnie
in the top photo. She'd been in the school's Legislative
Assembly, whatever that was. A quick scan of the small

print informed him that the group was responsible for "passing school laws and putting them into action."

Bonnie was seated on risers, feet on the floor, legs together, hands cupping her knees. She was dressed just the same as in the Art Club picture. In this one, her socks were even. Larry smiled. She had a bemused look on her face. Her bangs hung a little crooked, showing a vee of uncovered brow.

Larry brought the book closer to his face. Her head was turned slightly. Her hair was swept back behind one pale ear. She seemed to be leaning forward. Her blouse looked snug against her belly, and her breasts cast a vague, horizontal shadow across the white fabric.

He was about to turn to the index when he spotted Bonnie on the opposite page. She was in the top photo, front row, third from the right. A member of the Social Activities Committee.

"Ah-ha!" Larry whispered.

So she decorated the gym for dances, after all.

"I knew it."

In this photo she wore a crew-neck sweater with a large B on its chest.

A cheerleader?

Figures, he thought. I should've guessed.

Bonnie looked different, somehow. Larry stared at the picture. She had been caught without her smile. The glimmer was gone from her eyes, and her lips were pressed together in a soft, straight line.

Something was obviously troubling her.

Maybe she was feeling sick, that day. Maybe she'd messed up a test. Maybe her boyfriend had dumped her.

Something had happened. Something, at least for a moment, had robbed her of happiness.

It didn't seem fair. Bonnie's life should've been perfect—there'd been so little of it left.

Larry felt a tightness in his throat.

He turned quickly to the index, then searched out page 133.

Bonnie stood in line with six other girls. "Songleaders," not cheerleaders. They all wore light-colored sweaters with the huge B in front, and dark, pleated skirts. They stood with pompoms raised in their left hands, right hands on hips, right legs thrown high.

Bonnie looked as if she were having the time of her life. Her head was tossed back. The shutter had caught her laughing. She'd kicked up her leg higher than any of the other girls. Not straight toward the camera, but a little to the side. The toe of her white sneaker seemed about to collide with her left armpit. Her skirt hung down from the upraised leg. She wore no socks. Larry gazed at her slim ankle, the curve of her calf, and the sleek underside of her thigh. He saw a crescent of underwear not quite as dark as the skirt, rounded with the slope of her buttock.

He fought an urge to bring the book closer to his eyes.

He looked away from the picture. He picked up his stein and took a sip of beer.

Glanced again.

It's not actually her panties, he told himself. It's part of the outfit.

But still . . .

He turned his attention to the second picture on the page. Same girls. Same costumes. In this one they were all facing the camera and leaping, pompoms thrust overhead with both hands, backs arched, legs kicked up behind them. Bonnie's sweater had lifted slightly. It didn't quite meet the top of her skirt. A narrow band of bare skin showed. Larry glimpsed her flat belly, the small dot of her navel.

He shook his head. He took another sip of beer, but had a hard time swallowing. He turned to the index.

Only one more page number after Bonnie's name. He turned to 147.

And sucked in a quick breath.

A three-by-five close-up of Bonnie filled more than half the page.

"Jesus," he whispered.

He glanced at the caption. "Bonnie Saxon, 1968 Spirit Queen." On the same page were small photos of four other girls—princesses. Her court.

He postponed studying her picture. It was the last. He wanted to savor the anticipation.

On the opposite page was a photo of a tackled football player smashing to the ground. The heading beneath it read, SPIRIT WEEK HIGHLIGHTS FALL SEASON. Larry scanned a description of the festivities, which were apparently marred by Buford's loss of the game. Then he came to the part he'd hoped for. "Sherry Cain, Sandy O'Connor, Julie Clark, Betsy Johnson, and Bonnie Saxon were presented as homecoming princesses at halftime. Bonnie Saxon was crowned queen at the Homecoming Dance that night. In spite of the defeat of the varsity, tremendous spirit was shown." Nothing more about Bonnie.

Fantastic, Larry thought.

Homecoming queen.

"Good going, Bon," he muttered.

Then he turned his attention to the photo.

And flinched as someone knocked on his door. "Time to eat," Lane called.

"Okay. I'll be right there."

Larry glanced at the Spirit Queen, then shut the book.

He lay motionless in bed that night, staring at the ceiling. When the sounds of Jean's breathing convinced him that she was asleep, he crept out of bed. The air was chilly. He shivered with the cold and nervous excitement. At the closet he pulled his robe off a hook. He put it on as he stepped into the hallway. The soft velour felt warm on his bare skin.

In the living room he found Lane's book bag propped against the wall beside the front door. He opened it, searched inside with one hand until he felt the annual, and slipped the book out.

He carried it to his office. He shut the door, flicked on the light, and eased himself down onto his chair.

In spite of the warm robe, he was shaking. His heart felt like a pounding fist.

I must be crazy, he thought. What if Jean wakes up? Or Lane? What if one of them catches me at this?

They won't. Calm down.

With the book on his lap, he turned to the Spirit Queen.

God, so gorgeous.

She wore a dark top that left her shoulders bare.

He could look at her later.

He took an X-Acto Knife from his desk drawer, pressed the open book flat against his thighs, and drew the razor-sharp blade down the annual's gutter, neatly slicing off the page where it joined the spine.

He cut out every page that showed a photograph of Bonnie.

When he was done, he hid them in his file cabinet, sliding them into one of over fifty folders that contained copies of short stories he'd written over the years.

His pictures would be safe there, from Jean and Lane.

He sat down again and riffled through the yearbook. A few pages were loose. He touched their edges with glue and carefully inserted them.

He shut the book and peered at its top. Along the spine tiny gaps were visible where the pages had been removed. But only an extremely close inspection would reveal the damage. And if someone did notice, who was to say when the desecration had been performed? Maybe years ago.

Larry shut off the light and left his office. He returned

the annual to Lane's book bag, fastened the straps, and went to his bedroom.

From the doorway he could hear Jean's long, slow breaths.

He hung up his robe. He crept to the bed and slipped cautiously between the sheets. He sighed. He thought about the pictures.

They were his now. His to keep.

He remembered the way Bonnie looked in each of them. But his mind kept returning to the songleader shots.

Then she was alone on the football field. She thrust her pompoms at the sky and twirled, her long golden hair floating, her skirt billowing around her and rising higher and higher.

Twenty-two

Larry woke up in the morning and remembered cutting the pages from the book. He was suddenly certain that the librarian would notice the damage. Lane would catch hell. It would be his fault.

He realized that he'd done a lot of things lately that left him feeling guilty: threatening Pete with the gun; bringing Bonnie home and keeping her presence a secret; wandering out to the garage, apparently in a drunken stupor, and not even knowing what he did out there; and now, defacing the library book, maybe getting Lane into trouble.

Before finding Bonnie out there in that ghost town, he'd never done much to be ashamed of. About the worst, he thought, was having a few lustful thoughts about other women. That seemed pretty harmless.

But all this.

What the hell's happening to me?

Too hot, he flipped onto his back and tossed the blanket aside. Jean was already up. Good. He didn't want any company just now. Especially not Jean's. She might sense that he was upset and start asking questions.

Oh, nothing's wrong. I've got a corpse hidden in the garage. And you know that library book? Well, it had these terrific photos of the dead gal . . .

I had to have those pictures, he told himself. Nobody was about to let me keep the book. Photocopies wouldn't have been any good: they're fine for printed stuff, but the pictures would've looked awful.

I bet nobody's even opened that book for the past twenty years.

Nobody'll notice the pages are gone.

You hope.

So if they give Lane shit, I'll pay for the book.

Lot of good that'll do. She's never been in trouble. It'd kill her.

Nobody will notice a damn thing. She'll return the book, and that'll be it.

No point in worrying, anyway. The damage is done. You can't put the pages back in, even if you wanted to.

They're mine now.

He closed his eyes and let his mind dwell on the photographs. The memories of them soothed him. He filled his lungs with the mild, morning air. He stretched, savoring the solid feel of his flexing muscles, the softness of the sheet against his skin, the images of Bonnie.

He stayed in bed until he heard the soft grumble of the Mustang's engine.

He spent the day on *Night Stranger,* closing in on its finish. The writing was hard. His mind kept wandering. It slipped away from the story and tortured him with miserable thoughts about Lane being confronted by an outraged librarian. It tantalized him with thoughts of Bonnie.

Frequently he looked away from the computer screen and stared at his filing cabinet. The drawer where he'd hidden the yearbook pages was within reach. He longed to pore over them. But Jean was in the house. What if she came into his office while he had the pictures out?

Shortly after two o'clock Jean knocked on his door and opened it. "I thought I'd run over to Safeway. Anything you want me to pick up while I'm there?"

"Not that I can think of," he said. "Have fun."

"See you later."

She closed the door.

Larry stared at the computer screen. He heard the faint thump of the front door shutting. He rubbed his moist hands on the sides of his shorts.

He waited for a while, then rolled his chair back, left the office, and reached the living room in time to see Jean's car pass the windows.

Gone. She's gone!

He glanced at his wristwatch. A quarter past two. Give Jean ten minutes to reach the store, at least ten inside, and another ten to get home.

He had at least half an hour.

Stomach trembling, he hurried to his office, shut the door and pulled out the steel drawer of the file cabinet. He'd slipped the pages into the folder for his short story "The Snatch." He took out the entire folder, left the drawer agape, dropped onto his chair, flicked open the cover, and Bonnie smiled up at him.

The Spirit Queen photo.

"God," he whispered.

Bonnie seemed even more beautiful than he remembered. Lovely, fresh, innocent.

No wonder she was voted queen.

He gazed at her flowing blond hair. It swept softly down her forehead, slightly longer on the right, so that it brushed the curve of her eyebrow. It didn't quite touch her left eyebrow. The sides of her head were draped by shining tresses. Her eyes sparkled. Larry supposed that their gleam was a reflection of the camera's flash. Her lips were together, and curled upward just a bit at the corners with the mere hint of a smile. She looked serious, but pleased and proud.

Her jaw cast a shadow that slanted across her neck and puddled in the hollow above her right collarbone. Her shoulders sloped down gently, bare to the borders of the photo. The top she wore looked black. Only its upper edge showed. It eased downward to a point in the center of her chest. Not quite low enough to show any cleavage.

Larry placed an open hand across the bottom of the picture.

With the garment covered, she might have been naked.

He gazed at her face, at the smooth, pale flesh of her chest. Faint shadows revealed the hollow of her throat, the curves of her collar bones.

If the picture extended downward, his hand would be resting across her breasts. He imagined firm mounds with skin like warm velvet, nipples erect and pressing into his palm. He moved his thumb downward. It would reach to the golden curls between her thighs.

Suddenly shocked at himself, Larry jerked his hand away from the picture. He slapped the folder shut.

God!

What's wrong with me?

Face burning, he lurched out of his chair. He stuffed the folder back into the cabinet and shoved the drawer shut.

He returned to his chair. He stared at the computer screen. The sentences there seemed empty, meaningless. No point in trying to write more of this novel. Not today.

He signed off and replaced the disk with the one labeled "Vamp."

"Vampire," he muttered. "No way. Not Bonnie."

He brought up the directory, then the last chapter he'd written on Saturday night.

A lot of catching up to do.

He exited that chapter.

He gazed at the blank screen.

Good luck, he thought. How in hell do I write about ending up in the garage with her? Say I was wearing pajamas, for starters.

Any way you slice it, you're going to look like you're losing your grip. Like you're obsessed, or something.

And what about the annual? Tell the world you cut a library book to pieces? Figure out some kind of lie, maybe.

No matter what you write, Lane will know the truth. She'll read the damn book.

The photos *have* to go in it.

Shit.

Cross that bridge when you come to it.

And be *really* careful when you write about seeing the pictures. Understate it. For godsake, don't let it look like the things turned you on. The girl's dead.

She wasn't dead when the pictures were taken.

She was so alive then. So glorious.

And now . . .

In his mind Larry saw the way she looked now. Hideous. A withered mummy with a stake in her heart.

That wasn't done by any jealous boyfriend. Some bastard actually thought she was a vampire.

Murdered her.

Hid her body under the hotel stairs and hung a crucifix on the wall for good measure.

And padlocked the front doors?

That was a brand new padlock, Larry reminded himself. And someone had placed boards across the broken landing.

Bonnie's killer?

Someone was certainly watching over the hotel. The coyote eater? Had he been hanging around Sagebrush Flat for more than twenty years—a mad sentry guarding the tomb of his slain vampire?

Still there.

By now, he knows she's gone.

I've got her, you bastard.

How could you do that to her? How could you take my Bonnie and drive a stake through her heart?

Larry stared at the computer screen.

His fingers went to the keyboard.

They jabbed the keys, and amber words appeared.

SOMEBODY OUGHT TO RIP YOUR HEART OUT, YOU MOTHERFUCKER.

Somewhere in the house a door bumped shut. Larry quickly backspaced, erasing the words.

Larry managed to write four pages after Jean's return from the store, and was busy describing his clean-up of the garage when footsteps approached his office. He scrolled up quickly to clear the screen. A knock on the door. The door opened.

Lane stepped in.

His stomach shriveled, but he managed a smile.

"Hi ho," he said. "I thought you were staying late."

"So did I." She shrugged. "Mr. Kramer had a parent conference, so I came on home."

One hand was hidden behind her back.

Probably holding a gun, Larry thought.

But she didn't seem upset.

"What've you got there?" he asked.

Her hand came forward. It held a chocolate chip cookie. "Fresh from the oven," she said. "Want it?"

"Sure."

He reached for the cookie. His hand was shaking. Lane noticed. "Are you feeling okay?"

"Hard day at the office," he said, and took the cookie. "How was your day?"

"Okay, I guess."

"You returned the yearbook?"

She frowned. "You said you were done with it."

"Yeah. I am. Thanks a lot for the help. I owe you."

Smiling, she said, "Right, you owe me. One pair of boots."

"I don't have to pick them out for you, do I?"

"Just lend me your credit card. I'll take care of the dirty work."

Larry laughed softly. "My wallet's in the bedroom. Help yourself."

When she left, Larry ate the cookie. It was soft, still warm from the oven. But his mouth was dry, and he had a hard time swallowing.

Twenty-three

When the public library opened its doors at nine o'clock Wednesday morning, Larry was waiting. He felt nervous, approaching the librarian. She was a young, attractive woman with a cheery smile. But he half expected to be shunned, thrown out on his ear.

She's not psychic, he told himself. She has no idea I cut up the high school's annual.

"I'm doing research on 1968," he explained. "Would you have copies of the *Mulehead Evening Standard* going back that far?"

Minutes later she produced a box of microfiche. She showed Larry to the reader-printer.

Yes, he knew how to use it.

The librarian told him there was a charge of ten cents per page for hard copies, and he could pay at the desk before leaving. Her name was Alice. She would be around and more than glad to help if he needed any assistance.

He thanked her.

She left.

Larry began his search at the June 1, 1968 edition of the newspaper. High school graduation had probably taken place around the middle of the month. Because of the ring, he assumed Bonnie had graduated. But he might be wrong.

The paper from Saturday, June 22, settled the question. Graduation ceremonies had occurred the previous night, and the list of eighty-nine matriculating seniors included

Bonnie's name. Photographs of the festivities showed the school principal, the head of the Board of Education, and two students who had given speeches. No Bonnie.

But he had found what he needed: evidence that she was alive and well as of June 21.

He pushed a button at the base of the machine. Seconds later a copy of the page slid out.

He went on.

He watched for Bonnie's name. He watched for stories about murders and disappearances. But he kept his mind open, hoping to notice any story that might have a bearing, no matter how remote, on Bonnie's fate.

The story he found in the July 16 edition wasn't remote. Larry saw the headline and gasped. His heart thudded as he devoured the paragraphs.

TWO SLAIN IN SAGEBRUSH FLAT

Elizabeth Radley, 32, and her daughter Martha, 16, were brutally murdered last night in their rooms at the Sagebrush Flat Hotel. Their bodies were discovered by Uriah Radley, the husband and father of the victims.

According to a county sheriff's spokesman, Uriah had yesterday driven into Mulehead Bend for supplies. During the course of his return in the evening, his truck broke down fifteen miles outside Sagebrush Flat. He traveled the remaining distance afoot, and arrived at the hotel at approximately midnight to find his wife and daughter murdered.

The nude bodies were discovered in their beds, both apparently having sustained multiple wounds of a fatal nature. The nature of the murder weapon, or weapons, has not been disclosed. Nor has it been revealed, as yet, whether the deceased were victims of sexual assault.

Uriah Radley was questioned by authorities, but is not being held in connection with the murders. No suspects are in custody at this time.

Larry read the article again. Incredible. Two murders at the same hotel where they'd found Bonnie.

There's *got* to be a connection, he thought.

He copied the story.

In the next day's *Standard* was a follow-up.

SAGEBRUSH HOTEL MURDERS

Authorities remain baffled by the brutal double homicide which occurred sometime before midnight this past Monday in Sagebrush Flat. Autopsies of the victims, Elizabeth Radley and her daughter Martha, revealed that both died from exsanguination, or blood loss, as a result of multiple wounds.

Authorities have few leads, and no suspects at this time.

According to County Sheriff Herman Black, "We're of the opinion that they were victims of opportunity. That is to say, they were in the wrong place at the wrong time. Sagebrush Flat was no place to be living. I'd warned the Radleys on several occasions about the dangers of staying there, now that the town's as good as dead. For the past couple of years, we've had lots of troubles with undesirables vandalizing the place and generally raising Cain."

The sheriff went on to point out that biker gangs had frequently used the town as a site for wild parties. During the past twelve months, no fewer than three rapes and half a dozen beatings had been reported as occurring in the town's abandoned buildings, either at the hands of bikers or other transient types.

"It would be my guess," said Sheriff Black, "that Elizabeth and Martha Radley ran afoul of some bikers. That's a rough lot, and two women alone wouldn't stand much chance."

Uriah Radley, along with his wife and daughter, had continued to reside in Sagebrush Flat during the town's decline and eventual abandonment following the closure of the Deadwood Silver Mine in 1961. In the resulting economic chaos, businesses shut their doors and the citizens migrated to greener pastures, many of them settling in our own Mulehead Bend.

By early 1966, only Holman's general store and Uriah Radley's hotel remained in operation. Later in that year, the fate of the town was sealed when Jack Holman died as the result of an apparent suicide. In an ironic twist of fate, his body was found hanging by a rope in his general store by Martha Radley, then 14 years of age, who was murdered along with her mother on Monday night.

Though Holman's went out of business following the demise of its proprietor, the Radley family continued to reside in the Sagebrush Flat Hotel. The hotel ceased operations last year, but the Radleys remained. Uriah made weekly visits to our town for supplies, and he is known to be well liked.

Elizabeth and Martha were active members of our own First Presbyterian Church.

Martha attended Buford High School, where she completed her sophomore year this past June. She was a member of the school band and the Art Club.

Services will be held Sunday at First Presbyterian.

Larry copied the story.

He felt as if he'd discovered a treasure. The town had a grim history: suicide at Holman's, a pair of grisly murders at the hotel, "rough" types using the abandoned buildings for their fun and games. Great material.

To top it off, Martha had been in the Art Club. Like Bonnie. They must've known each other.

They'd been in the same club. And Martha had lived, and finally died, in the very hotel where Bonnie's body had been hidden.

That made two connections.

Larry knew he was on to something.

He suddenly realized he had a picture of her. Probably. If Martha wasn't absent on the day the Art Club's photograph was taken, she would be standing in the group with Bonnie.

Fantastic luck, he thought.

Hell, it's more than luck. It's no coincidence. Somehow, all this is related: the hotel, Martha's death, both girls in the same club, Bonnie's death. All linked.

He kept on searching.

Monday, July 22.

SERVICES HELD FOR SLAIN MOTHER AND
DAUGHTER

Funeral services were held Sunday at the First Presbyterian Church for Elizabeth Radley and her daughter Martha, who were murdered last Monday night at the Sagebrush Flat Hotel.

The ceremony was attended by numerous friends and by the husband and father of the deceased, Uriah Radley, who accepted the ashes of his wife and daughter following the service.

That was all.

Larry made a copy.

He wondered if Bonnie had attended the funeral.

He thought about the ashes. The two women had been cremated. Not unusual, but interesting. Larry knew plenty of vampire lore. The wide belief was that a vampire's victims would become vampires themselves. Burning their bodies would prevent the women from coming back. Was *that* the reason Uriah had his wife and daughter cremated? Did he have some reason to think they'd been killed by a vampire?

The paper had been vague about the nature of the wounds and murder weapons. More than likely, the cops kept that information to themselves. A common practice. You don't tell the press everything.

Suppose the wounds were bites, the weapons teeth?

The women had died of blood loss.

Uriah, discovering the bodies, certainly saw the wounds. And maybe he noticed that there wasn't much blood on the beds. He might conclude that they'd been murdered by a vampire.

Right, Larry thought. If he's crazy.

But what if he *did* believe a vampire'd killed them? What if, for some reason, he thought the vampire was Bonnie? And he went after her. And he pounded the stake through her heart. And he hid her under the stairs of *his* hotel. And he's still out there, after all these years, living in the hotel and standing watch over the remains of the vampire who murdered his loved ones.

It works, Larry thought. My Christ, it works.

Which doesn't make it true, he told himself.

Flights of fancy were his way of life. He'd built his whole career on daydreams, constructing them into a semblance of reality. You make up an unlikely situation, you make up characters and motives and causal links, and pretty soon the situation takes on a certain kind of sense.

Real life, he knew, didn't work like a book. People acted out of character. Motives were often murky. Chance and coincidence could make a shambles of looking for a neat chain of causes.

Maybe bikers killed Elizabeth and Martha, just as the sheriff speculated. Or maybe a serial killer, passing through. Or maybe Uriah himself.

Whoever killed them, vampires might've been the furthest thing from Uriah's mind when he requested the cremations.

It might be pure coincidence that someone had selected Uriah's hotel as the hiding place for Bonnie's corpse.

On the other hand . . .

Everything fit together so neatly if Uriah blamed Bonnie for the killings and put her out of commission.

Pounded a stake through Bonnie's chest.

The crazy bastard.

How could anyone think that Bonnie was a vampire?

I did, he reminded himself. Just a little bit, maybe. At the start.

But he knew better, now. She was a beautiful, innocent girl, murdered by some deluded human garbage who obviously believed in the most outlandish superstitious nonsense.

Very likely Uriah Radley.

After eating a hamburger at a café down the block, Larry returned to the library. He smiled a greeting to Alice, took the box of microfiche off the circulation desk and returned to the machine.

He resumed his search where he'd left off, at July 24, 1968.

In the July 27 edition he found this:

LOCAL GIRL DISAPPEARS

Foul play is suspected in the disappearance of 18-year-old Sandra Dunlap, daughter of Windy and William Dunlap. The young woman was discovered to be missing from the bedroom of her parents' Crestview Avenue home early this morning.

According to authorities, the front door of the house showed evidence of forced entry, and traces of blood were found on the bedsheets of the missing girl.

Sandra, a recent graduate of Buford High School, was last seen Friday night when she attended a movie with her boyfriend, John Kessler, and two other friends from high school, Biff Tate and Bonnie Saxon. The three youths, interviewed early today by police officials, all indicated that Sandra was dropped off at home shortly before midnight and that she was seen to enter the house without mishap.

Windy and William Dunlap stated they were asleep at the time of their daughter's return from the double-date.

The disappearance is believed to have occurred between midnight Friday and sunrise today.

Anyone who may have noticed unusual activity in the area near the Dunlap residence during that period, or who has any knowledge about the present where-abouts of Sandra Dunlap, is urged to contact the Mulehead Bend Police Department immediately.

The story was accompanied by a small, grainy photograph of the girl. It showed the head and shoulders of a pretty, smiling brunette. She wore a dark sweater. Larry guessed that this was her "senior picture," the same one that probably appeared in the school yearbook.

If he still had the annual . . .

Forget it, he told himself. You got away with cutting out Bonnie's pictures. It's pressing your luck to try the same thing with Sandra. Pressing Lane's luck.

No way.

He went back to the part of the story about Bonnie. She and her friends were actually the last people to see Sandra.

Incredible.

Okay, he thought, maybe not "incredible." It's a small town, only eighty-nine kids in the graduating class. Bonnie was "Spirit Queen," without question one of the most popular girls in her class. It would be strange if she *didn't* know every other kid her age. She was probably close friends with several of them.

Sandra must've been one of her very best friends, though. You don't go double-dating with just anyone.

What about this Biff Tate? Bonnie's boyfriend, obviously. Stupid name. He was probably a football star, or something.

Bonnie was probably making it with the guy.

A goddamn jock. Larry could just hear him bragging in the locker room. "Sure, I slipped it to her. Had her begging for more."

Come off it, he told himself. It's stupid to be worrying about her boyfriend. Kids Bonnie knew were getting nailed. Two down in less than two weeks.

Had to be tough on her.

Yeah, and I bet good ol' Biff was more than eager to comfort her in her grief.

Larry muttered, "Shit," then glanced at Alice across the room. Her back was turned as she shelved books. She didn't react, so he assumed that she hadn't heard him.

He copied the story about Sandra Dunlap and returned to his search of the newspapers.

A brief piece in the July 31 edition indicated that the girl was still among the missing, that her parents feared the worst, that the police were again asking witnesses to come forward with information.

On August 10, 1968, Linda Latham vanished.

The photo showed a cheerful, blond girl with freckles and a cute, uptilted nose. This didn't look like a school picture. She wore a T-shirt, and a ball cap with its bill turned sideways. Larry gazed at the girl's young, innocent face. It saddened him, stifled the excitement he felt about discovering another victim.

TOWN STUNNED BY KIDNAPPING
Linda Latham, 17-year-old daughter of Lynn and

Ronald Latham, was apparently abducted late Friday night while walking home from the house of a friend, Kerry Goodrich.

At approximately midnight, Linda's parents grew concerned about her absence and telephoned the Goodrich residence, only to learn that their daughter had left more than an hour earlier. The walk, a distance of four blocks, should have taken the girl no longer than ten minutes.

Alarmed, her parents searched the area between the two homes. Finding Linda's handbag near the curb approximately a block from the Goodrich house, they promptly called the police.

Though the area was canvassed by authorities, no information about the apparent kidnapping was obtained.

Linda Latham is the second teenage girl to disappear under suspicious circumstances in recent weeks. On July 26, Sandra Dunlap vanished from her home on Crestview Avenue, and her fate remains unknown to date.

Police point out that there is little similarity in the circumstances of the two disappearances. "The M.O.'s are completely different," according to police spokesman Captain Al Taylor. "It would be premature, at this point, to speculate that both crimes were the work of the same perpetrator. In spite of that, we do need to recognize that two teenagers have been abducted over a short period of time. There certainly *is* cause for concern. I would advise parents to keep a close watch on the activities of their adolescent children, particularly females. The youths, themselves, should exercise extreme caution until the perpetrator or perpetrators have been apprehended."

Captain Taylor went on to suggest that teenage girls refrain from going out alone, that they carry whistles in case of an emergency, and that they report any encounters of a suspicious nature.

Authorities are conducting an all-out search for the two missing girls. Anyone with information about either disappearance is requested to contact the police immediately.

Nothing about Martha Radley, Larry realized. Didn't the police see a connection there? Obviously not, or they'd be even more concerned.

One murder, two disappearances. That's three down.

Larry removed the bottom page from his small stack of copies—the list of 1968 graduates from Buford High School. He found the names Dunlap, Sandra and Latham, Linda. The Radley girl wasn't there, of course: she was only sixteen.

But she'd been in the Art Club, and Sandra and Linda had both been Bonnie's classmates.

Bonnie knew all three.

God, she must've been devastated. And scared.

Something like that happens, and you've got to start wondering who will be next.

Maybe you.

He copied the story.

He continued searching. He copied three follow-up stories, none of which provided any new information. The girls were still gone. The police had no suspects.

Bonnie was next.

He found her picture and story on the front page of the *Mulehead Evening Standard*'s August 14 edition.

He stared at the screen with a horrible feeling of loss.

What did you expect? he told himself. You knew she was dead, you've got her body. This shouldn't come as any great blow.

But it was as if part of his mind had held on to a wild

hope that Bonnie's story would have a happy ending, after all. Somehow.

The newspaper crushed that hope.

He moaned as he stared at the photo. He knew it well. It was her senior picture. He had it in his filing cabinet. Reluctantly, he read the story.

BONNIE SAXON VANISHES

Bonnie Saxon, voted Buford High School's "Spirit Queen" during the fall, 1967 homecoming festivities, disappeared during the night from the Usher Avenue home where she lived with her mother, Christine.

The 18-year-old girl was last seen by her mother when she returned home following a date Friday night with her boyfriend, Biff Tate. The next morning, Bonnie was gone. Her bedroom window was found to be broken, and blood was noted on her sheets.

This marks the third disappearance, since late July, of local teenage girls. On July 26, Sandra Dunlap, 18, vanished from her home. Like Bonnie, Sandra was apparently taken during the night from her bedroom. In both cases, there was evidence of forced entry, and blood was found on the bedsheets. The second disappearance occurred on August 10, when Linda Latham, 18, was the victim of an apparent kidnapping while she walked home after visiting a friend.

According to Police Chief Jud Ring, "It looks now as if we have a definite pattern, especially between the Dunlap and Saxon cases. It's reasonable to conclude that all three girls were abducted by the same perpetrator. This is a very nasty situation. We still hope that the girls will be found alive, of course. But we just don't know what has become of them. What we do know is this: there is every reason to believe that such crimes will continue if we fail to apprehend the person responsible for these outrages.

"Our department," he went on, "is conducting a full-scale investigation of the matter. No avenue is being overlooked. I have every confidence that we'll soon have the perpetrator in custody. Until then, however, it's imperative that all our female citizens exercise the utmost caution in their daily affairs."

Bonnie Saxon is a graduate of the Buford High School Class of 1968. In addition to being voted "Spirit Queen," Bonnie was on the honor roll and was active in numerous school activities. She and her mother are members of the First Presbyterian Church, where Bonnie sang in the Youth Choir. This energetic and beautiful young woman is a familiar figure to a great many citizens of our town, and it is hoped that her widely recognized appearance may prove useful in locating her.

Anyone with information about the abduction or present whereabouts of Bonnie Saxon, Linda Latham, or Sandra Dunlap is urged to contact the authorities at once.

She was gone.

Dead.

Whoever wrote the story didn't know it, but somebody had pounded a stake through her chest. Killed her.

Larry knew he should go on, but he didn't have the heart.

He checked his wristwatch. Three o'clock. It was early to quit. If he stopped now, he would need to come back tomorrow.

He didn't care.

He made a copy of the story and shut off the machine.

Twenty-four

When the bell rang, the students began to file out of the classroom. Lane slowly gathered her books from the rack under her seat so it wouldn't be obvious to the others that she was remaining.

No point letting the whole world know she was staying to help. Some of the kids would think she was brown-nosing. Not that I care what they think, she told herself. Still, it seemed wise to keep a low profile.

Jessica stopped in the doorway and looked back at her.

Lane slid her stacked books toward her chest as if preparing to stand.

"You're leaving?" Mr. Kramer asked.

"No, uh-uh. Not if you have something for me."

Nodding, he smiled. "I have a job, if you don't mind a little manual labor."

"No, that'd be fine." She glanced toward the door. Jessica, frowning, turned and walked away.

"Come on up here," Kramer said. He reached into his briefcase but kept his eyes on Lane as she approached.

She hoped she looked all right. Jim had certainly thought so. During the lunch period, he'd snuck his hand under the loose bottom of her blouse several times before she finally lost her temper. "If you don't like it," he'd said, "you shouldn't wear that kind of thing."

The white pullover blouse had a cowl neck, short sleeves, and a hem that reached just to her waist. It wasn't meant to be tucked in. Neither, however, was it meant as an open invitation for Jim to explore the bare areas just out of sight above her belt.

That morning, when Lane chose to wear the blouse and her short denim skirt, she hadn't been thinking about Jim's reaction. Her mind had been on Mr. Kramer. She'd wanted to look good for him. And maybe just a little sexy.

If Kramer appreciated her outfit, he gave no sign.

He turned his attention to his briefcase as she stepped around the back of the table. He pulled out a file folder, turned toward her and opened it. Inside was a stack of eight-by-ten pictures.

"Whitman?" she asked, peering at the upside-down face of the top portrait.

"Very good."

"I used to play 'Authors' a lot when I was a kid."

"How would you like to hang these up? Give the kids something worthwhile to gaze at while they're daydreaming."

"Great," Lane said. "Where do you want them?"

He pointed out a strip of corkboard high on the front wall between the chalkboard and the ceiling. "Think you can manage that? You'd have to stand on the stool, I'm afraid."

"No problem," Lane said.

"Fine. Just fine. I'd give you papers to correct, but all I've got are essays. I really have to do those myself."

"Oh, this'll be okay."

He took a clear plastic box of thumbtacks from his desk drawer and gave it to her along with the folder of pictures.

"Any special order you want them in?" Lane asked.

"Doesn't matter." He brought the stool from the corner of the room.

It was as high as Lane's waist, with metal legs and a disk of wood for a seat. Each room seemed to have just such a stool. Teachers often perched on them, but Mr. Kramer never used his, preferring to sit on the front table when he addressed the class.

He carried it to the far end of the chalkboard. "Maybe I'd better hold something."

Lane handed the pictures and tacks to him. He stood beside her, watching, frowning slightly.

"Don't worry, I'm not planning to fall."

"I'm sure you know what Burns said about the best-laid plans and schemes."

"Promise you'll catch me if they 'gang a-gley'?"

"I'll give it my best."

She stepped onto a rung, planted her other knee on the seat, and braced herself against the chalkboard as she got to her feet.

"You okay up there?"

"Yeah, I think so." She looked down at him and managed to smile. Her position *did* feel precarious. There was little room for her feet and nothing to hold onto. But the corkboard was just in front of her face, so she wouldn't have to stretch for it.

"Try one, see how it goes." He passed the Whitman picture to her. Lane took it in her left hand. She reached her right arm across the front of her body, and Mr. Kramer dropped two tacks into her palm.

She raised the picture and pressed it flat against the corkboard. Holding it in place with one hand, she shoved a tack into its upper right corner.

And knew what her blouse was doing. She knew that she'd made a mistake when she selected it. But she'd thought she would be correcting papers, not climbing onto a stool and leaning forward with both arms extended and Mr. Kramer below her.

The hem was brushing the skin of her back at least an inch above the top of her skirt. Lane couldn't see the front. She didn't have to. She could well imagine the way it must be hanging away from her body. If Mr. Kramer happened to be looking in the right direction, he could probably see all the way up to her bra.

The knowledge gave her a hot, crawly feeling.

She pushed the other tack into place, lowered her arms and looked down at the teacher.

He nodded. "So far, so good," he said, smiling. He gave her a photograph of Mark Twain.

"I can probably manage," Lane said, "if you want to go ahead and correct the papers. Just give me the box of tacks and set the pictures on the chalk tray."

"Sure you don't want me here as a spotter?"

"I think I'll be okay."

He handed the tacks to Lane, then removed the short stack of pictures from the folder and propped them up on the chalk tray. He didn't leave.

The hell with it, Lane thought. No big deal.

She went ahead and lifted Mark Twain up to the cork-board.

"Get him right there next to Walt. Maybe overlap the edges a little. You could use the same tack for both."

He isn't paying attention to me, anyway, she told herself.

Yeah? Don't bet on it.

If he's like most guys, he's probably staring straight up my blouse. Or crouching for a peek at my panties.

She tucked the plastic box under her chin to free her right hand, and pried out the tack at the corner of the Whitman picture.

By now, she thought, Jim would have a hand sliding up my leg.

Mr. Kramer's not Jim, thank God.

Besides, I'm a student. He wouldn't dare touch me, even if he wanted to.

She overlapped the edges of the pictures and pushed in the tack. It held Mark Twain in place while she took the box from under her chin, crouched down, and lifted a por-trait of Charles Dickens off the chalk tray. As she straightened up, she looked around at Mr. Kramer. He nodded with approval.

"Looks as if everything's under control," he said.

"Yeah."

"Just give a whistle if you need me," he told her, and headed for his desk.

He sat down. He bent over a stack of papers and picked up a red pen.

Thank goodness, Lane thought.

She felt strange, though—not just relieved that he no longer stood below her, but a little disappointed, a little abandoned.

Guess he wasn't all that impressed, she thought.

She rammed a tack through the corners of Dickens and Twain.

I didn't *want* him looking up my clothes!

Maybe he didn't even take advantage of the opportunity.

She climbed down from the stool, adjusted its position, and saw Mr. Kramer turn to watch her mount it. "Careful," he said. She smiled and nodded.

And a terrible thought struck her.

What if he thinks I dressed like this to turn him on?

Fire spread over Lane's skin.

He must think I'm a slut.

As she tacked up a picture of Tennyson, beads of sweat slid down her sides.

I did want to look nice for him, she told herself. But I had no idea . . .

She wished to God she had worn jeans and a long-tailed blouse. A blouse she could have tucked in tight.

I would've, she thought. So help me, I would've if I'd had any idea . . .

I'm not a slut.

What if he thinks I did it for grades?

A lot of kids were known to flirt with their teachers in hopes of getting higher marks. Some probably even offered sex. Though Lane didn't know of anyone who'd done that, she supposed it sometimes happened.

I'm already getting an A from him, Lane told herself. He can't think I dressed like this for a better grade.

For that matter, why should he even suspect I wore this stuff for *him?* He probably just thinks I'm just trying to look good for a boyfriend.

Lane began to feel better as the sickening heat of embarrassment subsided.

Sure, she thought. He can't suspect I dressed for him. He's no mind reader.

She continued to put the pictures up, balancing on the stool, bending over for new ones, reaching out, tacking them to the corkboard, frequently climbing down and moving the stool closer to Mr. Kramer's desk.

Often, she glanced at him. Usually, he was busy reading the essays. A few times, however, she found him looking over his shoulder at her. When that happened, he never tried to turn away and pretend he wasn't watching. He never acted guilty. He usually just smiled or nodded, and made a comment: "You're doing a good job," or "Glad it's you and not me up there," or "Don't push yourself if you start getting tired."

Lane finally began to suspect that he didn't care about the way she was dressed.

I might as well be wearing coveralls, she thought.

She wondered if he might be gay.

Give it a break, she told herself. What do you want? He's a teacher.

She stepped down to the floor once again and moved the stool a couple of feet nearer to his desk. Swiveling his chair around, he scanned the high row of pictures. "Terrific," he said. "They add a nice touch to the room, don't you think?"

"Be nicer if they weren't all *dead* guys."

"Well, unfortunately, the literary community doesn't

hold much stock in living writers. You can't be a 'major author' till you're dead."

Lane thought he was wrong about that. Though she felt reluctant to question his views, he usually seemed to enjoy discussions with his students. Besides, if she stopped talking, he would return to the essays.

"Dad says that's a myth," she told him, and climbed onto the stool. She lifted a picture of Hemingway from the chalk tray and raised it to the corkboard. "Most of these guys were enormously successful and famous in their own time." She punched a tack through its corner. "Only a few weren't recognized till after they died. Like Poe, for instance."

Bending down for a picture of Steinbeck, she looked over her shoulder. Mr. Kramer was smiling, nodding his head.

"And Poe was *all* screwed up," she added.

Mr. Kramer laughed. "I suppose he had to be, to write the way he did."

"I don't know." She straightened up and pressed the picture into place. "Dad writes worse stuff than Poe, and he seems fairly normal. I've met scads of horror writers—going to conventions and stuff." She pressed in the tack, then turned carefully atop the stool to look down at Mr. Kramer. "Some are even really good friends of Dad's, guys I've known forever. Almost none of them are weird. In fact, they seem more normal and well-adjusted than most people I've known."

"That's hard to believe."

"I know. You'd think they'd be raving lunatics, wouldn't you?"

"Or at least slightly weird."

"You know what *is* weird? Nearly all of them I know have this incredible sense of humor. They're always cracking me up."

"Strange. Maybe their humor is a reflection of their somewhat off-kilter worldview."

"More than likely." Lane climbed down from the stool,

moved it closer to Mr. Kramer, and mounted it again. As she rose, she lifted a picture of Faulkner from the chalk tray. She pressed it against the corkboard and tacked it into place. Hearing a squeak, she glanced back. Mr. Kramer had turned his swivel chair around. He was looking up at her.

He didn't say anything.

Lane crouched for another picture. As she raised it, she said, "You know how we were talking about dead writers and fame?"

"The myth."

"Right. Well, you want to know something odd? The reverse is actually true. At least nowadays." She tacked the picture of Frost to the cork. "When a writer kicks the bucket, he's screwed."

She heard her teacher laugh. Turning around, she smiled down at him. "Publishers want to *build* a writer. Once he's dead, they don't want to touch him."

More laughter.

"It's true. Unless he's a real biggy. With most guys, they just lose interest. I know about an agent, and one of his best writers died, and he *kept it a secret.* She was a big writer of romances, you know? He stood to lose a fortune. So what he did, he actually got some hack to start writing imitations, and he sold them using the dead writer's name. Do you believe it?"

"Gives a new meaning to 'literary immortality.' "

"Yeah, I'll say."

Lane turned away and took a picture of Sandburg off the tray. Rising, she realized she should have moved the stool. Frost was already some distance to her left. Sandburg would mean a stretch. She supposed she could manage it, though.

Easing herself forward, she braced her right forearm against the chalkboard. She leaned to the left. She reached way out with the picture of Sandburg and pressed it to the wall and the stool flipped.

Lane heard herself gasp, "Oh shit!"

Part of her mind seemed to disconnect, to step back and observe this ridiculous and embarrassing event. She saw herself dropping sideways, arms waving in the air beyond her head, her right leg high as if the overturning stool had thrown it toward the ceiling. Her skirt was up around her hips. Her blouse was halfway up her chest.

Wunnerful wunnerful.

She heard a crash, but it wasn't her. Not yet. Maybe Kramer's chair slamming against his desk.

He coming to the rescue? she wondered. Or just trying to get out of the way.

Coming to the rescue, she realized as one of his hands jammed under her armpit and another clapped the bare skin of her upraised leg, high against her inner thigh. She felt the hands thrust upward. Then she slammed against the floor, grunting at the impact.

The hands went away.

"My God, are you okay?"

Nodding, gasping, Lane rolled onto her back. Mr. Kramer was kneeling over her. His face was red, his eyes wide, his lips twisted in a grimace.

"Guess I'll live," she muttered. She started to sit up.

"Don't." He gently pushed her shoulder. She eased back down. "Don't try to get up. Just rest a minute." He kneaded her shoulder. "That was a nasty fall."

"Thanks for catching me."

"Well, I tried. It happened so fast."

"You broke my fall some."

"Not much."

"I feel like such a dork."

"These things happen." His other hand patted her belly. "I just hope you're all right. You really gave me a scare."

His hand settled there, big and warm against her bare skin just above her belt. "Where do you hurt?" he asked.

"My side, I guess."

He leaned farther over her. His hand slid across her belly to her hip. "Here?"

She nodded. "And my ribs."

"Hope nothing's broken."

"I don't think so."

Lane closed her eyes. Gently, Mr. Kramer rubbed her hipbone and the side of her rump. His other hand brushed her blouse upward. "Pretty red," he murmured. "You'll probably have a whale of a bruise."

"Moby bruise," she said, then sighed as he began to massage the side of her rib cage.

"Tender?" he asked.

"Yeah. A little."

His hand roamed higher, fingers kneading, soothing the soreness.

"Any sharp pain?" he asked.

"No." She moaned when his wrist brushed against the underside of her breast.

"It hurts here?" he asked, pressing her ribs. The wrist moved slightly, rubbing her.

"Just kind of an ache," she murmured.

He massaged her side, his wrist staying against her breast, caressing Lane through the thin fabric of her bra.

Doesn't he realize it's there? she wondered.

She hoped not.

If he realized, he would stop.

His other hand eased lower. Lane's skirt was no longer in its way. She felt him stroking and squeezing the side of her leg, high up.

"Better?" he asked.

"Yeah."

He continued to rub her.

Doesn't he know what he's doing to me? she wondered.

Lightly, he patted her leg. "Okay," he said. "Why don't we get you to your feet now?"

Lane considered telling him she wasn't ready. Any more of this, though, and it might become all too obvious that his touch was doing more than just soothing her injuries.

He took a firm hold on her upper arm, placed his other hand at the base of her neck, and helped her sit up.

Her blouse unrumpled and drifted toward her waist. Her skirt was as high as she had suspected. She glimpsed glossy blue between her legs, and dropped a hand to conceal it.

A little late for modesty, she thought.

Mr. Kramer held onto her arm until she was standing.

"Thanks," she murmured.

When he let go, she looked down and straightened her skirt.

"Are you all right?"

"Yeah. I think so." She raised her eyes. "At least I was wearing clean undies," she added, and smirked, and couldn't believe she'd said that.

"Always should," Mr. Kramer said, a smile spreading across his face. "You never know when you might be in an accident."

"As Mother says."

"As all mothers say."

"Shit," she muttered, and lowered her head.

He put his hands on her shoulders, rubbed them. "I'm just glad you're all right. I feel responsible, you know."

"I'm such a klutz."

"You're a terrific young lady. Don't ever think otherwise."

Lane looked into his eyes. They were clear blue, gentle, knowing. "Thanks."

"I mean it. Now, you'd better run along."

"But I haven't finished putting up the—"

"I'll take care of the rest. If I were you, I'd take a long, hot bath. Really soak. That'll help the soreness."

"I will."

Lane waited until after dinner that night, then went into the bathroom. She still wore her school clothes. She lay down on the floor. There, she hitched up her skirt and blouse so they were just as they'd been after the fall. She arranged her legs to match her earlier position: left leg straight and flat against the carpet; right leg raised a little, bent at the knee, angled outward. Bracing herself up with her elbows, she stared down at herself.

This is how I looked to Mr. Kramer.

Holy cow.

Then she noticed that her right leg had a faint purple hue. The imprint of Mr. Kramer's hand? *That must be where he grabbed me to break my fall,* she realized. It was just below her groin.

"Man," she whispered.

She thought she could still feel his hand there, as if it had left a ghost of itself.

If Jim had grabbed me there . . .

Forget Jim, she told herself.

She got to her feet, stepped in front of the mirror and again lifted her skirt. Her panties were tight and clinging, the blue fabric nearly transparent.

She grimaced at her reflection. Her face was very red.

"He sure got an eyeful," she whispered.

But he never got funny. He acted like a perfect gentleman. That's the difference between a mature, sensitive man like Mr. Kramer and a horny teenager like Jim.

Lane stoppered the tub and ran water for her bath. While the tub filled, she took off her clothes. She returned to the mirror. There were bruises over the jut of her left hipbone and low along the side of her rib cage.

She stared at her left breast. Leaning backward, she studied its underside where Mr. Kramer's wrist had rubbed it through the bra. The skin looked smooth and white.

What did you expect? she asked herself.

But it didn't seem right for there to be no visible evidence of his touch.

Shaking her head, Lane turned to the tub. She crouched and shut off the faucet. Then she climbed over the side.

She settled down into the hot water. She sprawled beneath it, squirming under the fluid caress, and once again arranged her body to match its position on the classroom floor. She closed her eyes.

She remembered the feel of Mr. Kramer's touch. In her mind the teacher stopped massaging her ribs. His hand closed gently over her breast and he sank down onto her and covered her mouth with his. She wrapped her arms around him. She squeezed him hard and sank into the moist heat of his kiss.

Twenty-five

Jessica woke up. Keeping one eye shut, she squinted at her bedside lamp. Then at her alarm clock. Almost three. In the morning?

What is this? she wondered. What's the lamp doing on? She rolled onto her back and sat up.

Kramer, naked, stood with his back to the closed door of her bedroom. His left hand rested against the switch plate. His right hand, down at his side, held a straight razor.

Jessica felt as if her heart had been stomped.

"Aren't you glad to see me?" Kramer asked. He spoke in a normal voice, not a whisper. It was very loud in the stillness.

Jessica struggled for a breath, then whispered, "My folks'll hear you."

"Think so?" he said, speaking even louder than before.

Maybe not, she told herself. Her door was shut. Her parents' room was at the other end of the hallway, and they were sound sleepers.

Kramer let his hand fall away from the light switch. He stepped slowly toward the end of the bed.

Jessica gazed at the razor swinging near his side.

Why did he have that?

He'd warned her that he might come back with a razor. She panted. She couldn't seem to get enough air into her lungs. "I didn't tell," she said. "I didn't . . . tell on you. What do you want?"

He said nothing. A corner of his mouth curled up. He stopped at the foot of the bed. Eyes on Jessica, he reached down with his left hand and dragged the covers toward him.

She didn't move.

The blanket and top sheet slid off her lap, down her legs, and dropped off the end of the mattress. Her short nightgown, rucked up and twisted while she slept, left her bare below the waist.

"Nice," Kramer said. "Now, lie back and relax."

She shook her head. She lifted her left arm and rested its cast against her thigh, her hand blocking the teacher's view.

"That's no way to behave. You'll get low marks for co-operation." He lifted the razor close to his face and shook it in a scolding gesture.

Jessica moved her arm aside. She lay down.

The mattress shook as Kramer crawled onto it. He knelt between her legs. He lifted her nightgown and slit it up the middle until it parted between her breasts. With the end of the blade, he flicked the fabric aside.

"Don't cut me," she whispered. "Please."

"I'm not happy with you, Jessica."

"I didn't tell."

"I know."

She whimpered as cold steel slid down her belly. Raising her head, she saw that it was the blunt side of the blade.

"But you might," Kramer said.

"I won't. Never."

"I saw how you looked at Lane this afternoon. You were thinking about it, weren't you?"

"No."

"Thinking about warning her."

"No. I wouldn't. Why should I care what you do to her? I don't even like the bitch."

He flipped the blade and cut her. A quick, curling slash. It didn't hurt much, but she flinched rigid and sucked in her belly. A red S appeared above her navel. Its curving line thickened. Dribbles spread out from it like tendrils. They blurred as tears filled Jessica's eyes. Her sobbing made them shimmer and wiggle.

"Please!" she gasped.

"Shouldn't have called Lane a bitch."

"I'm *sorry!*"

Kramer hunched down. Braced on his elbows, rump high, he lapped up the spreading blood. With the tip of his tongue he probed the shallow cut. Jessica shuddered as his tongue spread the raw edges.

She crashed her cast against the side of his head, crying out as pain lanced up her arm.

The blow knocked his head sideways.

Twisting, she rammed a knee into his hip.

He toppled, and the edge of the bed wasn't there to catch him. He dropped out of sight, slammed against the floor.

Jessica rolled, grabbed the side of the mattress and looked down at him. He was flat on his back, an upraised knee resting against the box springs, his other leg straight out, one arm against his side, the other flung out limp against the carpet, its hand open, the razor a few inches beyond his fingertips. His jaw drooped. His open eyes were rolled upward as if gazing at something beneath his upper lids.

He's out, she thought.

She knew out when she saw it; she'd seen enough boxing matches with Riley.

Gasping for air, trembling and nauseous, she swung her legs down. She rose from the bed and stepped over him. With one foot she pinned his right wrist to the carpet. She crouched and picked up the razor. Once she had it, she ground her heel against his wrist.

He groaned.

Coming to! Jessica's heart lurched. Her stomach seemed to shrink and go cold.

She stepped off his wrist, turned around and looked down at him. His eyes were squeezed shut, his teeth bared.

She had to do something fast!

She took a deep breath, about to cry out *"Dad!"* But she stopped herself.

Kramer would talk. If he lived, he'd talk. Everyone would find out she'd been sleeping with him. Everyone. Her folks, all the kids at school, Riley.

Can't let him talk.

A chill swept up Jessica's body. Her skin prickled with goose bumps.

Nobody'll blame me. It's self-defense. He broke into the house and attacked me.

She looked down at her wound. Blood still spilled from the S-shaped slice. The skin below it was slicked with shiny red. Her pubic hair was matted and drops trickled down her thighs.

That's my proof, she thought. He cut me. He came to rape and murder me. I had to defend myself.

Kramer opened his eyes.

Jessica rushed to his side and rammed her foot down, driving her heel into his belly. Breath whooshed out of him. His eyes bugged. He half sat up. She dropped onto him, knees landing on his chest and stomach. As his back struck the floor, she swept the razor down at his throat.

His left arm shot up faster than she could imagine. It met her descending forearm just above the wrist. Pain streaked to her shoulder. The razor flew from her tingling fingers.

Kramer's other hand punched her in the spine. As she jerked rigid, he grabbed her hair. He yanked it and bucked beneath her knees, hurling Jessica backward. She crashed against the floor. The impact jolted her, knocked her breathless.

Kramer had one of her legs. He raised it, dragged her by it, propped it high.

Jessica lifted her head and saw her right leg stretched upward, heel on the edge of her mattress. Before she could move, Kramer stomped her knee. As if her leg were a branch. She heard the sharp crack, watched her leg cave in beneath his foot, felt an explosion of agony that turned her vision bright red, then black.

When she woke up, she was on her bed. Kramer was on top of her, in her, grunting and thrusting. Her right leg felt as if it were burning from the inside, as if her bones were ablaze. The pain was so fierce that Kramer's ramming penis seemed incidental. She just wished he would get it over with and stop bouncing on her leg.

When she tried to move her outstretched arms, she realized they were tied at the wrists. Probably to her bedposts.

No chance of fighting him.

At last Kramer finished.

But she knew he wasn't done.

It didn't seem to matter much. She knew it ought to matter, she ought to care. But her mind was fuzzy, couldn't seem to focus on anything except the pain.

The pain couldn't get any worse.

But it did.

It got a lot worse when he started with the razor. So bad that she screamed, and wondered why she hadn't screamed earlier. Dad would hear it. Dad would save her.

Kramer stuffed a rag into her mouth.

He kept on cutting.

Where's Dad?

She passed out.

When she came to, Kramer was hunched over her, lick-

ing and sucking on her wounds. He raised his face and
gazed at her. Except for his eyes, his face was smeared
with blood. Even his teeth were red.

He pulled the rag from Jessica's mouth. He tossed it
aside, dropped flat and squirmed up her body. His penis
pushed into her. His tongue filled her mouth. He rode her
hard as if trying to pound her through the mattress.

Later she saw him standing beside the bed. He was
clean. He was dressed. He had a bundle of newspapers
under one arm. He crouched out of sight.

She heard the crackle of papers being crumpled.

She heard the snick of a match.

Kramer stood over her.

"Sleep tight," he said. "Don't let the bedbugs bite."

On his way out, he turned off the light.

But the room wasn't dark for long.

Twenty-six

Bonnie came to him. She stepped silently toward his bed. She looked lovely, glorious, her blond hair floating around her face. She wore the pleated blue skirt and golden sweater of her songleader costume, but her feet were bare.

Stopping beside Larry's bed, she gazed at him with solemn eyes. "I've been waiting for you," she said, her voice as soft as a caress. "Why haven't you come to me?"

"I . . . I don't know. I've *wanted* to, but . . ."

"Don't you know that I love you?"

Her words quickened Larry's heart.

"You do?" he asked.

"Of course. Why wouldn't I?"

"Why *would* you?" he asked. "We don't even know each other."

A sweet smile lifted the corners of her mouth. "We know each other with our hearts. I love you so much, Larry. And you love me, don't you?"

"Yes," he said, and felt a hot rush of joy. "Yes, I love you."

Then a thought came to him that seemed to crush his heart.

"But you're dead, Bonnie."

Her laugh was a quiet rush of breath. "Don't be silly. Do I look dead?"

"You look . . . so beautiful."

Bonnie stepped closer. She bent over him, her hair drifting down until its tresses brushed against Larry's cheeks. Then her lips met his. They were soft, warm, moist. They parted, and he felt her breath enter his mouth.

He lifted his arms out from under the covers. He placed his hands on Bonnie's sides, caressed her through the sweater, felt the heat of her flesh, the gentle curves of her ribs.

She eased her lips away. "Do I feel dead?"

"You sure don't," he murmured through the tightness in his throat. "You feel wonderful."

"I've longed so much for you, Larry."

"I've longed for you, too."

He slipped his hands under the bottom of her sweater. A tremor swept through him as he touched the velvety skin above her hips.

Then he remembered something else, and again his joy sank into anguish. Though he ached for her, he pulled his hands out from under the sweater and let them drop to the mattress. "I'm married, Bonnie."

"Do you love her?"

He wanted to say no. But he couldn't. "Yes," he said. "I'm sorry. God, I'm sorry. I love Jean, but I love you, too."

"That's all right," she whispered, her warm breath touching his lips. "You can have us both."

"I don't think Jean would like that."

"She'll never know. I promise. It'll be our secret."

Larry felt the covers glide down his body, felt the cool morning air chill his skin. Bonnie kissed the side of his neck. She kissed his shoulder, his chest.

"No," he whispered.

"You don't mean that, darling." Her soft lips pressed his nipple.

He moaned with an agony of desire and loss.

"It wouldn't be right," he said.

"Love is always right."

"I don't know."

"Yes," she whispered. "Yes, my love." She crawled onto him. She straddled him, upright on her knees, her light cotton skirt draping him and keeping out the morning chill. The heat of their bodies seemed to mingle in the air beneath it. Larry knew, somehow, that she wore no panties. He ached for her to sink down, to impale herself, to let him plunge high up into her slick, hugging warmth.

But she didn't. Not yet.

Smiling down at him, she drew her sweater up. He watched it rise slowly, unveiling her sleek belly, the rise of her rib cage, her breasts. They were twin, creamy mounds with pink nipples standing erect. They lifted slightly as she pulled the sweater up past her face. Keeping her arms high, she slipped out of the sleeves. She tossed the sweater to the floor.

Larry raised his hands to her breasts. Lightly, he caressed them. He thought that he had never touched anything so fine.

Smiling down at him, Bonnie guided one of his hands to the smooth valley between her breasts. She moved it up and down, stroking herself with his fingertips. "Not even a scar," she whispered.

He remembered the stake.

"Oh," he said. "That's right."

"I'm as good as new. And I'm yours. I'm yours forever."

She began to ease herself down.

Larry groaned.

This is wrong, he thought. I can't do this. Even if Jean never finds out . . .

But Bonnie was moving slowly lower, lower. He squeezed her breasts. Lower. He felt as if his penis were being sucked toward her dark, waiting center.

The alarm clock blared.

Larry's eyes flew open.

Bonnie was gone.

A dream. It had only been a dream, and the alarm had cheated him out of its best moments. His chest ached. He felt as if he might weep.

But he felt lucky, too. A few more seconds and there would've been a mess.

He was sprawled on his back, covered only by a sheet. The sheet jutted up like a tent over his groin.

If Bonnie had slid down onto him . . .

He rolled onto his side. Jean was braced on one elbow, her back to him. As the alarm went silent, she flopped faceup and closed her eyes.

Larry reached out and put a hand on her belly. Her skin felt hot through the thin fabric of her nightgown. Her head turned toward him. Her eyes opened a bit and she made a lazy smile. "Morning, fella," she whispered.

He said, "Mmmm," and moved his hand up the slick nightgown to her breast. Not like Bonnie's. No fire coursed through him when he touched it. But Jean's breast was soft and warm and familiar, and he felt a fresh stir of arousal as her nipple rose stiff against his palm. He brushed the strap off her shoulder and slipped his hand inside the loose pocket of fabric. Jean moaned. She squirmed as he caressed her. Then she rolled toward him.

"We're sure feeling our oats this morning," she murmured.

"Yeah."

Her fingers curled around his erection. "You'd better shut the door. Lane'll be getting up any minute."

On his way back from shutting the door, he watched Jean kick the sheet down to the end of the bed and pull her nightgown up. When it covered her face, Larry's mind flashed an image of Bonnie taking off the songleader sweater.

Their bodies looked very much alike.

Don't think about Bonnie, he told himself. That was just a dream.

And it's crummy to think about her. It's like cheating, like adultery.

But he couldn't stop.

He didn't want to stop.

He closed his eyes as he made love with Jean, and the woman under him ceased to be his wife. She was Bonnie, the Bonnie of the yearbook photos, the Bonnie of his dream: eighteen, beautiful, innocent, eager and gasping and writhing with lust, ramming up against him to meet his thrusts. His Bonnie. His Spirit Queen.

He seemed to explode. He flooded her.

When they were done, she hooked her legs around Larry as if to keep him inside forever. She hugged him hard. He opened his eyes.

Jean gazed up at him, looking haggard and happy.

He kissed her mouth.

He felt like a total shit.

"Something wrong?" she asked.

He shook his head. "Just that I've gotta go back to the library today. I hate wasting time with research."

"Why don't I fix you a nice big breakfast before you go?"

"Great."

Lane smelled frying bacon as she struggled into her jeans.

They're having breakfast? she wondered. What's the big occasion?

She left the zipper down to give herself breathing room, sat on the edge of the bed and pulled on the new, blue denim boots she'd bought after school yesterday.

Standing up, she admired the way they looked with her white jeans.

Too bad I didn't wear this stuff yesterday, she thought.

A blush spread up her skin as she remembered standing on the stool in her short skirt and loose blouse, Mr. Kramer standing below her, and the disarray of her clothes after the fall. Then she remembered his touch. She still felt warm, but her embarrassment turned to pleasure.

Known he'd play doctor, she thought, I would've fallen sooner.

Lane smiled and shook her head at herself as she stepped past the closet mirror.

She took a bright blue and yellow plaid blouse off its hanger, stepped back in front of the mirror and started to button it.

And stopped.

What if I take off my bra?

The idea made her stomach flutter.

Don't be a dork, she thought. Nobody'll even realize except Jim, and he'll be wanting to paw me. Mr. Kramer probably wouldn't even notice the difference.

Mr. Kramer doesn't have anything to do with it, she told herself. It'd feel good, that's all.

Besides, my ribs are sore.

Good enough reason.

She took off her blouse and checked herself in the mirror. Sure enough, the side panel of the bra was pressing against her bruised ribs.

She reached back, unclasped the bra and pulled it off. Holding it between her knees, she slipped into her blouse again. She buttoned it, tucked it in, and fastened her jeans.

She smiled at herself.

Aren't you the daring one?

The soft fabric, taut against her breasts, felt very good.

Should do this all the time, she thought.

No way. With most of her blouses, it would show. But this one had dark, bright colors, and a pocket over each breast. With the double thickness of the fabric there, it was hardly even noticeable that her nipples were erect.

Nobody'll know the difference, she thought. Just me.

It sure does feel good.

She turned in a circle once for a final check, then returned her bra to the dresser drawer. Grabbing her handbag, she headed down the hallway.

What if Mom and Dad notice?

They won't. Ease up.

The aromas of bacon and coffee made her mouth water as she entered the kitchen. Her parents, still in their robes, were seated at the table, bacon and fried eggs on their plates. "What's with breakfast?" she asked. "This doesn't *feel* like Sunday."

They both looked at her. Neither seemed interested in her chest.

"I'll be spending the day at the public library," Dad said. "Mom figured she oughta fill me up."

"Yeah, I'd hate for him to perish among the tomes."

Stepping up beside her father, Lane said, "You could sustain yourself with bookworms."

"Come on, I'm eating."

"Mind?" she asked, and reached for a strip of bacon on his plate.

He jabbed his fork at her hand. He stopped just short of poking her.

"I wish you wouldn't fool around like that," Mom complained. "You might slip."

"I might indeed," he said.

Lane took the bacon and bit it in half.

"There goes my nourishment."

"Hey, I'm a growing girl."

"I could certainly start making breakfasts for you," Mom said. "Just say the word."

"The word is 'yuck.' Who can stomach food at this ungodly hour?"

"You seem to be stomaching my bacon all right," Dad said.

"Gotta go." She bent down and kissed his cheek. He swatted her rump. She hurried around the table, kissed her mother, then grabbed her lunch bag out of the refrigerator and hurried from the kitchen. "See you guys later. I'll probably be late again."

"Have a good day, dear," Mom called after her.

From Dad, "Have fun."

"I'm going to *school,* guys," she called from the living room. She checked her book bag, dropped her lunch inside, then took the car keys from her purse and rushed outside.

The sun felt warm on her shoulders. The mild breeze stirred her hair. A gorgeous day.

The back of the car seat was cool through her blouse, reminding Lane of the missing straps. As she waited for the engine to warm up, she squirmed against the upholstery, savoring how it felt against her back.

Nice.

She cranked her window down and eased slowly out of the driveway.

She headed for Betty's place. On the radio Anne Murray was singing "Snowbird." Lane joined in. She swung her arm onto the windowsill and felt the blouse pull snug against her left breast.

Very nice.

Steering with one hand, she swung the car around a corner.

"Snowbird" ended.

A jingle came on signaling the start of a news break.

"This is Belinda Bernard with the top local news stories of the hour."

"Top of the morning, Belinda," Lane said.

". . . died in a fire early this morning in their Cactus Drive home."

Lane glanced at the radio. Cactus Drive? Died in a fire?

"The deceased were identified as Jerry and Roberta Patterson and their seventeen-year-old daughter Jessica."

"My God," Lane muttered.

"Flames were first noted by neighbors at approximately four-thirty A.M. Firemen arriving at the scene were unable to enter the house to attempt any rescue. Due to the heavy conflagration, however, it's believed that the family expired from smoke inhalation some time prior to the arrival of the fire department. This was confirmed later, when the bodies of the three family members were found in the rubble, still in their beds. The cause of the fire is under investigation, but it is believed that it started in the bedroom of the daughter, Jessica."

Smoking in bed? Lane wondered.

"The Board of Education met last night—"

She turned off the radio.

She felt cold and numb inside.

Jessica dead.

The girl'd been a royal pain, but God! Dead.

How could something like that happen?

Jessica smoked like a chimney. Spent half her life in the girl's john, puffing away. She must've fallen asleep with a cigarette.

Didn't they have a smoke alarm?

Lane rounded a corner. Betty was waiting beside the street. Lane stopped the car, stretched across the passenger seat and unlocked the door.

"Did you hear?" Betty asked, swinging the door open.

"Yeah."

"Holy smoke!" She hurled her book bag into the rear and dropped onto the seat. The car shook. "I knew that bimbo'd come to a bad end." She slammed the door.

"She's dead," Lane muttered.

"Well Jesus, I guess *so*."

Lane stepped on the gas. "She didn't deserve that."

"Smoking in bed, it'll get you every time."

"God, I can't believe it."

"I can. Boy, I sure can. Good riddance to bad rubbish.

Know what happened yesterday? I went to take a leak after third period, and there she was, sitting on a john with the door wide open, sucking on a butt. I go, 'Those things'll give you cancer, you know.' And she gives me this look." Betty demonstrated, wrinkling her nose and curling up her lip. "And she goes, 'Fuck you and the horse you rode in on, lardass.' So like I can't say I feel any great amount of sympathy, you know? She did it to herself."

"And her parents."

"Yeah. Too bad Riley Benson wasn't sleeping over. That piece of greasy-haired shit would be improved considerably by a good dose of smoke inhalation. Know what I mean?"

Lane nodded. It seemed wrong, knocking Jessica and Riley. But she didn't feel like defending them. They *were* creeps.

She wondered if Riley might actually have been in love with Jessica.

Hard to imagine him loving anyone.

But maybe he did.

"That babe did have some rotten luck," Betty went on. "First she gets herself creamed, next thing you know she's a crispy critter."

Lane turned the radio on, volume high. Willie Nelson and Ray Charles were singing "Seven Spanish Angels."

"A hint? A subtle but effective hint?"

"I just don't think we should be bad-mouthing her."

Ahead, Henry waved from his perch on the boulder in front of his house. He hopped down and picked up his briefcase. "Salutations, merry-makers," he said, as Lane stopped the car.

Betty climbed out. She held the seat back forward while Henry scrambled in behind it. Following him, she pulled the door shut.

Lane glanced back at them. Betty had an eager look in her eyes. "You haven't heard," she said.

"Heard what?" Henry asked.

Lane started driving.

"Jessica got toasted last night."

"Huh?"

"Burnt, charbroiled, cooked, incinerated."

"You mean she's dead?" He sounded perplexed.

"Dead dead dead. She bought the farm. She bit the weenie. Dead."

"Holy shit," Henry whispered.

"It would appear that Miss Congeniality fell asleep smoking a cigarette."

"We're talking about Jessica *Patterson?*"

"Who else, numbnuts?"

"Holy shit," he said again. His hand clamped over the corner of Lane's seat back. "Is she shitting me?"

"No," Lane said. "It's true. Jessica and her parents were killed in a fire last night."

"Oh, man."

"Good riddance," Betty said.

"Hey, cut it out."

"Oh, and like she's suddenly a saint now that she's cooked?"

On the radio, Belinda Bernard's voice said, "We now have an update on the fire that rushed through the home of . . ."

"It just isn't . . ." Henry began.

"Quiet," Lane said. "News."

They went silent.

". . . are now indicating that a preliminary examination of the charred remains has revealed that all three members of the Patterson family sustained massive, possibly fatal injuries, prior to the fire. Details are still sketchy, but it appears that an intruder may have slain the trio, after which the fire was deliberately set in order to destroy evidence of the crimes. We also have word that a youth seen entering the house earlier last night has been taken into

custody for questioning. The identity of the underaged suspect has not been disclosed."

"Benson," Betty said. "Betcha."

"We now return you to . . ."

"Holy shit," Henry muttered. "They were *murdered.*"

"I bet it *was* Benson. Wouldn't put anything past that
slime-bag."

"This is awful," Lane murmured.

"Speak for yourself."

"Cool it," Henry said. "It's not funny."

"Maybe not funny, but . . . somehow, deeply satisfy-
ing."

Twenty-seven

Alone as he drove to the public library, Larry at last had time to himself, time to ponder what he'd done that morning and try to relieve himself of the shame.

He'd betrayed Jean.

Not really, he thought. It wasn't that big a deal. You had a little fantasy, that's all.

You really wanted Bonnie.

Jean didn't know that. She thought it was great.

The girl's dead, for godsake.

I must be nuts, having a dream like that.

Hell, it's perfectly natural. I've been *studying* the poor kid—looking at pictures of her, reading about her—*I've got her in the garage!* Who wouldn't start dreaming? I ought to just be glad it wasn't a nightmare. What if she'd paid her visit the way she looks now!

Maybe better if she had. Might have scared the shit out of me, but at least I wouldn't have ended up with a hard-on and all this damn guilt.

Take it easy, he told himself. It was your subconscious. You can't control your subconscious.

Bullshit. It was a wish fulfillment dream. I *wanted* her to come to my bed. And it wasn't my subconscious that made me take out my lust on . . .

The radio news interrupted his thoughts.

A family of three murdered here in Mulehead Bend. Their house set on fire.

One of them, a seventeen-year-old girl.

He wondered if Lane knew the girl. The name didn't sound familiar, but she must've been a senior at Buford High. Lane almost had to know her.

They couldn't have been very good friends, he thought, or I would've heard the name before. Jessica. No. It didn't ring any bells.

Even if they're just acquaintances, it'll be a shock to Lane. A girl in her own class murdered.

Isn't *anywhere* safe?

Of course not. What are you, an idiot?

You know damn well Mulehead Bend hasn't been exactly a haven. Bonnie, Linda, and Sandra are pretty good indications of that. And don't forget Martha Radley. She was over in Sagebrush Flat, but that's right next door.

All high school girls.

Jessica, too.

Larry felt a small tremor of excitement in his belly as he wondered if there might be a connection between Jessica and the others from so long ago.

Didn't seem likely.

What if we triggered something? What if taking Bonnie's corpse . . . ?

That's ridiculous.

Besides, the radio'd said that a young man had been taken into custody. More than likely, this was some kind of a lovers' quarrel. Most murders come down to that, or an argument between friends, or robbery.

Maybe this Jessica jilted a guy and he flipped out.

Nailed her parents, too.

In a way, he supposed, that was fortunate. Better they should be dead. Easier on them.

If someone ever did that to Lane, *I'd* rather be killed on the spot than . . .

No, I'd want to kill the bastard first. Cut him up *real* slowly. Make him feel it. Make him . . .

Stop it!

Larry shook his head sharply, trying to jar apart the idea of Lane being killed.

It won't happen! It can't happen!

It could.

Christ! Why do I do this to myself? She's fine. We're *all* fine. Forget it.

He swung into the library's parking lot, shut off the engine and slumped back against his seat. He felt as if he were suffocating. He took deep breaths, trying to calm himself. The armpits of his shirt felt sodden. He wiped his sweaty hands on his pants.

He sighed.

"Me and my damn imagination," he muttered.

Didn't have that, he thought, wouldn't be an infamous and semi-successful author of horror tales.

Might be happier, though.

He sighed once more, then climbed from the car and headed for the library entrance.

Alice smiled a greeting at him from behind the circulation desk.

"Morning, Alice," he said. "Back for another look at those 'sixty-eight *Standards*."

"Oh, I think that can be arranged."

She vanished into her office and returned with the box of microfiche.

After thanking her, Larry settled down in front of the reader-printer. He searched through the box until he found the fiche labeled *Mulehead Evening Standard,* August 15, 1968—the day after the story of Bonnie's disappearance. He slipped the plastic card out of its envelope, inserted it into the viewer, and brought the newspaper's front page onto the screen.

Pictures of the three missing girls.

The headline read, URIAH RADLEY SOUGHT IN DISAPPEARANCES OF MULEHEAD TEENS.

"Oh, man," Larry muttered. He'd expected follow-up stories, but nothing like this.

Uriah Radley, whose wife and 16-year-old daughter were mysteriously slain at the Sagebrush Flat Hotel on July 15, is being sought by authorities in connection with the recent disappearances of three Mulehead Bend teenagers.

This startling development was revealed early today by Police Chief Jud Ring, who stated that a witness has identified the former hotel proprietor as the man he saw sitting in a pickup truck near the residence of Bonnie Saxon shortly before the girl vanished.

An attempt to apprehend Uriah Radley ended in failure early this morning when a party of Mulehead Bend police officers, together with County Sheriff's deputies, raided the Sagebrush Flat Hotel but failed to locate the suspect.

It is believed at this time that Uriah Radley has fled the immediate area. A bulletin for his arrest has been issued throughout California, Nevada, and Arizona.

Bonnie Saxon, 18, former "Spirit Queen" of Buford High School, disappeared from her Usher Avenue home on Friday night. The broken window of her bedroom indicated forced entry, and blood was found on her bed. She was the most recent of three local girls to vanish under mysterious circumstances.

On August 10, Linda Latham was abducted while walking home from a friend's house. Prior to that, on July 26, Sandra Dunlap vanished from her home under circumstances nearly identical to those surrounding the disappearance of the Saxon girl.

The information that Uriah Radley had been seen near the Saxon residence Friday night is considered to be a major break in the matter of the three abductions.

"We're very interested in having a chat with Mr. Radley," commented Chief Ring. "He may or may not have committed the crimes, but we'd certainly like to find out what he was doing in front of the Saxon place at that hour."

Authorities have speculated that all three teens were the victims of the same perpetrator. It is now believed that the apprehension of Uriah Radley may lead to information regarding their fates and present whereabouts.

While the suspect has so far eluded the law, police and deputies are carrying out an exhaustive search of Sagebrush Flat in hopes of locating Radley and/or the missing teens.

A sidebar story told of Christine Saxon, Bonnie's widowed mother, issuing a "tearful plea" over a local television station. In a "choked voice" she begged the kidnapper to release her daughter unharmed. Reading it, Larry's throat tightened.

God, he thought. The poor woman.

The story pointed out that her husband had died in a car accident. Now, she'd lost her only daughter.

He wondered what had become of her. She would probably be in her sixties now, if she was still alive.

Check the phone book?

What would I tell her? I've found your girl's body?

I can't do that. No way.

He knew it would probably be a consolation for the woman to learn, at last, what had happened to Bonnie. She would want to give her a proper burial.

She'll find out, one way or another, when the book comes out.

Hell, she might be dead.

Larry hoped so, then felt guilty for wishing such a thing, then told himself that the woman was probably better off dead, at peace, spared from her endless grief.

But maybe she's still alive, he thought, clinging to the fragile hope that she might someday be reunited with her daughter.

The book will destroy her.

Worry about it later, he told himself. Who knows, she *might* be dead. Or she might be somewhere out of touch and never hear about the book. For that matter, the book might never even be published. What's the point in stewing about her now?

Trying to forget about her, Larry copied the two stories. He put away the microfiche and slipped the next day's *Standard* into the machine.

BIZARRE FINDINGS AT
SAGEBRUSH FLAT HOTEL

Though yesterday's search of Sagebrush Flat failed to locate either Uriah Radley or any clues as to the whereabouts of the three Mulehead teens who disappeared in recent weeks, authorities have revealed the discovery of several strange items in a hotel room which apparently served as the suspect's residence.

The door and windows of the second-floor room were found to be decorated with strands of garlic cloves. In addition, no fewer than four crucifixes were said to be in evidence, though it is believed that the Radleys were of the Presbyterian faith, and not Roman Catholics.

By far the most startling discovery, however, was the presence of a hammer and half a dozen shafts of wood which had been whittled to sharp points.

Commented Chief Ring, "I saw enough movies when I was a kid to know this looks like a man who was in the business of killing vampires. I realize it sounds crazy, but why else would a fellow surround himself with garlic and crucifixes, not to mention making himself a batch of wooden stakes? Uriah always was a strange sort. It could be that the loss of his wife and kid unhinged him completely."

The chief went on to speculate that Uriah Radley may have believed vampires were responsible for the slaying of his family. "Somehow, he just might've gotten it into his head that Sandra Dunlap, Linda Latham, and Bonnie Saxon were the guilty ones and that they were vampires. We're operating on that assumption, right now, in our search for the girls."

Asked about the prospects of finding the three teens alive, Chief Ring responded, "I can only say that we'll continue searching and hope for the best."

Larry sat back in his chair and stared at the screen.

My God, he thought, I was right!

He remembered his own speculations, yesterday, after reading about the cremations of Uriah's wife and daughter. He'd wondered, then, if the crazy bastard had vampires on his mind when he ordered the bodies burnt. The possibility had seemed remote.

But the guy had garlic, crucifixes, and stakes in his room.

He *did* go after the girls thinking they were the vampires who murdered his family.

Incredible!

Larry frowned, wondering why he hadn't heard of all this before. After what was found in Uriah's room, the news media should've gone wild. You'd think there would've been nationwide coverage.

Probably did get a lot of attention in rags like *The National Inquirer,* along with the usual array of stories on UFO visits, disemboweled cattle, men giving birth, that kind of thing.

The legitimate media may have covered it in some small

way, but Larry couldn't recall anything about the situation. There *were* bigger stories in the summer of 1968: the assassination of Robert Kennedy; the capture of James Earl Ray for the April shooting of Martin Luther King; rioting in the streets because of Vietnam and the King assassination. Hardly surprising if little or no attention was paid to a crazy man running amok in a desert town and kidnapping three teenagers he thought were vampires. Especially if the bodies were never found, if Uriah never got picked up.

Larry copied the story, then continued his search.

A small article in the August 17 issue of the *Standard* indicated that a thorough search of Sagebrush Flat and "its environs" had failed to turn up the missing girls. Uriah Radley was still at large.

A piece in the August 22 issue indicated that there were no new developments in the matter.

On Sunday, September 1, a service was held at the First Presbyterian Church for Sandra Dunlap, Linda Latham, and Bonnie Saxon. Families and friends of the missing girls were present. The girls were remembered. Prayers were offered for their safe return and for the comfort of their loved ones during this terrible ordeal.

Larry noted that the service wasn't called a "memorial." The girls were "remembered," not "eulogized." Prayers were said for their return.

He supposed they all knew the poor kids would never be seen again, but they were still clutching onto the small, frail shadow of a hope.

Larry copied the story, swept the other pages across the screen, found nothing of interest, and went on to the next fiche in the box. He scanned one after another, but finally came to the end of September without finding more stories about Uriah or the missing girls.

Neither was there news of any further disappearances. The series had ended with Bonnie. It came as no surprise. After that, Uriah had fled the area.

He'd been gone by the time the cops arrived at Sage-brush Flat. He must've known he'd been recognized while he waited in front of Bonnie's house.

Larry guessed he had taken her back to the hotel and hidden her body under the staircase before striking out for parts unknown. But what about Sandra and Linda? He wouldn't have been in such a hurry with them. Maybe he took their staked bodies out into the desert and buried them in unmarked graves.

On the other hand, maybe he hid them in town the same as Bonnie. All those abandoned buildings. He might've boarded them inside walls or under floors.

I wonder if we could find *them,* Larry thought.

The cops didn't have any luck. Hell, though, they weren't able to find Bonnie, and she was right under their noses when they searched the hotel.

Under their noses.

Well, the area under the stairs was enclosed. Hot and dry. She didn't decompose so much as she mummified: that was obvious from looking at her. So maybe there wasn't much to smell.

Larry remembered the smell under the staircase. Dry, dusty, a little bit like the odor of old books with their pages turning brown.

And the aromas from his dream came back to Larry. There was the cozy wool odor of her sweater. Her hair, drifting against his face, had smelled like a fresh morning breeze. Her skin had a faint cinnamon scent. Her breath had been like mint, as if she'd recently brushed her teeth.

Larry leaned back in his chair. He closed his eyes. He could almost smell Bonnie now.

You didn't smell a thing, he told himself. It was all a figment of your imagination.

So real, though.

So real that the memory of it made him long for her.

Had she smelled that way, he wondered, when she was alive?

Would she smell that way if she *came back to life?*

She's not a vampire, Larry told himself. But just suppose she is. Just suppose I pull out the stake and she really is a vampire. Would she be just the same as the Bonnie who came to me this morning?

Would she smell the same? Look the same?

Would she *act* the same?

Would she love me?

Twenty-eight

With a minute to spare before the start of sixth period, Lane entered the classroom. About half the seats were still vacant. Including Benson's. Including Jessica's.

Walking toward her desk, Lane gazed at Jessica's empty seat.

The girl would never sit there again.

The idea of that seemed black and vast, and Lane felt a hot sick feeling in the pit of her stomach. She sat down and slumped forward, elbows on her desktop, hands on her cheeks, eyes straightforward.

Mr. Kramer, she saw, had finished tacking the author pictures to the corkboard. She'd fallen while reaching out with Sandburg, whose calm and solemn face, white hair draping one eye, was now in place next to Frost. After Sandburg, Mr. Kramer had put up T.S. Eliot, F. Scott Fitzgerald, and Thomas Wolfe.

I only had four to go, she thought.

The fall had seemed like such a major deal: her clumsiness in letting it happen, her embarrassment at the way so much of her body was revealed to Mr. Kramer, the thrill she felt when he touched her. Now none of that mattered very much. Jessica's death seemed to shrink the importance of everything.

She'd hardly known the girl. She hadn't even liked her.

But ever since hearing the news of the murder, Lane had felt small and insignificant—as if her own life were nothing more than a performance. She was acting in her own stupid little play. And while she dwelled on her petty problems and hopes and desires, safe on her tiny stage, *real* things were happening in a real world nearby. A frightful, alien place full of darkness and violent death.

She didn't like the feeling, not at all. It made everything she did seem so trivial. Even worse was the nagging worry that somehow, sometime, she might *herself* be dragged into the same real world where Jessica and so many other people—everyone, maybe, sooner or later—got crushed.

It scared the hell out of her.

All day, whenever she was reminded of Jessica, Lane had broken into a sweat. Stopping in the rest room on her way to sixth period, she'd sniffed her armpits. They'd smelled okay, thanks to her deodorant, but her blouse was damp under there. Right now it felt sodden. Perspiration was sliding down her sides, tickling slightly. With no bra to soak up the droplets, they kept going until they were absorbed by her blouse just above her belt.

She wished, again, that she'd worn her bra to school. Not because of the sweat. Because of Jessica. Because leaving it at home seemed like part of her own little drama, childish and coy in light of the real world's horrible intrusion.

Also, she would've liked the security of it. Earlier she'd savored the loose, free feelings. But after hearing about Jessica, she'd stopped feeling free. Just vulnerable.

The bell rang, startling her.

She sat up straight as Mr. Kramer entered the room. He put down his briefcase, took out a small brown book, then stepped to the front of the table. He sat on its edge, resting the book on his thigh. The room fell silent. He scanned the rows. His face looked grim, a little haggard.

"I'm sure you're all aware, by now, of the tragedy that occurred last night. Everyone's talking about it. I imagine some of your other teachers have spoken to you about the situation."

Pressing his lips together, he shook his head. He frowned at the empty desk.

"Jessica was my student. She was your classmate. Obviously, her death is a shock to all of us, and we'll miss her."

He looked up from her desk. His eyes briefly met Lane's, then turned away and roamed from face to face.

"I don't have any magic words," he said, "to ease the grief we share. But I'm a teacher, and there is a lesson to be learned from this. The Bible tells us that, in the midst of life, we are in death. But the reverse is also true. 'In the midst of death, we are in life.' We need to keep that in mind. Life is a precious gift. We should never forget that, or take it for granted. We should savor every moment that is given to us."

Lane felt her throat tighten.

"We have the present, and that's all we can ever really be sure of. So many of us and I'm as guilty as anyone— allow our present moments to pass us by unnoticed, unappreciated, while we occupy our minds with other thoughts. Certainly, we need to work and plan to help things turn out right in our futures. But we even lose our futures if we spend them worrying about what may come next. When the future arrives for us, it comes as single moments, present moments.

"So if we're to learn anything from what happened to Jessica and her parents, it's this—we need to live life now. We need to notice each second, and fill ourselves with its wonders and mysteries . . . and its joys."

His final words brought tears to Lane's eyes. She blinked and wiped them away.

He's so right, she thought. Each moment is precious.

This moment is precious, sitting here, listening to Mr. Kramer. She realized that she had never felt closer to him, not even yesterday when he was touching her.

"I want to share a poem with you. Then we'll get on with class." He lifted the slim volume off his leg and opened it to a bookmark. "This is by Allan Edward De-Prey. It's called, 'Grave Musings.' He lowered his eyes and began to read, his clear voice low and solemn:

> If I should sleep, this moonless night,
> Nevermore to rise,
> I'll keep with me the shimmering light
> Of the love in my lady's eyes.

> I'll keep the touch of dewy grass
> Wet on my feet at dawn,
> And how it smells, so sweet, alas!
> After the rain is gone.

> I'll keep the flavors I have known
> Of bread and meat and wine,
> And cherish them when I am bone
> Because they taste so fine.

A few of the kids tittered. Mr. Kramer looked up from the page. "If you'd rather not hear the rest of this . . ."

"Go on," Lane urged him.

"Maybe I *should* skip over some of this," he said. "It gets pretty long." He took a few moments to search the poem, apparently trying to decide where he should resume reading. Then, he continued:

> Into the grave with me I'll take
> Each sight and smell and sound
> And pray that they will not forsake
> Me in my sleep beneath the ground—

> If memory, in truth, survives,
> The reaper's savage knife
> I'll keep with me my golden prize
> Of what I loved in life.

But if an empty darkness waits
Bereft of all I've known,
I shall not curse the cruel Fates
That cast me there alone.

For I was given years to taste,
To smell, see, feel and love.
Though doomed, at last, to charnal waste,
I had my glorious days above.

Someone in the room said, "Yuck," and a few kids laughed.

"I admit the poem has its grim aspects, but I think De-Prey's point is well taken—'I had my glorious days above.' We have to always keep ourselves aware of those glories." He shut the book and set it aside. "Okay," he said, nodding. "Let's take out our textbooks and pick up where we left off yesterday."

When the bell rang, Lane stayed in her seat. The other students filed out. She remembered how, yesterday, Jessica had stopped in the doorway and scowled at her.

The girl should've been enjoying the time she had left, Lane thought. Not giving me crap.

Hell, she didn't know.

None of us knows. Any one of us could die tonight.

Instead of striking fear into Lane, the thought reminded her again of Mr. Kramer's advice to savor every moment.

She watched him step behind the table and load his briefcase. He met her eyes. He smiled. "How are you feeling today?" he asked.

"A lot better, thanks."

"Bruised up?"

"Yeah, some."

"Well, you'll have to stay out of bikinis for a while."

Lane felt the warmth of a blush spread over her skin. "Good thing summer's over," she said.

"I promise not to make you stand on any more stools."

"Do you have some papers or something for me?"

"So happens, I do." He walked to his desk and began searching through stacks of file folders. "Ah, here we go. Spelling sentences." He came toward her with the folder and a red pen. "Make sure you check for everything: spelling, punctuation, grammar. Five points off for each mistake."

"Right."

Stopping in front of Lane, he set the folder and pen on her desktop. "If you have any questions . . ."

"I really liked what you said at the start of class," Lane told him. She felt daring and embarrassed. "About appreciating each moment. It was very . . ." She shrugged, and felt her blouse brush softly against her nipples. "I don't know. It made me feel a lot better about things."

He looked down at her, sorrow in his eyes. "I'm glad if it helped. This was a terrible thing. I guess everyone's pretty shocked about it. I know I am, even though Jessica was a bit of a problem in class. Were you friends?"

A corner of Lane's mouth curled up. "Hardly. But even still . . . When something like that happens . . ."

"I know. It makes us aware of our mortality. If it can happen to her, why not to us?"

"Yeah. I was feeling . . . *little*. Like everything in my life is so petty and trivial compared to the big stuff."

"You shouldn't." His hand reached out and stroked Lane's hair. "You shouldn't feel that way at all."

"I guess I know that now," she said, feeling slightly breathless as his hand slipped down to her shoulder. It moved from side to side, sliding the blouse against her skin. "Each moment is something . . . to be treasured."

"Exactly."

Did he notice there was no strap on her shoulder?

"Nothing is trivial," he said. "Everything counts."

"Yeah."

He rubbed the side of her neck. "You're one very tense young lady," he said. "Your neck muscles feel like rock."

"Yeah. Hasn't been exactly a banner day."

"Same here."

The gently kneading hand sent warmth flowing through her body.

"Does that feel better?"

She nodded. Her head felt heavy.

Mr. Kramer stepped behind her. She heard a desk squeak against the floor as it was pushed out of his way. Then both his hands were on her shoulders, rubbing, squeezing.

"How's that?"

"Wonderful," she murmured. His fingers moved up and down. The front of Lane's blouse moved with them, caressing her breasts. She took a shaky breath. She lowered her head.

He swept her hair out of the way so it hung past the side of her face. Then he rubbed her neck just below her ears. She felt drowsy, felt as if he were squeezing warm fluid into her head. She shut her eyes. She sighed.

"Nothing like a neck rub to make things right," he said. His hands moved lower, his gently plying fingers easing down inside the collar of her blouse. They were warm and smooth on her bare skin.

She wondered how she could feel so lazy and so excited, both at the same time.

She felt powerless to move.

Her head wobbled as he massaged her.

The top button of her blouse popped open. Lane knew where his hands were. He hadn't unfastened the button. It had simply pulled out of its hole because of the way he was spreading her collar.

She wished he *had* done it.

She imagined him unbuttoning her blouse, spreading it open, taking her breasts in his big, powerful hands.

"I'd better call it quits," he said, "before you get too relaxed to mark the papers for me."

"Just a little more?" she asked, her voice a quiet murmur.

His hands went away from under her collar. They squeezed her shoulders. "Some other time. Hey, someone might come in and get the wrong idea."

She supposed that was true. She couldn't expect Mr. Kramer to risk his job for the sake of giving her an innocent massage.

He patted her shoulder in a coachlike fashion. "Now let's see you grade those papers." He stepped out from behind her and started walking toward his desk.

"Mr. Kramer?"

Looking around at Lane, he raised his eyebrows. His face was slightly red.

"I feel a whole lot better now. Thanks."

"Glad to help." He continued to his desk, sat down, and started shuffling through papers.

Lane began to check the spelling sentences. Her neck and shoulders seemed to keep the warmth of his touch. She felt as if she were glowing inside.

She realized that the neck of her blouse was still spread apart. Hunched over the desk, she looked down at herself. Below where the button had pulled open, she saw the shadowy side of her right breast.

Had Mr. Kramer noticed?

Probably not, she decided. After all, he'd been standing behind her.

She didn't fasten the button or straighten her blouse, and she remained pleasantly aware of the small gap as she went on correcting the papers.

She hoped Mr. Kramer was aware of it, too.

Each time she looked up, however, she found him bent over his papers.

Finally he stood up and carried a folder to the far side

of the table. He slipped it into his briefcase. "How's it going, Lane?"

"I've just got a few left."

"Well, I'm afraid it's time to close up shop. I'll finish them off tonight."

"Fine." She arranged them neatly inside the folder, eased out of her seat and approached the table. Stretching across its top, she handed the folder and pen to her teacher.

As he took them, she saw his eyes lower briefly. A glimpse, then he was looking at her face. "I sure appreciate the help, Lane."

"Glad to be of service." Bending over, she placed her hands on the table and stared at the small book from which he'd read "Grave Musings."

She could feel the way her blouse was hanging, its front not touching her chest at all. I can't believe I'm doing this, she thought. Why don't I just rip it open instead of being so tricky?

She felt as if she were blushing from head to toe. But she couldn't bring herself to straighten up.

She opened the book's cover and flipped to the title page. *"Collected Poetry of Allan Edward DePrey,"* she said. "I've never heard of him," she added, keeping her eyes on the book.

"Few people have," Mr. Kramer said. "He's a rather obscure poet from upstate New York, lived around the turn of the century. I happened onto that little volume in a secondhand store when I was a teenager. For a while there he was my favorite poet."

"Is everything in here as grim as 'Grave Musings'?" Lane asked, turning to the table of contents. Though she glanced at the listed titles, none of them registered.

"Oh, that's one of his more pleasant pieces. He had quite a morbid turn of mind."

"I wonder if Dad's ever heard of him. Sounds like De-Prey might be right up his alley."

"I tell you what. Why don't you take the book home tonight, let him have a look at it."

"Could I?" she asked, finally looking up at him.

He smiled. He had tiny speckles of sweat in the whiskers above his lip. "Just don't lose it."

"Oh, I won't." She lifted the book and stood up straight, feeling her blouse pull against her breasts. "Maybe I'll even read it myself, since he's a favorite of yours."

He laughed softly. "Hope you enjoy it. Now, you'd better run along. Thanks again for your invaluable services."

"My pleasure," Lane said.

She returned to her desk, gathered her books and binder, and headed for the door. Stopping with one foot in the hallway, she looked around. Mr. Kramer was staring at her. "Hey," she said, "thanks again for the neck rub."

"My pleasure," he said.

"Bye."

"Have a nice evening, Lane."

My evening, she thought, will be a drag after this. But she said "Thanks" before leaving the room.

In the corridor she fastened her button.

Twenty-nine

The alarm clock startled Larry awake Friday morning. As Jean stopped the noise, he rolled over and pressed his face into the warmth of his pillow. The bed shook slightly. Jean getting up. He heard her quiet footsteps on the carpet, then the door latching shut.

Alone in the room, he wondered whether he'd dreamed of Bonnie. If so, he couldn't remember it. He felt a little disappointed. Mostly, though, he felt relieved.

His stomach tightened as he remembered last night's decision.

After supper Pete had phoned.

"Hey, man," he'd said, "what's going on? You freezing me out, or something?"

"No, uh-uh. I've just been busy, that's all."

"Yeah, well, you could've let me know what's going on. You still working on our book?"

"It's coming along fine."

"Can you talk? Anyone in earshot?"

"No. Okay here." He'd grabbed the extension in their bedroom. Jean, he knew, was in the kitchen cleaning the dishes. Lane was in the living room, reading the poetry book her English teacher had loaned her.

"I've got a little privacy myself," Pete told him. "Barb's taking one of her marathon baths. So look, I think we've gotta talk about this thing. You were going like gangbusters over the weekend. Are you all caught up, or what?"

"Pretty much."

"Well, what's next? Seems to me like we oughta get this show on the road. I've been shopping. I got a good deal on a VHS camcorder. Set me back about thirteen hundred, but I figure it'll be worth it so we can make a video when we pull the stake. Which we oughta *do*. How about tomorrow night?"

"Tomorrow night?" Larry hadn't been able to keep the shock out of his voice.

"Why not? That's what this is all about, right? Why delay it?"

"There are some loose ends."

Silence. When Pete spoke again, the pushy edge was gone from his voice. He sounded excited. "What do you mean? What kind of loose ends?"

"I know who she is. I think I know who killed her."

"Holy shit."

"It's a long story. Look, why don't we meet tomorrow during your lunch break. I'll tell Jean I'm going to the library. I'll tell you everything then. How about Buster's?"

They agreed to meet there at noon.

Now, lying in bed, Larry wondered if he should go through with it. He'd made the suggestion, mostly, as a delaying tactic. Pete had taken him off guard, demanding that they pull the stake tonight.

Larry wasn't ready for that. He wasn't sure he would *ever* be ready for that.

What do you want to do, he asked himself, keep her up there forever?

The stake's the mystery, he thought. Once we take it out, Bonnie won't . . . she'll just be a corpse.

She *is* just a corpse.

No. As long as she has the stake in her heart, she's more than that.

What, a vampire?

Uriah thought so.

And Larry knew he was clutching a faint hope that she *might* be one. It was a ridiculous hope, of course. But pulling the stake would take it away. Bonnie would just lie there, a dried-up cadaver with a hole in her chest, and it would be over.

He would lose her.

He wouldn't even be able to pretend she might come back to life, fresh and young and beautiful—and his.

So you're stalling Pete, he thought, trying to keep your stupid dream for at least a while longer.

What's the harm in that?

Larry climbed out of bed. He stepped to the window and gazed out across his sunlit yard at the garage. He imagined Bonnie in the dark of the attic, lying in her casket, the end of the stake jutting upright from her chest. He seemed to hear her voice, as clear and sweet as it had come to him in yesterday's dream. *Free me. Pull the stake, and I'll come to you. I love you, Larry. I'll be yours forever.*

Sure, he thought. Fat chance.

Shortly before noon he told Jean that he needed to check on a few things at the library. He took a large manila envelope with him when he left the house. He drove to Buster's, a diner near the south end of town, not far from Pete's shop.

He found Pete waiting in a booth at the rear, and scooted in across the table from him.

"Long time no see, *compadre.*"

"Yeah, sorry about that."

A waitress came, set places for them, and asked if they would like to see menus.

Pete shook his head. "I'll have the Buster-Burger with the works, chili fries and iced tea."

"Guess I'll have the same," Larry said.

"Making it easy on me, huh, fellas?" she said. Then she went away.

"So what's the story?" Pete asked.

Larry dug into his pants pocket, took out Bonnie's ring and set it down in front of Pete. "It's hers."

"What?" Pete picked up the ring and squinted at it.

"I found it on her hand."

Pete frowned at him. "And you didn't tell me?"

"I'm telling you now."

"Well shit, when did you find it?"

"Sunday morning. Before you came over. I know I should've told you about it, but—"

"Damn right . . ."

"I wanted to check on a few things first."

"Why you been holding out on me?"

"I don't know, Pete. I just wanted to see where it would lead. I figured I'd lay it on you once I got the whole story."

"My pal," he muttered, then studied the ring again. "Bonnie Saxon."

Hearing Pete speak her name, Larry felt an ache of loss. She was no longer his alone.

"You think that's her name?" Pete asked.

"I know that's her name. She was graduated from Buford High in 'sixty-eight. Like I said, I did some checking." He opened the manila envelope.

I don't want to do this, he thought.

But he was already committed. Besides, Pete would find out everything, sooner or later. Best to get it over with.

He slid out the Spirit Queen photograph of Bonnie. It fluttered in his trembling fingers as he passed it to Pete and took the ring back.

Pete's eyes widened. He pursed his lips. "This is *her?*"

"Yeah."

"Man!"

"Yeah."

"She's a fuckin' *knockout.*"

"I know."

He shook his head. "So this is our babe."

Our babe. I shouldn't have done it. Should've kept her to myself.

"Where'd you get this?"

"A school yearbook."

"Man, you *did* do some checking. What else have you got?"

"Let me have it back," Larry said, holding out his hand. "Somebody might see it. There could be people in here who knew her."

Pete stared at the picture for a few more moments, then gave it back to him. Larry slipped it inside the envelope. He pulled his stack of photocopies halfway out. "There's too much here for you to read right now. I'll make copies of them, if you want."

"What do they say?"

Larry let them slide out of sight and set the envelope down beside him. "It's a long story. I had to spend a couple of days searching back issues of the town paper."

"Come on, man. Give."

Larry waited while the waitress approached with their meals. She set down the plates and drinks. "Enjoy, fellas," she said. Then she was gone.

"It started with two murders in the Sagebrush Flat Hotel." While they ate, he told Pete how the town had been abandoned after the mine failure; how the Radleys had remained, living in their hotel, after everyone else had left. He told about Uriah's trip to Mulehead Bend, the trouble with his pickup, and how he'd walked the final miles only to find his wife and daughter slain in the hotel. He gave Pete the official speculation that bikers or other transients were responsible.

"But Uriah thought they'd been killed by vampires," he said.

"That wasn't in any newspaper," Pete said.

"He had his wife and daughter cremated so they wouldn't come back to life."

"You guessing, or what?"

"Just let me go on."

"Well, how about sticking to the facts?"

"Okay. Facts. The Radley women were murdered on July fifteenth. On July twenty-sixth a teenage girl named Sandra Dunlap was abducted from her parents' home right here in Mulehead. Blood was found on her bed. On August tenth another girl vanished. This was Linda Latham. She was apparently kidnapped on her way home from a friend's house. Bonnie Saxon—"

"That's *our* gal . . ."

"Right. She was taken from her mother's home on the night of August thirteenth. Blood was found on her bed the next day."

"Just like the other one, huh? Dunlap?"

"That's right. All three girls were about the same age. They all disappeared within a month after the Radley murders in Sagebrush Flat. The police had absolutely nothing to go on. Until Bonnie was taken. That night, a witness spotted Uriah Radley waiting around in front of her house."

"The guy from Sagebrush?"

"Right. So the cops went looking for him. They searched the hotel. They didn't find him or the missing girls, but they found some pretty interesting stuff in one of the rooms: crucifixes, garlic cloves, a hammer and some pointed wooden stakes."

"Holy shit. So you're telling me this Uriah guy is the one who snatched the teenagers?"

"It sure looks that way."

"And he's the one who staked our gal."

"Probably the others, too."

"Man, this is *far* out."

"You're telling me?"

"Were the other two found?"

"Not that I know of. Neither was Uriah, apparently."

"So what do you think?" Pete asked. "You think this Uriah guy went off his rocker and thought he was killing the vampires that nailed his family?"

"It sure looks that way."

"Jesus, our book's gonna be a blockbuster for sure! Now, if we just pull that stake tonight and she *is* a vampire—gangbusters!"

Larry's heart quickened. "Not tonight."

"Why the hell not? We've got the whole story. Everything but the finish."

"There's still a loose end."

"Okay. Your famous 'loose end.' What is it?"

Larry didn't know. But he had to find a reason to delay the pulling of the stake.

Suddenly he saw the loose end. It was obvious.

"Who put the brand new lock on the hotel door?" he asked. "Who covered the break in the stairway landing? I think it might be Uriah. I think he's returned to Sagebrush Flat."

Pete, wiping his mouth with a napkin, stared at Larry. He lowered the napkin. He stroked one side of his thick mustache. His eyes narrowed. "God Almighty," he muttered. "I bet you're right. Maybe he's our friend the coyote eater."

"What if we can find him?"

"What if we can *bust* him! A citizen's arrest! Jumping fucking Judas, the *publicity!* Lar, you're a genius!"

A genius? He felt as if he had just stepped off a cliff.

"We'll go out there tomorrow," Pete said. "We'll tell the wives we're going target shooting. They didn't want to come along last time, they'll be glad to get rid of us. And we'll drive out to Sagebrush Flat and nail us a killer."

Thirty

"I asked Henry and Betty to come with us tonight," Lane said.

Jim, chewing a mouthful of apple, suddenly looked as if he'd gnashed a worm. His voice came out muffled. "You gotta be kidding."

"You don't mind too much, do you?" she asked.

"Mind? Shit! You *are* kidding, right?"

"I think it'll be nice."

"How could you do this to me? We haven't been out together in *weeks,* and now we've gotta take along those two rejects?"

"They're my best friends, Jim."

"That doesn't mean you've gotta take 'em everywhere you go. Shit. They'll ruin everything."

"No, they won't."

"Oh, right. Sure. *Damn.* Can't you just tell 'em you changed your mind?"

Lane shook her head. "I knew you'd cause a stink about this."

"Then why'd you do it?"

"I felt like it, okay?"

Scowling, Jim turned away from her and bit out a chunk of apple with an angry snap of his teeth.

Lane gazed at the remains of her ham sandwich. She thought she might choke if she tried to eat any more.

A rotten trick to pull on the guy. Maybe I *should* tell them I changed my mind.

Damn it, though, she didn't want to be alone with him. Asking Henry and Betty to come along had been a way to squirm out of the situation: either Jim would call the whole thing off, or the presence of her friends would keep him in line. At least as long as they were in the car. Once Jim dropped them off, she'd be on her own.

I can handle him, she told herself.

But maybe I won't have to.

"Would you rather skip the whole thing?" she asked.

Jim faced her. His scowl was gone. There was a look of hurt in his eyes. "Is that what you want?"

He does care about me, she reminded herself. Maybe he even loves me.

Lane knew she didn't love him. Maybe once. Not anymore. She'd seen too many samples of his juvenile behavior: his pettiness, his meanness toward her friends, his constant preoccupation with sex as if all he really cared about was her body, as if his whole aim in life was to score with her. Why couldn't he be kind and sensitive? If he were only more like Mr. Kramer, there wouldn't be a problem.

But they'd been very close. She supposed she still cared about him. She knew she didn't want to hurt him.

She put a hand on his arm. "No. Let's go out tonight. I want to."

"I guess I can stand those two for a few hours. If I have to."

"Who knows? You may even end up having a good time."

"Sure," he muttered.

"Let's see a smile."

He bared his upper teeth.

"A smile, not a snarl. You look like an old hound with a burr up its ass."

That brought a real smile, and a small laugh.

"Much better," she said.

She realized that her appetite had returned. She bit into her sandwich. As she chewed she said, "Just wait and see. We'll have a great time."

Jim reached behind her. He rubbed the middle of her back, sliding her blouse against her bare skin. "Nice," he said softly. "Nothing in the way. You'll leave it off for me, won't you? Tonight? I'll be real nice to your pals."

"We'll see," she muttered.

"Oh, come on. You been coming to school without it, you won't need it for the movies."

"In school you have to keep your hands to yourself."

"Don't *have* to. I'm just too much of a gentleman to take advantage."

"Sure."

He grinned. "Besides, I'm no idiot. If I got cute, you'd start up wearing the damn things again."

"You better believe it."

He continued to caress her back. "I love it," he said, "just knowing you got nothing on in there."

"Cool it, huh?"

When Lane entered the classroom just before the sixth-period bell, she found Riley Benson in Jessica's seat. He was slumped low, legs stretched out, ankles crossed. He didn't look at her.

Why's he at Jessica's desk? she wondered.

It came as no surprise that Riley was back in school. She'd learned from news reports that "the suspect" had been released by the authorities, and she'd already seen him a few times today in the hallways and cafeteria.

But it seemed pretty weird to plonk himself down at Jessica's desk instead of his own.

Lane could only think of one reason for that: he missed

her. Sitting where she used to sit, maybe he felt closer to her.

She looked at him.

Poor bastard, she thought.

His head turned and he glared at her. "What're *you* staring at?"

"I'm sorry about Jessica," she said.

"Yeah? Well, fuck you."

"I was just trying to be nice," she muttered.

"Yeah? Who needs it?"

In a soft voice she said, "You don't have to be such a tough guy all the time."

"You don't have to be such a fuckin' goody-two-shoes."

"Did the police treat you okay?"

"Cram it, huh?"

"Why won't you let anyone be nice to you?"

"*You* wanta be nice to me?" He suddenly drew in his legs and lunged sideways, leaning out over the aisle and grabbing Lane's arm. He tugged her from her seat. As her rump hit the floor he dragged her closer.

"What're you *doing?*" she cried out. "Stop it!"

She heard other kids in the classroom suddenly shouting: "Leave her alone!" and "Benson, you turd!" and "Somebody *do* something!"

Riley released her arm. Clutching her hair and chin, he twisted her face upward. "Wanta be nice to me, huh?"

"Somebody stop him!" a girl yelled.

Riley spit. The saliva spattered Lane's tight lips. He let go of her chin and rubbed the spit around her mouth and cheeks.

"What's going on here?" A shout. Mr. Kramer's voice.

Riley thrust Lane away. She caught herself with an elbow, and winced as pain shot up her arm. With the back of her other hand she wiped the spittle from her face. The stuff had a sweetish, sickening odor like the smell of a sneeze.

"Benson, you son of a bitch!"

"Fuck you, man!"

Sitting up and holding her elbow, Lane watched Mr. Kramer stride toward the front of the desk where Riley sat.

"Hey, man, you better not touch me!"

The teacher leaned over the desk, clutched the long hair on top of Riley's head, and jerked him into the other aisle. His right fist smashed Riley's face. The boy's head snapped sideways. Lane saw spit fly from his mouth. Mr. Kramer released the hair, and Riley slumped to his knees.

"Apologize to Miss Dunbar."

"Eat shit, fag."

"Cream him!" a guy advised from the rear of the room.

Riley looked up at Mr. Kramer. The way the boy's face was red and contorted, Lane thought he might start to cry. In a shaky voice he said, "You're gonna get it. You hit me, you fag bastard. I'm gonna have your job."

Mr. Kramer picked him up by his shirtfront, glared in his face and shook him. "Apologize to my student."

"It's all right," Lane said, getting to her feet. "Please. Can't we just forget it?"

"Say you're sorry, Benson."

"Okay, okay, I'm sorry."

"Tell her."

Riley turned his face toward Lane. He said, "Sorry." He looked as if he wanted to kill her.

"Very good," Mr. Kramer muttered. "Now get the hell out of here." He shoved the kid backward and let go. Riley stumbled, tripped over his own motorcycle boots and fell sprawling.

A few kids laughed, but most watched in silence.

Riley scurried to his feet and ran for the rear door. "You're gonna be sorry!" he shouted back, his voice high-pitched and trembling. "Both of you! Just wait!" Then he darted into the hallway.

When he was gone, Heidi began to clap. The rest of the class joined in, and in seconds the room was thundering with applause.

"Stop it," Mr. Kramer said. "Everybody settle down." He stepped over to Lane. "Are you all right?" he asked.

She nodded. "I'd like to wash my face."

"Maybe you should see the nurse."

"No, that's okay. I'm not hurt. Really. I just want to wash off the spit. If I could have a rest room pass . . ."

"I'll escort you there myself, then drop by the principal's office to have some words about our friend." Turning to the class, he said, "I'll be out of the room for a few minutes. Take out your books and make good use of the time. When I come back, I want to find everyone quiet and busy. Understood?"

He followed Lane into the hallway. She looked both ways. No sign of Riley or anyone else.

Side by side they walked toward the rest room. Her legs felt weak and shaky.

"What started off Benson, anyway?" Mr. Kramer asked.

"I don't know. I told him I was sorry about Jessica, that's all. I was trying to be nice to him, and all of a sudden he grabbed me."

"Some people are best just left alone."

"Guess so. Thanks for coming to the rescue."

"I'm just sorry I wasn't quicker about it. Seems like I'm never quite on time when it comes to helping you out of jams."

Oh yeah, she thought. My fall, too.

"Sorry I keep causing you all this trouble," she said.

"No trouble. But I'm starting to wonder if you might be accident prone, or something."

"Didn't used to be."

"Just in my room, huh?" He smiled.

"Looks that way."

They stopped at the double doors of the girls' rest room. "I'll wait here while you go in and take a look around."

"You don't think Riley . . . ?"

"Never hurts to be careful, Lane."

She pushed open one of the doors and entered. The air reeked of stale smoke. Though the place appeared deserted, she checked each of the stalls. About half the toilets were unflushed, all the seats looked wet, and so did the tile floor around each fixture. But Riley wasn't lurking about. Feeling a little disgusted, she returned to the door and opened it.

"Nobody here, Mr. Kramer."

"Fine. I'll see you back in the room."

As he walked away, Lane let the door swing shut. She stepped up to a sink, turned on the hot water, and pumped greenish-yellow liquid soap into her palm. Though her face was dry, she could still smell Riley's saliva. She started washing.

Sure isn't my day, she thought.

The crud. Why would he want to do something like that?

I should've known better than to mess with him. Now he'll really want to get me.

Even worse, Mr. Kramer might get into trouble for slugging him.

Lane wished she had stayed home. If she'd been absent, none of this would've happened with Riley. She even would've had a good excuse for breaking off tonight's date. Should've just stayed in bed this morning and pretended to be sick.

It'll be all right, she told herself. It isn't the end of the world. And Mr. Kramer was terrific.

She dried with paper towels. When she finished, she saw in the mirror that her skin was a little red around her mouth and chin. Her eyes had a weird, dazed look. She shook her head as if to wake herself up. Then she tucked in her blouse and left the rest room.

Arriving at the front door of the classroom, she glanced in. Mr. Kramer hadn't returned yet. She heard quiet murmurs and laughter. Sounded like everyone was behaving—sort of. But she didn't want to step inside until the teacher was there. Everyone would stare at her, ask questions, offer comments. So she stepped away from the door and leaned back against a locker.

Finally Mr. Kramer came strolling up the corridor. She stood up straight when he stopped in front of her.

"Are you feeling all right?" he asked.

"Yeah. How did it go in the office?"

"I explained the situation. It looks as if our friend Benson will find himself transferred to Pratt."

Pratt was the "alternate school," mostly designed as a holding pen for students with chronic behavior problems.

"God, I feel like it's all my fault."

"Benson already had one foot in Pratt's door. This just nudged him the rest of the way. My only regret is that you had to be one of his victims. It makes me sick when something like that happens to a sweet kid like you."

His words set a pleasant warmth flowing through her.

"Come on," he said. "I've got a class to teach."

She followed him into the room.

With a minute remaining before the final bell, Mr. Kramer read off the names of the four students chosen to accompany him to the city college production of *Hamlet*. "Are all of you still planning to make it?" he asked.

They nodded, muttered "Yes" and "Sure."

"Okay. Jerry and Heidi," he said to the alternates, "it looks like you're out of luck. Sorry. Maybe there'll be another opportunity later in the year. I want you others to stay in your seats for just a second after the bell rings, and I'll fill you in on the situation."

Class ended. Everyone filed out except Lane, George, Aaron, and Sandra.

"Okay," Mr. Kramer said. "Curtain is at eight-thirty tomorrow night. I'll pick each of you up in my car between about seven and eight, so write your address on a piece of scrap paper and hand it to me before you leave the room. Any questions?"

"What should we wear?" Sandra asked.

"I think a sport coat and tie would be appropriate for the guys. As for you two young ladies, this isn't the prom, but I'd like you looking good. After all, you'll be representing Buford High. Anything else?"

There were no more questions.

Lane took out her binder. She wrote her address on a sheet of loose-leaf paper and waited at her desk while the other students gave their slips to Mr. Kramer. When they were gone, she approached him.

"Thank you," he said, taking her paper.

"Do you have some work for me?"

Smiling, he shook his head. "This is Friday, Lane. Why don't we both knock it off early? Besides, after what Benson put you through, I'd think you might want to get out of here."

"Oh, I kind of enjoy helping you."

"There's always next week, if you're that eager."

"You're sure you don't want me to stay?"

"I'm sure. Thanks, though."

"Well, let me get the poetry book for you." She returned to her desk and crouched to take it from the rack under the seat. "Dad read quite a bit of it," she said, looking over her shoulder. "He'd never heard of DePrey. He thought the poems were pretty neat."

"Glad to hear it. I'm looking forward to meeting him tomorrow night."

Lane stood up, turning, and handed the book to her teacher. "I read the whole thing, myself."

"Terrific. I hope you didn't have any nightmares."

She smiled. "None that I remember."

"Why don't you get your things together?" he said. "I'll walk you out to the parking lot. I'm sure Benson's long gone, but—"

"Never hurts to be careful," she interrupted, repeating what he'd told her in front of the rest room.

"I couldn't have put it better myself."

"I'll have to stop by my locker," she said.

"No problem."

It took Mr. Kramer a few minutes to get ready. Finally he said, "All set," and they left the room. Several kids were still in the hallway, standing in front of open lockers or heading out, some talking with friends, some laughing. Lane wished they were all gone, the school deserted except for herself and Mr. Kramer.

Right. And what would you do, throw yourself into his arms?

They walked in silence. Lane searched her mind for something to say—something that might force him to see her as a woman, not just as a student.

Ask about his love life, she thought, and rolled her eyes upward. *Sure thing. That'd be subtle. Besides, what if he* is *gay? No way. He couldn't be. Not Mr. Kramer.*

She arrived at her locker. "It'll just be a second," she said.

"No rush."

She shifted her load of books to her left arm and hugged them against her chest.

"Here, I'll hold them for you."

"Oh, I can—"

"Chivalry ain't dead yet," he said, setting down his briefcase. His left hand braced the bottom of the stack. His right hand slipped between the top book and her breast. It pressed against her, warm through the blouse. A knuckle rubbed her stiff nipple. She felt a warm, trembling rush. Then his hand was gone.

She turned to her locker, bent over, and began to spin the dial of its combination lock.

Did he touch me there on purpose? she wondered. No. It was just an accident. But there was no possible way he could've not noticed what was against his hand.

She got the combination wrong.

She got it wrong again.

"You're sure this is the right locker?" he asked.

"Yeah. I'm just not thinking straight."

"Rough day."

She smiled at him. "It's getting to be the story of my life. If I'm not falling off a stool, I'm getting attacked."

She tried the combination again. This time it worked. She opened her locker. Mr. Kramer didn't touch her at all when he returned the books. She put some away, kept others, struggled to concentrate on which of those in her locker she would need for homework. Finally she took out her denim book bag. When it was full, she buckled it shut and closed her locker. She lifted the bag by its shoulder straps.

"All set?" Mr. Kramer asked, picking up his briefcase.

"Yeah. I'm sorry it took so long."

"I assure you, I have nothing in my immediate future more important or enjoyable than the task of escorting a beautiful young lady to her car."

Lane felt herself blush and smile. "I bet you do," she said, and started walking beside him.

"To be honest, I don't have much of a social life."

"Oh, sure."

"It's true, I'm afraid."

"Well . . . what do you do with your spare time?"

"I read. I go to movies and plays."

"Don't you . . . see anyone?" Lane grimaced. She couldn't believe she had asked that.

"No," he said. He glanced at her, then looked quickly away. "I was engaged to be married. Her name was Lonnie. She was a lot like you, Lane: lovely, intelligent, cheerful, quick to poke fun at things, including herself. But . . ." He shook his head sharply. "Anyway, I guess I'm still not over her."

"I'm sorry."

She wanted to ask what happened to Lonnie, but didn't dare. Already her probing may have opened a wound.

"Well," he said, "I guess we all have our crosses to bear." He pushed open the heavy exit door and followed Lane outside.

The sun was warm on her face. A stiff autumn wind was blowing. It tossed her hair, fluttered her blouse, pressed her skirt against her legs, caressed her. She took a deep breath, savoring the fine feeling of walking with Mr. Kramer on such an afternoon.

He thinks I'm just like Lonnie, she told herself. The woman he loved.

"It's the red Mustang, isn't it?" he asked as they entered the parking lot.

She turned to him, smiling, and the wind flung wisps of hair across her face. "How did you know?"

"I notice things," he told her.

The way he said it, Lane knew he had more in mind than her car. Did he want her to realize that he'd noticed the feel of her breast when he took the books from her? Or maybe that he was aware of her feelings for him? Could he sense that she'd fallen in love with him?

I'm not in love with him, she told herself. Good God, he's a teacher. He's probably ten years older than me.

Ten years isn't such a big deal, she thought. And he won't be my teacher after I graduate.

Dream on, stupid. Don't kid yourself. He's not interested.

She stopped beside her car and took out the keys.

"Well," Mr. Kramer said, "I guess you didn't need a bodyguard, after all."

"I'm glad you walked me out, anyway. Thanks." She opened the door, swung her book bag onto the passenger seat and climbed in. While she folded the sun shade, she said, "You won't be in trouble for hitting Riley, will you?"

"I doubt it. He had it coming."

She twisted around and tossed the cardboard shade onto the backseat. Then she smiled out the open door at Mr. Kramer. "You know, you'll be a legend around here once it gets around that you cleaned his clock."

"Well, that would be unfortunate. It's a shame when people are admired for acts of violence. I'd much rather be known as someone who is caring and sensitive."

"You already are that," Lane said. "At least as far as I'm concerned."

"Thank you, Lane." For long moments he stared into her eyes. Then he swung the door shut.

She cranked the window down. "Do you need a ride or anything?"

"My car's just in the other lot."

"I could give you a ride over to it."

Dumb! Can't you be a little more *obvious?*

"That's all right. Take it easy, now. I'll see you tomorrow night."

"Okay. Bye, Mr. Kramer."

Lane watched him walk away, the wind mussing his dark hair and making his shirt cling to his back. She gazed at his broad shoulders, the curves of his shoulder blades, the way his shirt tapered down to his waist. Today he didn't have the wallet in the back pocket of his slacks. The fabric was tight against his rear. The mounds of his buttocks took turns flexing as he walked.

I notice things, too, she thought.
Then Mr. Kramer stepped behind a parked car.
Lane slid her key into the ignition.

Thirty-one

Lane knocked, opened the door, and leaned into her father's office. "Jim'll be here any minute," she said. "Do you want to come out and harass him?"

"I'll give the kid a break tonight," he said, pushing a key to make his computer screen go blank as she stepped into the room.

"Writing more dirty stuff?"

"Yep."

Lane lowered a finger toward the "page down" button on his keyboard.

"Ah-ah!" He swatted her hand away.

"Aw, come on. I'm a big girl."

He looked up at her, smiling. Then his smile slipped away. "You'll be careful, won't you?"

"Yes, Daddy."

"I mean it. I'm not at all sure you should be going out tonight, what with this Benson character and everything."

"This isn't one of your books, you know."

"I know. It's real life, and that's worse. Look what happened to that Jessica girl."

"Riley Benson didn't do that."

"What makes you so sure?"

"Well, the cops let him go."

"Cops have been known to make mistakes, honey. And even if he had nothing to do with it, he showed himself to be violent in class today. And he threatened you. So don't pretend there's nothing wrong. I want you to be very careful."

"I will be. And it's not as if I'll be alone. Nobody is going to attack me with Betty around."

Dad laughed. "Nasty."

"Inherited it from you, along with my allergies."

She heard the doorbell ring. "He's here," she said. Bending down, she kissed her father. "See you later."

"Have fun. And I mean it, keep your eyes open."

"Righto," she said, turning away. *"Adios."*

She pulled the door shut and hurried into the living room. Jim was talking to her mother. He smiled at her. He looked handsome in his tan chamois shirt, corduroy pants, and sneakers. She realized she was glad to see him in spite of their frequent quarrels.

"Hi ho," she said.

"Lane," he said. A red hue colored his face. She wondered what had brought that on. Jim wasn't a guy who often blushed. "You look very nice," he said.

She said, "Thanks." If he was disappointed, it didn't show. But Lane knew he couldn't be very happy that she'd worn tight blue jeans instead of a skirt, and a thick vee-neck sweater over her blouse.

She kissed her mother.

"Have a good time, you two," Mom said. "And don't stay out too late."

"We will and we won't," Lane told her.

Mom shook her head, rolled her eyes upward.

"Have a nice evening, Mrs. Dunbar," Jim said.

She thanked him. As they walked across the yard, Lane heard the front door bump shut. She glanced back. The porch light came on, lighting the entrance with a yellow glow.

Jim's car was parked at the curb. He opened its passenger door for Lane, then strode around the front of the car and climbed in behind the steering wheel. He inserted the ignition key but didn't start the engine. He turned to Lane. "You really do look terrific," he said.

"I figured it's too cold for a skirt."

"That's okay." He was silent for a moment. Then he said, "Are you wearing it?"

"Wearing what?"

"You know."

Lane grinned. "Aren't you the guy who can spot that sort of thing a mile away?"

"Yeah. But the sweater." He reached out. His hand curled around the back of Lane's neck. She scooted across the seat, turned to Jim, kissed him. The hand on her neck slid upward, fingers pushing into her hair and easing her head forward, pressing her lips harder against his open mouth. His other hand closed on her right breast. "Yeah," he said into her mouth.

"Happy?"

"Yeah."

It was nothing like the gentle, accidental touch of Mr. Kramer's hand. Jim rubbed her breast hard through the sweater and blouse. His tongue thrust into her mouth. He squeezed her nipple. The pain made her squirm. She forced his hand away and freed her mouth.

"That's enough," she whispered. "Come on. We've got to pick up the others."

"Yeah, okay. Shit."

"You promised to be nice," she reminded him.

"I know. Just watch. I'll be great. I love you so much, Lane."

"Or at least my boobs, huh?"

A mean thing to say, she realized. Jim couldn't help it if they turned him into a sex maniac. After all, she thought, he's just a horny teenager.

"I love everything about you," he said, not sounding offended by her remark. "And I'd like to kiss you everywhere."

"Oh, man. Cool off, huh?"

"I'm cool, I'm cool," he said, and started the car.

Lane scooted across the seat and fastened her seat belt. As he drove, she gave him directions to Betty's house. "Henry'll be there, too," she added.

"I can hardly wait."

"You promised."

"I'm a man of my word," he said. "Do we have to sit with them at the movies?"

"Yep."

"God, the things I do for you."

"I'm worth it, right?"

"You know it." He reached over and squeezed her thigh. His hand stayed there, rubbing her through the denim. It felt good. But when he moved it higher, she guided the hand down to her knee.

"Behave," she said. "And make a left."

He made the turn onto Betty's street, and Lane saw her two friends standing together in front of the mobile home.

"Here goes nothing," Jim muttered. He stopped.

Lane twisted around in her seat and unlocked the back door for them. "Greetings, good folks," Henry said as he scurried in. "James, Lane. Sounds like a picturesque London Road. James Lane."

"Hiya, guys," Betty said, squeezing into the car.

"Hello," Jim said. He sounded pleasant enough.

"How's it going?" Lane asked, looking back at them.

"We're fine," Betty said. "What about *you?*"

"Great."

"Really?"

"Yeah," she insisted.

"Why wouldn't she be?" Jim asked, sounding a little annoyed as he made a U-turn.

"Oh, I don't know. Unless maybe it has a tad to do with a certain Riley Benson."

Lane felt her skin go hot.

"What about Benson?" Jim asked.

"Oh, nothing. Just that he jerked Lane out of her seat in English class today and hocked on her face."

"What?" Jim blurted.

"Christ, Betty."

"That's what Heidi told me, and she was there."

"Did he really spit on you?" Henry asked. He sounded concerned.

"Yeah."

"Benson spit on you?"

"It's no big deal," Lane said. She had realized everyone would find out about it, sooner or later. But she wished it hadn't happened this soon.

"I'll kill the cocksucker!"

"I'll help," Henry said.

"Mr. Kramer already punched him out," Lane explained. "And he's being sent to Pratt."

"I'll send the fucker to Hell."

"Take it easy, Jim. Okay? My God, his girlfriend was just murdered. He's having a tough time."

"It'll get a lot tougher . . ."

"It's no reason to take it out on you," Henry told her. "That guy's such a rectum. He always has been."

"That's right," Betty said. "He was a shit chute long before Jessica got her ticket canceled."

"Look," Lane said, "I'm the one he messed with. I'd like to just forget about it, all right? It's over. It's finished. Now, why don't we talk about something else and enjoy ourselves?"

"I'm gonna kill him," Jim said.

"Shut up about it!" Lane snapped.

He did.

There was a long silence.

Finally Lane said, "I guess I'm lucky to have friends like you guys. I don't want anyone trying to nail Riley Benson because of me, but it's nice to know you care enough to be pissed at him."

"I'll piss *on* him," Jim said.

"Hey!"

"Okay, okay, I won't."

"Besides," Henry put in, "Benson would probably enjoy it. He'd be right in his element."

"Hen," Jim said, "I'm starting to like you."

"You're not so bad yourself."

"The jock and the nerd," Betty said. "What a pair."

"You got a nifty pair yourself there," Henry said, and Betty squealed as he did something to her.

Jim glanced back and grinned.

"Keep your eyes on the road," Lane warned.

Betty cried out, "Don't you . . . ! Ow!"

"Oh, that didn't hurt."

"Did, too."

"But this might."

"Don't you *dare!*" She shrieked, then giggled.

"Are we having fun yet?"

"No! Yes! No, *stop* that!"

"Hope they don't act like this in the movies," Lane said. "They'll get us all kicked out."

"Oh, I'll be a model of decorum," Henry assured her.

Betty yelped. It was followed by a smack, and Henry said, "Ow! You didn't have to slug me."

"Want another one, four-eyes?"

Jim looked at Lane and shook his head.

It was Henry's idea that they sit in the last row of the movie theater. "That way," he explained, "you don't have to worry about who's behind you."

"The dink won't sit anywhere else," Betty said, following Lane into the row. As they sat down she added, "He's paranoid."

Leaning forward, Henry looked past Betty and said, "Did you read *Curtains?*"

"Dad's book? Yeah."

"Remember he had that lunatic sitting behind people in the movies and slashing their throats? Makes a person think, you know?"

"Makes *me* think you shouldn't read that kind of book," Lane told him.

"Better a wall at your back than a stranger. You just never know. Until it's too late."

"Spare me," Betty muttered.

"I may be sparing us all. You'll thank me for it when nobody rips open your jugular."

The theater darkened and Previews of Coming Attractions started. "Want some?" Betty whispered, lifting her tub of popcorn toward Lane.

"No thanks." Though it smelled good, the popcorn would make her thirsty and she had no drink. She and Jim had decided to wait for the intermission before getting snacks.

Jim stretched an arm across her shoulders. As he caressed her upper arm, she leaned closer to him. He tried to push his hand under her arm, but she pressed it tight against her side. "No funny stuff," she whispered, "or I'll trade places with Betty."

"Anything but that," he said. He brushed his lips against the side of her forehead, then turned his face toward the screen.

About ten minutes into the feature attraction, he stopped stroking Lane's arm. The film was *Night Hunt,* about a young woman being stalked through the woods by a heavily armed killer. Jim seemed engrossed by it. The heroine was beautiful and running around in torn clothes. Lane suspected that had something to do with grabbing his attention. But the suspense was terrific. Soon Jim took his arm away and sat up straight. As Lane shifted in her seat, she noticed that Betty had stopped eating, though her tub of popcorn was still half full. She glanced past Betty at Henry. The boy's eyes were fixed on the screen, the lenses of his glasses reflecting the light. Betty gasped, and Lane jerked her eyes back to the film.

It seemed to be over very fast. When the lights came up, Jim gave her a look as if he'd been blown away.

"Pretty decent," she said.

"Man."

Henry said, "Was that totally awesome, or what?"

"Must've been," Lane told him. "Betty couldn't even finish her popcorn."

"Small oversight," Betty said, and stuffed a handful into her mouth. She said to Henry in a muffled voice, "I could go for a hot dog."

Henry and Jim headed for the lobby to pick up refreshments. They returned with loaded arms just as the lights dimmed. Lane took her Pepsi and nachos from Jim. He sat down beside her.

Leaning close to him, she whispered, "How are you and Henry getting along?"

"He's not so bad for a twerp."

She elbowed Jim gently in the ribs. The wrapper of a straw shot past her face and landed on Jim's far shoulder. She grinned at Henry.

"Sorry," he said. "Aim was off."

"He was trying for my eye," Betty explained.

As the movie began, Lane clamped her drink between her thighs and poked her straw through the X on its lid. She sipped her drink. She ate her nachos, leaning forward and keeping the cardboard dish under her chin, careful not to drip any of the melted cheese on her white sweater.

From the start it was obvious that this film, *Dance of the Zombies,* was a turkey. Henry started talking back to it. Once Jim was done with his nachos, he drew Lane closer to him. He caressed her arm and kissed the side of her face while she tried to eat the last of her chips.

"Pay attention to the movie," she whispered.

"It sucks," he said, and kissed the corner of her eye.

She stuck her last nacho chip into his mouth. "Suck on that," she told him.

As Jim chewed, she took the Pepsi from between her legs and drew the cold, watered-down soda into her mouth. She didn't expect his other hand. It had been resting on the far arm of his chair. But now it suddenly pressed tight against the crotch of her jeans. She flinched and shoved it away and choked on her Pepsi. The drink shot up her throat, sprayed from her mouth, burned inside her nasal passages and spilled out her nostrils. Hurling her cup to the floor, she hunched over and flung both hands under her face to catch the mess.

Jim pounded on her back as she coughed.

"Jesus, gal," Betty said, and joined in the pounding.

"Is she all right?" Henry asked. "What happened?"

Finally Lane could breathe again. She wiped her tearing eyes. With a napkin from Betty, she dried her face. The legs of her jeans felt damp. So did the front of her sweater.

"What happened?" Henry asked again.

"Went down the wrong pipe," she muttered. "I'm going to the john." Without a glance at Jim, she squeezed past the knees of Betty and Henry. She lunged into the aisle and shoved through the swinging door to the lobby.

In the rest room she used damp paper towels to clean the faint spatter of stains on her sweater.

Second time today, she thought. First Riley, now Jim. I'm spending half my life cleaning up after getting messed with by shitheads.

Why'd he *do* that?

My hands were full, that's why. Figured he'd get in a grab when I couldn't stop him. Rotten bastard.

Betty came in. "Are you okay?"

"No. And I'm not going back in there."

"What's the matter?"

"Jim. The bastard."

"What'd he do?"

"Never mind. I'm gonna call my dad and have him pick me up."

"Well, Jim's waiting right outside the door."

"Yeah?" Lane wadded the paper towels, tossed them into the trash bin, and shouldered open the rest room door. It missed Jim, but not by much. Henry was standing nearby, staring at the room as if embarrassed to be a part of all this.

"Are you okay?" Jim asked, frowning, all concerned.

"What do you think?"

"I'm sorry. Jesus, Lane. I didn't mean for you to choke."

"Yeah, Sure."

"I'm *sorry.*"

She turned away from him and strode toward the pair of public phones beside the drinking fountain. Jim rushed after her. "Hey, what're you doing?"

"Calling home. Go on back in and enjoy the movie."

"Hey, come on."

"Get lost."

"I didn't *do* anything."

"Right." She dug into her handbag, searching for change.

"You don't have to call anyone," Jim said. "I'll drive you home, if that's what you want."

"I'm ready to leave," Betty said.

"Me, too. The movie stank, anyway," Henry said.

"How about it?" Jim asked her.

"Okay," she muttered. "But you'd better just keep your fucking hands to yourself."

Jim grimaced.

Henry's head snapped toward him. Glaring, he snapped, "What did you do to her?"

"What's the trouble over here?" the manager asked, approaching.

"We're just leaving," Jim said.

They hurried for the exit doors. Henry, in the lead, kept glancing back at Jim with furious eyes. He held the door open for the group.

Outside he grabbed Jim by the arm. "What'd you do to Lane, you rotten scum?"

"Don't you touch me, asshole."

"You want to make me?"

"Henry!" Lane snapped. "Quit it. Let go of him."

"Better do like she says," Jim said, "before I wipe up the sidewalk with you."

"Oh yeah?" Though Betty tried to pull him away, he kept his grip on Jim's arm. "I've been beat up by tougher guys than you."

Jim cocked back his arm.

Lane kicked him hard in the rear. Crying out, he jerked rigid, freed his arm from Henry's grip and grabbed his rump. He started hopping up and down as if that somehow helped the pain. He turned around as he hopped. His face was bright red under the streetlights.

"That *hurt!*" he blurted, his voice high-pitched and accusing.

"It was supposed to. You want to beat up on somebody, try me. Better yet, why don't you team up with Riley Benson? You're no better than him. Maybe the two of you'd like a try at me."

"Oh yeah?" He stopped hopping. He stood there, gasping, clutching his seat with both hands. "Well, fuck you."

"Not in your lifetime."

"If you think I'm gonna forget this—"

"I sure hope not. Do me a favor and get lost."

"Yeah! I'll get lost, all right! You and your asshole friends can *walk* home, see how you like it."

"We'll like it just fine, thanks."

He turned away from her and hobbled past Henry and Betty.

"Ciao," Henry said, and Betty thumped the side of his head.

Jim scowled back at them, then turned his head more until his eyes met Lane's. "I wouldn't take you back if you begged me. Not a chance. It's over."

"I'm already eating my heart out," she called to him.

"Who needs you? You're a pain in the ass."

"Literally," Henry said.

Betty thumped him again.

"Try Candi," Lane suggested. "I'm sure she'll appreciate your finer traits."

Jim flipped her off, then vanished around the corner.

Joining her friends, Lane said, "Let's walk over to Antonio's and get a pizza. My treat. Then I'll call home and get Mom or Dad to pick us up."

"Spectacular," Henry said.

"I could go for some pizza about now," Betty said. "All this excitement sure stirs up the ol' appetite."

They started walking. Lane, stepping between Henry and Betty, put her arms across their backs. "You were great," she said to Henry.

"The nerd showed hair," Betty agreed.

"Our Henry's not a nerd."

He beamed.

"You almost got yourself creamed," Betty told him.

"That was sure some kick," Henry said. "Any harder, you would've knocked his ass out his mouth."

Lane laughed. "Well, I tried."

"Did you see the look on his face?" Betty asked. "I mean, that crud didn't know whether to shit or go blind."

"He'll wish he'd gone blind when he tries to sit down," Henry said. "Spectacular. You ought to try out for the football team."

"Anyway," Lane said. "That's over. I should've dumped that creep a long time ago."

"That's what we've been telling you," Betty said.

"I'm a slow learner."

"You're lucky to be rid of the slimebag," Henry told her.

"Yeah." They waited for a car to pass, then stepped off the curb and started across the road. "He wasn't *all* bad, though. Sometimes, he could be . . ." A lump suddenly closed her throat. Tears filled her eyes. ". . . He could be nice," she finished, her voice trembling.

Betty rubbed her back. "Hey, it's all right. You're better off without him."

"I know. I know."

"If you get desperate," Henry said, "there's always me."

"You ready to die, Hen-house?" Betty asked.

"Just a suggestion."

Lane squeezed both of them closer against her sides. "Quit it before I kick your butts."

Thirty-two

"Do you want to talk about it?" Larry asked after dropping off Henry and Betty.

Lane slumped in the passenger seat with her arms folded, turned her face toward him and said, "I kicked Jim in the butt. So he advised us to walk home."

"You *kicked* him?"

"You wouldn't believe what he did to me."

"Oh, I might."

"Guys are such pigs."

"Thanks."

"Not youuuu. But I mean it. Honestly. All they want to do is grab grab grab. They've got sex on the brain."

"And you don't, huh?"

"I don't go around grabbing . . . their private areas."

"Happy to hear it."

"You weren't like that, were you? When you were a teenager?"

He was glad there wasn't enough light coming into the car for Lane to see his face go red. He'd been in his office with the door shut when she phoned from the pizza parlor. Gazing at his pictures of Bonnie. Remembering all the details of his dream. Longing for her. A girl nearly the same age as Lane. Who even *looked* quite similar to her.

"I guess every teenager has sex on the brain," he said.

"But you didn't go around always trying to cop a feel, did you?"

"When I was your age? No. I dated sometimes, but I wasn't especially interested in the girls I went out with. So I didn't try much funny stuff with them."

"You weren't *interested* in the girls you dated?"

"We're talking about my high school days, right?"

"Yeah."

"Well then, no. Not much. I basically just went out with dogs."

"Dad!" She sounded shocked but amused.

"It's true. And I didn't want to get fleas, so . . ."

"Really, that's not nice."

"Okay, okay. Seriously? I wasn't exactly dashing, and I knew it. So I never even tried to go out with any of the girls I really thought were neat. They scared the hell out of me. If a girl looked like you, for instance, I'd just admire her from afar and maybe daydream about her. I sure wouldn't date her."

"Jeez, Dad."

"Weird, huh? Now I've got a kid who's one of *them*."

He looked at Lane and smiled. She shook her head. Then she reached out and patted his shoulder. "*I* would've gone out with you."

"A pity date."

"No way. I'll bet *you* would've been a perfect gentleman."

"A lust-crazed maniac!" He shot his hand under Lane's outstretched arm and thrust it into her armpit.

"Don't!" she cried out. Giggling, she clamped her arm down and squirmed.

He pulled his hand free, got it under her elbow and tickled her side.

"Dad! Stop!"

He returned his hand to the steering wheel. As he eased the car to the curb in front of their house, Lane grabbed *his* side and dug her fingers in.

"Don't!" he cried out, mimicking her and laughing. "Please. Stop!"

"You can give it but you can't take it," she said.

Writhing as she tickled him, he shut off the engine. Then he grabbed her forearm and pushed up the sleeve of her sweater. "Indian burn," he announced.

"No!" she gasped, breathless with giggling. "Don't! I mean it! I'll tell Mom!"

"Tattletale." He gave her the Indian burn. Gently. Then let go.

"Is that the best you can do?"

"Oh? You want me to give you a good one?"

"I think I'll pass, thanks," she said. She patted his arm. "Maybe some other time. Maybe . . ." She suddenly clutched his forearm with both hands and twisted, wringing its flesh.

"Yeeeoow!"

"That'll teach you, tough guy." Laughing, she hurled herself at the passenger door and scurried from the car. She ran to the house. But instead of using her key to let herself in, she waited on the porch for him.

Larry rubbed his arm as he walked toward her. It stung.

"I didn't really hurt you, did I?" she asked.

"I'll live. With luck."

Lane held out her arm. "Want to give me one?"

"No."

"Come on, I'll feel better if you get me back."

"You'd just scream and wake up your mother," he said, and unlocked the door. They entered the house quietly.

Lane looked toward the sofa. "Where is she?"

"In bed."

"Ah-ha. Gosh, I hope I didn't interrupt anything when I phoned."

Jean, complaining of a miserable headache, had gone to bed nearly an hour before the call, giving Larry his opportunity to be with the pictures of Bonnie. He said, "You'll never know."

"Ho ho ho."

"Well, it's time for me to hit the hay."

"Time for me to hit the shower," Lane said.

"Didn't you just have a bath before supper?"

Her smile fell away. "I'm feeling kind of grubby."

"Oh."

"Yeah. Everything that—" She pressed her lips together. Her chin began to tremble and tears glimmered in her eyes.

Larry's throat suddenly tightened. "I'm sorry, honey."

She wrapped her arms around him and hugged him. "Why do things . . . have to get so fouled up?"

"I don't know. It's life, I guess."

"Life's a bitch, then you die."

"Don't say that, honey," he whispered. "Everything will turn out fine."

"Yeah, sure."

"Jim isn't the only guy in the world. Just wait and see. You'll run into some fellow, one of these days, and fall head over heels for him."

"Good way to break your back," she muttered against the side of his neck. Relaxing her hold, she kissed his cheek. "Anyway, thanks." She stepped back and wiped her eyes on a sleeve of her sweater.

"You'll feel better in the morning," he told her.

"At least until I wake up."

Larry stretched out between the sheets of his bed. They were cool and felt good.

"Lane back?" Jean asked in a husky voice.

"Yep."

She sighed, and seemed to fall asleep again. Larry listened to her deep, slow breathing. Soon, he heard the distant windy sound of the shower.

He wondered if Lane would go right to bed when she was done.

You don't need to look at those pictures again, he told himself. Go to sleep and forget it.

What if Lane caught you looking at them? A girl her own age. A dead girl, to boot. She'd think you're no better than Jim. Worse. *Guys are such pigs.* Including Dad.

Just explain you're writing a book about her. She was murdered, and tomorrow . . .

Tomorrow.

Larry had struggled, ever since lunch, to push that out of his mind. Whenever he thought about returning to Sagebrush Flat, a sick hot feeling swept through him. It came now. He kicked free of the top sheet and blanket.

Call it off?

What do you tell Pete? Sorry, I changed my mind. Right. We've got to go through with it.

What if we find Uriah?

We won't. We were there twice before, and he didn't put in an appearance.

Maybe he just happened to be away the other times. Taking a stroll in the desert. Killing coyotes.

Or right there, hidden, watching us.

Terrific.

Now I'll never get to sleep, he thought.

Think about something pleasant. Think about Bonnie.

No! I've got to stop thinking about Bonnie. It's crazy. It's wrong.

He heard the shower go silent.

Lane was done. Give her fifteen minutes, he thought, to make sure she's asleep. Then it'll be safe to take out the pictures.

Might as well, if I can't sleep anyway.

No.

Besides, what's the point? She's dead. She won't come back.

She might. When I pull the stake.

Bullshit.

But what if she does?

She won't. There's no such thing as vampires.

"Pull it and find out," Bonnie said, her voice soft and teasing in his mind.

"You'd like that, wouldn't you?" he told her.

"Very much."

"I suppose it can be arranged." He straddled the coffin and smiled down at her.

It was confusing. He hadn't pulled the stake yet, but she was already alive, naked and beautiful and talking to him.

"How come you're already alive?" he asked.

She gave him a playful smile. "Vampire magic."

"So you *are* a vampire?"

"Never said I wasn't."

"I don't know."

"You want me, don't you?" Her hand reached up from inside the coffin and stroked him.

"It's not as simple as that, Bonnie."

"You want me, don't you?"

"But if you really are a vampire . . ."

Bonnie lifted her legs, spread them apart, and hooked her knees over the sides of the coffin. "You *do* want me," she said.

"I know, but—"

"And I want you." Her hands went to her breasts, caressed them, squeezed them. "Take out the stake, and I'll be yours."

He didn't want to pull the stake. He ached for her, but she had as good as admitted that she was a vampire. If he freed her, what would she do?

"I won't feed on you or your family," she told him, as if reading his mind.

"How do I know that?"

"Trust me. Pull it." Then her head lifted. It came up off the bottom of the coffin. As she writhed and massaged her breasts, her neck grew longer. Slender and white and curving forward. It lowered her head toward the jutting stake. Her tongue slid out, long and pink, dripping, and curled around the wooden shaft. Slid down to where the wood entered her chest. Cheek resting against the smooth skin above her breasts, she looked up at Larry and smiled. "Pull it," she urged him, somehow able to talk in spite of her extended tongue.

Larry watched, breathless, his heart slamming.

Bonnie's tongue, wrapped around the shaft, wound its way to the top. Her head followed. She drew in her tongue. And then she stretched her lips wide and lowered her mouth over the blunt end of the stake. She sucked on it.

She's going to suck it right out of her, Larry thought.

It's okay if *she* does it. As long as I'm not the one . . .

"Cop out!" A stranger's voice.

Bonnie's head jerked up, fluid spilling down her chin, her eyes furious. With her long neck, she reminded Larry of a cobra rising to the tune of a snake charmer. Her head swiveled toward the sound of the voice.

Larry looked, too.

The stranger wore the dark robe of a monk. Its hood hung low, hiding his face.

"Uriah?" Larry asked.

"Do not be deceived by the evil one," the stranger said.

"Kill him, Larry," Bonnie said, her voice low and calm, coaxing. "That's Uriah, all right. He's the one who did this to me."

"Get thee back to Hell, demon!"

"He's a madman," Bonnie said. Her voice sounded farther away. And different. There was nothing sly or seductive about it. She sounded very much like Lane. Larry felt his chest tighten. "He *murdered* me. And it hurt. It hurt so much."

Larry looked away from the stranger.

The coffin was empty.

For a moment, Larry thought, *Its too late! She sucked the stake right out and she's alive!*

Then he saw her. She stood on the other side of the coffin. Tears gleamed in her eyes. Her chin trembled slightly. There was no stake in her chest. Somehow, she now wore Lane's white sweater, jeans and boots. But she was Bonnie, beautiful and innocent and weeping softly.

Larry suddenly realized he was naked. He looked down at himself and sighed with relief. He now had his robe on.

"He killed me," Bonnie said, her voice trembling.

"Vampire!" Uriah bellowed. "Hideous slut!"

"Shut up," Larry snapped at him.

"I'm no vampire," Bonnie said. She sniffled. "Uriah's crazy. He . . . he murdered my friends and me. We never did anything."

Larry scowled at Uriah.

"She's lying, you fool."

"Oh yeah?" Larry snapped. "You goddamn maniac, you—" And he was suddenly rushing the man. "I'll kill you, you fucking maniac!"

Uriah hurled the severed head of a coyote at him.

The eyeless head tumbled through the air, blood spraying from the stump of its neck, its maw wide, fangs dripping. Larry flung up his arms to block it. The teeth snapped shut on his forearm. He yelped and flinched and woke up.

The house was dark and silent. He lay uncovered on the bed, trembling, his skin tingling with goose bumps and bathed in sweat. He sat up. The bottom sheet peeled away from his wet back. Looking past the vague form of his sleeping wife, he squinted at the alarm clock. Almost one. He couldn't have been asleep for more than half an hour.

Not even *close* to morning.

He ran his hand through his drenched hair. The muscles

along the sides of his neck felt tight and cold. They seemed to be squeezing pain into his head.

He climbed out of bed, stepped quietly to the closet and put on his robe. It clung to his damp skin. Knotting the belt, he went into the hallway.

He passed Lane's open door on the way to the bathroom. Her light was off, but he wondered if she was asleep. He didn't stop to check.

It doesn't matter, he told himself. I'm not going to look at the pictures.

What *will* I do? he wondered.

He knew what he wouldn't do—go back to bed. Not right away, at least. He felt wide awake. Besides, there was no point in trying to sleep until the headache subsided. And he didn't want to risk another dream. Not like that one.

At the end of the hallway he entered the bathroom. He shut the door but left the light off, knowing it would hurt his eyes. The mellow glow from the night-light was enough. As he stepped toward the medicine cabinet, he breathed deeply of the scents that still lingered after Lane's shower. Feminine, flowery aromas from her soap or shampoo or body powder . . . who knows what? But they filled the bathroom with her presence, and Larry felt himself relax a little.

He took two aspirin, washing them down with cold water.

He returned to the door. He took hold of its knob.

He realized that he didn't want to face the dark, silent house beyond the door. He didn't want to lie in bed and wait for sleep. He didn't want to sleep. He didn't want to sit alone in the living room and try to read or watch television. He didn't want to sneak into his office and slide open the file cabinet and take out his pictures of Bonnie.

I'm just fine right here, he told himself.

He thumbed down the button in the middle of the knob. The door locked with a loud ping.

He lowered the toilet seat and sat down. Leaning forward, he rested his elbows on his knees. He stared at the bath mat. Even in the faint light he could see where Lane's wet feet had matted down the nap.

He breathed through his nose, savoring the comfortable, familiar mix of aromas.

Bonnie can't get to me here, he thought.

A knock on the door startled him awake. The bathroom was gray with morning light. "Dad, my teeth are floating."

"Just a minute." He pushed himself off the floor, picked up the bath towel he'd used to cover his legs, hung it on the rack and straightened his robe. He flushed the toilet. Then he lifted its seat and stepped to the bathroom door. "What's the secret password?" he asked.

"I'm gonna pee on the floor!"

"That's it." He opened the door.

Lane rolled her eyes upward. "About time." As she side-stepped past him, she stopped and frowned. "Are you okay? You're looking kind of weird."

"Rough night," he said.

"Case of the trotskis?" she asked.

"Just a headache."

"Good. So you didn't stink the place up."

"Smells fine in there." It smells like you, he thought. He rubbed her mussed hair. She stepped past him and shut the door.

In the bedroom he found Jean still asleep. He closed the door, hung up his robe, and crawled into bed. The sheets on his side were cool. He rolled, and curled himself against Jean's back. He slipped an arm down across her belly. She was warm and smooth. He eased his face against her hair. The smell of her was like those that had kept him company through the night.

She and Lane must use some of the same stuff, he thought, snuggling against her.

"Time to get up?" she mumbled.

"Not yet."

"Good. Hold me for a while."

Thirty-three

"Try not to shoot each other," Barbara said through the van's open window. She gave Pete a kiss, then stepped backward.

Jean, by the passenger window, frowned at Larry and said, "Are you sure you're all right?"

"I'm okay."

Ever since getting up, he'd been plagued by stomach cramps and loose bowels. Jean had suggested he phone Pete and cancel the outing. He'd been tempted. But he knew that his problem was caused by nerves. If he called off the trip to Sagebrush Flat, Pete would insist on trying it again tomorrow. Better to get it over with.

"What's the problem, pardner?" Pete asked.

"A little indigestion," he said. He didn't want to discuss his runs. Not with Barbara standing there. "I'm fine now."

"Okey-doke. We're off."

Jean kissed Larry and moved out of the way.

Pete turned the ignition key. *Click-click-click.* He twisted it again. Nothing. "Shit!"

"Must be the battery," Larry said.

Pete tried again. Again he said, "Shit."

Larry felt like celebrating.

"Do you want to jump it?" Jean asked, approaching the passenger window.

"No. Damn it!" Pete whacked the steering wheel with his palm.

"Calm down," Barbara told him. "It's not the end of the world. Why don't we jump it, and you can stop by the service station on the way out and have the problem taken care of?"

"It's probably gonna need a new battery." He pounded the wheel again. "There goes the rest of the morning."

"It's not that big a deal," Barbara insisted.

"Maybe we weren't meant to go shooting today," Larry said.

"We'll take your car," Pete told his wife.

"Oh? Terrific. And how am I supposed to get to the grocery store?"

"You can walk, for all I—"

"Oh, sure thing. Why don't you—"

"Wait," Jean interrupted. "Hold it. Why don't you guys just take one of our cars?"

Thanks a heap, Larry thought.

"I don't know," he said. "I'd hate to take a chance on the Dodge overheating . . ."

"Take the Mustang."

"Maybe Lane has plans."

"Don't worry about it. If she wants to go someplace, she can take the Dodge."

Larry nodded. Why argue? We're meant to go after all, he thought.

They climbed from the van. They transferred the VCR camcorder, their firearms, food, and beer to the red Mustang. Larry settled in behind the steering wheel. Pete harnessed himself into the passenger seat.

"Let's hope this one works," Pete said.

"Yeah."

He knew it would work. Nothing was going to save him from his rendezvous with Sagebrush Flat.

He turned the key. The engine grumbled to life.

The wives stood side by side, smiling and waving as Larry backed the Mustang onto the road.

"Is this exciting, or what?" Pete said, grinning.

"Or what."

"Should be just around this next bend," Pete said.

Larry hoped he would find the town occupied. This was a Saturday, after all. Maybe some folks on an outing had stopped to explore the "ghost town." Maybe some kids had dropped by to decorate the walls with grafitti or shoot the place up. Even a biker gang would be a welcome sight. Anyone would do. Just so the town wasn't deserted and they had to give up their hunt for Uriah.

But he rounded the bend, and the broad main road through Sagebrush Flat stretched in front of him, glaring in the sunlight, empty except for a tumbleweed rolling lazily past the saloon.

"Stop the car," Pete said. "I'll get us some footage." He climbed out with his video camera. Standing in the middle of the road, he turned slowly from side to side, panning the area ahead. Then he stepped closer to Larry's window. "I'll get you driving in. Head on up there and park at the hotel."

"Seems kind of dippy to me."

"Hey. Did Doug MacArthur complain when he had to wade ashore at Bataan?"

"I don't think it was Bataan."

"Wherever. This is *us* returning, pardner."

"Right," he muttered.

He drove the rest of the way alone, swung off the road in front of the hotel and got out. Pete, still about fifty yards away, was walking slowly forward, the camera to his eye.

"Open the trunk!" Pete called. "Strap on your shootin' iron."

He opened the trunk, lifted out his holstered Ruger .22, and strapped the belt low around his hips. Squinting at

Pete, he tugged the brim of his battered old Stetson down across his eyes.

"Terrific!" Pete called. "Now, slap some leather!"

"Get real," he said.

"Well, at least *load* it."

He supposed that wasn't a bad idea. If they somehow did manage to run into Uriah, he didn't want to be standing there with an empty gun.

He sat on the rear bumper, dumped some .22 magnums into his hand and started feeding them into the cylinder. By the time he finished, Pete was only a couple of yards away.

"Gimme an Eastwood sneer."

"If Uriah's watching all this, he'll think we're clowns."

"Good. Give him a false sense of security."

"False, huh?" He dropped a handful of cartridges into the pocket of his shirt and set the box down inside the trunk. "Should we have a beer before we start?" he asked.

"Not yet. Here, take this. I don't want to be left out."

He gave the camera to Larry and showed him how to work it. Larry stepped away from the car, picked up Pete in the viewfinder and recorded him strapping on his gunbelt.

"A couple of real *hombres,* huh?"

"Yup," Larry said.

It felt good, he realized, to be dressed up in his boots, faded jeans, old blue workshirt, and cowboy hat. It especially felt good to have the holster against his leg and know it held a real six-shooter with live rounds in the cylinder. Like playing cowboys for real.

Pete, though smaller than Larry, looked twice as tough. He wore scuffed and dusty combat boots. The cuffs of his jeans were frayed. The sleeves of his plaid shirt were turned up, revealing his thick hairy forearms. The shirt, too tight across his chest, bulged with the push of his muscles. His dirty straw hat, sides curled up and front swooping low, looked like something he might've swiped off a drunken old-timer in an alley behind a saloon. But the best part was the black handlebar mustache, sprinkled with flecks of gray. The mustache was more than dress-up. It was real.

Leaning back against the car, Pete fed ammo into his revolver. His bullets looked about three times the size of Larry's.

"I'm gonna have to get me a forty-five or something," Larry said.

"Yeah. Get yourself a piece with some real stopping power." Pete holstered his magnum. Squinting into the camera, he poked a cigarette into the corner of his mouth. He lit it with a Bic. "Ready to go after our man?" he asked.

"How about a beer before we start?"

"Reckon that'd hit the spot."

They leaned against the side of the car while they drank. Larry kept looking up and down the road, hoping someone might show up and ruin their plan.

Pete finished his cigarette. He tossed it down and mashed it under his boot. "This'll be great in our book," he said, "the two of us coming out here to kick ass."

"Yeah. We probably won't find him, though."

"Hey, man, think positive."

"I am."

"Get outa here. You mean to tell me you came all the way out here *hoping* we won't find the guy?"

"I'm not exactly looking forward to it."

"You're not gonna chicken out on me, are you?"

"Came this far."

"That's the spirit."

"The thing about Uriah, though—" He stopped, shook his head, and drank some more beer.

"Yeah?"

"Nothing."

"Come on, man. Spit it out."

"Well, he's *real.*"

"No fooling."

"You've been to Vietnam and everything. It's different for you. The closest I ever came to real trouble was when some neighbors got shot up back in L.A. I just hit the floor and prayed none of the bullets would come our way. I've never actually *gone after* anyone."

"Me neither. I wasn't a grunt, you know."

"You've never shot anyone?"

"Nope. Or been shot *at.* Closest I ever came to getting plugged, ol' hoss, was when you drew down on me last Friday."

"Oh."

"Yeah, oh." He laughed. "Hey, buck up. It showed you had balls. If you can stick a gun in my face, you'll do it when it counts."

"Hope so," Larry muttered.

"Don't worry, you will." Pete stepped away from the car, tossed his beer can high and went for his gun.

"No!" Before he could clear his holster, Larry grabbed his wrist.

The can clinked on the street and rolled.

"Hey, man—"

"Are you out of your gourd? That cannon—"

"We didn't exactly *sneak* into town, Lar. If Uriah's around, I reckon he knows we're here."

"Well, Jeez."

"Okay, okay. You done there? Let's get this show on the road."

While Pete retrieved his can, Larry finished his beer and stepped to the trunk. They dropped both cans inside. "What about the camera?" Larry asked.

"It'll be too dark in the hotel."

"Better take this, then." Larry searched a corner of the trunk. Along with the jack, tire iron, and flares was a flashlight he kept there for emergencies. He took it out and started to shut the trunk.

"Whoa there. We might need this, too." Pete reached in. He lifted out the tire tool.

Looking over his shoulder, Larry saw that the hasp on the hotel doors still dangled loose. "Think we'll need the bar?"

"We're gonna check the rooms, aren't we?"

He hadn't thought of that. He realized, in fact, that he'd avoided thinking about what they would actually do once they were here. "I don't know about breaking into rooms."

Pete shook his head and chuckled. Tire iron in his hand, he closed the trunk. "You really *don't* want to find this guy, do you?"

"I sure don't want to shoot him," Larry said as they approached the front doors.

"I don't aim to shoot anyone, either. But it's nice to know we've got some protection." He patted the handle of his revolver. Then he slipped the tire iron under his belt, swung open one of the doors, and stepped into the hotel.

The light from the doorway swept across the lobby floor and faded, leaving the far areas of the room in darkness. Larry could barely make out the vague shape of the registration counter, could only see halfway up the stairs to his left. As he tried to see more, the light was squeezed out. The door bumped shut.

"Let's get our eyes used to it," Pete whispered.

Larry felt as if a black hood had been dropped over his face. But when he turned around, he found strips of sunlight coming through cracks in the boarded windows, and a glowing band across the bottom of the doorway.

Pete stood beside him, silent.

Larry faced forward again. Soon he was able to make out the faint shapes of things: the long counter, the cubbyholes behind it, the banister and stairs. They were almost invisible, but there. Soft around the edges. Flowing. Melting into the blackness. He saw some shapes he wasn't sure about. Something above the distant counter that might be a face. Something partway up the stairs that might be a man standing motionless, staring down at them.

It was better, he thought, when I couldn't see at all.

"The lair of the madman," Pete whispered.

"Cut it out."

"That'd be a good title for you, huh?"

"Shhh."

"You're gonna get a lot of good material from all this."

He wished Pete would hush. He wanted silence so he could hear if anyone . . .

"Go ahead and turn on the flashlight," Pete said.

He thumbed the switch. Swept the light up the stairs. His breath snagged as shadows from the banister squirmed on the wall. But nobody was there. The beam reached all the way to the top. It cast a dim glow into the second-floor hallway. Larry quickly swung it away and darted it across the top of the registration counter. Nobody there, either. Breathing more easily, he probed each corner of the lobby.

"Let me have it," Pete said.

Larry was reluctant, for a moment, to give up control of the light. Then he realized that it should belong to the one leading the way. He preferred Pete to be the leader. He passed the light to him and rested his hand on the grips of his revolver.

They started forward, their boots making gritty sounds on the sandy hardwood floor. Larry watched where the flashlight went. It stopped briefly on the crucifix. It moved around the edges of the panel, which was flush with the other sections enclosing the area under the stairway. It swept along the length of the counter and lingered on a closed door near the far end.

"Let's check that out," Pete said.

They climbed over the counter and dropped into the space behind it. Pete led the way to the door, eased it open

and leaned in. Larry peered past his head. The pale shaft
of light revealed an empty room with a boarded window
on its far wall.

"The hotel office," Pete whispered. "Let's try upstairs."
He pulled the door shut.

They swung themselves over the counter again and
crossed the lobby to the stairway. Pete aimed the light at
the top as if to make sure nobody was waiting up there.
Then he lowered it to the steps just above them. He started
to climb.

The landing was still covered by loose planks.

Seeing them, Larry wished to God that Barbara had
never broken through.

How can you wish such a thing?

The voice was Bonnie's, sad and accusing.

I thought you loved me.

"Think I'll take a peek," Pete said. He sank to his knees
and carefully lifted two boards out of the way. Ducking
low, he lowered his head into the gap. The flashlight followed. "I don't see anything," he said.

"What did you expect?"

"Who knows?" He straightened up, replaced the boards,
and got to his feet. Again he shined the light at the top
of the stairs. Then he began to climb.

Larry took a long stride to avoid stepping on the planks.

Just above him Pete switched the flashlight to his left
hand. With his right hand he drew the revolver from its
holster.

"Be careful," Larry whispered. "I mean, don't go blast-
ing anything that moves. There might be a bum living here,
or something."

"Don't worry, huh?"

"We're the ones trespassing, you know."

"Yeah, yeah."

One stair from the top Pete leaned forward and glanced
both ways. He stepped into the corridor. Larry followed.

The corridor ended just to the left of the stairway. To the right it stretched long and dark with doors on both sides.

They stopped in front of the first door. Pete pressed his ear to it, shoving his cowboy hat crooked. After listening for a moment, he moved back. "You wanta do the honors?" he whispered, pointing the flashlight at its knob. "I'll cover you."

Heart thudding, Larry gripped the knob. He tried to twist it, but there was no give. "Locked."

Pete tapped the muzzle of his revolver against the end of the tire iron in his belt.

Larry pulled the bar out. Holding it with both hands, he forced the wedge into the crack between the lock plate and the door frame. He looked at Pete.

"Well, go on."

"I don't know."

"Well, shit."

"We shouldn't be here."

"Don't go pussy on me now."

"Maybe we ought to just go shooting like we told the gals."

"The book, man. The book. Uriah's the missing piece, remember?"

He murdered me. Bonnie's voice again. *You can't let him get away with it. He's got to pay.*

"Okay," Larry muttered.

He put his weight against the iron bar. He felt it move a bit sideways, digging into the wood. There were soft crunchy sounds.

Then came the blare of a car horn.

He froze.

"Uh-oh," Pete said.

Larry jerked the bar free and spun around. "That was *our* car!"

Thirty-four

Pete in the lead, they raced down the stairs. The wood clamored and creaked under their pounding boots. The loose planks across the landing jumped and clattered. If the horn was still honking, Larry couldn't hear it.

His stomach was a ball of ice. His chest ached. He could barely breath. There was a tightness in his throat like a scream trying to force its way out.

Somebody was out there. Uriah? Curious strangers? A gang? Cops?

"Don't go running out with a gun in your hand," he gasped as he rushed after Pete to the front doors.

Pete stopped. Larry, at his back, grabbed his shoulder.

"Take it easy," Pete whispered, and eased the door open a crack. A strip of daylight jabbed Larry's eyes. "I don't see anybody."

"A car or anything?"

"Just yours." The daylight spread. Pete stuck his head through the gap and looked from side to side like a kid getting ready to cross a busy road. "Nope. Nothing." He holstered his revolver, swung the door wide and stepped onto the sidewalk.

Larry, just behind him, squinted at the bright red Mustang. He saw no one. He looked both ways. The street was deserted.

"The horn didn't honk itself," he muttered.

"Tell me something I don't already know."

"I don't like this at all."

"Join the crowd."

"You think he's behind the car?"

"Let's find out." Eyes on the car, Pete sidestepped his way to the middle of the street. There, he saw something that made him scowl and shake his head. He dropped to his knees, set down the flashlight and peered beneath the car. Rising, he stepped close to the driver's side and glanced through the windows. He took a deep breath. He looked at Larry. Nobody here," he said. "But we've got a flat."

"Oh no. Jesus." His head seemed to go numb inside. His legs felt wobbly as he staggered into the street.

The Mustang's left front tire was mashed against the pavement.

Crouching, Pete fingered its sidewall. "Slashed."

"He doesn't want us to leave," Larry said. His voice sounded far away.

"Either that, or he's just pissed off. You've got a spare, don't you?"

"Yeah."

Pete stood up and turned his back to the car. Eyes narrow, he scanned the storefronts across the street. "He's probably over there laughing at us."

"Let's change the tire and get out of here."

"This is our chance to get him."

"It might not even be Uriah."

"Bet it is."

"Well, I'm gonna change the damn tire." Larry dug the car keys out of his pocket and stepped toward the trunk. "Keep an eye out, huh?"

"Uriah, all right," Pete said. "And I'll bet he knows we're the guys who took his stiff. That'd explain why he slashed the tire. Wants to keep us here and nail us."

Larry moaned. He opened the trunk, leaned in and took out the jack.

"Maybe he thinks *we're* vampires."

"Jesus, Pete."

"I'm serious. What if he thinks we already pulled the stake and she bit us?"

"It's daytime, for one thing."

"So?"

Larry lifted the spare tire, swung it away from the trunk and lowered it to the pavement. As he rolled it toward the front of the car, he said, "Vampires can't survive in the sunlight."

"Maybe that's just movie crap."

"It's in all the books."

"You believe everything you read?"

"Of course not." He let the tire fall and hurried to get the jack. "I don't believe in *vampires,* for godsake."

He imagined Bonnie laughing at that, shaking her head, her golden hair swaying.

"But Uriah believes in them," Larry went on. "He believes in using crucifixes and garlic and stakes." Setting down the jack beside the spare, he reached up. Pete handed him the tire iron. "So he must know that vampires can't be out in the sunlight the way we are."

"Unless he knows different."

Larry pried the hubcap loose. It fell and clanked on the pavement. He covered one of the nuts with the lug wrench. He yanked on the bar. It slipped off and he stumbled backward.

"I'd better do it," Pete said. "You keep watch."

Larry gave him the tire tool, turned his back to the car and scanned the buildings across the street. A few of the doors stood open. Some of the windows were boarded, but others weren't.

"One down," Pete said.

The hubcap rang as a nut dropped into it.

"Besides," Larry said, "if he thinks we're vampires, he'd have to kill us with stakes."

"Good point. No way, right?" Another nut rang into the hubcap. "He must *think* he has a chance, though, or why the flat tire?" Pete grunted. Seconds later a third nut hit the hubcap. "Three down, one to go."

"Maybe it *wasn't* Uriah. Could've been anyone. A hermit, or somebody. Maybe doesn't like strangers, did it to teach us a lesson."

The last nut clanged into the hubcap.

"You got the emergency brake on?"

"Yeah." Larry looked around. Pete, on his knees, was putting together the jack. He dropped lower to study the undercarriage, then shoved the jack beneath the car and started pumping it up with the tire iron. The car began to rise.

The arrow missed Pete's hat, skimmed above the hood of the Mustang, flew across the sidewalk and thunked into the hotel wall.

"What the—" Pete blurted.

Larry whirled, crouching and drawing his gun. Nobody. Just shadows beyond the doors and windows.

"Shit! That's a fuckin' *arrow!*"

Then Pete was on his knees beside Larry, arm out, sweeping his revolver slowly from side to side.

"Where'd it come from?"

"Over there someplace."

"You were supposed to keep watch, man. Thing coulda *killed* me!"

"What're we gonna—"

Larry still saw nobody. But he saw the next arrow. It shot out of the gloom beyond a window directly across the street. The big display window of a shop, partly crisscrossed by weathered boards, mostly open.

"Pete!" he shouted as he threw himself at the pavement and the arrow hissed by. A moment later he heard it punch into something.

Then his ears were pounded. He felt as if they were

being slapped hard by open hands determined to destroy his eardrums.

Huge, horrible explosions.

Pete's .357 magnum.

Pete was on his knees, eyes narrow, teeth gritted, arms straight out and jerking upward as another blast struck the air. Larry fought an urge to cover his ears. Facing forward, he was hit by another explosion and saw a hole get punched through the wall below the window. There were three or four other holes nearby, spaced about a foot apart.

He started firing, aiming to the left of Pete's holes, making new ones he could barely see, stitching a line toward the open door. His gun made sharp, flat bangs that seemed insignificant compared to Pete's thundering weapon. But he knew the .22 magnums were strong enough to penetrate the wood. If the walls inside weren't lined with plaster or Sheetrock, his bullets would be flying through the room.

His hammer clanked on a spent round.

"Reload, reload!" he heard Pete yell through the ringing in his ears.

He rolled onto his side and started to eject the casings.

Pete, still on his knees, was shoving fresh cartridges into his cylinder. Then he was rising, rushing the window.

"Wait!" Larry shouted. Though his gun was still empty, he scurried up and ran for the door.

Lot of use I'll be, he thought.

He half expected Pete to dive through the window and come up inside firing like a movie cowboy. But his friend proved more cautious, and ducked below the windowsill and peeked in. Larry slammed his shoulder against the doorframe. Pressing his back to the wall, he flicked the last two shells from his revolver.

"I don't see him," Pete said.

"Think we got him?"

"I don't know." Pete dropped lower, turned around and

squatted, seeming to sag against the wall as he stared into the street.

Larry fumbled fresh cartridges out of his shirt pocket. He started thumbing them into the chambers. The cylinder made quiet clicking sounds as he turned it. Done, he snapped the loading gate shut.

Pete looked at him. "All set?"

"For what?"

"We're going in, aren't we?"

"Are we?"

"We're not going anywhere *else,* I'll tell you that much. I'm not changing any fuckin' tire with Tonto taking pot-shots at me."

"You want us to *go in?*"

"That's the idea." Pete started duck-walking toward him.

"I don't know about this."

"What don't you know?"

"What if he's waiting?"

"If you're chicken, I'll go first."

"I'm not chicken, but . . ."

Pete dropped to his knees, crawled past Larry and eased his head past the doorframe. "I think he's gone."

"If you catch an arrow in the face, Barbara's gonna kill me."

Pete rose slowly until he was standing in the middle of the doorway. Larry turned around and stepped up close beside him. The room was brighter than he'd expected. Light not only poured in from the front door and display window, but also from a smaller window at the rear.

"Bet he took off out the back," Pete said.

"What about over there?"

Over there was an L-shaped counter with a few bullet holes near its top. Behind it was the closed door of a room that occupied the shop's right rear quarter.

"If you're in here," Pete said in a loud voice, "show yourself right now."

Nothing happened.

He fired three times, the explosions slamming Larry's ears as bullets crashed through the counter at knee level.

"Christ! Did you have to do that?"

"Yep." Even as the word left Pete's lips, he raced at the counter. He vaulted it. His kick sent the door flying open. He rushed into the back room, then came out shaking his head. "Like I said, he beat it out the window."

Larry joined up with Pete and they reached the window together.

He yelled, *"Shit!"*

He shoved Pete. The force of the push sent them both stumbling, separating them, and the arrow sizzled between them.

As he fell to one knee, Larry's mind held a frozen image of the man he'd seen an instant ago. A man standing in the desert about a hundred feet beyond the back of the building, letting an arrow fly. A savage with wild gray hair, a bushy beard, and a black patch over one eye. Wearing a necklace of garlic cloves, a crucifix that hung in the middle of his chest, an open vest and skirt of gray animal fur, with a knife in the belt at his hip.

"Did you see *that?*" Pete asked.

Getting up, Larry said, "Uriah?"

"Fuckin' wildman of Borneo!"

They both peered out from the sides of the window.

The man was running away, hair streaming out behind him, the bow pumping up and down in his right hand, a quiver of arrows and some kind of cloth bag bouncing against his back.

Pete crouched. He braced his arms on the windowsill and took careful aim.

"You can't shoot him in the back!"

"Watch me."

Larry was ready to knock the gun aside, but an image of Bonnie filled his mind. He saw her alive, sleeping in her bed, the weird old man creeping toward her with a hammer and stake.

Pete fired.

His bullet kicked up a puff of dust a yard behind the sprinting lunatic.

His next shot chopped through the bow. The weapon was ripped from the man's hand, its string flinging the broken ends high, whipping them together.

"All *right!*" Pete cried out. "Now we've got him!"

As they climbed out the window, Larry saw him leap and drop out of sight.

"He's in the ravine," Pete said.

"Yeah." The ravine. The streambed where they'd found the old jukebox and the campfire with the remains of the coyote.

They started walking toward it, Pete reloading.

"We won't have to shoot him now," Larry said.

"Right. We'll take him alive, ask a few questions. This'll be great. We'll take him to the cops. Man, we'll be the guys that solved the disappearances."

"Yeah," Larry muttered. He knew he should feel good. They'd come here for Uriah. Pretty soon, they'd find out whether this was him.

Certainly wasn't the Uriah of his nightmares.

Probably him, though.

The guy who murdered Bonnie and the other two girls. They'd have him. Alive. He could tell them everything.

But Larry didn't feel good. He felt as if he were being strangled by fear.

Pete grinned at him. "You look like shit, pardner. You okay?"

"Yeah."

"Nothing to be scared of, man. What's he gonna do, *throw* arrows at us?"

"I don't know. But I don't like this."

"I do. Fantastic!"

Maybe we won't be able to find him, Larry thought. This is a guy who eats coyotes down there. Probably knows the ravine like the back of his hand. Maybe has special hiding places.

Or, once at the bottom, he might've taken off running in either direction. By the time we get there, he could be long gone.

God, I hope so.

Get him for Bonnie. He killed her. Make him pay.

When they were thirty or forty feet from the rim of the gap, Pete waved toward the left. "You go that way."

"Huh?"

"We'll split up and box him in."

"Split up? You outa your mind?"

Halting, Pete scowled at him. "Just do it."

"No! If we split up, one of us'll get nailed. Happens in every shitty splatter film I've ever seen."

"This ain't a fuckin' movie."

"We stick together, and that's final."

Looking disgusted, Pete shook his head. "Okay, okay. Shit."

"Besides, if we aren't together down there—"

In the corner of Larry's vision something moved. He jerked his eyes toward the ravine. Glimpsed the head and arm of the one-eyed wildman, the face leering, the arm snapping forward as it hurled a rock. "Watch out!" he shouted.

Ducking, he looked at Pete.

Pete ducked as he brought up his revolver. The rock caught the bridge of his nose, knocked his head back and bounced to the side. His hat flew off. He stumbled backward a few steps like an outfielder going for a high fly ball. Blood spilled over his mustache, dribbled into his open mouth and spread down his chin. The gun fell from his hand. He flopped to the ground. The back of his head thumped a flat slab of granite.

Larry cringed, watching all this, as if he could feel the sharp impacts himself.

Then he remembered Uriah. Or whoever it was.

He snapped his head sideways.

The man was gone.

He dashed for the edge of the ravine.

I'm gonna kill you, you rotten bastard! his mind shrieked. *Look what you did! What'm I gonna tell Barbara? Shit shit shit! You piece of shit, I'm gonna blow your fucking brains all over the desert! Wasn't enough you had to kill Bonnie, you goddamn fucking lunatic!*

He teetered on the rim and gazed down. The embankment below was steep, cluttered with boulders and scrub brush. But nobody was on it. Nobody was running along the flat bottom of the streambed.

"Where are you, you shit!" he yelled.

Then he was scrambling down, dodging the rocks and bushes in his way, arms waving for balance, digging his heels into gravel, skidding over the hard-packed earth. Halfway down he slipped. His rump pounded the slope. He slid on the seat of his jeans, throat going tight and tears filling his eyes. A boulder stopped his descent. He pushed himself up, stepped onto the outcropping, blinked his eyes clear and scanned the area below him.

No trace of Uriah.

But a lot of hiding places: boulders, thickets, deep cuts eroded into the walls of the ravine.

The bastard might be anywhere, he thought.

Or not even down here at all.

Instead of heading for the bottom after he threw the rock, he might've gone *across* the slope.

A chill swept up Larry's spine. He twisted around.

Nobody there.

But he felt exposed, vulnerable.

Might be anywhere. I've gotta get out of here.

The walnut grips of his revolver felt slippery. He

switched the gun to his left hand, rubbed the right dry on a leg of his jeans and wrapped it around the revolver again. Then, with quick glances all around him, he began to climb the embankment.

Might be anywhere.

He snapped his head from side to side. He glanced behind him. He squinted at the top. Behind him. To the left. To the right. Whenever he looked one way, he imagined Uriah leaping up from the opposite direction.

It's like backing out of a tight space in a parking lot, he thought. A busy lot. Other cars backing out of other spaces.

Exactly the same.

You don't know where to look first.

I'll have to remember that and use it sometime, he told himself. Christ, this is no time to think about your damn writing!

Took my mind off Uriah, though. At least for a while.

Long enough to get me the rest of the way to the top!

His head almost even with the rim of the embankment, he felt a great surge of relief.

You're not there yet, he told himself. This is when he gets you—when safety's in easy reach.

He looked to the sides. He looked back. No Uriah.

I *made* it!

He chugged for the top.

Uriah was kneeling beside Pete.

Holding a stake against the middle of Pete's chest.

Swinging his hammer down.

Thirty-five

Larry didn't take aim. No time for that. He pointed and fired.

The man's head jerked sideways. Dropping the stake, he grabbed his cheek, glared at Larry with a single, mad eye, twisted on his knees and flung the hammer at him. Larry jumped out of the way. The hammer tumbled by, just missing his shoulder.

"Freeze!" he shouted.

Though he aimed his cocked revolver at the wildman, he held fire. His first shot had been lucky. He didn't want to risk another. Not while his target was kneeling beside Pete.

But Uriah didn't freeze.

He didn't seem to care that a gun was aimed at him. Nor did he seem to care, anymore, about his wound. Blood spilled down both sides of his shaggy gray beard as he snatched the stake off the ground and leaped up and charged.

"Stop or I'll shoot!"

"Vampire!" he yelled, spraying blood from his mouth. He dashed straight at Larry, the stake raised in his right hand.

Larry fired.

The metal belly of Jesus caved in and the upper corner of the big wooden cross gouged Uriah's chest.

I hit Jesus! Christ saved Uriah.

Larry thumbed back the hammer, but he couldn't pull the trigger.

As Uriah bore down on him, he flung up his left arm to ward off the stake and whipped the barrel of his gun against the man's temple. The gun discharged. Hair and flecks of bloody flesh flew off the side of Uriah's head.

Larry was slammed to the ground by the man's limp weight. As his breath was knocked out, he drove his knees up. They jammed into Uriah's belly.

The vampire killer tumbled over Larry.

From the sound of him, he kept on tumbling.

Larry crawled to the rim and saw Uriah plummeting down the slope—rolling, twisting, bouncing over rocks, smashing through bushes, arrows flying from his quiver, his limp arms and legs flapping. Near the bottom he skidded on his back, headfirst, until his shoulder struck a knob of granite. The impact jarred him to a stop that sent his legs swinging up. He did a backward somersault and landed facedown on the floor of the ravine. He lay there motionless.

Larry gazed down at him.

Finish him off. It seemed to be Bonnie's voice. *Do it for me. If you love me, kill him.*

I can't.

If you don't care what he did to me, look at your friend Pete. Look what Uriah tried to do to you. He tried to kill you, too.

It would be easy, he realized. So easy to raise the revolver and empty it into the sprawled body.

Do it, the voice of Bonnie urged him.

But he thought about the way his bullet, fired point-blank at Uriah's chest, had been stopped by the crucifix. As if God himself had intervened to protect the man.

God had nothing to do with it. Uriah was just lucky, that's all. Finish him off, or you'll be sorry.

I've gotta get back to Pete.

Kill Uriah.

"No!" he blurted. Holstering his weapon, he turned away from the ravine. He snatched up his hat and hurried toward Pete.

You'll be sorry.

He dropped to his knees and sagged with relief when he heard Pete's raspy, gurgling breath. Out cold, but alive! Probably a broken nose. He looked like hell. The bridge of his nose was split and swollen. His eyes were swollen. Below his nostrils his face was sheathed with blood. A string of red saliva hung from the corner of his mouth.

Larry shook him gently by the shoulder, wobbling his head. "Pete. Pete, wake up."

Nothing.

Straddling him, Larry grabbed the front of his shirt and pulled him into a sitting position. As his head came up, bloody drool flowed from his mouth. He coughed softly, spraying out more, but didn't come to.

Now what?

I'll have to carry him. There's no other choice.

What about his stuff?

Sighing, Larry eased him farther forward until he hung slumped over his own legs. He seemed fairly steady that way. Letting go, Larry gathered the nearby revolver and hat. The gun went into Pete's holster. Larry shoved the hat down on top of his Stetson.

He crouched over Uriah's canvas bag. It contained six wooden stakes, their ends whittled to points.

Bring it along?

Just an extra burden, he decided.

Straddling Pete, he again tried to shake him awake. Then he gave up and grabbed him under the arms and hoisted him. He crouched, wrestling with the body until it flopped over his shoulder. Hugging the backs of Pete's legs, he forced himself upright and started to walk.

He made his way forward, eyes on the distant row of

buildings. There seemed to be no passageways leading to the street. He would either have to lug Pete all the way around the end of town or take him through a window. His legs were already straining and shaky under the weight. It would have to be a window.

Might as well be the one they'd climbed through when they went after Uriah.

Suddenly imagining Uriah rushing at him from the rear, he swung around and looked back.

Nobody there.

Probably still at the bottom of the slope, Larry told himself, and continued trudging toward the window.

He wondered if he *had* killed the man. The first bullet, he was pretty sure, had gone in one cheek and out the other. Certainly not fatal. The second bullet had buried itself in the crucifix or ricocheted off it. But the gun had discharged when he pounded Uriah with it. The bullet from that shot had struck the man's head. No telling what kind of damage it might've done. Maybe it only sliced across his scalp. Or it might've gone into his head. That one could've killed him.

At least I didn't finish him off, Larry told himself. If the guy died from that last shot, it was an accident. And self-defense.

Not that the cops are going to find out about any of this, he thought. Not if I can help it.

He was nearly to the window when Pete moaned and squirmed a little. He took another step, another.

"Uhhh. Put me down," Pete mumbled.

"Hang on." Larry staggered the final distance to the wall. Crouching, he pressed his friend against it.

"Look out, man." Pete shoved him away, sank to his knees, hunched over and heaved bloody vomit. Then he hocked and spit out gobs of red mucus. When he finished, he stayed down, his head hanging. "Fuckin' A," he mumbled.

"Are you all right?"

"Ohhh shit. You gotta be kidding." With one hand he fingered his face. "What happened?"

"Uriah clobbered you with a rock."

"I think my fuckin' nose is busted."

"Yeah."

"Feel like my head's split open."

"You hit a rock when you fell, too."

He moaned again. He touched the back of his head. Larry didn't see any blood in the hair.

"We'd better get you to a doctor."

"Fuck that. Take me to an undertaker." He pushed himself up and leaned against the wall. Holding the sides of his head, he squeezed his swollen eyes shut. "So what happened to Uriah?"

"He's down in the streambed."

"Did one of us get him?"

"Sort of."

"Huh?"

"It's a long story. Let's get to the car. I'll tell you about it later."

"Yeah, but is he dead, or what?"

"He might be. I don't know. Think you can get through the window okay?"

"Sure," he muttered.

Larry climbed into the building. There, he clutched Pete's arm and held him steady while he clambered over the sill. Keeping his grip, he led Pete through the shadowy room and out to the street.

The car was still resting on its jack.

The feathered shaft of an arrow jutted from the wall of the flat tire.

"Good thing we hadn't finished changing it," Larry said.

"Our lucky day," Pete muttered.

"It *has* been lucky."

"Trade heads, you won't think so."

"Could've been a lot worse."

"Yeah, sure. Get the trunk open, huh? Get me a beer."

"I'm not sure you should drink any alcohol. A head injury like that—"

"Who died and made you a neurologist?" Pete slapped the trunk. "Come on!"

Larry opened it, removed the lid from the cooler and took out two cans of beer. He popped their tops and gave one to Pete. Instead of drinking, Pete poured beer onto his handkerchief and started cleaning the blood off his face.

Larry stepped to the front of the car. The can was wet in his hand. He took a drink. The beer was cold and good. Squatting, he yanked the arrow from the tire.

"Let's see it," Pete said, tossing the sodden handkerchief to the pavement.

Larry gave the arrow to him.

"Just like I thought, Apache."

"Right."

"Nice souvenir."

"Good thing it didn't end up in one of us." Larry drank some more beer. "We're out here playing cowboy and a lunatic starts shooting arrows at us."

"Why don't you take off my hat? You look like a dork. If I laugh, it's gonna hurt."

He plucked Pete's hat off the crown of his own and held it out.

"On this head? You've gotta be kidding. Just toss it in the car."

He sailed it through the open window. It landed on the passenger seat. Taking another drink of beer, he squatted down and started pumping the jack handle.

"You sure we don't have to worry about that bozo jumping us again?"

"I shot him three times," Larry said.

"Holy shit."

While he worked on changing the tire, he told Pete about rushing down the embankment after Uriah had thrown the rock, being unable to find him, returning to the top just as the old man was about to hammer a stake into Pete's chest, and putting a bullet through his face. He told about Uriah yelling "Vampire!" and attacking him with the stake. About the bullet that was stopped by the crucifix, about the accidental shot and throwing Uriah down the slope.

When he finished, he looked around. Pete blew softly through pursed lips and muttered, "Are you shitting me?"

"Nope," Larry said. "It got pretty wild there for a minute."

"And I missed it."

"Sorry about that."

"The bastard was really gonna do a Van Helsing on me?"

"That's right."

"Sure glad you're good with that shootin' iron, old hoss."

"Me, too."

Pete tipped his can high and emptied it into his mouth. "I'm having another. How about you?"

Though Larry's can was still half full, he said, "Yeah." He used the lug wrench to tighten the nuts while Pete went for the beers.

Pete set the fresh one down beside him.

Larry started lowering the car.

"Sounds to me like the old buzzard might still be alive," Pete said.

"If he is, he's not feeling too spry. And his bow's busted, so he can't do us any harm."

"Wish you'd polished him off, though."

"I thought about it."

Pulling the jack out from under the car, he waited for Pete to suggest they go back and finish the job.

It didn't happen.

Instead Pete said, "What'll we do about him?"

"Leave him."

"I've got half a mind to go back there and put a bullet in his head. But the other half hurts too fucking much."

"Let's just get the hell out of here. We can worry about him later."

"Come back in a few days, maybe."

"Maybe," Larry said. He had no intention of returning. But why argue about it now?

He didn't feel like fighting with the hubcap, either. Instead, he took it and the jack to the trunk. Then he rolled the flat tire to the rear of the car and lifted it in.

Pete showed up beside him with the flashlight and arrow. "We're gonna keep this quiet, right?" he asked. "You aren't thinking we should tell the cops?"

"No way," Larry assured him.

"Or the wives."

"What'll we tell them?"

"We went target shooting, right? I tripped and smashed my face on a rock."

"Sounds good to me." He shut the trunk. He returned to the front, picked up his two beers, and climbed in behind the steering wheel. He finished the first can as Pete moved his hat out of the way and lowered himself gingerly onto the passenger seat.

Larry started the car.

"It's all gotta go in the book, though," Pete said.

He made a U-turn and sped for the end of town.

Pete grinned at him. "It's gonna be great in the book, huh, pardner?"

"Yeah. Great."

"Who would've figured it? We come out here looking for the bastard and we wind up in a fuckin' battle. Fantastic. Gonna have us a best-seller, for sure."

"And a lot of explaining to do."

"Hey, the guy's a homicidal maniac. What's to explain?"

"Plenty, I should imagine. The wives'll find out everything. The cops'll find out everything. We'll be up to our ears in crapola."

"Hey, you're not gonna pussy out on me, are you?"

Larry shook his head. He took a drink of beer as he sped past Babe's Garage and out of town. "After all this, nothing in the world could stop me from writing that damn book."

"My man."

Thirty-six

Uriah got slowly to his feet. He stumbled over to a boulder and sat down on it, wincing as his rump met the hard surface.

He knew he'd lost a lot of skin on his way down the slope. But the abrasions were nothing compared to the bullet wounds.

Leaning forward, he spit out some blood and bits of tooth. With his tongue he gently probed the hole in his left cheek. The pain made him cringe. The hole was pretty small, though. A lot smaller than the wound in his right cheek. Not only had the bullet exited there, but so had one of his molars.

Lucky that bloodsucking son of Satan just had a twenty-two, he thought.

Hurt like crazy, though.

Spitting out some more blood, he fingered the furrow in the scalp above his left ear.

I've been hurt worse, he reminded himself.

This was bad, but he figured nothing could ever hurt as much as the time one of the vampires stabbed the stake into his eye. Talk about a world of pain!

Uriah rubbed the bleeding gouge in the middle of his chest.

He saw the crucifix.

The gold-plated body of Jesus was broken in half at the stomach.

He stared at it for a long time.

My Savior, he thought.

You know I still have work to do.

That's why You helped me escape from the booby-hatch. That's why You brought me back home. That's why You saved me today from the hands of the evil ones. You knew I still had work to do.

Confined in the Illinois hospital for the criminally insane, Uriah had thought his mission was over. He hadn't destroyed every vampire, but he'd done his share. He'd whittled the army down some. He'd lost his eye. He'd been caught. Though they didn't know all he'd done, they knew he'd tried to kill that Charleston vampire, which was enough to get him put away. He'd hated to admit it, but he'd been glad it was over.

When he escaped, he'd had no intention of going after any more vampires. All he'd wanted was to make his way back to Sagebrush Flat and live in his hotel where he belonged.

But God was behind it, after all. God had led him back here, knowing in his infinite wisdom that trouble was afoot.

Uriah had been in town no more than a month before those people came and found the hiding place. He'd been out in the desert, hunting up supper. They were gone by the time he returned. When he spotted the broken floor of the landing, he'd prayed that they hadn't discovered the vampire. But his prayer was in vain. The panel enclosing its tomb was loose. The blanket was disarrayed.

He knew, then, that Satan had sent them to undo his work.

But why hadn't they pulled out the stake then and there? It didn't make sense. Had God intervened, somehow, to prevent it?

For days afterward Uriah had kept a vigil. He never left the hotel. At night, instead of retiring to his second-floor room, he'd slept in the lobby. It puzzled him that the intruders didn't return to resurrect the foul thing under the stairs. Perhaps they hadn't been sent by Satan, after all. Maybe pure chance had led them here, and they had no intention of coming back.

But if they were innocents, why hadn't they told the police about finding a corpse?

Day after day Uriah waited and pondered these things. He left the hotel only to relieve himself and to fetch water from the old well out back. He ate jerky from the small supply that he'd set aside for emergencies. When the last of the jerky was gone, he fasted for two days rather than abandon his watch to go hunting.

Finally, gnawed by hunger and knowing he would need all his strength to combat the evil that was sure to come, he'd set out into the desert. Not until after dark did the Lord provide him with a meal. He'd cooked up the coyote. It had spoken to him as he ate. It told him to beware. While he'd been guarding the vampire under the stairs, the intruders had found the other two and set them free.

He'd been sure it was the voice of God that had warned him. Terrified that the evil had been unleashed, Uriah had hurried back to the hotel. With candles and a rusty old spade from his room, he ran to the east end of town. The front door of King's Liquor had long since been broken open. Entering, he made his way to the rear of the empty shop. Holding a candle close to the floor, he was able to find the trapdoor.

It had been Ernie King's pride and joy—a secret entrance to the cellar where he kept his most precious bottles of wine. In the old days Ernie used to brag that nobody knew about the trapdoor except for his own family and his best pal, Uriah. They'd spent many fine evenings down there, sampling, before Ernie upped and left town along with nearly everyone else.

A thin layer of sand blown in from the desert covered the wooden hatch.

Sure didn't *look* as if anyone had opened it up recently.

But maybe the intruders had sprinkled sand around, afterward, to make the area look undisturbed.

Uriah took out his knife. He pried up the trapdoor and eased it down against the floor. Lifting his shovel, he descended the stairs.

The dirt floor didn't appear to have been dug up. That should've been another clue. But Uriah was not about to question the words of the Lord. By the light of the candles, sweating in spite of the cellar's chill, he'd dug for the bodies.

These had been buried deep. With these, he'd had plenty of time. He would've put the last vampire down here, too, but he'd been in too much of a rush. He'd been seen. So he'd just hidden it under the hotel stairs and fled town as fast as he could.

Digging in the hard earth of the cellar, he wished he hadn't put these two down so far.

Hours seemed to go by, and his last candle was down to a tiny stub before the blade of his shovel struck wood. He had buried the coffins next to each other. He wasn't sure which he'd found. But it didn't matter.

Standing in the shoulder-deep hole, he worked feverishly to clear the coffin's lid. The candle was guttering as he scooped out footholds on each side.

He straddled the coffin. He rammed the blade of his shovel under its lid. The nails squeaked. The candle died.

A chill of dread squirmed through Uriah as he worked in total darkness.

The Lord had told him that the vampires had been set free. Not that they were gone.

There might be a living vampire in the coffin below him.

My crucifix and my garlic will protect me, he told himself.

But his terror grew as he wrenched the top of the casket loose. He tossed his shovel out of the hole, bent down and lifted the lid. He brought it up between his spread legs. He hurled it out of the hole.

Carefully, he eased himself down until his knees came to rest on the narrow wooden edges of the casket. Gripping an edge with his left hand, he bent lower. He reached through the darkness.

His fingers slipped into soft, dry hair, and he felt as if a thousand spiders were rushing up his back.

He touched the parched, crusty skin of the vampire's face. When his fingertips met the edges of her teeth, he gasped and jerked his hand back.

"The Lord is my shepherd, I shall not want," he whispered, and forced himself to touch her again. He felt her neck. Her collarbone. "He maketh me to lie down in green pastures."

He touched the smooth roundness of the wooden stake. He curled his hand around it.

The stake was still buried in her chest, just as it ought to be.

Uriah knew, then, that the coyote had lied. Its voice hadn't been the Lord. Satan had spoken through the beast to trick him.

Throwing himself out of the hole, Uriah scurried through the darkness. He stumbled up the cellar stairs and rushed out to the sidewalk.

In time to see two men come out of the hotel carrying the coffin.

Angry, miserable with fear and guilt, he watched them slide the coffin into the rear of a van. They climbed into the front seats. Without headlights the van sped up the moonlit street. For a wild moment Uriah considered rushing out and trying to stop it.

But the Lord held him back.

Bide your time, He seemed to say. I won't fail you.

So Uriah had ducked out of sight within the store until the van was gone.

He had bided his time.

Today the Lord had brought the men back to Sagebrush Flat. They had come to kill him. Of that, he was certain. They had set the vampire free and become its undead brethren. They had come here to destroy the only man worthy of laying them to rest.

But they had failed.

Uriah touched his tongue against the raw inside of his cheek and winced.

They failed, he thought. But I didn't.

No, he hadn't succeeded in putting them at peace. But he would.

He would get them *and* the vampire who had slaughtered his family. All together.

He smiled. It sent fire through his cheeks and made his eyes water.

Reaching down, he plucked a slip of folded paper from between his belt and the skin of his belly.

Before honking the horn of their car to draw them out, he had searched the glove compartment. He had found what he knew must be there.

The vehicle registration slip.

Unfolding it, he blinked the tears from his eyes and gazed at the paper.

The car was registered to Lawrence Dunbar, 345 Palm Avenue, Mulehead Bend, California.

Mulehead Bend.

Uriah used to know that town very well.

It's where the vampires had come from before—when they came in the night to murder his Elizabeth and Martha. It's where they were gathering again, growing in numbers.

Some fifty miles off.

It'll take me a couple of days, he thought. I'd better get started.

He tucked the registration slip under his belt and began to climb the wall of the ravine.

Thirty-seven

Lane's hand trembled as she applied eyeliner. It's not a date, she told herself. Just a school function. Nothing more than a glorified field trip, really.

She'd been telling herself that all day, but it never seemed to help.

I probably won't even have a chance to be alone with him.

The doorbell rang, and her stomach gave a sickening lurch.

He's here.

Lane took a deep breath, trying to calm herself, then brushed mascara onto her lashes. She put the makeup away. She took her purse off the dresser and stepped back in front of the closet mirror.

I can't go dressed like this! she suddenly thought, and saw her face turn red. No, it's okay. He doesn't want us in evening gowns. He said it's not the prom.

Besides, she'd worn this outfit to mass a few times. If it's good enough for mass, it's good enough for *Hamlet*.

And I do look good in it, she thought. And it's *me*.

Lane lifted her arms. Though her armpits felt wet, no moisture showed on the tie-dyed blue denim. Probably because the blouse fit so loosely. Most of the perspiration just ran down her sides.

"Lane!" Mom called. "Mr. Kramer's here."

"I'll be right out!"

Quickly, she popped open the top snaps. She plucked some Kleenex from a box on top of the dresser, reached inside the blouse, dried her armpits, and applied a fresh coating of roll-on. Pinching the snaps shut again, she hurried from the room.

I *am* too casual, she thought when she saw Mr. Kramer in the foyer. He wore a necktie with a white shirt, blue blazer and gray slacks.

"Good evening, Lane," he said. Then he turned back to her father and raised the copy of *Night Watcher* in his left hand. "Thanks again for the autograph, Larry."

"Thanks for buying the book," Dad said. "I'm glad you could find a copy." His face was a little more red than usual, his voice a little thicker. But at least he didn't slur his words. He'd had a *lot* to drink before dinner. Lane hoped Mr. Kramer didn't realize he was pretty well polluted.

"And I can count on you for October thirty-first?"

"I'll be there."

"That's terrific. The kids'll get a great kick out of having a speaker like you on Halloween."

"I'll read 'em some *really disgusting* stuff from my books."

"I'm sure they'll love it." He nodded at Lane. "Well, I guess we'd better be on our way. Are you all set?"

"Am I dressed okay?" she asked. "I could put on something more—"

"No, no, you're perfect."

Mom, smiling, nodded in agreement. "You look just fine, honey."

"You shore do, little pardner," Dad said. "If'n you run into Hoot up the trail, be sure'n tell him howdy for me."

"Oh, Daaaad."

Mr. Kramer laughed. "It was very nice meeting you, Larry," he said, and extended his hand.

Dad shook it. "Nice to meet you, too. And I'll see you on Halloween."

Shaking hands with Mom, Mr. Kramer said, "A real pleasure meeting you, Jean. I can see where Lane got her looks."

She blushed. "Why, thank you."

As he opened the door, Lane kissed her parents. "See you later," she told them, and they wished her a good time. Then she was on the walkway with Mr. Kramer. His station wagon, parked at the curb, looked empty.

He *did* come here first!

Lane hoped it wasn't just a matter of geographical convenience, hoped he'd chosen to pick her up before the others so they could have some time alone.

"Are you warm enough in that?" he asked.

Did he realize she was trembling? "Oh, I'm fine," she said. Her shivers, she thought, had little to do with the chilly night air. "I'm just excited," she added.

He smiled at her. "It's great to have a student actually excited about going to a play."

That isn't it at all, Lane thought as he opened the passenger door. She climbed into the car. He shut the door, walked around the front, and got in behind the steering wheel.

"Excuse me," he muttered. Leaning sideways, he reached in front of Lane to open the glove compartment. "Don't want anything happening to the book." For just a moment, as he slipped the paperback into the compartment, his shoulder pushed against her upper arm. "There," he said. "Safe and sound." He sat up straight and started the car.

"Have you read it yet?" Lane asked.

"No, unfortunately." He pulled away from the curb. "I should be able to get to it next week, though."

"After you read that, you may want to reconsider having Dad speak to the class." She grinned. "You may not want him anywhere near a group of high school students."

"That bad, huh?"

"That nasty."

"He seemed like a very nice man," Mr. Kramer said.

"Oh, he is. You'd think he was a monster, reading that stuff, but he's awfully sweet. He had kind of a bad time today, though. In case you thought he was acting a little . . . weird. See, he went out shooting in the desert. With our neighbor, Pete." I'm running off at the mouth like a kid, she thought. He doesn't care about any of this. "Anyway, Pete had some kind of an accident."

"Not shot, I hope."

"Oh, no. Nothing like that. But he fell off some rocks and got knocked out cold. He actually broke his nose. Dad had to take him to the emergency room. So anyway, he wasn't exactly himself after he got done with all that."

"It doesn't sound like much fun."

"No. It wasn't. So, how have you been?"

"No complaints. How about yourself? You haven't had anymore run-ins with Benson, I hope."

"No."

"He'll probably leave you alone. But let me know if he causes you any trouble."

"I think you put the fear of God into him."

Mr. Kramer shook his head. "You never know, a guy like that. You'll have to keep your eyes open. Don't let him catch you alone. There's no telling what he might do, and I'd sure hate for anything to happen to my best student."

"I'll be careful," she said.

"Speaking of which, maybe you'd better buckle up."

"Planning to crash?" she asked, and reached for the seat belt.

"I'll sure try not to. But you may have noticed, you keep getting hurt when you're around me."

"Yeah. Guess you're bad luck." She drew the strap down between her breasts and snapped its metal tab into the buckle by her left hip.

"Now you won't have to worry about a rendezvous with the windshield."

"Yeah. I'd look lousy at the play with blood all over my clothes."

"I do like that outfit," he said, glancing at her. "You haven't worn it to school, have you?"

"Not this one."

"I've seen you in something similar, though. A blue denim jumper with white lace. A mini, as I recall."

"Oh, that." She felt a warm stir, pleased to find out that he actually remembered what she wore to school, but slightly embarrassed that he recalled the jumper. "Probably too short," she said.

"I wouldn't say that. You've got the legs for it."

"Thanks," she said, heat rushing to her face.

He swung the car to the curb and stopped. Lane gazed at him, her heart pounding. *Why'd he stop?* He turned on the overhead light. He smiled at her. Then he reached inside his blazer and took a sheet of paper from his pocket.

Just checking directions, she realized.

"Okay," he said. "Aaron's at 4980 Cactus. Should be just on the next block."

Lane felt a pull of disappointment. Their time alone was almost done.

She hoped she would get to sit with him in the theater, but it didn't work out that way. Sandra, bending his ear about something, followed him down the aisle and into the row. There was no way for Lane to get past her without making a spectacle of herself.

Mr. Kramer took a seat beside a college student. Sandra sat beside him, and Lane found herself between Sandra and George, with Aaron at the other side of George.

She felt cheated.

I'm here to see *Hamlet,* she reminded herself. Not to be with Mr. Kramer.

He likes me, though. He really does. He likes me a lot.

George, squirming in his seat, brushed against her arm. "Excuse me," he whispered.

"That's okay," she said without looking at him.

"I didn't mean to do that."

She looked at George and nodded. "I know. It's okay."

"I guess guys are probably always bothering you, you know? It must get annoying."

Lane shrugged. "It all depends on the guy."

"Yeah. I guess it would. That makes sense. Well, you don't have to worry about me. These seats are kind of close together. That's the problem."

"You shouldn't worry about it."

"I just don't want you to get the wrong impression."

"I won't."

"It was nice talking to you, though." George turned his face forward, leaned the other way and scanned the audience ahead of him. His lips were pressed together. With his far hand he adjusted his glasses and brushed some stray hair off his forehead.

"George?"

He jerked his head toward her so fast that Lane feared he might've hurt his neck.

"If it makes you so nervous sitting next to me, maybe you should trade places with Aaron."

For a moment he looked hurt. Then he said, "Sure. If you want me to."

"I don't."

His eyebrows lifted. "You don't?"

"Not unless you want to."

"Me? No. I mean—"

"You sit way in the back of the class. I don't think we've ever even talked to each other."

"No, we haven't."

"You're really good in English."

"You, too. You're the best in the class."

"When I don't lose my place?"

He smiled. "Oh, that was nothing. I lose my place all the time. I get to daydreaming, and that's all she wrote."

"I'll bet you want to be a writer, don't you?"

His head tilted. He frowned. "How did you know?"

"You have that look about you."

He wrinkled his nose, making his glasses rise slightly. "The look of the nerd."

"Don't let my dad hear that. He's a writer."

"A *real* writer?"

"He likes to think so. You've probably never heard of him. Lawrence Dunbar."

George's frown deepened. "No. I don't think so."

"He writes penny dreadfuls. Or, as he likes to say, $3.95 dreadfuls."

George laughed. "That's a good one," he said.

"I really liked the story you read in class. The guy whose bones dissolved?"

His face went bright red. "You did? Thanks."

"Have you got any more?"

"Are you kidding? I've got piles of them. My parents think I'm doing homework all the time, but I'm actually up in my room writing stuff. Boy, would they be pissed." He cringed. "Excuse me. That just slipped out."

"I say it all the time."

The theater lights went dark.

Lane leaned toward George. "I want to read some of your other stories, okay?"

"Do you mean it?"

"Sure." The curtain started to rise. "If you want, I'll even have Dad take a look at some of them."

"Jeez, I don't know."

On the stage it was night and two sentries stood on the parapet of Elsinore, looking very cold.

George settled back in his seat. When his shoulder brushed against Lane, he leaned away to break the contact. Lane swept her elbow up past the arm of the chair and nudged him. Again he snapped his head around.

"I don't bite," she whispered.

She tried to pay attention to the play. But her mind kept drifting.

She felt good about her talk with George. He seemed nice. A little like Henry. Not as weird, though. Those two should really hit it off.

Awfully shy, but he would get over that once they knew each other better.

And we will, she thought.

Maybe it was fate that she ended up sitting with him. And fate that she'd broken up with Jim last night.

George would never act like Jim. He probably never even would've had the nerve to talk to me, she thought, much less ask me out. Probably *still* won't ask me out. I can ask him, though. Why not?

I **ne**ver would've gotten anywhere with Mr. Kramer, anyway.

Thinking that, she felt a hollow ache.

He's a teacher, she told herself. He can't get involved with me even if he wants to.

But her mind dwelled on him, lingering on the way he looked, the things he'd said to her, the way he'd handled Riley Benson, the way he'd caught her when she fell from the stool, how his hands had felt when he touched her bare ribs and leg, when he'd accidentally touched her breast as he took the books from her yesterday.

He remembered her denim jumper, though she hadn't worn it for nearly two weeks. He recognized her car in the lot yesterday. Didn't those things prove that he cared for her?

Maybe he likes me as much as I like him.

She wondered how it would feel to kiss him.

The lights came up for intermission, and she realized she'd hardly paid any attention at all to the play. Not that it mattered. She'd read it a few times, and seen both the Olivier and Burton movies.

Mr. Kramer stayed in his seat and talked to Sandra. Aaron went off, probably to find a bathroom since he couldn't be going for refreshments—the theater had no snack counter. Lane turned to George. He was looking around the auditorium, but not at her. Intentionally not at her, she suspected.

"How do you get to school?" she asked.

"Me?" Now he looked. Straight into her eyes.

"Yeah, you."

"Oh, my mom drives me."

"Your place is just a few blocks from Henry Peidmont. I usually give him and Betty Thompson a lift to school in the mornings."

"Oh yeah, I know."

She smiled. "Spying on me?"

"No! Uh-uh."

"I was just joking."

He kept staring into her eyes. For a few moments he was silent. Then he smiled. "Me, too. I mean, I don't *spy* on you, exactly. But I notice you a lot. All the time. Whenever you're around, anyway."

"Really?"

"If you want to know the truth—" Grimacing, he shook his head. "Never mind."

"No, what?"

"You'd think I'm a dork."

"No, I wouldn't. Come on." She elbowed him gently. "Spill it."

"It's stupid. Never mind."

"All right. Anyway, what I was going to say is you can ride with us if you'd like. I could pick you up Monday morning on my way to Henry's. I've got room for one more pas-

senger. It'd save your mother a trip, and we'd be glad to have
you along."

George looked confused. "Why?" he asked.

"Why what?"

"Why would you want me along?"

"Why wouldn't I?"

"We don't even know each other."

"We do now. And I want to know you better."

His face went crimson. "You do?"

"Yes."

"Jeez."

"How about it?"

"Sure. Fine. I'll have to check with my parents, but . . ."
He shook his head.

"Why don't you give me your telephone number?"

"Yeah. Sure. Okay."

Lane opened her purse. She took out a pen and a small
notepad. George told her the telephone number. She wrote
it down, then wrote her own number on the next page,
tore off the sheet and gave it to him. He stared at it.

"You find out if it's all right with your folks, and I'll
give you a call tomorrow."

"Yeah. Okay."

"You don't *have* to ride with us."

"No, I think . . . that'd be neat. Henry's a cool guy,
and—"

"I've never heard him called that before."

George grinned. "Well, yeah, he is. I think so, anyway."

"Me, too."

"Betty's kind of obnoxious."

Lane laughed. "Ah, you know her."

"To know her is to fear her. But you're not so bad."

"Why, thanks. You're not so bad, either."

Thirty-eight

"Would you mind if we stop at the marina for a minute?" Mr. Kramer asked after he'd dropped off the others. They were back on Shoreline Drive, still a mile from the turnoff to Lane's house. "It'll save me an errand in the morning."

"That's okay with me," she said.

"Great. It won't take long. I just need to pick up a couple of things I left on my boat."

"You have a boat?"

"She isn't much, but she's mine."

"Gee, that's neat." Neat, Lane thought. Dumb. Stop talking like a kid.

He pulled the station wagon into the parking area in front of a hardware store, turned around and headed back the way they'd come. Lane was well aware that they had passed the marina shortly after leaving the college. Either Mr. Kramer hadn't wanted the rest of the kids to know about his boat, or he'd just remembered whatever it was that he needed to pick up. Either way, she was glad. This would give her a little while longer to be with him. And it made her feel special that he was willing to take her along, to let her have a glimpse of his real world.

I'm more than just a student to him, she thought. He wants me to see that he's not just a teacher.

"So," he said, "I guess you made a new friend tonight."

"George? Yeah. He's nice."

"He's a good student. He seems like quite a young gentleman. Did he ask you out?"

"No, not hardly."

"Well, then, he missed the boat. No pun intended."

"George is pretty bashful. But I might start giving him rides to school. He has to check with his parents."

"Always a good idea. Speaking of parents, it's almost midnight. I don't want to get you into any trouble."

"Well, they know it's a long play. I don't think they'll mind if I'm kind of late. Especially since I'm with you. Since you're my teacher, and everything."

"Good. That's good. This won't take long." Soon he turned into the marina parking lot. A few other cars and pickups were there, but Lane saw no people. "Come on down with me," Mr. Kramer said. "I'll show you the pride of my fleet."

"Great." She climbed out. She met him in front of his station wagon. Side by side they walked toward the dock. A chilly wind, blowing in off the river, swept her hair back and pressed the front of her blouse and skirt against her skin. She leaned into it. She folded her arms across her chest.

"Cold?"

"A little."

"Here." He started to remove his blazer.

"No, no. I can't take that. I'm fine. Really."

"I insist." Turning to Lane, his white sport shirt flapping, his necktie whipping this way and that, he draped the jacket over her shoulders. She clutched its lapels to keep it from blowing away.

"You're gonna freeze," she warned, her voice trembling.

"Naw. I'm of hearty, seafaring stock."

"If you say so."

He unlocked a chain-link gate and held it open while Lane stepped onto the dock. When he came toward her, his shoulders were hunched.

"You *are* freezing."

"Me?" Arching his back, he threw his chest out and pounded it with his fists.

Lane laughed. It felt strange to laugh with her lungs feeling so tight and shaky. It left her breathless.

"You can shield me," Mr. Kramer said. He turned her around. Holding her by the shoulders, he pressed himself against her back and steered her forward. She twisted her head to look at him. Their faces nearly collided. "Careful," he said. "Or we'll have *still another* accident."

The dock swayed under her feet. The boats moored along both sides bobbed and pitched on the rough surface of the river. Most were dark, but lights glowed from the cabins of a few. She wondered if there were people inside the lighted boats. She didn't see anyone. And hoped that no one saw her.

What if it got back to Mom and Dad that I was out here fooling around like this with Mr. Kramer?

"Hard to port," he said into her ear. Turning Lane to the left, he pushed her along an arm of pier. Past a rocking, dark sailboat. Past a catamaran. He halted her at the bow of a powerboat that must've been at least twenty feet long. Moonlight gleamed on its foredeck and cabin windshield.

He hurried ahead of Lane, and she followed him up a narrow strip of pier that reached alongside the boat. Near the stern he stepped onto the gunwale and hopped down. "Watch your step," he said. He held out a hand to her. She took it, hung onto his jacket with her other hand, and planted a foot on the rail. As she thrust herself up, he pulled. She dropped, landed on the pitching deck and staggered against him.

Mr. Kramer wrapped his arms around her. He squeezed her tightly against him. He said, "Brrrrr."

His face felt cool on her cheek. His chest was solid

against her breasts. His hands moved up and down her back. She could feel him shivering.

"Why don't we go below for a minute?" he gasped. "Warm up."

Lane nodded.

He turned away, unlocked the cabin door and slid it open. "Go on first. And watch your step."

She climbed down into darkness. Away from the wind. At the bottom of the stairs she found herself in narrow, cozy quarters. Moonlight came in through the portholes, casting a gray haze over cushions to both sides and in front of her.

She heard the door skid shut. It cut off most of the wind's noise.

"Sleeps three," Mr. Kramer said. "If they're munchkins."

"Nice," Lane whispered. She turned around, careful not to lose her balance, and saw the dim shape of Mr. Kramer coming toward her.

"A haven from the tempest," he said.

"That's for sure. You might as well have this back." She slipped the blazer off her shoulders.

"Just toss it down anywhere."

She folded the jacket. As she bent down to place it on a cushion, a hand stroked the back of her head and she flinched.

"Sorry. Did I startle you?"

"A little."

She stood up straight. The hand slipped down to her shoulder. Then both Mr. Kramer's hands were on her shoulders, gently rubbing them through the heavy denim. Her mouth went dry. Her heart thudded.

"Does that feel good?" he asked.

"Yeah. But . . . I really can't stay."

"I know. We'll go in a minute. But you like this, don't you? I know you liked it after school the other day. Really eases the tension."

He kept on massaging her, squeezing her shoulders, moving to the sides of her neck.

We shouldn't be doing this, she thought. Not here.

Her head felt heavy. She could hardly hold it up.

His hands eased down along her neck. Under her collar. The top snap of her blouse popped open. And his hands were inside, kneading her shoulders.

"Mr. Kramer," she murmured.

"Hal. Call me Hal."

"Hal. I'd better go now. Honest."

"It's all right," he said. "We're not doing anything wrong."

It *felt* wrong. But it felt good, too. Incredibly good.

His big, warm hands curled over her shoulders and down her upper arms. She realized they had taken her bra straps with them. Something low in her belly, something cold, seemed to jump.

"Now, you're smooth," he whispered, massaging her shoulders.

"We shouldn't. This isn't—"

He brushed his mouth against hers, and the words got lost. "Oh, Lane." His breath caressed her lips. His hands drifted over her cheeks as softly as a mild breeze. They went away. He kissed her again, his mouth open and warm and tender.

Lane had daydreamed about this. And this was much the same as her daydream. But more exciting. And more frightening. And somehow shameful. She hadn't expected the feelings of fear and guilt.

It's already gone too far.

But she felt helpless, trapped by the pull of his moist, warm mouth.

While he kissed her, he popped open the next snap of her blouse. And then the next.

Jesus, she thought.

After the last snap came apart, Hal slid his tongue into her mouth and spread her blouse open.

She turned her face away. His tongue came out of her mouth and spread a wet path across her cheek. "I have to go home," she gasped. "Right now."

"This is what you've been waiting for," he said, slipping the blouse off her shoulders. She tried to raise her arms, but he pressed them down and pushed the sleeves off. "It's what we've both been waiting for. You know that."

"No."

Embracing her, pinning her arms to her sides, he kissed her wet cheek and unclasped the back of her bra.

"No! I mean it!" She squirmed, but he hugged her hard against him.

"What's the matter with you?" he asked. She heard no anger in his voice. He sounded confused, even hurt.

"It's just not right. You're a teacher."

"You've been trying your best to seduce me. Well, I'm only human. You've won. You've got me."

She struggled in his embrace, but he held her fast.

"There's no reason to be frightened. Just calm down."

Lane stopped struggling.

"That's better. That's much better." He relaxed his hold. His hands roamed gently over her bare back. "Doesn't this feel good?"

"I guess so."

"You're a very lucky young lady," he said. "They *all* want me. You know that, don't you?" His hands slid lower. They rubbed her buttocks. "Every female in that school has the hots for me. But only a lucky few actually *get* me."

"I want to go home," Lane said, trying to keep her voice from shaking. "Please."

"I'll take you home." He found the button at the hip of her skirt. He opened it and slid the zipper down.

"No!"

"I'll take you home as soon as we've finished."

The skirt dropped around her feet. He slipped his hands inside the seat of her panties. His fingers kneaded her rump.

"Mr. Kramer, don't."

"It's Hal. Remember?"

He peeled the panties down around her thighs.

"Damn it!" She shoved him.

He stumbled backward and dropped onto a cushion. Sprawled there, he said, "You're a real disappointment, Lane."

She bent over. The bra fell away from her breasts, its straps sliding down her arms. She tugged her panties up. Bending lower, the bra drifting down to her wrists, she reached for her skirt. Before she could lift it, Hal stretched out a leg and pinned the skirt to the deck. "Take your foot off."

His leg jerked back. The skirt, hooked by his heel, tugged sharply at Lane's boots. Her feet skidded. With a gasp she lurched up straight and waved her arms, flinging her bra through the darkness. Just as she found her balance, Kramer ducked, grabbed the skirt with both hands and yanked it toward him.

Her feet flew out from under her.

"No!" she cried out as she fell.

The edge of a cushion caught her across the rump. Her back slapped the cool surface. She jammed her hands down and pushed herself up.

Kramer stepped between her knees. He grabbed her throat and shoved her down against the pad. With his other hand he punched her just below the sternum.

Pain blasted through Lane's body. Her breath whooshed out. She wheezed, trying to suck in more, but her lungs didn't seem to work. Nothing seemed to work. She felt as if her body had exploded apart from the center.

Kramer let go of her throat.

She tried to lift her head but couldn't.

"You'll be okay in a minute," Kramer said, his voice faint through the roaring in her ears. "I hit you in the solar plexus. It's a nerve ganglion, in case you're not up on your physiology. Somewhat the equivalent of a man catching one in the nuts. I'm sorry you made me do that to you."

Lane realized the agony was fading and she could breathe, taking small, painful gulps of air.

"But I'll do worse," he said, "if you give me any more trouble."

She felt one of her boots come off. Then the other. Kramer's hands moved slowly up her legs.

"We'll have a long, wonderful relationship, though. In spite of this rather shaky beginning. You'll see."

She felt his mouth against the crotch of her panties. She felt his lips and teeth, his squirming tongue. Then his mouth went away. He ripped apart each side of her panties and tugged the remnants of fabric out from under her rump.

"This is what you wanted," he whispered. She heard a tremor in his voice. "This is what we both want."

"You're home," he said. "Safe and sound. And it isn't even all that terribly late."

His words seemed to come from far away.

"Look at me."

Lane turned her head. Vaguely, she realized that Kramer was smiling.

"You had a wonderful time, didn't you? I know I did. We'll do it again, won't we? Maybe Monday or Tuesday. We'll work out where and when later. And you'll be there. Won't you?"

She managed to nod.

"I didn't hear that."

"Yes," she murmured. "I'll be there."

"And you'll never tell a living soul about our little party, will you?"

"No."

"And what happens if you do?"

"The razor."

"That's right." Kramer patted the pocket of his slacks. "And who gets the razor?"

"My parents. And me."

"Very good. You're an excellent student. Now, go on inside your house. Your folks are probably waiting up for you, so you'd better look lively. You'd better put on a good show. If I so much as suspect that you've betrayed me, you know what'll happen."

"I know."

"And don't think the cops can save you. They can't. Even if they take me in, I'll be out. You know what bail is."

"I know."

"And you know what'll happen when I get out."

"I know."

"Okay. Good night, now, darling."

She concentrated on her hand, and watched it pull the door lever. The door swung away from her shoulder. She felt a cool wind.

"Sweet dreams," Kramer said.

Then she was standing on the curb, watching Kramer's car until it disappeared around the corner. She turned slowly until she was facing the house. Its porch light was on.

How can I pretend . . . ?

She took careful steps toward the house. She felt as if Kramer had shoved a thick branch deep inside her, a branch of embers that any quick motion would set ablaze.

They'll know something's wrong, she thought.

I'll say I got my period.

At the front door she halted under the light and looked

down at herself. Her skirt was crooked. She straightened it. She supposed she looked as if nothing had happened. As long as they couldn't see under the skirt.

Kramer had kept her panties.

A souvenir of our first date, he'd said.

What am I going to do?

She tried to focus her mind.

All that matters right now, she told herself, is getting past Mom and Dad. I can't let them suspect.

She found her keys, unlocked the door, and stepped slowly over the threshold.

The television was on.

Dad lay on the sofa, snoring.

Mom wasn't in the room.

Thank God.

Silently, Lane shut the door. She crept past the sofa, out of the living room and into the hallway. "Is that you, honey?" Mom called. Her voice sounded groggy, as if she'd been asleep.

"Yeah." Fixing a smile on her face, she stepped to the doorway of the master bedroom. Her mother was propped up in bed, an open book resting on her lap.

"How was the play?"

"Pretty good."

"Did you go somewhere after?"

"Yeah. Mr. Kramer took us all out for pizza."

"Oh, that was awfully nice of him." Mom yawned, patted her mouth, and squinted at Lane. "Are you feeling all right?"

"I've got a miserable headache. And cramps."

"Oh, I'm sorry. Hope it didn't ruin your time."

She shrugged. "I'll be okay after I've had a shower and some aspirin."

"What's your father doing?"

"Snoozing on the sofa."

"He overindulged."

"Yeah. He was upset about Pete's accident."

"Whatever. I think I'll just let him stay there."

"Okay. Night, Mom."

"Sleep tight."

Lane went to her bedroom. When she came out with her robe, light no longer spilled into the hallway from her parents' room.

In the bathroom she turned on the light and locked the door. She took off her clothes. Sitting on the toilet, she removed the tampon.

Don't want you ruining your nice skirt, Kramer had said before pushing it into her.

He actually kept a supply on his boat.

The tube was sodden with blood and semen.

Lane knew she shouldn't flush it down the toilet, but she couldn't leave such evidence in the wastebasket. She had never used tampons. If Mom noticed it . . .

She flushed it away.

Leaning back, she looked down at herself. Her skin was red where he had punched her. Red where he'd squeezed her. Red where he'd sucked her. She thought she could smell his saliva. A sickening, sweet odor. But not as sickening as the taste in her mouth.

Groaning, she leaned forward and peered down. Her blond curls were matted flat, dry now but sticking to her skin. Under the sparse hair, her skin had a reddish hue like her breasts. She saw no blood. Or anything worse. Kramer had licked her clean.

Her vulva looked like a raw wound, the lips crimson and shiny.

Lane winced when she eased her legs together. She stood up, hobbled to the sink and started to brush her teeth. The toothpaste had a minty flavor that overcame the taste of Kramer.

She stared at herself in the medicine cabinet mirror as she brushed. Her hair looked windblown. Her eyes were pink where they should've been white, and had a strange, dazed look about them. They hardly seemed to be her eyes at all.

This *isn't* me anymore, she thought. It's somebody else. Somebody who got fucked.

Really fucked.

I'm ruined, she thought. Wrecked, fucked.

And I'm dead meat if I tell. Dead meat if I don't let him do it to me again.

Like *hell* I'll let him do it to me again!

A thick foam of toothpaste spilled over Lane's lower lip. In the mirror she watched it roll toward her chin. She suddenly gagged. Eyes going blurry, she whirled away from the sink. She dropped to her knees in front of the toilet, grabbed its seat with both hands and heaved into the bowl.

When she was done, she crawled to the bathtub.

Thirty-nine

Lane patted herself gently with the towel, taking care not to awaken hurts. Then she draped it over the bar and put on her robe. The soft fabric stuck to her skin where she'd missed wet areas.

Her toothbrush lay in the sink, its bristles and handle still coated with white goo. She rinsed it off. Knowing she could never put it into her mouth again, she dropped it into the wastebasket.

I'll say it fell on the floor and got hair on it, or something, she thought.

In a cabinet under the window, she found her leather traveling case. She took out her spare toothbrush. She brushed her teeth again. When the paste thickened inside her mouth, she gagged once and her eyes watered. This time, however, she didn't throw up. She spat out the paste, rinsed, and put her brush into the holder.

She took aspirin, washing down three caplets with cold water.

After checking the toilet and finding no traces of vomit, she gathered her clothes and left the bathroom.

The hallway felt cool. Light still glowed at the far end. She wondered if her father was still snoring on the sofa.

Mom always got pissed off when he drank too much.

It's not such a big crime, Lane thought.

Mom ought to be glad she's married to someone like him, and not give him crap about little stuff like that.

She stepped into her bedroom. With an elbow she nudged the light switch up. She carried her denim boots to the closet and set them down.

And stared at them.

Her present, her reward for getting Dad the yearbook.

God, she thought. If Kramer hadn't helped me get the yearbook, I wouldn't have started staying after class. None of this might've happened.

You got me raped, Dad.

Bullshit. It was all my fault.

Grievously did she sin, and grievously did she pay.

What's that, Shakespeare?

Kramer rigged that coin toss for *Hamlet,* she suddenly realized. He had it all planned.

She stepped over to the bed with her clothes. She tossed her skirt and blouse down and lifted her bra close to the lamp. It didn't appear to be soiled.

Soiled enough, she thought. The bastard touched it.

As she inspected her blouse and skirt, her mind went back to the coin toss. When was that? Before Mom and I went to Grandma's last weekend. Friday. He did it on Friday, and it wasn't till this last Monday that he got the yearbook for me.

If he rigged the coin toss, he must've had it all planned by Friday to get me tonight. *Before* the yearbook. *Before* I started staying late and fell off the stool and started acting like an idiot and leaving my bra home and *everything.* It had nothing to do with all that.

The bastard picked me like a target.

Lane brought her mind back to the present task. Her blouse and skirt were okay. She might never wear them again, but they weren't spoiled by stains.

She tossed her garments into the hamper.

She stared at her bed.

She didn't want to get in it. She wouldn't be able to sleep. She would lie there, thinking. All her worst thoughts came when she was trying to sleep, and she didn't want to face those that were waiting tonight.

Did he get me pregnant? Did he give me AIDS? Is he going to sneak into the house with his razor, some night, and murder us all?

Shit.

Who needs to be in bed to think about that shit?

He probably didn't get me pregnant, not with my period due so soon. What about AIDS, though? Even if he's got it, the chances . . .

There I go, thinking about it.

And it'll be *worse,* lying there with the lights out.

Be nice to just sit up all night and watch television.

The TV's *on,* she remembered. And poor Dad's an outcast on the sofa.

She left her room, uncertain what she planned to do. Maybe sit down and stare at the tube. Or maybe turn it off and wake up Dad so he could have a good night's sleep in the bed where he belonged.

At any rate, the TV and lamp shouldn't be left on all night.

Lane made her way toward the living room, walking slowly. Though she ached all over, the pains seemed rather mild. Maybe the aspirin had helped. Certainly the shower had helped. And the long, hot bath she'd taken after cleaning herself under the spray.

The virus could've gotten in when he busted the old maidenhead. Wouldn't that be ironic? I died because I was a virgin. Shouldn't have been so fucking chaste.

I'll be all right, she told herself. I'll be all right.

The television was still on, its screen fuzzy with snow. The lamp at the end of the sofa was still on. But Dad was gone.

Lane heard the soft rumble and thump of a door sliding shut.

What's he doing? Going out back?

She went into the kitchen and cupped her hands against the glass. Dad was out there, all right. Walking funny, as if he wasn't completely awake—or awfully soused. He made his way toward the garage with a lurching, staggering gait, weaving a little.

Lane slid open the kitchen door. She almost called to him, but realized that a shout might wake up her mother. Whatever Dad might be up to, Mom was sure to interfere and give him some grief about it.

As Dad opened the garage door, Lane stepped outside and eased the kitchen door shut.

"Dad?" she called, not too loudly.

He didn't seem to hear her. He vanished into the darkness.

Lane frowned. Maybe I should just go back in, she thought. But what if he isn't okay?

What's he doing in the garage, anyway?

The wind parted her robe below the cloth belt and swept it away from her legs. She liked how the caresses felt, supposed that the cold didn't bother her because she was still heated from the bath.

What if Dad can see me?

Reluctantly, she pulled the robe shut. She clamped its soft fabric between her thighs.

Something suddenly glowed white inside the darkness of the garage. The light seemed to be moving. Lane realized it must be the battery lantern that she'd given Dad for Father's Day. It had a fluorescent tube instead of a regular flashlight bulb.

Is he looking for something? she wondered.

Because of her bare feet, Lane stayed off the grass. She walked across the concrete sun deck. She was nearly to the garage door when she saw him.

He had the lantern in one hand. He was standing on the small wooden platform beneath the trapdoor to the attic, his head tilted up, his back to Lane. His other hand waved overhead in an attempt to catch the dangling rope.

The wind tossed Lane's hair across her eyes. It bared her right side, curling gently over her skin. As she halted to close her robe again, she saw her father grab the cord and pull the trapdoor down. He set the lantern on the platform at his feet. He unfolded the ladder.

"Dad?"

Acting as if he didn't hear her, he picked up the lantern and began to climb.

Is he deaf?

She hurried toward him, afraid he might fall.

It wasn't like Dad to ignore her. Something was definitely wrong with him. Either drunk senseless or . . . *sleepwalking?*

She stopped beneath the ladder. He was almost to the top.

Maybe I'd better get Mom, she thought. If he's walking in his sleep, this is serious. What if he finishes whatever he's doing up there and doesn't know he's in the attic and falls right through the opening?

He could do that while I'm going for Mom, she realized.

Dad scrambled off the ladder and crawled out of sight.

Lane started to climb.

What'll I do?

Somewhere, she'd heard that sleepwalkers often dropped dead if you woke them up. Probably just a stupid myth. What if it's true, though?

I'd better just keep an eye on him, try to keep him from getting hurt.

Through the opening above her, Lane saw the garage's slanted roof, its crossbeams casting bands of shadow against the ceiling planks. The lantern had to be nearby, but she couldn't see her father.

She climbed higher. The rungs pressed into the bottoms of her feet. She noticed that her legs were shaking.

When she stepped onto the next rung, her head lifted

above the attic floor. She stopped. Not much more than a yard in front of her face was a long, wooden box.

A coffin?

No way. That's ridiculous.

But shivers crawled up her back. Her heart began to thud, pumping throbs of pain through her body. She felt as if her muscles, already sore and trembling, were melting into warm mush. She clutched the ladder's top rung in case her legs should give out.

And gazed at her father.

He was standing at one end of the box.

It can't be a coffin!

Standing there, staring down into it. The lantern, held close to the side of his chest with his one hand, left smudges of darkness on his face.

"I know," he said.

The words seemed to suck out Lane's breath. She knew he wasn't talking to *her.*

"I've missed you, too," he said. "So much."

He nodded as if he heard a voice in his head. Then he straddled the box and sat down on its end. He rested the lantern on his left knee.

"Forever?" he asked. After a moment he said, "That would be so wonderful, Bonnie."

Lane forced herself to climb higher. Dad didn't seem to notice.

She knelt on the attic floor.

She saw over the edge of the box.

She went numb.

It *was* a coffin, and it wasn't empty, and the thing inside looked like a fucking Egyptian *mummy* that someone had unwrapped—a *girl* mummy with a horrible grin, a stub of wood jutting out of her chest between breasts that look like oblong flaps of leather. She didn't wear a stitch. And Dad was sitting above her feet where he could see *everything,* and he was staring at her and *talking* to her!

This can't be happening, Lane thought. I must be sleeping, and . . .

He's the one sleeping.

"I know," he said, but not to Lane. "But I'm afraid."

He nodded.

He scooted forward on the edges of the coffin. Just above the mummy's pelvis, he stopped. If Lane reached out, she could touch his left leg.

"I love you, too," he said. There was agony in his voice. "But I love my wife and daughter. I can't give them up, not even for you."

Those words seemed to scatter the fog in Lane's mind.

"Do you promise?" he asked.

He's talking to a corpse! About me and Mom!

"If you do anything to hurt them . . ."

Again, he nodded. "All right. I'll do it." Leaning forward, he reached down toward the chest of the mummy with his right hand. His fingers wrapped around the stake.

"Dad!" Lane punched the side of his knee. The impact shot his leg inward. The lantern tumbled off. Dad's leg slammed the coffin. The lantern struck the attic floor. It went out.

Black fell across Lane's eyes. She scurried forward.

"Huh?" Dad's voice. Confused. Then he bellowed, "Yeeeeeahhhh!"

Lane found his leg. He flinched rigid and his yell turned into a shriek. She wrapped her arms around his waist. "Dad," she gasped as he tried to twist free. "Dad, it's me. It's Lane. You're okay."

He stopped screaming, stopped trying to struggle free. He made choked, whimpering noises.

"It's all right," she whispered. "It's all right."

She felt a hand press against her back. Another hand touched the side of her head, moved forward and stroked her face, the fingers fluttering against her cheek. As he caressed her and sobbed, he slowly seemed to calm down.

He started to murmur "Oh, my God" over and over again.

Lane kept whispering "It's all right."

After a while he said, "I don't know what I'm doing here."

"I think you were walking in your sleep."

"She made me. She brought me here. Oh, my God. Did I pull the stake?"

"I don't know."

"Oh, God."

The hand went away from her face. She felt him lean forward.

"What're you doing?"

She felt a shudder pass through him.

"Dad?"

"It's still there. Thank God."

"Come on, let's get out of here."

"How could I *come* up here?" he blurted.

"It's all right, Dad. Let's just try and get down without breaking our necks." She let go of him and turned around. Dad kept a hand low on her back.

"Be careful, sweetheart."

"You, too."

The opening was a gray rectangle. His hand went away. She heard him moving, climbing off the coffin as she sat down and swung her legs toward the dim gap. "Why don't you wait up here till I can turn on the garage light?"

"You've got to be kidding," he said.

He sounded almost like Dad.

Lane scooted forward. She lowered her legs until her heels found a rung of the ladder.

"You okay?" Dad asked.

"Yeah." Gripping the side rails, she pushed herself off the attic floor. She climbed down slowly, her back to the ladder, rungs rubbing against her buttocks and dragging open her robe until nothing covered her front except the cloth belt loose against her belly.

She hoped Dad couldn't see her.

For a moment she pictured herself lying naked in the coffin up there, Dad sitting above her with that light.

Who is she?

Lane's feet found the wooden platform. She thrust herself away from the ladder, stood up straight and tied her robe shut before turning around.

Dad came down facing the other way. When he reached the platform, he folded the ladder, took hold of the dangling rope and swung the trapdoor up. It shut with a soft bump.

He stepped down. Lane went to him and put an arm around his back. He hugged her against his side.

Together they walked to the house.

"I guess we need to talk," he said.

"What's that thing doing in our garage?"

"It's a long story. Why don't you make a pot of coffee? I'll go and get your mother."

"You're going to tell Mom?"

"Yeah. I think I'd better."

"If you're afraid I'll snitch . . ."

"No, it isn't that. I've gotta tell her what's going on."

He left the kitchen. Lane threw out the used filter, put a fresh one into the machine's plastic basket, added coffee grounds and slipped the basket into place. She poured water into the top of the brewer. She thumbed the on switch. A red light came on. She gazed at it.

The times are out of joint.

Understatement of the fucking year, she thought.

Forty

He sat on the edge of the bed and shook Jean gently by the shoulder. Groaning, she rolled over. She squinted up at him. "Huh? Wha's—"

"You need to get up," Larry said.

Suddenly she looked alarmed and wide awake. "What's wrong?"

"It's not a fire or anything. Nobody's hurt. We just need to talk."

"Oh, my God. What? Tell me!"

"Lane's waiting in the kitchen."

"Is she all right?"

"She's fine. This is about me. I'll explain everything in a few minutes."

Jean sat up. She had a strange look in her eyes. A look of pain and fear. She caught her lower lip between her teeth.

"Don't get all upset," Larry said.

"Are you leaving us?"

"No, no. God, no." A strap of her nightgown had slipped off, baring her shoulder and right breast. Larry curled his hand over the breast and kissed her mouth.

Pulling her head back, she stared into his eyes. "You're having an affair?"

"No. I love you, Jean." He lifted the strap onto her shoulder and kissed her again. Her arms went around him.

She hugged him fiercely. "Come on now. Lane's waiting." She released him.

Larry stood up. He waited while she climbed out of bed and put on her bathrobe. Then he took her hand and led her from the room. As he entered the kitchen he smelled the comfortable aroma of coffee.

"It'll be ready in a couple of minutes," Lane said. She exchanged a rather sick-looking smile with Jean.

"Do you know what this is all about?" Jean asked.

"Not really."

They both faced Larry. "Go ahead and sit down," he said.

They sat at the table. Larry stood behind his chair and gripped its back. To Jean he said, "Do you remember that body we found?"

"What about it?"

He looked at Lane. "When your mother and I were out exploring in the desert with Pete and Barbara, we found a body in an abandoned hotel in Sagebrush Flat. That's a ghost town about fifty—"

"That's where you found *her?*"

"Yeah."

Jean frowned. "I thought we agreed not to tell Lane . . ."

"I didn't tell her." He felt a grimace twisting his face. Here goes, he thought. He took a deep breath. "Lane saw it. Tonight. It's up in our garage attic."

Jean gaped at him. The color drained from her face. In a low voice she said, "You're kidding."

"Pete and I went out and brought it back with us. While you two were in Los Angeles."

"You're kidding," she said again.

"He isn't," Lane told her.

Larry turned away from the table. Coffee had stopped streaming into the pot. He opened a cupboard. "We're doing a book about it. *I'm* doing the book."

"A book," Jean muttered.

"A vampire book," he said, taking down three mugs. "Nonfiction." He started to fill the mugs. His hand shook, slopping coffee onto the counter.

"You're telling me . . . you and Pete *took* that hideous *thing* out from under the stairs and brought it *home* with you, and it's out in our garage?"

"That's right. I'm writing a book about it."

"A vampire book," Lane murmured. She sounded as if she were talking to herself.

Larry brought the mugs to them. Lane seemed to be staring at the center of the table. Jean looked up at him as he set the mug in front of her. "You're out of your mind," she said.

"I know." He sat down. "I knew you'd be upset . . ."

"Upset? Me? Why would I be upset? My husband brings a goddamn *stiff* home and hides it in our garage."

"Boy, Dad."

"I'm sorry. I know it was a stupid thing to do. But Pete and I figured—"

"Pete." Jean's eyes narrowed. "I'll just bet it was his idea."

"Well, it was. But I went along with it. We're talking about a major book. It could make us rich."

"So would robbing a bank," Jean said. She put her hands on the table. She pushed her chair back. She got up and walked to the phone. "Does Barbara know about this?"

"No. What're you doing?" Larry asked.

She didn't answer. She jabbed buttons on the handset.

"Oh, boy," Lane muttered.

Larry groaned. He wished he hadn't mentioned Pete. But it *was* Pete's idea.

Now we'll have two wives going apeshit.

It would be nice, though, to have Pete here for some moral support.

"This is Jean." Her voice sounded calm. "I'd like to

speak to Barbara . . . No, I'm not kidding . . . Yes indeed, 'uh-oh' . . . Hi, Barbara, Jean . . . Yes, I'd say so. Something is quite wrong. I'd like you and Pete to come over here right away . . . Let's just say our dear husbands pulled a certain stunt. Bring something sharp. We may want to kill them."

At least she hasn't lost her sense of humor, Larry thought.

Jean hung up. "They'll be right over," she said.

"Wonderful."

She sat down, took a sip of coffee, put down the mug, scowled at Larry and said, "What were you doing out there with it tonight?"

The question made his heart lurch. He felt heat rush to his face. "Nothing."

"What do you mean, nothing? You were out there with it, weren't you?" She faced Lane. "Wasn't he?"

"He walked in his sleep," Lane said. "He didn't know what he was doing."

"What *was* he doing?"

Lane looked at him. She pressed her lips together.

"Go ahead and tell," he said. "Then we'll both know."

"Dad was talking to . . . the body. I guess he was dreaming or something, and they were carrying on a conversation." She turned her eyes to Larry. "I think she was trying to talk you into pulling out the stake."

"*Oh*-for-godsake," Jean gasped.

Lane's head jerked toward her mother. "He didn't do it," she said very fast. "I mean, I didn't realize that thing was supposed to be a vampire, but . . . I woke him up before he could take the stake out."

"And what were *you* doing out there, young lady?"

"I was worried about him. I didn't think Dad should have to spend the whole night on the couch just because he had a couple of drinks too many." She gave Jean a frown. "So after I finished my bath, I went to wake him up so he could go to bed, and he wasn't there. He was on his way to the garage. So I followed him. I was afraid he'd get hurt. You could tell something was wrong. He was walking in his sleep. He didn't know *what* the hell was going on."

"You followed your father into the attic and saw him talking to a corpse." She looked at Larry. "I hope you're proud of yourself."

"I couldn't help it, Jean. I was asleep."

"He really was, Mom. You should've heard him scream when I woke him up."

The doorbell rang. Without saying a word, Jean got up from the table. She stepped closer to Lane. Shaking her head, she slid a hand gently down the girl's hair. Then she hurried from the kitchen.

"I'm really sorry," Larry said.

"That's okay. Mom's really pissed, isn't she?"

"I'm afraid so. It's a big shock. For both of you."

"I'm just glad you didn't take that stake out."

"So am I. I was going to do it, huh?"

"Yeah. You had your hand on it when I woke you up."

"Jesus."

"You don't really think it would've . . ." She shook her head.

"Come back to life? I don't know. Probably not. But I'm still glad you stopped me." He managed a smile. "And I also appreciate the way you stuck up for me."

"That's all right."

"You're a good kid, no matter what everyone says."

She laughed softly and winced. Her eyes widened as if she were surprised by a sudden pain. Color drained from her face.

"What's wrong?"

She gave him a very strange look. For a moment Larry thought she was on the verge of telling him something terrible. But she said, "Nothing. I'm just not feeling very swift. Cramps. You know."

"Are you sure that's all?"

"Isn't it enough?"

"You could go to bed. You don't have to stick around for the fireworks."

"I wouldn't miss this."

Pete was first to enter the kitchen. He wore a blue bathrobe over white pajamas, and had moccasins on his feet. His nose was bandaged. From the look on his face, he might've been a fourth grader caught red-handed putting a tack on his teacher's chair. Meeting Larry's gaze, he mouthed "What's happened?" but didn't utter a sound.

Larry felt his lip curl up. He shook his head.

"I don't know what you boys did," Barbara said as she followed her husband through the doorway. "But I've got a feeling you're both neck deep in runny shit." She leaned back against a counter. Her hair was tangled and sticking out in odd places. Though she obviously hadn't brushed it, she must've taken time to dress. She wore white sneakers, tight red sweatpants, and a loose gray sweatshirt with an emblem on the front that read, "Alcatraz Swim Team."

Any other time, Larry thought, I'd be wondering if she had anything on under the clothes.

He realized he *was* wondering.

Guess I'm not totally out of it, he thought.

As Pete sat down, Jean came in with an extra chair from the dining room. She placed it near a corner of the breakfast table. "You'd better be seated for this," she told Barbara.

"That bad?" She pushed herself away from the counter and stepped toward the chair. Larry watched her breasts jostle the front of the sweatshirt. Obviously no bra, he decided.

He imagined Bonnie in her cheerleader outfit, the sweater jiggling just a bit with her movements. He saw the sweater rising above her belly as she leaped. When she came down, her pleated skirt billowed high.

"Larry." Jean's voice. "Are you with us?"

"Huh? Sure." He felt a rush of guilt.

Jean was already sitting down. To Barbara she said, "It appears that our two geniuses, here, decided to do a book about the body we found in Sagebrush Flat. So they snuck back and brought it home with them. It's in our garage."

"Holy shit," Barbara said.

Pete gave her a lopsided grin that lifted one side of his mustache.

She cuffed him high on the arm, and Larry watched the Alcatraz emblem swing.

"Hey! No need to get physical. It's a brilliant idea, honey. I'm in for twenty percent of the take."

She socked him again.

"Cut it out, huh? I've got a broken nose, for Christ-sake."

"I oughta smack it for you. Shit! Are you outa your fucking *gourd?*"

"We knew it'd upset you ladies," Larry said. "That's why we tried to keep it a secret until the book was finished and we could get rid of the corpse."

"Lane caught him in the garage with it tonight."

Now *Pete* looked angry at him. "Jesus, man."

"It wasn't his fault," Lane said. "He was walking in his sleep."

"Oh, sure. Jesus, man."

"You were sleepwalking?" Barbara asked. "That's wild."

Sensing an ally, Larry said, "Yeah, it was weird. Ever since we brought that body back with us, I've been having all kinds of strange dreams." He decided not to mention the other sleepwalking incident. "It's almost as if Bonnie's been trying to *communicate* with me. Like it's telepathy, or something."

"Bullshit," Pete said. "You're just obsessed, that's all."

"Bonnie?" Jean asked.

"That's her name," Larry explained. "Bonnie Saxon."

"You know who she is?" Barbara sounded excited.

"She was wearing a school ring. She went to Buford High, graduated in 1968."

"The yearbook," Lane muttered.

"Yeah. I found pictures of her. She was a cheerleader and the Homecoming Spirit Queen."

"Holy shit," Barbara said. "That yucky corpse . . . ?"

"And she was murdered the summer after graduation," he went on. "Somebody thought she was a vampire."

"Uriah Radley," Pete added. "The guy who broke my nose."

"What?" Barbara blurted.

He grinned at her, settled back in the chair and folded his arms across his chest. "We lied about target shooting."

She didn't punch him. She gazed at him. She looked astonished.

"We went out there figuring we might take him in for the murders," Pete explained. "He also killed two other high school girls. Right, Lar?"

"It looks that way." He turned to Jean. "You know all that time I spent at the library this week? I was studying up on her."

"God, you've been lying about everything."

He grimaced. "Not about everything. Just about this vampire stuff."

"You went out *gunning* for this guy?" Lane asked. She sounded just as intrigued as Barbara.

Larry nodded.

Pete said, "Yep. And we almost got him. Should've seen the bastard slinging arrows at us. He thought *we* were vampires."

"He *shot* at you?" Barbara asked.

"This is mad," Jean muttered.

"He was about to pound a stake into Pete, but I managed to stop him."

"Saved my ass. Or at least my heart."

Barbara's lips moved but no words came out. Pete gave her a martyred look. She stretched an arm toward him and rubbed his shoulder. "Oh, honey."

"This is incredible," Lane said.

Larry smiled at her. "Make a good book, huh?"

"Yeah."

"The thing about the book, it'll all be true."

"It'll sell *millions*," Pete said. "Just like *The Amityville Horror*. We'll be rich and famous."

*"In*famous," Jean corrected him. "People read something like that, they'll think you're a couple of assholes. Like that guy who got 'beamed up' by space monsters." She glared at Larry. "You want to be the laughingstock?" In a dopey, hick voice, she said, " 'Hey, there goes Larry Dunbar. Him's the dork that believes in vampires. Yassir.' "

"It won't be like that," he said. "It's just an account of what happened. I've got a lot of it written already, and—"

"God, I've gotta read it!" Barbara blurted, her hand going motionless on Pete's shoulder.

"When it's done," he said. "It'll just be a couple more weeks. But the thing is, I make it clear in the book that I *don't* believe in vampires. I tell it exactly the way it happened . . . how Pete and I thought it'd be a neat idea for a book. Neither *one* of us really believes it's a vampire."

"Not me," Pete said.

"But it's not really a vampire story anymore. It grew into a lot more than that. Now it's a murder mystery. Those three girls disappeared in 1968, and nobody knows what happened to them. Nobody but us."

"And Uriah," Pete said.

"We know who killed them, and why, and we've even got one of the bodies."

"In our garage," Jean muttered.

"And you almost got yourselves killed," Barbara said.

"But we've got the story," Larry said. "We've got it. I didn't think we had anything at first. It's like you said, Jean. I thought we had nothing but a couple of nuts cart a body home 'cause it might be a vampire, and they've got nothing else to do but pull out the stake to see if she comes alive. And then they do it, and she just lies there. Zip. Big deal. The whole thing falls flat. But it doesn't *matter* if she's a vampire. She's a *homicide,* and we can name her killer."

"Killed her because *he* thought she was a vampire," Pete put in.

"Uriah's wife and daughter were murdered," Larry said. "Somehow, he got it into his head that they were the victims of a vampire. He had their bodies cremated so they wouldn't come back. Then he went hunting. He got Bonnie and two other girls."

Frowning at him, Jean said, "You guys didn't make any of this up?"

Larry realized she had actually been listening. Though she didn't seem fascinated like Lane and Barbara, her anger had melted. She was interested.

"Some of it's speculation," he admitted.

"More than some, I should imagine."

"Not all that much," Pete said. "Lar's got a whole stack of newspaper stories."

"This is big," Barbara said, her voice low.

"Big?" Pete said. "Enormous. Now, if we just pull the stake and it turns out she *is* a vampire . . ."

"She'll suck all our blood and there won't be any book," Lane said.

Everyone looked at her.

"Just kidding," she muttered, blushing.

"There's no such thing as vampires," Jean said to her.

"I know. I know that."

"We all know that, don't we?" she asked. Her gaze

roamed the group. She was met by nods of agreement. She looked at Larry. "You've got that thing here just so you can pull the stake?"

"Yeah. I guess so."

"That's all you need it for? Once you've taken out the stake and proved she isn't a vampire, that's it? You'll be done? We can get rid of it?"

"Yeah."

Pete scowled, apparently recalling his plans to take the body on the talk show circuit.

Larry said to him, "We'll have to turn her over to the authorities." To Jean he said, "They can take up the investigation from there, and go out and try to pick up Uriah."

Jean nodded. "Okay. Let's go out to the garage and do it."

He stared at her.

She raised her eyebrows. "I mean it. You want to pull out the stake, we'll do it right now. I want that thing off my property. Tonight."

"It might be better to wait for daylight," Pete said.

Jean sneered at him. "Get real."

"Just in case," Larry said.

Her sneer turned on him. "In case of what?"

"Yeah!" Barbara pitched in, her voice loud and cheery. She was beaming. "What *are* you guys, a couple of pussies? Let's yank the fuckin' stake, see if the babe sits up and says hi."

"What the hell," Pete said.

"Okay," Larry said.

"Oh, boy," Lane said. She looked scared.

Forty-one

Pete went home for his video camera. Jean and Lane left the kitchen to get dressed. Barbara, still seated in the extra chair from the dining room, had her arms folded beneath her breasts and kept shaking her head.

Larry, trembling and wondering if his teeth might begin to chatter, took a sip of coffee. It was lukewarm. He realized they'd neglected to offer any to their guests. "Want some coffee?" he asked.

"Thanks, but I don't think so. I'd probably wet myself. God, this is exciting."

"Yeah," he muttered.

"It *is* like something from a book. One of your books."

"Hope it doesn't turn out like one."

"You and me both, buster." She let out a nervous laugh. "I'll be in it, won't I?"

"Sure. You already are." He managed a smile. "You're the one who found the body."

"Pete found it. But I'm the one who busted the landing, right?"

"Yeah."

"You don't describe me as a big lummox, I hope."

"No way. You'll like it."

Her head nodded, bobbing slowly up and down a few times, then switched directions and shook from side to side. "I can't believe you guys actually *did* all this."

"Neither can I."

"Jean can, though."

He groaned. "Don't remind me."

"She'll be okay," Barbara said. "Once it's all over and she realizes what's going on. You know, the fact that it's true. It's gonna be hot."

"Hope so."

"I bet there'll even be a movie. De Niro'd be perfect for Pete. They'd need someone big for me. Not big famous, necessarily. Big big."

"How about Susan Anton?"

She beamed. "Hey, that'd be great. Now, what about you and Jean? Somebody kind of small and cute for Jean. What about that gal with the husky voice from *An Officer and a Gentleman?*"

"Debra Winger."

"Yeah. She'd be perfect for Jean. For you, we've got a choice."

"Really?"

"Nick Nolte or Gary Busey."

He chuckled and felt his face heat up. "Thanks a bunch."

"No, they'd be great. Either one of them."

"At least you didn't suggest George Kennedy."

Larry heard slow footsteps coming toward them. Lane stepped into the kitchen, dressed in sneakers, jeans, and a heavy plaid shirt. The shirt was very large. It wasn't tucked in.

In her right hand she held a crucifix.

The one that belonged on the wall of her bedroom.

It looked identical to the crucifix that Larry had seen hanging around Uriah's neck. The one that had stopped his bullet.

"Don't let your mother see that," Larry warned.

"You're probably right." She slipped it underneath the front of her shirt and worked some of the long end down inside the waistband of her jeans. When she finished, the loose shirt showed no trace of the crucifix.

"You wouldn't happen to have a spare?" Barbara asked.

Lane spread the shirt's neck and lifted out the small golden cross. The cross, on its thin chain, had come from Larry's parents. They'd given it to her as a first communion present. He hadn't noticed Lane wearing it in a long while.

"Bring a vampire around," he said, "people start discovering religion."

"You're sure prepared," Barbara told her.

"Here, you take it." Lane started to fool with the clasp behind her neck.

"No, no. Hey, I'm not worried about vampires."

"Take it anyway," Lane said, and held the necklace out to her.

"Well . . ." She looked at Larry.

"Why not?"

"Right. Why not?" She slipped the chain around her neck and fastened it. Then she dropped the golden cross down the front of her sweatshirt. "Thanks, hon. If it looks like the babe might start chomping on me, I'll just whip this out and send her packing."

"That's the idea," Lane said. "Mom always wears hers, so she's protected."

They're all protected, Larry thought. He told himself that he didn't believe in vampires. He told himself that the crosses wouldn't protect them from squat. But still, he was glad they had the things.

Barbara patted her hair. She curled her upper lip. "You wouldn't have a brush handy, would you? Since Pete's gonna record this for posterity . . ."

"Sure," Lane said. "I'll get one."

Barbara stood up. Saying, "I'll need to use a mirror," she followed Lane out of the kitchen.

Larry sat alone at the table.

Oh, man, he thought. This is it.

At least we'll get it over with. No more wondering.

God, Bonnie. So what's it gonna be?

I'll be yours, she seemed to tell him.

Sure thing. Right. You'll just lie there dead.

Don't count on it.

What if she kills all of them but me?

He pictured himself pulling the stake. And Bonnie suddenly changing. Very suddenly. One second a dried-up grinning hag, the next second a gorgeous teenager, the next second throwing herself out of the coffin with a mad shriek and attacking. Hurling bodies, breaking necks, ripping open throats with her teeth. And Larry stands there helpless, watching the slaughter, too stunned to feel the pain of losing Jean and Lane, Pete and Barbara.

When they're all dead on the garage floor, Bonnie comes to him, her naked body sheathed with gleaming blood. She raises her dripping hands toward him. *Now we'll be together forever.*

Come off it, Larry told himself. My goddamn mind. It's not going to happen that way. Not a chance.

But he started to imagine himself back in the scene, so he shoved himself away from the table. He hurried into the living room. Barbara was standing in front of the fireplace, watching herself in the mirror above the mantel as she brushed her hair. Lane, beside her, seemed to be gazing into space. He put an arm across her back. She flinched, then looked at him and settled against his side.

As a toilet flushed, off in the distance, the front door swung open and Pete came in. He wore boots and jeans and a blue turtleneck sweater. A leather strap crossed his chest like a Sam Browne belt. He held the video camcorder on his shoulder. In his right hand was a bow.

"All set 'n' rarin' to go?" he asked.

"We're just waiting for Jean," Larry said, staring at the bow.

"Man, I can't believe we're finally gonna do it."

"Me neither," Larry told him.

"At night, no less."

Barbara turned away from the mirror and looked at him. "What are you doing with *that?*"

"This?" He raised the bow. "Got the idea from Uriah." To Larry he said, "I used to hunt deer with this baby."

"Oh, give me a break," Jean said, coming in from the hallway. "You're not serious."

"Wooden arrows, darlin'. Just as good as a stake when it comes to dispatching vampires. Better. You don't have to get up-close and personal."

"I thought we all agreed we didn't believe in any of this nonsense."

"It can't hurt to take precautions," Larry told her.

"God, you guys really take the prize."

"If it bugs you," Pete said, "just consider it a stage prop. There'll be a video of this, you know."

Jean obviously knew that, all right. She had not only brushed her hair, but put on lipstick. She'd dressed in her blue velour jumpsuit and white boots. She'd even knotted her Anne Klein silk scarf around her neck.

Larry realized that two of them—Jean in her scarf and Pete in his turtleneck—had chosen to wear garments that covered the region traditionally preferred by thirsty vampires. He wondered if they'd done it on purpose.

Pete raised the viewfinder to his eye, and the camera began to purr. He pivoted slowly to get everyone. Then he kept the camera on Jean as she crossed the room to join Larry and Lane. She smirked at him and shook her head. Stopping beside Larry, she put her arm around him. Barbara got into the picture, moving in close to Lane.

"Here we are," said Pete as he panned the group. "The dauntless, intrepid team as it prepares to go outside and remove the stake from the heart of the cadaver."

"Does that thing have sound?" Jean asked.

"Yes indeed," Pete said. "Any famous last words before we embark on our adventure?"

Larry shook his head.

"Say something," Barbara urged him.

"Well . . . None of us actually believes in vampires. I want to make that clear. But the body we found—a girl named Bonnie Saxon—was murdered by a man who very much believed in vampires. He believed *she* was one, and killed her by pounding a stake into her heart. In just a few minutes we're going to pull out that stake. We'll see what happens."

"Terrific," Pete said. "Anybody else?"

Nobody offered to speak.

"Okay," Pete said. "Let's do it."

They went out back through the kitchen door. Jean was first to reach the garage, and turned on the overhead light before the others arrived.

When they were all inside, Pete said, "Why don't we close the door?"

"Let's not," Larry said.

"Yeah," Barbara said. "You never know, we might have to run for our lives."

"Give me a break," Jean muttered.

Larry left the garage door open. He stepped onto the platform and reached up for the dangling rope.

"Just a minute," Pete said. "Here Barb." He handed the camera to her.

"What am I supposed to do with it?"

"Get us bringing the coffin down." He showed her how to hold the camera. "You look through this. What you see is what you get. Just hold this button down, and that's all there is to it. Okay?"

"I think so."

Pete set his quiver and bow on the concrete floor. Joining Larry on the platform, he glanced around at Barbara. "Okay, get her going and keep her going till I say to stop."

"Yessir."

Larry caught hold of the rope. He pulled the trapdoor down, and Pete helped unfold the ladder. "Be my guest," Larry told him.

Pete started to climb. Halfway up the ladder he looked over his shoulder and waved. "Famous last wave," he said.

"Quit screwing around," Barbara told him.

Larry smiled at her. Jean and Lane were standing close to Barbara. Jean's hands were stuffed into the front pockets of her jumpsuit. Her shoulders were hunched and she looked as if she were gritting her teeth. Lane's teeth were bared. Her arms were wrapped tightly across her chest. She met his eyes and said, "Be careful. Don't fall or anything."

Murmuring "Thanks," he turned to the ladder just as Pete's boots disappeared beyond the edge of the floor.

"No!" Pete cried out. *"In the name of God, no!"*

Larry's heart kicked.

He heard gasps from the women.

"Watch out!" Jean's voice.

From above came the sound of Pete laughing.

Behind Larry something crashed. He heard glass break.

Pete's grinning face appeared at the top of the ladder. "Just kidding," he said.

"You bastard!" Larry yelled. Turning around, he saw Barbara sprawled on her back. The crotch of her red sweatpants was dark, the patch growing, urine seeping out and dribbling onto the concrete floor between her legs. The camcorder lay about a yard beyond her head.

"What's wrong?" Pete asked.

Larry scowled up at him. "You idiot! You scared Barbara so bad she fell down. I think your camera bit it."

"No!"

This time the outcry was real.

"Yes," Larry told him.

As Pete hurried down the ladder, Jean and Lane helped

his wife up. She rose to her feet, grimacing, rubbing her rump as she stared down at herself. "Oh shit," she said. Her voice was pitched high and trembling. "I don't believe this." She started to sob.

Pete halted in front of her. "Don't hit me," he said.

She stared at him and wept. Then she rushed from the garage, leaving dribbles on the concrete, and hobbled down the driveway bow-legged.

"I did it this time," Pete muttered.

"You sure did," Jean said.

"Oh, man." For a moment he looked as if he might go after Barbara. Then he shook his head. He glanced at the small puddle on the garage floor, shook his head again, then stepped over it and crouched in front of his camera. He picked it up. He picked up a few pieces of plastic and glass. He stood and raised the viewfinder to his eye. "Oh, man," he said.

"Serves you right," Jean said.

"I'm sorry. Man, am I sorry."

"Save it for Barb," Jean told him.

"Yeah. I really blew it, huh?"

"Now what?" Lane asked.

Pete frowned at Larry. "Can we call this off for now? I mean, we've just *gotta* get the whole thing on video. I bought this camera especially . . . God, why did I have to fuck around?"

"Do you think it can be repaired?" Larry asked.

"I don't know. I'll have to check it out. Even if I can fix it, I wouldn't be able to buy any parts tomorrow."

"You mean today?" Lane asked.

"Yeah. Sunday. Can we put this off till Monday? I'll either have it fixed by then or get a new one. Okay?"

"It's up to Jean," Larry said. "Can you wait till Monday?"

She sighed. "I don't want to be the one to ruin . . . Yeah, I guess it's okay. You've waited this long." She shook her head with disgust. "On one condition. We lock the garage doors till then. Padlock them." She peered up at Larry. "I don't want you coming out here again, sleep-walking or otherwise."

"Neither do I," he told her.

"That's great," Pete said. "Thanks."

"You'd better go home," Jean said, "and look after Barbara."

"If she'll let me in the house. God, she's probably on the phone trying to get a divorce lawyer. Or busy loading my magnum."

Larry, somewhat pleased by Pete's agony, patted him on the shoulder. "If we hear shots, we'll call an ambulance."

"Thanks a load, pardner."

Forty-two

When Lane woke up, her bedroom was full of sunlight. For just a moment she felt good. Then the memories of last night with Kramer crashed down on her. Sickened with shame and terror, she threw her covers aside, sat up and hugged her belly. She couldn't think straight. Her mind was a torrent of horrible images that kept her heart racing, her skin burning, her stomach knotted.

She fought the images. Like trying to shove dozens of writhing snakes down inside a box. Their heads kept popping up, striking at her, sinking in their fangs. But at last she got them all shoved down and slammed the lid. Though they were out of sight, she still thought she could hear them hissing and thumping around, eager to escape and hurt her.

She sat on the bed gasping, sweat trickling down her face, nightshirt clinging to her skin.

I'll kill the bastard, she thought.

Oh, sure I will.

What am I going to do?

Last night hadn't been enough for him. He'd made that very clear. And if Lane gave him any trouble about it, he'd get her with the razor. Her parents, too. He would kill them all.

The same way he killed Jessica and her family.

My God, she thought. Where'd that idea come from? Kramer certainly hadn't told her any such thing.

But he'd killed them. Lane was suddenly sure of it. Jessica'd been in his sixth-period class. He must've been getting it off with her until she gave him trouble. He was the one who beat her up, who broke her arm. Not Benson, after all. Kramer had taught her a lesson about cooperating, but that wasn't enough. Maybe she wouldn't have any more to do with him. Maybe he was afraid she might talk. So he crept into her house last week and slaughtered the whole family and set the place on fire.

He'll do the same to us.

Dad gave her a sheepish smile when she entered the living room. He was in his easy chair, a paperback in his hands, a mug of coffee on the lamp table beside him. "Good afternoon," he said.

She kissed him on the cheek. It was scratchy with whiskers. "Where's Mom?"

"She went to the twelve o'clock mass."

"Glad she didn't wake me up for it."

"Figured you needed your sleep. How's it going?"

"Okay, I guess."

"Hope you didn't have any vampire nightmares."

"I don't think so," Lane said. If I had nightmares, she thought, they wouldn't have been about vampires. "How about you?"

"Your mother and I were up till after sunrise."

Lane managed to smile. "Having a little discussion?"

"It turned out okay. Better than I deserved, I guess. When you see her, just don't bring up the subject of our guest in the garage."

"I wonder how Pete fared."

"We didn't hear any gunshots."

"That's a good sign."

"I don't think your mother would've been quite so forgiving if *she'd* been the one who wet her pants."

"Daaaad."

He chuckled softly and shook his head. "Anyway, there're some sweet rolls in the kitchen."

"Yuck. Maybe I'll eat something while I'm out. I've got to pick up a few things at the drugstore. And maybe I'll drop by the mall. Need anything?"

"I'm getting a little low on pipe cleaners."

"Okay." She headed for the front door. "See you later."

"Have fun," he said.

Outside, she took the keys from her denim shoulder bag. She locked the front door and hurried to the Mustang. She slid in behind the steering wheel and swung her heavy bag onto the passenger seat.

As she drove away from the house her stomach began to flutter. The car was hot inside, but she kept the windows up and didn't turn on the air conditioner. Though the heat didn't stop her from shivering, she found it comforting.

A block from home she stopped the car. She reached into a pocket of her blouse. She took out a folded sheet of paper and opened it. While she studied the first of the two addresses she'd copied from the telephone book, she eased her hand between the buttons of her blouse and gently rubbed her left breast. Both her breasts were sore, but the left hurt more than the right. It had been purple with bruises when she looked at herself before dressing.

She finished memorizing the address, took her hand out of her blouse, folded the paper again and tucked it gently into her pocket.

She drove to the address.

She parked at the curb and stared out the passenger window at the mobile home. It was on a foundation some distance back from the road, a battered pickup truck near one end, a motorcycle in front of the pickup. There was no driveway, no lawn. Just the home and the vehicles sitting on a patch of desert.

It looked like the kind of place where you'd expect to find throwbacks.

It looked exactly like the kind of place where Lane expected to find Riley Benson.

I must be out of my mind.

She grabbed the strap of her bag and dragged it behind her as she climbed from the car. She lifted the strap onto her shoulder. On wobbly legs she made her way around the front of the car, stepped onto the curb, crunched over gravel, and climbed a few stairs to the front door.

She thumbed the door-bell button, but no sound came from inside. So she knocked.

"Yeah?" A woman's voice. "Who is it?"

"A friend of Riley's," she called.

The door opened. The woman standing on the threshold looked too young to be Riley's mother. Maybe in her late twenties. Her blue eyes seemed too pale for the deep tan of her face. Her blond hair, neatly brushed, hung to her shoulders and draped her brow. Her tank top, tie-dyed pink, was cut off to leave her midriff bare. Lane could see her nipples through the fabric. She wore cutoff blue jeans low on her hips. Her feet were bare.

She doesn't look like *anybody's* mother, Lane thought. Maybe Riley's sister. Or maybe he'd already found himself a replacement for Jessica.

"Don't just stand there gawking," she said. "Come on in."

"Is Riley home?" Lane asked, climbing the steps.

"You say you're a friend of his? You sure don't look it."

"Well, I knew Jessica."

"That poor thing."

Inside, the mobile home smelled good—a coffee aroma blended in with hints of perfume and maybe floor wax.

"Have a seat, darling. I'll tell him you're here."

Lane sat at a table in the kitchen area and watched the woman stride down a narrow passageway. The jeans were frayed where the legs had been cut off, and strands of ragged denim dangled against the backs of her thighs. Her right thigh was smudged with a nasty bruise that reminded Lane of those she'd seen on herself today.

Near the far end of the corridor she rapped gently on a door. Then she rolled it open and stepped out of sight.

"You've got a visitor, honey." Though she spoke in a hushed voice, Lane easily heard her.

"Huh?"

"Well, take the blessed headphones off."

"What?"

"You've got a visitor."

"The cops?"

"No, it's not the cops. It's a nice young gal who says she's a friend of Jessica's."

"Oh, Jesus."

"You watch your tongue."

"I don't wanta see nobody, Mom."

She *was* his mother?

"Put on your shirt and go on out and talk with her. And try to keep a civil tongue in your head."

As Riley's mother came out of the room, Lane turned her eyes away. The salt shaker on the table was a little plastic dog, the pepper shaker a red fireplug.

"He'll be right along," she said. "I ought to warn you, though, he's been in a mighty foul mood lately. First it was Jessica's murder, then the police bothering him, and then he got into trouble with some gal at school and got himself expelled. This has been a mighty bad week for him, the poor kid."

"I'm really sorry," Lane said. "Some of it's my fault, I guess. I'm the one who got him kicked out of school."

Riley's mother frowned. "I hope he didn't hurt you. I heard what he did, and—"

"*You!*"

The mother looked around. "Be nice, honey."

Riley stepped around her. "What're you doing here, Dunbar?"

"I just want to talk a minute."

"Whatever you've gotta say, I don't wanta hear it."

The mother turned on him, scowling and shoving her fists against her hips. "Did you hear what I said about being nice?"

"Mom, for godsake!"

"I just want to talk to you a minute," Lane said. "It's really important."

"Maybe the two of you should step out front. There isn't much privacy in this place." She fixed her eyes on Riley. "You be a gentleman, or you'll be sorry."

He wrinkled his nose. Glaring at Lane, he said, "Okay. Let's go out. But make it quick."

Lane stood up. "It was nice to meet you, Mrs. Benson."

"Nice to meet you, honey." She held out her hand. "The name's Melanie. You can call me Mel."

Lane shook the woman's hand. "I'm Lane Dunbar."

"Hope to see more of you around here."

"Don't hold your breath," Riley told her.

He led the way outside. Lane followed him to the road. He sat down on the hood of her car. "Okay, what's the fuckin' idea?"

"Your mom's nice."

"Yeah, sure, a sweetheart. She's probably got an eye on us, or I'd take you apart, you fuckin' cunt."

"I came here to tell you who killed Jessica."

He sneered. "Yeah, sure."

"Kramer did it."

The sneer fell away. He stared at Lane. He said nothing.

"Kramer got me alone last night. He beat me up and raped me."

Riley's eyes narrowed. "You don't look beat up." His voice came out quiet, uncertain.

"He didn't hurt my face."

"How do I know he did *anything* to you?"

Lane checked the area ahead. On the other side of the street was empty land, a barren hillside. Keeping her back to Riley's home, she fumbled open three buttons. She spread the front of her blouse wide enough for him to see her breasts. "That's just some of it," she muttered, closing the blouse.

"Kramer did that to you?"

"And plenty more. And he had a razor with him. He said he'd use it on me if I talked. He said he'd kill me and my family. I think that's what happened to Jessica and her parents."

Riley slumped forward and clutched his knees. His head lowered. For a while he just sat like that on the car's hood, staring down. Then he raised his head and met Lane's eyes. "Jessica looked like that. After she got herself pounded. She said it was a gang of spics got her behind the mini-mart."

"It was Kramer."

"I'm gonna kill him," Riley said.

"I'm gonna help you."

Lane swung the denim bag forward. Clutching it to her belly, she reached inside and took out a revolver. "It's my dad's," she said. "It's just a twenty-two, but—"

"That'll do just fine," Riley said.

Lane waited in the car while Riley went back inside his home. A few minutes passed. Then he came out and climbed into the passenger seat. "I told the old lady we're going to a matinee."

Lane took the paper out of her blouse pocket. She checked the second address.

"What's that?"

"It's where Kramer lives."

"All *right.*"

She put the paper away and started to drive.

"I've got something for him," Riley said. He tugged up a cuff of his blue jeans, reached down and came up with a knife. Lane glanced at it. The thing looked wicked. Its blade must've been eight inches long.

"Here's how we're gonna work it," he said. "You keep the motherfucker covered with the gun. *I'll* do him. Don't you go shooting him up unless he makes a break for it."

"We'll be each other's alibis," Lane said, her voice shaking.

"Fuck alibis. I don't care if they get me for it."

"I do. And I'm sure your mother does. If we're caught, we might not get charged with anything, or end up with suspended sentences. I mean, I don't think a jury's going to put us away for this. But let's try to work it so the cops don't come looking."

"Oh yeah? How do you figure we can manage that?"

"Why don't we make it look like suicide?"

"Fuck that. I'm gonna cut his dick off. I'm gonna cut his head off."

"Maybe we can make him write a suicide note. Make him confess what he did to Jessica. On paper. Then we hang him. Right there in his house."

"You read too many fucking books."

"It's worth a try."

On Kramer's street, two blocks from where his house should be, Lane swung the car to the curb. She faced Riley. He had the knife in his right hand, rubbing its blade along the leg of his faded jeans.

"Why don't we walk from here?" she said. "That way, nobody's likely to connect the car with what happens to Kramer." She paused and tried to catch her breath. She hadn't been *doing* anything, but she felt as if she'd just finished dashing up a few flights of stairs. "I'll go on ahead first. Give me a couple of minutes head start."

"You'll be alone in there with him."

"Don't I know it," she muttered. She lifted the bag onto her lap and dropped the keys inside. After a quick look around to make certain no one was in sight, she took out the revolver. She set the bag on the floor. Leaning back against the seat, she untucked her blouse, lifted its front, and slid the muzzle under the waistband of her skirt. It only went down an inch before pushing against her pubic mound. Lowering the blouse, she held the gun against her belly. She opened the door and climbed out.

"Good luck," Riley said.

"Thanks." She shut the door. Facing the car, she slipped the revolver farther down until it was snug between her skirt and body. She glanced down at herself. The hanging front of her blouse concealed the bulges.

The back of the blouse was glued to her skin. She peeled it away, but as soon as she let go, it stuck again.

There was no sidewalk in this neighborhood, so she walked along the edge of the road. The barrel pressed her groin. The front sight sometimes scraped the inner side of her left thigh, so after a while she nudged the gun butt sideways. Then the muzzle was stroking her right thigh with each step she took. But it was smooth, and didn't scratch her the way the sight did.

She remembered last night with the bottom of the crucifix stuffed in her jeans.

Last night, a cross. Today, a revolver.

It's a weird damn world, she thought.

She glanced back. The Mustang was a block away, Riley still in the passenger seat.

She kept walking.

A mortal sin, she thought. I'll be risking Hell, murdering Kramer. Even if it's Riley who does the dirty work. I'll be just as guilty as him in the eyes of God.

What am I supposed to do, let Kramer go on raping me? Let him kill Mom and Dad?

It's self-defense. Lane didn't know a lot about Church policy, but it seemed like allowances were made for killing people in self-defense, war, that kind of thing. She sure hoped so.

At the next corner she took the paper out of her pocket. She unfolded it. Squinting as the white paper glared sunlight, she read the address again: 838.

She looked back. Riley was out of the car.

She put the paper away. She rubbed a sleeve across her face to dry the sweat. She continued walking. The sun felt like a hot blanket on her back. She wanted to reach around and pluck at the seat of her panties, but Riley was sure to see her do it.

The house to her right was 836.

Next door was Kramer's. A small, adobe house with a picture window. Its driveway was empty.

Gasping for breath, heart slamming, leg muscles feeling as soft as pudding, she walked up the driveway.

No garage. A carport instead.

The station wagon wasn't in the carport.

It wasn't anywhere in sight.

He's not home!

After all this, she thought, he *has* to be.

She mounted the front stoop. She rang the door bell, and heard quiet bells from inside the house.

She waited.

She wished she could catch her breath.

She slipped a hand under the front of her blouse and wrapped sweaty fingers around the grips of her father's revolver. The barrel moved, nudging her groin. She thought about Kramer's mouth down there.

"Come on, you bastard," she muttered.

They found his station wagon fifteen minutes later in the crowded parking lot of the marina.

The chain-link gate, which had been locked last night, now stood open. Lane didn't pass through it. She stood there, alone, and peered at Kramer's deserted slip.

Then she went back to the car. She opened the door, pulled the revolver up high enough so its barrel wouldn't dig into her, then slid into the driver's seat.

"He's out in his boat," she said.

"Shit."

"God, I don't know. Maybe it's just as well." She took the gun out of her blouse and stuffed it into her denim bag.

"Just as well, my ass."

"Would've been tough getting away with it here. Awful lot of people around."

"Yeah, but we could've deep-sixed him in the river."

"I know."

"Shit," Riley said again.

"There's nothing we can do about it. We'll have to figure out something else."

"Like what?"

Shaking her head, Lane backed up the car. She drove toward the parking lot exit. "He's gonna want me again. He said Monday or Tuesday. He'll probably want me to meet him someplace. Someplace where we'll have privacy. Maybe I can let you know ahead of time. You can be waiting."

"Sounds good."

Lane steered onto Shoreline. "Want to go to the mall?"

"Okay with me." He gave her a strange look. "Do you?"

"Yeah, I think so. It'll give me time to calm down."

"You forgetting who you're with?"

She glanced at him. "Riley Benson. Tough guy. Just don't try getting tough with me, okay?"

"Not with you," he said. Then he added, "Lane."

Forty-three

During the day, Uriah stayed in a dry wash some distance from the road.

He had tried to eat jerky that morning, but found that he couldn't chew it without sending horrible pulses of pain through his jaw and cheeks. He was able to drink water, though some dribbled out through the holes in his face. And he was able to sleep.

He dreamed the vampires got him. He recognized all of them. All were demons he had slain, but they were slain no longer. They came shrieking at him through the desert sunlight. They brought him down. They stripped off his animal skins. They took the hammer and stakes from his pack. Holding him down, they pounded the wooden spikes through his hands and feet. They nailed him to the ground. Crucified him. As he writhed in torment, one ripped the patch off his eye. He looked up out of the depths of the socket, thinking, *How strange!* He could see with both eyes. The vampires were all around him, down on their knees, hunger and delight in their eyes, drool spilling down their chins. Their hands moved over his body as if trying to awaken his lust. Horrified, he realized they were succeeding. *I must resist,* he thought. *I am God's warrior.* The faces lowered onto him. He felt their mouths all over. Sucking him. Instead of pain, he felt ecstasy. *This is wrong!* Lips pressed against his mouth. A tongue thrust in. Other tongues slithered through the holes in his cheeks.

Another pushed into his anus. As he wondered how that was possible, flat on his back the way he was, a tongue entered the tip of his penis and snaked in deep and he squirmed. Another slid into his empty socket. He realized he was not pinned to the ground by stakes. The wooden shafts had turned into vampire tongues that writhed inside the holes in his hands and feet. Then tongues were sliding into his body where he had no openings, melting in through his flesh, filling him.

Uriah twisted and bucked in an agony of exquisite pleasure and woke up as pain flared in his right cheek. He found the tip of his forefinger inside the bullet hole. Wincing, he eased it out. He sat up and gently held both sides of his face.

Night had come.

In the frenzy of his dream he'd tossed his blanket away. He dragged it toward him and clutched it around his shoulders. But he couldn't stop shaking.

Satan had visited that dream upon him. Trying to tempt him. Trying to weaken his resolve.

I am God's warrior, he told himself. *I won't fail.*

He got to his feet, picked up the satchel that held his weapons and useless food, wrapped the blanket around himself, and climbed the loose gravel wall of the wash.

Soon he came to the road. He looked both ways. There were no headlights.

During the whole of the night, as he made his way toward Mulehead Bend, Uriah encountered no headlights. Not once was he forced to flee from the road and hide. He made good time.

When the horizon began to go pale, he climbed to the top of a bluff. From there he could see the Colorado River in the distance—a broad, twisting ribbon of slate bordered by lights like hundreds of stars that had fallen to the desert near its shores.

Streetlights. A few slowly moving headlights. Porch

lights. Maybe even lights from the windows of homes where people had already started their day or spent a sleepless night.

Uriah wondered which of the lights might be glimmering from the lair of the vampires.

Maybe none.

Tomorrow night he would be in among those lights. He would sneak into the lair and put Satan's children to rest.

Forty-four

A hand gently shook Lane awake. "Time to rise and shine, honey," her mother said.

Monday morning.

Her stomach clenched.

"Okay," she muttered. When she was alone, she rolled onto her side, hugged her belly and drew her knees up.

I can't go to school, she thought. I just can't.

I've got to.

Yesterday she'd told Riley that she would talk to Kramer after class and arrange to meet him.

But that was yesterday. It was easy to make brave plans when you were safe with someone else and talking about tomorrow. Now she was alone and this was the day she had to do it. Not quite the same. Not the same at all.

Curling up more tightly under the covers, Lane pictured herself in sixth period. Sitting at her desk. Right next to Jessica's empty desk. Right in front of the table where Kramer always perched when he talked to the class. He would be sitting up there, all smug and handsome, acting as if nothing had happened. But sneaking glances at her. Calling on her sometimes. And all period long he would be thinking about how she looked naked, remembering the things he'd done to her, daydreaming about what he would do the next time he got her alone.

I can't go, Lane thought. I can't sit there in front of him. Not for an hour, not for a second. I'd go crazy.

So don't.

Right away she felt better.

Uncurling, she rolled face down. The mattress pushed against her bruised body, but didn't hurt very much.

The pressure against her breasts reminded Lane of opening her blouse for Riley yesterday. She felt the heat of a blush spreading over her skin. She hadn't been embarrassed at all when she did it, but now she could hardly believe she'd shown herself to him. Right by the street in broad daylight. It seemed as if someone else had done that. A different Lane.

The same, different Lane who'd walked up to Kramer's door with a gun shoved into her skirt.

I must've been crazy.

What if Kramer'd been home? What if we'd actually murdered him?

Didn't happen, she told herself.

Her breasts were starting to ache now, so she rolled onto her side, pushed away the covers and sat on the edge of the bed. She'd worn a jersey nightshirt instead of a nightgown, just in case Mom or Dad should see her without a robe. The gowns were either low-cut or diaphanous, or both, and no good for concealing her injuries. The crewneck jersey hid everything. Though not at the moment. Her rump was bare from scooting across the mattress, and the nightshirt was rumpled on her lap.

Lane glanced at the closed door, then peered down at herself. Her thighs were bruised, but some of the areas that had looked chafed and red now seemed okay. She pressed the gathered fabric to her belly and leaned forward. The edges of her vulva no longer looked raw. She lifted the nightshirt above her breasts. They were looking better, too. The bruises weren't so dark. They'd changed from deep purple to a greenish-yellow color.

A few more days, Lane thought, I'll be good as new.

On the outside.

Next time, maybe he won't hurt me.

There won't be a next time!

She let the nightshirt drift down to her waist, raised herself off the bed for a moment while she pulled it beneath her, then sat again and spread the fabric snug against her thighs.

There has to be a way out of this, she told herself.

Yeah, kill him.

Yesterday she could've done it. Or helped, at least.

But now the idea of murdering Kramer seemed so much bigger. Enormous. She felt as if it would cast a black cloud over her life that might never go away.

I can't kill him. I can't tell on him. I can't let him get me again.

I could kill *myself.*

The idea shocked Lane, sent a sickening flood of heat rushing through her body.

If I kill myself, he won't have any reason to go after Mom and Dad. But it'd *ruin* them. I'd burn in Hell, for sure. And everything . . .

Fuck that.

She stood up quickly, walked to the closet and put on her robe.

There *has* to be a way out.

Yeah, stay the hell home from school. That's a way out, at least for today. Worry about tomorrow tomorrow.

Maybe Riley'll take care of him without me. If I just stay out of it long enough. If Kramer doesn't come after me in the meantime.

Lane stepped into her slippers. She left her bedroom, made a quick trip to the toilet and relieved herself, then headed for the kitchen. Mom, unloading the dishwasher, looked around at her. "You're not dressed."

"I'm really feeling rotten today," she said, giving her voice a low, groany tone.

"What is it?"

"You name it. Cramps, a headache, the trots. I've got it all."

"Oh, I'm sorry, honey."

She shrugged and frowned. "I'll live, I guess. But I don't think I'm up for school."

"What about Henry and Betty?"

Lane grimaced. She'd forgotten about them. About George, too. She'd phoned George yesterday after coming back from the mall, and he'd sounded eager to ride with them. "I guess I could go ahead and take them, and then just come home."

"No, if you're not feeling good enough to go to school . . . I suppose I can pick them up. Just this once. Since they're expecting you."

"That'd be great."

"They have other ways of getting home, don't they?"

"Oh, yeah. They can always work something out. There's a guy named George, too. We got to know each other at the play. I was going to give him a ride today."

Mom nodded. "All right. Well, get me their addresses and I'll take care of it."

"That's wonderful. Thanks a lot, Mom."

"Would you like me to make you something before I go?"

"I don't feel much like eating. I'll come out when I get hungry, okay?"

"Well, suit yourself. You'll feel better, though, once you have some food inside you."

Lane poured herself a mug of coffee, then went into the living room. Dad was in his usual chair, dressed in the sweat clothes he usually wore after getting up, a mug in one hand, a paperback in the other.

"Morning, sweetheart," he said. "How's it going?"

"Not so hot. I'm staying home sick. Mom said it's okay."

"A touch of the flu?" he asked.

"Something like that, I guess. Anyway, I feel rotten. I'm going back to bed pretty soon." She took a sip of coffee. "Are you all excited about tonight?"

He wrinkled his nose. "I don't know whether I'm excited or just scared."

"If it bothers you, why not skip it?"

"Not that simple," he said. "What would I do about the ending of my book?"

"That can be the ending. You make an ethical choice, or whatever, not to meddle with the thing. Let sleeping dogs lie. That could be the theme of the book."

Nodding, he laughed softly. "Not a bad idea. Do *you* think we shouldn't take the stake out?"

"Hell, I wouldn't have brought any corpse home in the first place."

"I *wish* we hadn't. God knows." He shrugged. "But now that she's here . . ."

"I don't know, Dad. You've always warned me not to mess with weird stuff like Ouija boards and fortune-telling . . ."

"Yeah."

"Remember when I bought that voodoo doll in New Orleans?"

"It still holds," he said.

" 'You don't want to monkey with the supernatural.' That's what you always told me. And now you're planning to pull a stake out of a dead person to see if she's a vampire?"

"No good can come of it," he said, sounding like the voice of caution from an old mad-scientist movie.

"So why do it?" Lane asked.

His smile came back. "Because it's there?"

"Try again, Pops."

"You don't sound so sick to me."

"Maybe you *should* forget it. I'm serious. Make up your mind not to pull out the stake, and you'll be amazed how much better you suddenly feel."

"Will it make you feel better?"

"Maybe. I don't really care. I can always stay in my room when you do it, but you'll have to be out there. You know? This isn't my thing, it's yours. I've got my own problems."

"What kind . . . ?"

"I'm just saying," she hurried on, "you shouldn't let Pete or anyone else push you into doing something that you're against. You're the one who'll have to live with it."

"You think it's morally wrong to pull the stake?"

"It is if she's a vampire."

"Of course, we know she isn't."

" 'There are more things in heaven and earth, Horatio, than you've dreamt of in your philosophies.' "

"Hey, pretty good!"

She smiled. "I'm off to bed."

" 'Good night, sweet princess. And flights of angels sing thee to thy rest.' "

"Oh, thanks. I'm not dying, I'm just going to take another nap. I hope."

She left the room, wrote down the addresses of her friends, gave them to her mother in the kitchen, thanked her again for taking care of the matter, then returned to her bedroom.

Propped up against pillows, she tried to read. Though her eyes moved over the sentences, her mind kept straying, tormenting her with thoughts of Kramer. After a while she set the book aside. She snuggled down beneath the covers.

She *wished* she had her father's problems. He doesn't know how lucky he is, she thought. How nice it would be if the biggest worry in her life was whether or not to pull a piece of wood out of a corpse.

Dad had said the girl—Bonnie?—was the Homecoming queen. She must've been beautiful. Maybe just Kramer's type.

Drifting toward sleep, Lane imagined getting all her

friends together: Betty and Henry and George and Riley. *I need your help,* she told them. She explained her plan, and they all seemed eager to join in. So they crept into the garage and sneaked out with the corpse. They tied the coffin to the roof of her Mustang. They drove through the night across town to Kramer's house. His station wagon wasn't there. He was still out on his boat. While her friends waited on the front stoop, she broke a back window and entered the house. She opened the door for them, and they brought the coffin inside. They took it to Kramer's bedroom. They lifted the body onto his bed and hid the empty coffin in a closet.

Lane volunteered to pull the stake. *I'm not scared,* she said. And she wasn't. Not of Bonnie. Bonnie was not the enemy. Bonnie was her ally, her weapon. She drew the stake out of the girl's chest. The hole melted shut. The cadaver began to expand like an inflatable rubber doll with air being blown in. Its dry, leathery skin uncrinkled, took on a healthy glow of life. Except for the bruised places.

Lane was startled when she realized that Bonnie looked like her own twin. No, she thought, she's not a twin. She's me. This is even better than I hoped. Kramer'll think I came to him.

The Lane on Kramer's bed opened her eyes. *Don't worry,* she said. *I'll take care of him.*

Lane woke up feeling as if a terrible burden had been removed. She didn't know why, but she felt good. Then she remembered the weird plan of her daydream. It had only been a fantasy. Nothing was changed. Her spirits sank and dread returned to its nesting place in the pit of her stomach.

She looked at the clock beside her bed. Almost one.

She'd been asleep for a long time, and she was glad. If only she could just *stay* asleep.

But she was hungry. So she got out of bed, put on her robe and slippers, and left the room.

The house seemed deserted.

But the door to her father's office was shut. She knocked. Opening it, she glimpsed a page of black and white photos as Dad swept a folder shut. He smiled at her, but he looked startled and his face was red.

She wondered what he'd been looking at. Whatever it might be, he seemed ashamed of it. She decided not to ask. "Sorry to bother you," she said.

"No problem. Feeling any better?"

"A little. Hungry, though. Have you already eaten?"

"Yeah. We had lunch an hour ago. Do you want me to make you something?"

"No, that's okay. I can manage. Where's Mom?"

"She went to the store. We decided to ask Pete and Barbara over for dinner, so she had to pick up a few things."

"Barbara's recovered?"

"Apparently. Your mother dropped in on her. Sounds as if she's a little embarrassed about her accident, but she's eager to resume the adventure. Pete's already picked up a new video camera."

"Let's hope Barbara doesn't break this one."

"She probably won't get her hands on it."

"If Pete's smart. What time are they coming over?"

"Around six."

"If I'm not around, make sure you get me up. I wouldn't want to miss anything."

"You're sure about that?"

"Absolutely. See you later." She pulled the door shut and went to the kitchen.

While she made herself a grilled cheese sandwich, she thought back to the folder that Dad had shut so quickly. She tried to remember the look of the paper inside. Glossy, with two or three pictures on it.

Like a page out of *Buford Memories.*

"Oh, boy," she muttered. He must've torn it from the 1968 annual. And there had appeared to be more than one in that folder.

Pictures of Bonnie. He'd been studying pictures of Bonnie. God, if ol' lady Swanson ever found out . . . I would've been in such deep shit . . . How could he do that to me?

Pete had called him "obsessed." Right here in the kitchen, when Dad was talking about his weird dreams.

Obsessed, all right.

Lane slid her sandwich onto a paper plate. She took it to the table and sat down.

Dad just wanted the pictures for his book, she told herself as she started to eat. Nothing weird about that. He looked so guilty in there because he stole them from the yearbook, doesn't want me to find out. That's all.

Maybe that isn't all. He's been dreaming about her. Walking in his sleep. He went out there to pay her a visit.

Lane remembered the way she'd found him staring at the naked corpse. What if he *is* obsessed with her? Maybe he wants her to be a vampire, wants to see her change back into a beautiful girl, wants to . . .

Come on. This is Dad, not Kramer. Dad wouldn't . . .

The things he was saying to her. But he was asleep. He was talking to her in his dream. Awake, he wouldn't . . .

Awake, ten minutes ago, he was staring at her pictures. What was he thinking? Was he wondering what it might be like if she comes back to life tonight?

He's just a man.

No, he's not. He's Dad. He's doing this for his book, not because he's horny over a high school girl.

Lane couldn't finish her sandwich. She threw the remains away, took a drink of water, and hurried back to her bedroom. She shut the door. She tossed her robe across a chair. She kicked her slippers off. She drew the covers up around her neck, curled on her side and hugged her belly.

Dad isn't like that, she told herself. He's not a pervert. He loves me and Mom.

He even told Bonnie that he loves us.

The way someone might say it to his mistress.

He claimed he loved us, but he went ahead and started to pull the stake.

He was asleep, for godsake!

But what if I hadn't been up there?

The girl is dead, Lane told herself. She's dead. She's not a vampire. She wouldn't have come back to life. That's bullshit, and Dad knows it.

That's the end of it.

But maybe . . .

She started to recite an "Our Father," softly mumbling the words. To stop herself from thinking. To calm herself down. She did another "Our Father," not speaking this time, going through it in her mind. And then another.

A gentle rapping on the door woke her up. She rolled onto her back as the door eased open. Dad looked in. "Are Pete and Barbara here?" she asked.

"Not yet. But you have a visitor."

"Was she asleep?" came a voice from the hallway behind Dad.

Lane lost her breath.

"She's awake now," Dad said.

"Really," Kramer said, "there was no need to disturb her."

"That's all right," Dad said over his shoulder as he entered the room. "It was time to get her up, anyway. We're having some other guests pretty soon." He gestured for Kramer to come in.

"Daaaad."

458

"What's the matter?"

"I'm in bed."

I'm dreaming this.

"If she'd rather . . ."

"It's fine. She's just doing her shy routine."

Kramer came into the room.

He's in my bedroom. The bastard's in my bedroom.

Lane tried to force herself to smile.

Kramer's smile looked tentative and concerned. "I just dropped by to see how you were doing. I hope you didn't catch a bug, or something, while we were at the play Saturday night."

Wasn't a bug, she thought.

He stepped around Dad and approached the bed. He had a manila folder in one hand. Like the one in which Dad kept his pictures of Bonnie. "Just in case you might be down for a while," he said, "I thought I'd bring you this week's assignments."

"Thank you," she muttered.

"That's very nice of you, Hal," Dad told him.

Kramer smiled back at him. "Wouldn't want my ace student to fall behind." He set the folder down on her nightstand. "How are you feeling?" he asked her.

"Not very swift."

"I'm sorry to hear that. Do you think you'll be up and around . . . ?"

Far away, the telephone rang.

"I'd better get that," Dad said. "Jean's taking a bath."

He left the room.

I don't believe this, Lane thought. *It's a nightmare.*

Kramer sat on the edge of the bed and smiled down at her. "Obviously, you've kept our little secret."

She nodded. She didn't think she *could* talk.

"That's very good, darling. But I'm not happy about you staying home today. I missed you." He slipped a hand beneath the covers. Staring into her eyes, he gently squeezed her right breast. "You missed me, too, didn't you?"

Lane gasped for breath. She shuddered.

Kramer laughed softly. He glanced toward the open door, then fixed his gaze on her face and moved his hand down the front of her nightshirt.

She choked out, "Don't."

"Shhhh. I've got a sharp friend in my pocket." His hand found her bare skin below the rumpled jersey. Lane pressed her legs together. But his hand pressed between them. She started to whimper. "I could easily slash your throat in an instant. And then do the same to your father. And your mother. She's taking a bath. That might be fun."

Kramer took his hand away.

"See you later," he said. He went out to the hallway and shut the door.

Forty-five

After hanging up the kitchen phone, Larry went into the living room and found Hal in front of the bookshelves, looking at the collection of his works.

"You've got quite an output," Hal said.

"Seventeen novels, so far."

"That's fantastic."

"Well, things have been going okay. I'm not as successful as I'd like to be, but who is?"

"What are you working on now? Or is that a secret?"

"No big secret, I guess. Would you like a drink?"

"Oh, I don't want to impose. I just came by to check on Lane and—"

"You don't have to rush off. I was about to fix myself a vodka tonic. What can I get you?"

"Sounds good to me," Hal said, and followed him into the kitchen.

"That was a friend who called," Larry said as he started to prepare the drinks. "Another writer. Quite a coincidence. He's putting together an anthology of vampire stories, and asked me to contribute."

"Well, congratulations."

"Thanks. It's nice to be at the point where they're *asking* for stories. I don't even write short stories anymore unless I'm asked for one. That's a big step from the old days when I used to send them out to magazines and collect rejection slips."

"Must be very gratifying. You mentioned something about a coincidence?"

"Oh, yeah. Pretty weird. He wants a vampire story, and I've been up to my neck in vampire stuff for the past few weeks."

"So, you're working on a vampire novel?"

"Not exactly." He handed a cocktail to Hal, picked up his own and led the way back to the living room. He sank into his easy chair. Hal sat across from him at the end of the sofa. "Here's how," he said.

They drank. Hal smiled and said, "Hits the spot."

"I'm doing a book about vampires, but it's not a novel. Nonfiction."

"A study of some kind?"

"Actually, it deals with personal experiences."

Hal shook his head, smiling as if he thought Larry was putting him on. "You've had personal experiences with vampires?"

"Yep."

I'd better quit talking about it, he thought. Then he thought, why? The guy's certainly in no position to steal my story. And it might be worthwhile to get an outsider's reaction.

Everybody will know about it anyway, after tonight, when we turn Bonnie over to the police.

"Want to hear about it?" Larry asked.

"Sure!" He took a sip of his drink and leaned forward like a kid eager for a spooky tale.

"Well, it all started a few weeks ago when Jean and I went out in the desert to explore a ghost town with some friends. Peter and Barbara. They'll be coming over for dinner in a little while, so you'll have a chance to meet them."

"Great."

"In fact," Larry said, "how would you like to join us for dinner?"

He hoped Jean wouldn't object. Probably not. She had

a roast in the oven. There was undoubtedly more than enough to feed an extra guest.

We'll get him to stay for the big event, if he wants. Have an objective observer.

"I hate to impose," Hal said.

"We'd be glad to have you. This is a rather special occasion. You'll see why, once you've heard the whole story."

"Well, I'd be delighted to stay. If it's all right with Jean."

"She'll be happy to have you."

Hal shrugged. "If it's okay with her . . ."

"Great. Okay." Larry took another drink. "So, the four of us went to this ghost town about an hour's drive from here. It's called Sagebrush Flat."

As he told the story, Hal watched him and drank. Sometimes the teacher shook his head as if he couldn't believe his ears. A few times he murmured his astonishment. After finishing the part about bringing the body home, Larry left the room briefly to refresh the drinks. Then he sat down again and resumed his tale. Carefully leaving out the details of his infatuation with Bonnie. Concentrating on the facts. He enjoyed Hal's reactions. The man was clearly fascinated.

"And so," he finished, "tonight's the night we finally pull out the stake. Right after dinner."

"Holy shit," Hal muttered.

"You're welcome to stick around for it. You can play the role of the disinterested observer."

"Get myself killed?" He laughed. It sounded a trifle nervous.

"I don't imagine it'll come to that."

"No, I don't, either. I may be superstitious, but I don't think I'm ready to believe in the existence of vampires."

Grinning, Larry nodded. "If she comes to life, I guess we'll all be in for a shock."

"I'd certainly hate to miss it, though."

"No reason you should."

Excusing himself, Larry went down the hall to his bedroom. He found Jean putting on makeup. She wore her jumpsuit, boots, and scarf.

"Are they here?"

"Not yet. But Hal Kramer is. He came by to see Lane and bring her some assignments."

"That's certainly above and beyond the call of duty."

"I think he felt a little guilty. He was afraid her absence might have something to do with Saturday night."

"He did keep her out awfully late."

"Maybe he thought she got sick on the pizza. Anyway, it was nice of him. I've asked him to stay for dinner."

Jean frowned in the mirror. "Won't that kind of put a damper on things?"

"I told him all about it."

"You told him about the *vampire?*"

"Sure. Why not? It's no big secret. Or it won't be, once we've called the police."

"Still, you shouldn't have . . . You're always *blabbing*, Larry. God."

"What's the big deal?"

"I'm not saying it's a big deal, just that I wish you'd be more careful about what you say to people. Everybody doesn't need to know our business."

"I just wanted to get his reactions."

"Now he'll probably think we're all nut cases."

"Hardly. He was blown away."

Jean sighed. She glanced at her wristwatch. "Well, what's done is done. I just wish you'd—"

"I know, I know."

"Right, you know. Anyway, Pete and Barbara should be arriving any minute. Would you like to make sure Lane's about ready?"

"I shouldn't leave our guest abandoned . . ."

"It'll only a take a minute."

Wishing Jean wouldn't be so negative about everything, he left the room and went to Lane's door. He knocked.

"Yeah?" she called.

"Are you decent?"

"Yeah."

He opened the door. Lane was still in bed, hidden under the covers except for the back of her head. She didn't look at him.

"I thought you'd be up and dressed by now."

"I had a relapse."

"Do you feel good enough to have dinner with us?"

"I don't know."

Concerned, he went to the bed. He sat down on its edge and stroked Lane's hair. She looked up at him with solemn eyes. Her face was slack and pale. "Are you okay?"

"If I was okay, I wouldn't be lying here."

"I mean, do you think it might be something serious? Maybe we'd better get you to a doctor."

"I don't need any doctor. I'll be fine."

"I really hate to see you like this, honey."

"I'm sorry.

"Look, if you're not up to having dinner with us, we could bring it in for you."

"Are Pete and Barbara here yet?"

"Not yet. But Hal's still here. We've asked him to join us. For dinner and for the big event."

Closing her eyes, Lane muttered, "Wonderful."

"What's the matter?"

"Nothing. I just feel awful, that's all."

He gently caressed her cheek, then stood up. "It'd be nice if you can join us. It's up to you, though. Wouldn't want you barfing on the table."

Lane didn't crack a smile.

She *is* sick, Larry thought.

"Like I said, we'll bring you something."

"Thanks."

He went out to the hallway and closed her door, feeling depressed. It's probably nothing serious, he told himself. But he thought, What if it's spinal meningitis? Or bone cancer? Or . . . Knock it off!

Jean was no longer in the bedroom.

He found her in the living room, sitting on the sofa near Hal, saying, "I know the whole thing sounds crazy, but . . ." She looked up at Larry.

"Lane's feeling worse. She might not make it out for dinner."

Jean scowled. "I'd better go see her. Larry, why don't you get Hal another drink?"

Her mother shut the door when she left the room. A few minutes later Lane heard the doorbell. That would be Pete and Barbara arriving.

She heard faint, cheerful voices. Some laughter.

It all seemed too weird to be real: the group drinking and eating and having a merry old time while they prepared to conclude their business with the "vampire," never suspecting they had a *real* monster in their midst.

The Devil hath the power to assume a pleasing shape.

Kramer hath a pleasing shape, all right.

God, if only they knew what he was really like.

Lane imagined herself getting out of bed and going into the living room. "Hey, guess what Kramer did to me." Then he gets out his "sharp friend" and has at them all. Maybe Dad and Pete could nail him, but he was sure to cut someone.

She pictured the straight razor slashing a quick gash across her father's throat.

I'm not going to risk Mom and Dad, she thought. Better to let him keep on messing with me than . . .

Lane suddenly realized how vulnerable she was, lying

in bed with nothing on but her nightshirt, and Kramer in the house.

They're probably all drinking. Kramer says, "Mind if I use the facilities?" Somebody points out that the john is just at the end of the hall. Of course, nobody escorts him. He excuses himself from the group and comes straight to my room for another round of threats and feelies.

Lane climbed out of bed. She turned on the lamp. At her dresser she took panties from a drawer and put them on. Though flimsy, the snug fabric felt shielding. She pulled off her nightshirt and stuffed it into a drawer. Shivering, she slipped into a bra. As she fastened its hooks, she remembered the times she'd gone to school without one, hoping to attract Kramer's attention.

You attracted it, all right.

Had nothing to do with that, she reminded herself. Kramer picked me before I started anything.

For additional protection Lane put on a T-shirt. At the closet she took a pair of thick corduroy pants off a hanger. She stretched the T-shirt down to her thighs, drew the pants up over its tails, and fastened the waist button and closed the zipper. Now, to get at her skin, Kramer would have to yank the shirt up out of her pants. She slipped a belt through the loops and cinched it tight. Then she put on her big, plaid shirt. She buttoned its front but didn't tuck it in.

She glanced at herself in the mirror.

Not exactly armor, but a lot better than the nightshirt. If Kramer paid another visit, he would have a tough time finding any bare skin below her neck.

Lane climbed into bed. She pulled the top sheet and blanket up to her chin. It felt strange to be completely dressed beneath the covers.

Not only strange, but hot.

Better a little discomfort, she thought, than to let that slimy bastard put his hands on me again.

She listened for his footsteps. She *knew* he would come.

Suppose he comes, and I've got Dad's gun under the covers and I blow him away? They'll find the razor on his body.

Lane's heart began hammering as she thought about it. *I'll get it.*

She climbed out of bed. When she eased the door open, voices and laughter flooded in. They're having one hell of a party, she thought.

The hallway was clear.

She rushed to her parents' room. Leaving the light off, she made her way toward the closet where Dad kept his revolver.

In the dim glow from the hallway, she saw the telephone on the nightstand.

And felt a rush of relief.

She turned on the bedside lamp, phoned directory assistance, and got the number for Melanie Benson. She tapped out the number.

As she listened to the quiet ringing, she watched the door. "Come on, come on," she muttered.

After the fourth ring, someone picked up.

"Yeah?" Riley, sounding annoyed by the interruption.

"It's me, Lane."

"All *right!* What's up?"

"Kramer's here. He's at my house."

"No shit?"

"He's having *dinner* with us, for godsake."

"What the hell . . . ?"

"Never mind. Look, he's probably going to be here for a couple more hours. I can't get away, but . . . I don't know, I just thought I oughta let you know. He'll probably be going back to his house afterward, you know? Maybe you want to be waiting for him."

"Fuckin'-A."

"What do you think?"

"Fucker's gonna be in for the surprise of his life. The *last* surprise of his life."

"Be careful, okay? He carries that razor with him."

"When they autopsy the fucker, they'll find it up his ass."

"Good luck, Riley."

"Yeah, sure. See you around, Lane." He hung up.

Lane cradled the telephone. She rubbed her sweaty hands on the legs of her corduroys, turned off the lamp and hurried to the bathroom. She locked herself in.

Sitting on the toilet, she hugged her belly and hunched over and tried to stop shaking.

Forty-six

"Well, here she is," Pete announced, lifting his cocktail as if toasting Lane as she came into the living room.

"Can't keep a good woman down," Hal said.

Larry felt a surge of relief, but it was mixed with apprehension. "Feeling better, honey?" he asked.

"A lot better."

"That's terrific."

"The gang's all here," Barbara said.

Now I can relax, Larry told himself. While everyone else had been drinking and munching snacks and apparently having a good time, he'd been drinking and worrying about Lane.

But she must be okay. Thank God.

In a way, though, he'd been comforted by the knowledge that she would be staying in her bedroom away from the action when it came time to pull the stake.

The way she was dressed, she obviously intended to go out there with them. She even wore the same shirt that she'd had on the other night—the one she'd used to conceal the big crucifix from her bedroom.

Barbara seemed to notice the same thing. Smiling at Lane, she patted her belly and said, "You got it?"

Lane looked perplexed for a moment.

"You know." She patted her belly again.

"Oh, that." Lane glanced around.

"Jean's in the kitchen," Barbara told her.

"It's on my wall. I'll get it when the time comes."

"What's that?" Hal asked her.

Lane glanced at him and looked away, her face going red, as if she were embarrassed to admit such a thing to her teacher.

Barbara leaned sideways and put a hand on Hal's knee. "We're discussing our protection." With her other hand she lifted the gold chain out of her sweatshirt and showed him Lane's cross. "She loaned me this for big event. She's got a giant one for herself. Has to hide it under her shirt so her mom won't know about it. Jean's superstitious about being superstitious."

"Better eighty-six Barb," Pete said.

"I'm fine," she protested.

"Must be fine," Larry said. "Anybody can say 'superstitious' twice in one sentence without messing up . . ."

"You're the one who'd better watch it, buster," Barbara told Pete. "You go pulling another stunt like last time and you'll—"

" 'This little piggie went wee-wee-wee-wee all the way home.' "

Barbara's face went crimson. "You shut up."

"Chow time," Jean called from the dining room.

"Saved by the bell," Pete said.

Hal laughed. "Is that B-E-L-L-E?"

"Good one, Hal. The belle of the ball."

Barbara showed Pete her teeth. "Here's one belle you won't ball till Hell freezes over."

"Oooh, the lady's pissed. No pun intended."

"Come on," Larry said, getting quickly to his feet. "Let's put on the nose bag."

"Let's *muzzle* Peter."

When they were all seated at the dining room table, Pete raised his glass of wine and toasted, "To Bonnie. Will she or won't she?"

"Only her hairdresser knows for sure," Barbara said.

Larry took a sip of his wine. He felt more than a little light-headed. We've all been drinking too much, he thought. Joking around too much. Doesn't anyone realize . . . ?

Going out to fool with a dead person.

"Let me say something," he said. They all looked at him except Lane. She was sitting beside Hal, frowning at her empty plate. "Bonnie Saxon was a sweet and beautiful young woman, murdered. She was just a little older than Lane, and she would've had a whole life ahead of her if some goddamn nut hadn't—" Larry's voice started to tremble, and tears filled his eyes. "It shouldn't have happened. It was a cruel—" He sobbed. He shook his head. "I'm sorry," he muttered.

"You'd better lay off the stuff," Jean warned.

"Eighty-six Lar," Barbara blurted.

"I think what Dad said is right." Lane sounded upset. She looked angry. "This isn't a movie, you know. That corpse out in the garage wasn't put together by a special effects department. She was a real girl. Some damn bastard—"

"Lane!"

"I'm sorry, Mom, but *really*. You're all kidding around about this thing like it's fun and games. Will she or won't she sit up and say boo! Well, it's real, and she's really dead. Just because she's got a stake in her chest, it's a Halloween party. How do you think her parents would feel if they were here listening to all this shit?"

"Watch your language, young lady."

"What if that was *me* out there? Would you all party it up and go out with a video camera . . . ?"

"Stop it!" Jean snapped.

Lane lowered her head. "I just think you should leave the poor girl alone. It's not right."

"Nothing good can come of it," Larry muttered.

"Well, I'm in agreement with that," Jean said. "I just want the body gone."

"Now, hold on a minute," Pete said. "None of us are

ghouls, here. Me and Larry know this is serious business. God knows, we faced down her murderer Saturday and damn near got ourselves wasted. So maybe we're all a little edgy about this business, and maybe we're carrying on a bit too much. But that's no reason to call things off. Somebody's gonna take that stake out of her. If it isn't us, it'll be people from the cops, or the coroner's, or someone. It might as well be us. Our book depends on it, right, Lar?"

"Yeah," he muttered.

"We've gone this far. We've gotta see it through." Looking at Lane, he added, "It's not like we'll be desecrating the body. The girl's already been desecrated by that lunatic Uriah. We pull out the stake, we'll be un-desecrating her. It'll be doing her a favor."

"Especially if she's a vampire," Barbara said.

Jean, groaning, rolled her eyes upward.

"What do you think, Hal?" Barbara asked.

Solemnly, he shook his head. "I'm just here as an impartial observer. But I have to say that Larry and Pete won't have much of a book if they don't go ahead with pulling out the stake."

"My man," Pete said.

"I think we should eat before the roast gets cold," Jean said.

Nobody spoke much during the meal. Larry felt ravenous. As he forked beef and mashed potatoes into his mouth, he noticed that the others were also gobbling their food as if they'd been starved. Everyone except Lane. When the others were done, her plate looked as if it had hardly been touched.

"Are we ready, pardner?" Pete asked.

"As we'll ever be," Larry said, his heart suddenly thumping so hard he felt dizzy.

"Hang on, I'll get my camera."

"Think I'll pay a visit to Mr. Toilet," Barbara said.

They both left the room.

"That was a delicious dinner, Jean," Hal said.

"Well, thank you. I made some Black Forest pie for dessert, but I think we should wait and have it afterward. Let the boys get this nonsense out of their systems first."

Pete returned with the camcorder he'd left in the living room. "Let's hope this one survives the night," he said.

"Just don't pull any cute tricks like last time," Jean told him.

"Not a chance."

When Barbara came back, she said, "All set."

They went to the kitchen door. As Larry slid it open, Jean said, "I think I'd better pay a visit, too. Go on ahead. I'll be out in a minute."

"Right," Pete said. "Let's not have any more accidents."

The others followed Larry outside. He started to shudder as he strode toward the garage. Hunching over, he hugged his chest. He clenched his teeth.

Oh Bonnie, he thought. Here we come, ready or not.

Stopping at the garage door, he dug into a front pocket of his pants. He brought out the keys. The padlock felt like ice in his hand as he tried to hold it steady. The key shook, but finally he got it in. He twisted it and the lock dropped open. He removed it, flipped away the latch, and tugged the door sideways a few feet. He dropped the padlock into his pocket, where it pressed heavy and cold against his thigh.

Jean entered ahead of them. Seconds later the overhead bulb came on and the others stepped into the garage.

Larry was surprised to see the ladder down. Had someone been in here?

Then he remembered that they hadn't put it up again after the last try.

He stared at the dark opening to the attic.

"What's this?" Hal nudged Pete's bow, which lay on the concrete floor beside the quiver of arrows.

"Our insurance," Pete told him. "Just in case she gets lively after we take out the stake. Hey, maybe you'd like to keep her covered with that. I'll be busy filming. Any good at archery?"

"I used to be pretty fair," he said, as he picked up the bow. "I'm no William Tell but—"

"It'll be point-blank."

"It won't be necessary," Jean said to Hal. "Just more of their foolishness."

"Well, I'll be happy to play along." He left the quiver on the floor, but slipped an arrow out.

"Good man," Pete said. "Just go for the heart if she turns out to be Dracula's daughter."

Hal chuckled softly and nodded.

Pete took a step toward his wife and raised the camera toward her.

"No way, José."

"Hey, come on."

"And break this one?"

"Don't be such a pussy."

"Screw you."

"Come on, Barb! This is no time to be—"

"I'll do it," Jean offered. "Show me how it works."

"Great. Just get us coming down with the coffin. Then I'll take over and get Larry when he unsticks the babe." He gave the camera to Jean, showed her how to hold it, and pointed out the viewfinder. "It's all set," he said. "Automatic focus, the whole ball of wax. Just push this button here, and you're rolling."

He turned away from her. He grinned at Larry and rubbed his hands together. "Anything you want to say for our home viewers?"

"Let's just do it," he said. His voice came out shaky.

Pete slapped his upper arm, then hurried past him to the ladder. As he started to climb, he glanced back at Jean. "You getting this?"

"Yeah."

Larry waited until Pete crawled onto the attic floor. Then he began climbing. Though he didn't feel especially cold, he couldn't stop shaking. His bowels ached. His legs seemed so weak that he feared they might give out.

In a few minutes, he told himself, it'll all be over.

I'll be yours forever, Bonnie seemed to whisper in his mind.

What if it's true? he thought.

It's not. She's dead. Her "voice" is nothing more than my damned imagination trying to mess with me.

What if she *does* come back to life?

As Larry's head rose into the gloom of the attic, he saw himself in bed, Bonnie straddling him, naked and more beautiful than any woman he'd ever had.

What if it could be that way?

He paused, his mind full of her. He could feel her warm hands roaming over his skin, feel the moist softness of her lips, her breasts brushing against his chest, and then her slick tightness sliding down as she slowly impaled herself.

"What're you waiting for?" Pete asked. "Losing the ol' nerve?"

"I'm okay," he muttered. Clambering onto the attic floor, he realized he *was* okay. His dread had melted in the warmth of his fantasies.

It can't turn out that way, he told himself. But wouldn't it be nice?

No! It *wouldn't* be nice. What's the matter with me?

In the faint light from below, he saw Pete kneeling at the head of the coffin. He made his way toward the other end. His hand came down on the fluorescent lamp he'd brought up the night Lane caught him here.

Lane.

Wanting Bonnie was a betrayal of her. Even worse, it was a betrayal of Jean.

He moved the dead lamp out of the way, crept over the

floorboards to the foot of the coffin and put his hands on its corners.

Inside, the coffin looked black.

He couldn't see Bonnie in there at all.

In a whisper Pete said, "Hey, wouldn't it be something if she *does* come back to life?"

"Yeah," he murmured.

"She was one fabulous babe, wasn't she?"

"You're married to a fabulous babe."

"Yeah, but *Bonnie*. I haven't been able to get that picture out of my head, you know?"

"She doesn't look like that now," Larry said, and he was glad that he couldn't see her corpse in the black depths of the coffin.

"In the movies they come back good as new."

"This isn't the movies, Pete."

"Too bad, huh?"

"Yeah."

"What are you guys doing up there?" Barbara called from below.

"We're on our way," Pete called. Speaking softly, he said, "Ready?"

"Yeah." Clutching the wooden corners, Larry began to crawl sideways, looking over his shoulder and scooting the foot of the coffin toward the lighted gap in the floor. He stepped down onto the ladder. Left hand gripping the top rung, he braced the end of the coffin with his right.

"Let's hope she doesn't fall out this time," Pete said.

The panel tilted against Larry's hand and the coffin eased forward.

"Got it?" Pete asked.

"Yeah." Larry stepped slowly downward, holding the end high. It didn't seem to weigh much.

Just as he wondered if it might be empty, Pete said, "Ugly mother." She was in there, all right. The box probably felt light because Pete was supporting most of the weight.

When it started to tip, Larry released the ladder and grabbed it with both hands.

"Be careful," Barbara said.

"I think I'm—"

"I've got you," she told him, and clasped the sides of his legs just above the knees. She held him steady, her hands moving up his thighs as he stepped lower. Then they were on his hips. They pressed against his back, and she said, "Okay, one to go."

He stepped onto the platform, and her hands left him. He backed away from the ladder.

"Watch it," she warned as he approached the edge of the platform.

"Thanks." He stepped down to the concrete and slowly lowered the coffin to keep it level while Pete descended the remaining rungs of the ladder.

The edge sank beneath his chin. He glimpsed the corpse's brown, withered legs and quickly looked away. The box nudged his chest. He backed up until Pete was off the ladder, off the platform.

They set the coffin on the garage floor.

Hal hurried forward. "Good God," he said. "You people weren't kidding." Holding the bow and an arrow at his side, he bent over for a closer look.

Barbara came up beside him. "Yuck," she said. "I'd forgotten just how disgusting—"

"It's like she's mummified," Hal said.

"Jerky," Barbara said.

"Let's everybody quit admiring her," Jean said, "and get this over with."

Hal reached in. His fingertips prodded Bonnie's thigh. "Tough," he muttered. Then he rubbed the leg with his open hand.

"Cut it out," Larry told him.

"Sorry."

"Come on, everyone," Jean said.

"Yeah," Pete said. "Let's get this show on the road. Larry, get on the other side of the coffin."

Larry stepped around to the other side. Pete took the video camera from Jean, raised it to his shoulder and peered into the viewfinder. "Everybody clear away," he ordered. "Hal, get ready with the bow."

Larry crouched beside the coffin. The others stood together a few yards away, gazing at him. Hal raised the bow and nocked his arrow.

"Okay," Pete said.

"Hold it," Barbara said. "Shouldn't we wait for Lane?"

Do it now while she's not here, Larry thought.

He lowered his gaze to the body in the coffin. He looked at its straw-colored hair, its sunken eyelids, its hollow cheeks and horrible grin. Then he stared at the stub of wood protruding from the hole in its chest.

Take it out and I'll be yours.

He wrapped his right hand around the stake.

Closing his eyes, he saw Bonnie alive. He saw her striding toward his bed, hair drifting around her face, her eyes innocent and loving, the tip of her tongue moist at the corner of her mouth. Her flawless skin gleamed. Her breasts jiggled just a bit. Her nipples stood erect. Her pubic curls glinted like filaments of sunlit gold. Kneeling on the mattress, she swung a leg over Larry. On hands and knees she hovered above him.

Pull the stake, she whispered. *We'll be lovers forever.*

Larry's hand tightened around the wooden shaft.

He opened his eyes and looked at Jean. Her fists were planted on her hips. She was scowling at him. "Well, go on," she said.

Shifting his gaze toward Pete, he looked into the camera lens. "Forget it," he said. "I'm not going to do it. *We're* not going to do it. None of us. It's over. Forget it."

Lane moved in from the darkness beyond the garage door. She halted. She looked at Larry. Then at Hal.

"No!" she yelled, and ran at her teacher.

Forty-seven

Once the others were out of the house, Lane waited at the kitchen door and watched until they were inside the garage. Only then was she convinced that Kramer wouldn't break away from the group and come in for a visit.

She went into her bedroom. There, she removed her crucifix from the small nail on her wall.

Pushing the bottom end of the cross under her waistband, she thought about the revolver.

She could take the gun instead of the cross.

And do what with it? Blow Kramer away? Make him confess, first. It'll all be on videotape.

I can't.

I don't have to, she suddenly realized. She'd made the phone call to Riley. Right now he was probably waiting in Kramer's house eager to nail the bastard for murdering Jessica.

I'll be in the clear. He'll be dead, and nobody will ever have to find out what he did to me.

If Riley doesn't botch it.

He won't.

Leaving her room, Lane decided to go ahead and use the toilet. She went to the end of the hall, turned on the bathroom light and shut the door. She locked it just in case Kramer might decide to come back, after all. She took out the crucifix, set it down by the sink, lowered her corduroys and panties and sat on the toilet.

Maybe I should just stay here, she thought.

She finished, dried herself, and didn't get up.

Just stay here and I'll never have to see Kramer again. I can read about him tomorrow in the newspaper. Buford High School English teacher brutally slain in his home.

Nobody will ever know what he did to me.

Unless they get Riley for it. Then I'd have to testify for him.

Maybe that won't happen. Maybe it'll just go unsolved forever, and Mom and Dad will never have to know.

Lane wondered if they were waiting for her. They might not pull the stake until she was there. Maybe they would send someone in to get her. Maybe Kramer would volunteer.

He can't get me with the door locked.

Hell, *anybody* could unlock the damn thing. All it takes is something that'll fit into the keyhole. You could almost do it with a fingernail.

Besides, I should be there for Dad.

With the crucifix tucked into the front of her corduroys and out of sight under the draping shirt, Lane left the bathroom. She walked slowly down the hallway. No need to hurry. The longer she took, the less time she would have to spend in the presence of Kramer.

Not that it had been too bad, being around him tonight. With all the others in the same room, he didn't seem very threatening. Or maybe he didn't seem so threatening because she knew what was waiting for him.

He was a dead man. He just didn't know it yet.

In the kitchen Lane rolled open the sliding door. She stepped outside and pulled it shut. The wind swept her hair back. Though it fluttered the front of her shirt, the T-shirt underneath kept her from feeling much chill. She walked toward the driveway.

The garage door had been pulled back no more than four or five feet. Light spilled out onto the pavement, but she couldn't see anyone inside until she stepped through the opening.

Dad was squatting on the other side of the coffin, his hand inside, gripping the stake. The others were watching him. Pete had the camera on him.

Hal had an arrow aimed at him. At Dad.

"No!" she yelled.

Dad looked confused. Everyone else whirled around as she ran at Kramer, shouting, "You bastard!" Even as the words left her mouth, she realized her mistake. Kramer hadn't been about to shoot Dad; the arrow was meant for the vampire. *You blew it,* she thought.

She saw shock in Kramer's eyes. He yanked back the bowstring. Barbara rammed an elbow into his side at the same instant he released the string. The arrow zipped past Lane, missing her right arm by less than an inch.

Almost on him, Lane hunched down. The top of her head struck the bow, knocked it aside, and rammed Kramer in the chest. He staggered backward. She wrapped her arms around him. She heard shouts of alarm. A knee punched into her belly, striking the crucifix and driving it against her skin, lifting her off her feet. Kramer's arms went under her. He swung her sideways and let go.

She hit the floor rolling, the concrete pounding her bones, the crucifix falling out of her shirt. She came to a stop on her back. Breathless, she struggled to sit up. Kramer's knee had blasted out her strength. She could lift her head, but that was all.

Dad, a look of shock on his face, still squatted behind the coffin as if frozen. Barbara was down on her back. Mom was behind Kramer, an arm clamped across his throat, riding him, swinging as he spun around and slashed at Pete with his straight razor. Pete thrust the camera out, blocking the blade.

Lane shoved at the floor. This time she managed to sit up. She got to her feet.

"Stay put!" Dad's voice boomed.

She looked at him.

Their eyes locked. Lane had no breath to tell him what Kramer had done to her. But Dad seemed to know.

His eyes lowered.

And Lane saw him begin to rise from his crouch, his face twisting with rage, lips peeling back from his teeth, left hand shoving down against Bonnie's chest as he rose, right hand drawing out the stake. It came out, a long shaft of wood, stained dark just below his grip, tapering to a point. Like a madman with a butcher knife, he bounded over the coffin yelling, and rushed Kramer.

Mom had lost her chokehold. She was on her knees behind Kramer, hugging his thighs. Barbara was scurrying toward the quiver of arrows. Pete took a slash across the chest as he brought the camera down with both hands, crashing it against Kramer's face.

The blow knocked the teacher's head back. He waved his arms, fighting for balance, about to topple over Mom.

Dad punched the stake into his throat.

Kramer's knees folded. His rump hit Mom's back, driving her to the floor. Dad, still clutching the embedded stake, went down to his knees. Snarling, he put his other hand to work. He used them both, shoving down and working the stake deeper into the man's throat.

Kramer kicked and twitched and flapped his arms. Blood gurgled up around the stake. His eyes bulged as if they might explode from his head. His mouth gaped, tongue stretched out and jerking as he made gagging noises.

Then came a violent spasm that seemed to shake the

last of Kramer's life out of his body. He sagged. Lane heard a soft fart. A stench of excrement came, and she covered her nose and mouth.

Dad, using the stake like a handle, dragged Kramer's body off Mom.

He left it in the man's throat and straightened up, gasping for air. He looked at his dripping hands. Then he looked at Pete. "Are you okay?"

Pete was holding his bloody chest, staring down at himself, shaking his head.

Barbara held an arrow in each hand. She let go, and they clattered against the floor. She put an arm around Pete's back. "God, honey."

"Are *you* okay?" Pete asked her.

"Just had my wind knocked out."

"Jean?" Dad asked.

Mom was on her knees, staring at the body. Instead of answering, she got up. She lifted her arms toward Lane. She had tears in her eyes and her nose was runny, but she didn't look hurt. Lane stepped closer, and they embraced.

"What did he do to you?" Mom asked.

"He hurt me," Lane said, making sure her voice was loud enough for everyone to hear. "He raped me. After the play Saturday night. He's the one who murdered Jessica Patterson and her parents. He said he'd kill us, too, if I told on him."

"Oh my God," Barbara murmured. "You poor kid."

"Fuckin' bastard," Pete said. Lane heard a quick thud. Someone kicking Kramer?

She heard footsteps. Then Dad pressed against her back. His arms went around Mom, and Lane was enclosed between their bodies. She felt Dad's breath stirring her hair, warm against her scalp.

"Our pal Bonnie didn't come out of it," Pete said.

Turning her head, Lane saw the dark cadaver stretched

out motionless in its coffin, a hole where the stake had been.

Pete said, "Guess she wasn't a vampire, after all."

"Thank God," Dad muttered.

Forty-eight

"I don't wanta leave you holding the bag," Pete said from the backseat of his car, where he was stretched out with a towel hugged to his chest.

"Don't worry about it," Larry said through the driver's window.

"We'll come back," Barbara told him. "It shouldn't take more than an hour or so . . ."

"If they don't have to send out for more thread," Pete said.

"The cops'll probably still be here."

"I wouldn't be at all surprised." Barbara took a hand off the steering wheel, gently patted Larry's cheek and said, "Don't worry. Nobody's gonna throw you in jail for killing that maggot."

"If they do," Pete said, "you can write a book about it."

"Thanks a bunch, partner."

"Come on, babe. Let's move it. I'm turning into vampire dessert back here."

"Take care," Larry said. Then he stepped back from the car. Jean held his hand, and they stood side by side while Barbara steered out of the driveway.

Lane, sitting on her parents' bed with the phone book open on her lap, picked up the handset and punched in Kramer's number. She listened to the first ring, and imagined the phone suddenly blaring in Kramer's dark house, probably startling Riley, making his heart jump.

Two more rings, then the line opened.

Before she could speak, Kramer said, "I'm not available to answer your call right now. At the sound of the tone, please leave your name, number, and message, and I'll get back to you as soon as possible."

"Like hell you will," Lane muttered over the sound of his "thank you."

She heard an empty, windy sound like the desert at night.

What if Riley isn't there and the cops end up with this?

The beep came.

"Hey, pick up. It's goody-two-shoes. You know? Goody-two-shoes with the spit on her face. Pick up. It's urgent."

She heard a click. "Lane?" Riley's voice.

"Yeah, it's me. Take the tape out of the machine and put it in your pocket."

"Sure. What's up?"

"Do it now, okay?"

A few seconds later he said, "Okay, I've got it. What's going on? Is he leaving?"

"He's dead."

"What?"

"My Dad killed him about ten minutes ago. I don't have time to tell you about it now. The thing is, you can go on home."

"Damn it!"

"You oughta be glad."

"I wanted to—"

"I know, I know."

"Maybe I'll burn the fucker's house for him."

"No, don't do that. There might be some kind of evidence."

"Oh yeah, there's plenty of that, all right."

"Really?"

"Hey, the fucker's got a regular museum here in a closet—pictures on the walls. You, Jessica, half a dozen—"

"Me?" Lane asked, feeling as if her breath were being sucked out.

"Sure as shit. Must be thirty, forty of 'em. He's got a darkroom here, all kinds of cameras, telephoto lenses, you name it."

"My God."

"A lot of girl's stuff, too. Panties, bras, nightgowns. Fuckin' pervert. Looks like he used 'em to—"

"Just leave everything the way it is. For godsake, don't burn the place. The cops've gotta find that stuff. It'll help keep my dad out of trouble."

For a few moments there was silence. Then Riley said, "I don't know. Some of the shots he got of Jessica . . . I don't want a bunch of cops seeing her like that."

"They have to know what Kramer was doing."

"Yeah? Bet you wouldn't be saying that if you saw what he's got on *you.*"

"He couldn't . . ."

"He was following you around, Lane. He was out to your house, too, from the looks of it. You better start learning to shut your curtains better."

"Jesus," she muttered.

"Still want me to leave everything?"

Squeezing her eyes shut, she groaned.

Pictures of me on his walls. Taken through the windows? Her skin went hot and crawly.

"Leave everything," she said. "Please. You've got to."

More silence. At last Riley said, "I'll leave some of it. Enough so the cops get the idea. Okay? I'll take the worst ones of you and Jessica and burn 'em."

"All right. Thanks." She heard the front door bump shut. "Look, I've gotta hang up. My folks just came in. I'll be in touch. You get out of there." She hung up the phone and hurried to the hallway.

* * *

From his hiding place behind a cactus cluster across the street, Uriah watched the lair of the vampires and wondered what had happened there.

Everyone else in the neighborhood must've been wondering, too. He counted more than twenty rubberneckers wandering around the street and sidewalks, all of them strange in the flashing lights of the police cars and coroner's van.

After a long time a couple of gurneys were rolled down the driveway. As they were being loaded into the coroner's van, Uriah caught glimpses of bulky dark bags.

A lot of the gawkers cleared out, once the meat wagon was gone.

One by one the police cars left. The last of them stayed for quite a while. Only a few neighbors were still hanging around by the time a pair of cops stepped out of the front door, went to the remaining car and drove away.

Uriah sat down on the gravel behind the cactus, wrapped the blanket around himself to keep off the chill, and waited.

Whatever had gone on across the street, he still had to go in and carry out his mission. The cops hadn't taken care of any vampires, he was sure of that. Cops might be good at some things, but they didn't know beans about Satan's bloodthirsty children.

That's where I come in, he thought.

"Guess that's that," Pete said, and yawned. He was reclined in the easy chair, wearing one of Larry's shirts over the bandages that had been applied in the emergency room. "Score one for the good guys."

"I just wish you would've told us," Jean said, looking at Lane with weary, sad eyes.

"Let it go, honey."

"I was just so scared," Lane murmured.

"It's all right," Larry told her, and stroked her hair. "It's over now."

She nodded, her cheek rubbing against his shoulder. "Is it okay if I go to bed now?"

"Sure, go on."

Lane got up from the sofa. She said good night to Pete and Barbara, kissed Jean, came back to Larry, whispered, "Night, Dad," and kissed him. Then she walked out of the living room, moving slowly, her head hanging.

When she was gone, Barbara said, "Poor kid. The hell she must've gone through . . ."

"You got the bastard, Lar."

"With a little help from my friends."

"Man, you nailed him good."

"Let's not talk about it anymore," Jean said. She slumped forward until her elbows met her knees, and seemed to stare at the carpet.

"Come on, Pete," Barbara said, getting up. "Let's go before you pass out." To Larry she said, "They doped him up pretty good at the E.R."

"I'm fine."

She took his arm and helped him out of the chair.

"I'm okay, I'm okay." Pulling away from her, he staggered toward the sofa. He shoved a hand toward Larry.

Larry reached up and shook it.

Pete held on. "So I guess we did good, huh, pardner?"

Larry shrugged. He didn't feel as if he'd done good. He felt dazed, sick and weary and sad.

"Too bad old Bonnie didn't perk up for us."

"Just as well," Larry said.

"Still got us a hell of a book, though, huh?"

"No book," Larry said. "Not about this."

"Hey, man—"

"We never had a vampire, anyway. Even if we did, I couldn't write the truth. I couldn't write about Kramer. About Lane. I won't."

Pete stared down at him, eyes still blackened from his encounter with Uriah's rock. He stared for a long time. Then he sighed. His grip on Larry's hand tightened. "Good man," he said.

"You, too. We'll do a different book together."

A corner of Pete's mouth tilted up. "All *right*. I'm full of ideas. We'll—"

"You're full of Darvon," Barbara broke in, putting an arm around him. "Now, come on. Let's go home and get some shut-eye."

When they were gone, Larry turned off the lights and walked with Jean toward their bedroom. At the end of the hallway a glowing band showed beneath the bathroom door. He heard water running.

"I've gotta take a shower, too," he mumbled.

"Don't be long," Jean said. "I don't want to be alone."

"I'll hurry," he told her. They entered the room. He went to the master bath, turned on the light but left the door open.

He took off his clothes. When he lifted the lid of the hamper to drop them in, he saw the wadded, bloody shirt he'd been wearing when he killed Kramer. The sweatsuit covered it. He shut the lid, stepped to the tub and turned on the water.

Under the hot spray he thought of Lane in the other bathroom. Like him, trying to cleanse herself of Kramer.

He was weeping when the shower curtain rattled open. Jean stepped into the tub. She slid the curtain shut and put her arms around him. Her face pressed against the side of his neck.

They didn't speak. They held onto each other hard.

Lane draped her towel over the bar and slipped into her nightshirt. Where she had missed a patch of water, low on her back, the soft fabric hugged her skin.

She left her clothes hanging in the bathroom and stepped out.

The house looked dark except for light from the open door of her parents' bedroom.

She went to her own room, flipped on the light and stared at her bed. As weary as she felt, she knew that sleep wouldn't come easily or soon. She would lie in bed, wide awake, remembering.

No, I won't, she told herself.

She was in her room just long enough to pick up her pillow and blanket. Holding them to her chest, she turned off the light and walked silently down the hallway.

She glanced into her parents' room. They weren't there, but she heard a windy sound of rushing water from their bath.

Moving through darkness, she made her way to the sofa. She dropped her pillow and blanket onto it, stepped to the television and turned it on.

A Christopher Lee movie. She changed the channel, recognized Jimmy Stewart in some kind of Air Force story, and returned to the sofa.

There, she lay down and covered herself with the blanket. Curled up cozy on her side, she watched the show. When Kramer forced his way into her mind, she made herself remember the people zipping the rubber bag shut around him, taking him out to the van along with Bonnie.

They're both gone now, she thought. Kramer can never touch me again. And I don't even have to worry about Bonnie. They're gone. I'm safe. Mom and Dad are safe. Everything's okay.

She wondered if she should go to school in the morning.

They'll have a substitute in English.

It would be nice to see Henry and Betty and George.

Not tomorrow, though. It's so late. I'd be a space case.

The Jimmy Stewart movie ended. Lane wondered what

would come on next. Before she could find out, however, a warm fog seemed to fold itself over her mind, and she closed her eyes.

Forty-nine

In the first light of dawn Uriah left his hiding place. The neighborhood was silent. He crossed the empty street and glanced at the red Mustang of the vampires as he walked by.

Getting his hands on its registration had made things so easy. The first time he'd gone after Bonnie, he didn't have that. All he knew, then, was what kind of car she drove.

One of those Volkswagen bugs had gone by on the road while he was hiking back to Sagebrush Flat after his pickup broke down. It had a pale color in the moonlight, and he'd glimpsed enough of the driver to see she was a girl.

Not much to go on. He couldn't even be sure the bug was on its way to Mulehead Bend, though that was the first town to the east, the direction the car had been heading. So that's where he went looking.

It took him a while, but he found the girl vampire who had a yellow VW. He put her to rest. But then another turned up, and then another. They were all girls, all about the right age, and they all had light-colored Volkswagens. They were all vampires, too.

During his search was when he came to learn they didn't behave like vampires should. They didn't sleep in coffins. The sunlight didn't burn them up. They could go around in daytime, just like regular girls. All the sun did was weaken them.

The sun would've made them easier to kill, but he'd been so headstrong back then that he'd gone after them at night. When he thought about it afterward, he figured it must've been a kind of death wish on his part. He'd wanted his revenge, all right, but he hadn't really cared whether he kept on living.

That had been a fool way to go about it. But the Lord stood by him and kept him from harm.

The Lord had a mission all set up for Uriah. He planned to send his warrior all across the nation to hunt out the legion of vampires doing Satan's work in every corner of the land. So He'd let Uriah slip by, even though he went about killing the first three vampires in such a foolhardy fashion.

Uriah hoped the Lord would allow him to retire after today. If he survived.

Going up against five of Satan's children would be no easy task. He figured his chances were slim, especially since he didn't have his bow and arrows.

But if the Lord stuck with him, he planned to stake them all, and cart them back to Sagebrush in the van that belonged to the vampire he'd almost put to rest on Saturday. It was in the driveway of the house on the right. He would go to that house after finishing here.

Uriah tried the front door. He found it locked, so he made his way around to the side. He let himself in through a gate. Up ahead was the garage. It had a yellow plastic ribbon across the front—the kind of thing police put up in places where there'd been a crime.

That's where the vampires must've killed those two people last night. What kind of story had they told, anyway, to make it all right?

The police couldn't have kept them long, anyway.

Only one thing will do the job on those creatures, and that's what I've got.

At the rear of the house Uriah found a window that was

open just a crack at the bottom. He set his satchel down on the concrete, pulled his knife, and cut an opening in the screen. He tried holding the knife in his teeth to keep it handy, but clamping his jaw shut tight just hurt too much, so he sheathed the knife at his side. Then he reached through the split screen and pushed the window up.

He slung a strap of his satchel over his shoulder and climbed in.

A bathroom. It smelled flowery and nice.

The door was open. Beyond was a hallway, dim in the early morning light.

Before leaving the bathroom, Uriah took off the bag. He removed his hammer and one stake, then slipped the strap onto his shoulder again and crept into the hallway.

He stopped at an open door. A bedroom. But he saw nobody in it.

He kept moving, and came to another bedroom. There, he found the vampire who'd shot him. Uriah tongued the hole in his right cheek. It made him wince, and his eyes watered up.

This one's chest was exposed. He was sprawled on his back, bare to the waist where the covers were rumpled up.

A woman vampire slept next to him. She was covered to the shoulders, lying on her side with her face toward the other. She wasn't Bonnie.

As much as Uriah wanted to kill the one who'd given him such hurt, he'd already decided to take care of Bonnie first. She'd made these two into vampires after they brought her here. So they were new at it. They wouldn't be near as dangerous as Bonnie.

Besides, Bonnie was the demon that killed Elizabeth and Martha.

The two girls he'd staked before Bonnie were vampires, but she was the one who killed his family. The Lord had told him that. So she needed to be the first, here, to be struck down.

Silently he stepped past the bedroom. As he continued down the hallway, he heard a quiet sound of voices. His heart almost stopped. But then he heard music, too, and realized the noises must be coming from a radio or television.

He paused to catch his breath. Then he went on.

In the front room he found the television. Some kind of news report was on, the volume very low.

On the sofa he found Bonnie.

She looked just as Uriah remembered her. Satan's vermin, disguised as a beautiful young woman. She lay on her back, her golden hair spread out against her pillow, a blanket up around her neck.

Uriah gazed at her. She looked so peaceful, so innocent, so lovely.

He lowered his satchel to the floor, then stepped between the coffee table and the sofa. He slipped the stake under his right arm. Holding it against his side, he bent over and slowly drew the blanket down. Bonnie didn't stir. Uriah, though trembling and breathless with the sight of her, didn't rush. He eased sideways, taking the blanket with him. At last it no longer covered her at all. He left it heaped on the end of the sofa.

Satan took such beautiful ones for his own.

The leg closer to Uriah was stretched out straight. The other was bent a little, heel against the cushion, knee resting against the back of the sofa. Slim, bare legs, softly tanned, but bruised up around the thighs.

In her sleep of the undead, her red nightshirt had slipped up around her hips. Uriah stared between her legs. He licked his dry lips. His heart pounded so badly he feared the sound of it might wake her up. He felt his hardness rising against the coyote hide of his skirt.

She's a vampire, he reminded himself. She's a vile daughter of Satan, a bloodthirsty demon.

Get on with it! he told himself.

He stepped sideways, but he couldn't help himself from looking back. From here he could see her fine golden curls, but not the tempting region lower down.

He rubbed the back of his hand across his lips. Then he took the stake out from under his arm.

He looked at her chest.

I've got to look, he told himself. Have to see where I want to plant the stake.

He stared at her breasts, smooth mounds under the nightshirt, nipples pushing at the fabric.

The cloth was so thin that Uriah knew the stake would poke right through it—almost as if it wasn't there at all. Still, having it out of the way would be better.

She'll wake up, sure as hell.

But Uriah had to do it.

He set the hammer and stake on the floor at his feet. He drew his knife. Ever so slowly, starting at the neck, he sliced his way down the nightshirt. Bonnie stirred once or twice, but she didn't wake up.

At last he sheathed the knife. He carefully spread the severed edges.

She was mighty bruised up. Someone had used her in a rough manner. It surprised Uriah to see injuries. He'd thought such demons couldn't be damaged except by the stake.

Her breasts looked smudged with faint shadows. So did much of the skin around them. He saw a bruise the size of a fist just below her rib cage.

And a shape like a cross on her belly. A cross, for sure. It looked just like the one on Uriah's own chest after he'd been saved from the bullet. The beams of the cross had bruised her, and its edges had gouged her skin. The scraped places looked raw and shiny.

A wound from a cross on the vampire's belly. Uriah wondered what it could mean.

Had someone else come after her? Someone armed with a crucifix?

Those bodies the police took away last night . . .

Are there more of us? Had the Lord sent a couple of other warriors, afraid I might fail?

Well, they're the ones that failed.

Uriah picked up his hammer and stake.

She had no bruise at all where he had planted the stake the last time. There, her skin looked flawless, a silken cream in the gloomy light.

He let his eyes roam once more down her slim, smooth body. Then he eased the stake forward. He brushed its point against her left nipple and wished he could put his mouth there, wished he could kiss it and suck on it—but she would wake up for sure if he did that, and kill him. Besides, his mouth was in no shape to suck on anything.

He guided the stake to the place where he'd put the other one in. It shook slightly, its tip trembling half an inch above her skin.

Then he raised his hammer.

Fifty

The alarm didn't go off that morning. When Larry awoke, he found Jean still asleep beside him. He sat up and looked past her at the clock. Eight-fifteen.

Lane's going to be late for school, he thought.

Then he realized she probably wouldn't be going today. Not after all that had happened.

All that had happened. Kramer raped her. Oh Jesus. Oh God. My girl.

I killed the rotten son of a bitch.

Good. Good good good good.

Larry started to cry, and quickly got out of bed before his sobbing could wake up Jean. At the closet he took down his robe. He used it to rub the tears off his face, but more came. He put the robe on and went to Lane's room.

Her bed was empty.

He felt a rough grip of panic.

She's okay. Kramer's dead.

What if she's done something stupid?

He rushed through the house, trying to choke back his sobs, trying to tell himself that Lane's a strong girl, a brave girl, she'd had something terrible happen to her, something terrible beyond words, but she was a survivor.

He found her in the front room.

On the sofa.

Asleep, covered to the neck by her blanket.

"Thank God," he whispered.

Bending over the sofa, he caressed Lane's cheek. It felt very warm, as it always did when she slept.

He went into the kitchen to start the coffee.

His breath flew out as if he'd been kicked. He dropped to his knees.

He thought, It's a good thing I can't breathe. If I can't breathe, I can't scream. Don't want to wake up Lane. Don't want her seeing this.

Uriah Radley was sprawled belly down on the kitchen floor beside his canvas bag. He wore his vest and skirt of coyote skin, but the skirt was held up by the handle of a hammer that jutted up between his buttocks.

His head was twisted around so he wore it backward.

Much of his neck had been eaten away.

The blunt end of a wooden stake filled his mouth, and he had a stake in each eye. The eyepatch hadn't been removed first. It must've been pushed right in by the stake. The broken side of its black band lay across Uriah's forehead, but the other side was there at the corner of the socket like a bloody worm that had tried to creep out between the stake and bone.

Larry staggered into the living room. Lane was still asleep.

Did she . . . ?

No, that was impossible.

Someone turned his head around.

Stepping closer to her, Larry stubbed his toe on a leg of the coffee table. He grunted at the sudden pain, and Lane opened her eyes.

She frowned. "What happened?" she asked, her voice husky.

"Bumped the table," he said.

"You look awful."

"Lane, somebody . . . Let me have your blanket."

"What's going on?"

"I'm not sure."

As Lane sat up, the blanket slid to her lap. She reached down for it and gasped. Larry glimpsed her bare chest and belly. She jerked the blanket up again. She looked at him, eyes wide, mouth hanging open. "Daaad?"

"Oh, my God," he murmured.

"What's happening?"

"Uriah got into the house last night, honey."

"Uriah?"

"It's okay. He's dead. He's in the kitchen."

"The guy that killed Bonnie?"

"Somebody got him. Somebody . . . he's really messed up. Go to our room, honey. Stay with your mother, and don't either of you come out until I say it's all right."

Hugging the blanket around herself, Lane rose from the sofa. She faced Larry. She looked haggard, frightened. "Who killed him, Dad?"

"I don't know. I just don't know. But I don't think we're in any danger."

She stared at him, lower lip caught between her teeth. Then she turned away and headed for the bedroom.

Larry returned to the kitchen. He crouched beside the body, being careful not to look at it, and took a stake out of Uriah's bag. He left Uriah's hammer where it was.

Outside, the morning was sunny and still. He broke the police seal, opened the garage and stepped into the shadows. The concrete floor was cool on his bare feet. Casting a glance at the attic ladder, he felt gooseflesh scurry up his back. He hurried on. At the workbench he found his hammer.

"You're the one, aren't you?"

He went numb. The hammer slipped from his fingers and thudded the top of the workbench. He snatched it up again. He whirled around.

In front of him stood Bonnie.

Larry knew he was gazing upon a monster. Only a monster could've done such things to Uriah. Only a monster could be standing before him now, radiant and beautiful, though she'd been dead two decades, though last night she'd been a hideous, withered hag.

But she was Bonnie, the girl of the yearbook pictures, songleader and Spirit Queen. Bonnie, the girl who had haunted his dreams.

Her eyes flitted from his right hand to his left, from the hammer to the stake. A smile lifted a corner of her mouth. "You won't need those, will you?"

He struggled to breathe.

"Hey, calm down. You'll give yourself a coronary." One of her hands reached toward him. There was no blood on it. There was no blood on her at all that Larry could see.

Her hand caressed the side of his face. It felt smooth and warm.

"This can't be. It can't be."

"Hey, come on." She pulled his ear. The way she did it seemed playfully affectionate. "Are you okay?"

"No. Jesus."

"Look, I'm sorry." Frowning, she put both hands on Larry's sides. They rubbed him gently through the robe. "I thought you'd be glad to see me. I didn't mean to freak you out or anything."

"You . . . you did that to Uriah?"

She lowered her eyes. "Yeah," she murmured. "Pretty gross, huh? You must think I'm awful."

"How could you do something like that?"

She looked up at him. "Hey, I'm a vampire. Remember? Besides, he had it coming."

"But what you did to him . . ."

"I know, I know. Look, you don't have to rub it in. But he was all set to do a number on the girl."

"What do you mean?"

"He was going to kill her. The girl on the couch."

"God," Larry muttered. "You saved Lane?"

"Is she your kid?"

"Yeah."

"I'm extra glad I saved her, then."

Moaning, he eased forward against Bonnie. Her arms slipped around him. He dropped the stake and hammer to the floor and embraced her.

"What's your name?" she asked.

"Larry. Larry Dunbar."

"I'm Bonnie."

"Yeah, I know."

Her face pushed against the side of his neck.

It passed through his mind that she might sink her teeth in. But he wasn't frightened.

Nor was he aroused.

This wasn't like his dreams at all. He caressed the smooth skin of her back. He felt her breasts pushing against his chest. He knew that only his loosely belted robe kept their bare bodies from meeting. But he felt no heat in his groin, just a mellow warmth in his chest and belly.

"You saved my girl," he whispered.

Bonnie squeezed him hard, then kissed the side of his neck. "It was the least I could do for you. I'm just glad I got here in time."

"How . . . ?"

"No sweat." Tilting her head back, she gazed up at him. "I just came back to say thanks. I figured . . . hell, you're the guy who took the stake out of me. I wanted you to know the truth, too. You would've found out, anyway, I guess. I mean, you were bound to hear about my disappearing act at the morgue. But I wanted to thank you in person. You mean a lot to me, Larry. A hell of a lot. Anyway, I just happened to get here in time to nail that bastard. He's the same guy that murdered me. A real lunatic."

"He knew you were a vampire."

"Oh, he didn't know shit."

"But you *are* one."

"Yeah, but I didn't touch his wife and kid. That was Linda Latham, not me. Hell, you don't go around ripping people up. Not if you want to last long. You just give 'em a little kiss while they're asleep. A little suck. Take a pint, maybe. They wake up the next day, and half the time they don't even know anything happened. You don't go around *wasting* people. Linda did that 'cause her boyfriend dumped her for Martha Radley."

"A jealous vampire?"

Scowling with indignation, Bonnie dug her fingers into his sides.

He squirmed. "Don't. Hey."

"What do you think, we've got no feelings?"

"I don't know what to think. I can't even believe you're here right now."

Bonnie put her arms around him again. "I'm here, Larry. And everything's okay. Everything's just fine. The dirty bastard's dead, and Lane's alive."

"Because of you," Larry murmured.

"You gave my life back to me, or I couldn't have done it. You pulled that damn stake out of me. I'm so—" Her voice trembled. She looked up, and Larry saw tears glimmering in her eyes. "I'm so glad to be back. I'll always love you for that, Larry. I'm so happy I could . . . could do something good for you."

Lowering his head, he kissed each of Bonnie's eyes. They were wet. Her tears tasted salty.

She sniffed. "Look, I'd better amscray."

"You can't leave," he said. "It's morning."

She rubbed her face against the front of his robe, sniffed again, then sighed. "I'd like to stay, but . . . too much has happened here. I'll go off somewhere, start over."

Bonnie eased away from him, but he caught her by the shoulders.

"You'll burn up," he said.

"You've seen too many movies, Larry. I love the sun." She spread her arms, tilted back her head and closed her eyes. "It's like warm hands. Warm hands caressing me." She sighed. "I think I'll go to the ocean and be a beach bum."

"I don't want you to leave."

Her eyes met his. She smiled a little sadly. "Want to keep me in your garage?"

"We could figure out—"

She touched a finger to his lips, silencing him. "I can't stay. You know that. But I'll always love you." She curled her hands over his shoulders, drew him down and pressed her lips gently to his mouth. Then she kissed his cheek. Then the side of his neck.

There, her lips parted and her teeth slid into his flesh.

A cold stab of panic quickly melted away. He felt the pull of her mouth, heard the soft sucking sounds. A pleasant, warm languor spread through him. Closing his eyes, he saw Bonnie standing naked on a beach, arms spread out, face raised toward the sun, a mild breeze stirring her golden hair.

She stopped sucking. Her teeth eased out of him and he felt a harsh ache of loss. She licked the side of his neck. She kissed the wounds. Tilting back her head, she gazed up at him with such tenderness and love that he thought his heart might break. Her lips gleamed with his blood.

"Now you'll always be with me," she said, her voice husky.

"You mean . . . you made me a vampire?"

A smile trembled on her red lips. "Nooo." Stepping away from him, she placed her open hand between her breasts. "From now on, you'll be with me here." She lifted the hand. She tapped her fingers against the side of her head. "And here. If you ever need me, I'll know it."

"I need you now."

"No. Not now, but maybe someday. And if that ever happens, I'll come back."

"But—"

She was gone. She didn't turn and walk away. She didn't vanish in a puff of smoke. She didn't dissolve. Suddenly, she was simply there no more. Larry stared at the daylight glaring in through the garage door.

"Oh, Bonnie," he whispered.

As tears filled his eyes, he lowered his head.

There on the garage floor, between the hammer and the stake, stood a pure white sea gull looking up at him.

Larry crouched down.

With a quick flap of wings, the sea gull perched on his knee. It cocked its head to one side.

"You've got to be kidding," he murmured.

The bird pecked his knee. But not very hard. Then it took flight. It circled his head once, buffeting him with the soft breeze of its wings, then flapped its way to the garage door and soared into the sunlight.

A World of Eerie Suspense
Awaits in Novels by Noel Hynd

THRILLS AND CHILLS
The Mysteries of Mary Roberts Rinehart

__The After House	0-8217-4242-6	$3.99US/$4.99CAN
__The Album	1-57566-280-9	$5.99US/$7.50CAN
__The Case of Jennie Brice	1-57566-135-7	$5.50US/$7.00CAN
__The Circular Staircase	1-57566-180-2	$5.50US/$7.00CAN
__The Door	1-57566-367-8	$5.99US/$7.50CAN
__The Great Mistake	1-57566-198-5	$5.50US/$7.00CAN
__A Light in the Window	0-8217-4021-0	$3.99US/$4.99CAN
__Lost Ecstasy	1-57566-344-9	$5.99US/$7.50CAN
__Miss Pinkerton	1-57566-255-8	$5.99US/$7.50CAN
__The Red Lamp	1-57566-213-2	$5.99US/$7.50CAN
__The Swimming Pool	1-57566-157-8	$5.50US/$7.00CAN
__The Wall	1-57566-310-4	$5.99US/$7.50CAN
__The Yellow Room	1-57566-119-5	$5.50US/$7.00CAN

Call toll free **1-888-345-BOOK** to order by phone or use this coupon to order by mail.

Name _____

Address _____

City _____ State _____ Zip _____

Please send me the books I have checked above.

I am enclosing	$_____
Plus postage and handling*	$_____
Sales tax (in New York and Tennessee only)	$_____
Total amount enclosed	$_____

*Add $2.50 for the first book and $.50 for each additional book.

Send check or money order (no cash or CODs) to:

Kensington Publishing Corp., 850 Third Avenue, New York, NY 10022

Prices and Numbers subject to change without notice.

All orders subject to availability.

Check out our website at **www.kensingtonbooks.com**

Get Hooked on the Mysteries of
Jonnie Jacobs